ALSO BY AMANDA SCOTT

Series

THE BATH TRILOGY
The Bath Quadrille
Bath Charade
The Bath Eccentric's Son

BORDER NIGHTS
Moonlight Raider
Devil's Moon

THE BORDER TRILOGY
Border Bride
Border Fire
Border Storm

THE BORDER TRILOGY 2
Border Wedding
Border Lass
Border Moonlight

THE DANGEROUS SERIES
Dangerous Games
Dangerous Angels
Dangerous Illusions
Dangerous Lady

THE GALLOWAY TRILOGY
Tamed by a Laird
Seduced by a Rogue
Tempted by a Warrior

THE HIGHLAND SERIES
Highland Fling
Highland Secrets
Highland Treasure
Highland Spirits

THE ISLES/TEMPLARS SERIES
Highland Princess
Lord of the Isles
Prince of Danger
Lady's Choice
Knight's Treasure
King of Storms

The Reluctant Highlander

The Reluctant Highlander

A HIGHLAND ROMANCE

AMANDA SCOTT

OPEN ROAD
INTEGRATED MEDIA
NEW YORK

Copyright © 2017 by Lynne Scott-Drennan

Cover design by Lesley Worrell

ISBN 978-1-5040-1619-3

Published in 2017 by Open Road Integrated Media, Inc.
180 Maiden Lane
New York, NY 10038
www.openroadmedia.com

To Tom & Kathleen Fashinell,
two very special friends,
for always being there, again & again.
Thank you!

AUTHOR'S NOTE

Until the mid-1600s, the town of Perth, Scotland, was St. John's Town of Perth, after its namesake. Perth was the entire region now known as Perthshire.

Medieval Highlanders rarely used surnames, because most people in a given area belonged to one clan. In this book, for example, Gaelic *Mòr*, as in Glen Mòr and Shaw Mòr, means "the Great."

Kilts were nonexistent until the sixteenth century. But dyes came from local plants, so woven wool garments in one area might have colors and/or patterns distinctive to that area. Clan tartans came along much later and became popular after Queen Victoria visited Scotland (1842) and acquired Balmoral (1852).

GLOSSARY

For readers' convenience, the author offers the following:

- *Àdham(h)*: pronounced "Adam" in medieval days, now YAH dav
- *Catriona*: Ka CHREE na
- *Clerical hours*: Prime = 6 a.m.; Terce = 8–9 a.m.; Vespers = 4:30–6 p.m.
- *Father Prior*: the proper form of address for lead prior of a monastery
- *Gillichallum Roy*: Gilli HAL um; Gillichallum = "Young Malcolm"; Roy = red
- *Glen Mòr*: the Great Glen
- *Inver*: mouth of the river (i.e., Inverlochy; Inverness)
- *Ivor*: EE vor
- *Keekers*: eyes
- *Jack-o'-plate*: sleeveless jacket with inserted plates of iron or other padding
- *Plaid*: pronounced "played"; an all-purpose garment from a length of wool kilted up with a belt. Wearer flings excess length over his shoulder.
- *Sark*: long shirt (thigh length)
- *Wheesht* (as in "Hold your wheesht"): Be quiet

The Reluctant Highlander

'S math an còcaire an t-acras,
'S mairg 'ni tailleas air biadh,
Fuarag eòrn' a sàil mo bhroige,
Biadh as fhearr a fhuair mi riamh.

—Alexander Stewart, 12th Earl of Mar,
September 1431

Hunger is a good cook,
It is pitiful to scorn food,
Cold barley gruel from the heel of my shoe,
The best food I ever got.

—English translation by David Gressett,
master Gaelic instructor, 2016

PROLOGUE

———— ⌒⌒⌒ ————

Lochaber, Scottish Highlands, 23 June 1429

A lone dark-bearded, steel-helmeted Highland warrior stood on a steep, forested hillside, south of the river Spean, watching the chaotic scene below. Catching his breath, he tried to determine whether his fellow Highlanders' odds of defeating the enormous army of invading Islesmen had improved or grown worse.

Weeks ago, Alexander MacDonald, third Lord of the Isles—believing he should be lord of all in northern Scotland—had marched ten thousand Islesmen up the loch-filled rift in the earth that Highlanders called Glen Mòr, a difficult march of nearly eighty miles over rough terrain, to the royal burgh of Inverness on the Moray Firth, the glen's north end.

The Islesmen had burned the town and besieged its castle for over a fortnight. Then, lacking supplies to support his vast army much longer, Alexander turned his men homeward, only to meet days of cold, pelting rain and harsh winds that left muddy bogland in their wake.

Meanwhile, James Stewart, first King of Scots by that name, learning of his cousin Alexander's siege of a royal castle and outrageous declaration that he was not subject to the King but equal to him, had led the royal army northwest from Perth into the Highlands. En route, hearing that Alexander and his Islesmen had left Inverness, James had changed course to intercept them at Loch Lochy.

Two days before, the royal army had ambushed the Islesmen on the boggy east shore of the loch, which had overflowed its banks during the deluge. Battle had raged along its shore and uphill along the Spean since then, littering miles of ground with bodies and turning much of that vast area red and slippery with blood.

The young warrior was a skilled archer, swordsman, and woodsman. Under orders from the captain of his confederation to attack the Islesmen on the south flank of the battle with his bow, he had retained his mud-streaked green hunting plaid for warmth and concealment in the forest. Collecting spent arrows as he went, by routes learned in childhood, he'd made his way to the south bank of the Spean.

To be sure, as muddy as everyone was, he could scarely tell one side from another. However, many among the king's recently arrived royal forces wore breeks, helmets, shirts of mail, even light armor, while most of the bare-legged clansmen and Islesmen wore only quilted, saffron-dyed sarks or tunics because they had cast aside their woolen plaids to fight.

For a time, the archer had darted from tree to tree, reducing the number of Islesmen on the opposite bank. Now, breathless from his efforts but noting diminishing action across the river, he felt hopeful that the tide of battle was turning to favor the King.

Movement a half mile to the northwest drew his gaze to a line of warriors moving south along a narrow, cliff-shaded path on Loch Lochy's west shore.

That path, he knew, led to a perilous ford on the river Lochy. The newcomers' visibly cleaner, leaf-green plaids told him they had not traveled far, and he knew that the area west of Loch Lochy was mostly Cameron country.

Few men in the thick of battle would notice the newcomers. But they were close enough for the keen-eyed archer to recognize the large dark-green oak-leaf Cameron clan badge on their white standard.

Impulsively, he set off to meet them.

As he wended his way downhill amid the trees, sudden childish shrieks of pain issued from the thinning woodland ahead. With his bow in his left hand, he reached with his right for the sword in its baldric across his back, resting his hand on its hilt as he quickened his pace.

Soon, he saw two bearded louts in muddy plaids revealing the jacks-o'-plate beneath them. The taller one was taking a stiff tawse to the backside of an eight- or nine-year-old boy while the other held the shrieking lad in place.

"Hold there!" the warrior commanded loudly enough to make himself heard above the shrieks and the continuing clamor across the river.

"This be nae affair o' yours," snapped the man belaboring the lad's breeks-clad backside. "Stay till we finish, and I'll teach ye tae mind yer own business."

Cruelty to a child or animal always stirred the archer's ire. As he rested his bow against a nearby tree, a sweeping glance ahead through the foliage assured him that the men he had seen still had a distance to go before reaching the ford.

"Let the lad go, or face my sword," he said.

"Aye, then, I'll face ye," the spokesman replied. "Give the wee feardie a few more licks," he told his henchman, tossing him the tawse. "I'll tend tae this upstart."

Pausing only long enough to see his man catch the tawse, the spokesman snatched his sword from its sheath and leaped toward the warrior.

Stepping lithely aside at the last possible moment, the warrior caught his attacker a thunderous clout to the head with the edge of his blade.

The man collapsed near his feet.

Seeing him fall, his comrade shoved the lad aside, turned tail, and vanished uphill into the forest.

The skinny, sobbing urchin in his ragged breeks and filthy, too-big shirt stood rubbing his backside, his blue eyes wide, tears streaming down his cheeks.

Curly flaxen hair hung damply to his shoulders, and a small gray cap lay on the ground near his feet.

"Pick up your cap, lad, and take yourself off and away from here," his rescuer said. "You are too small to linger so near such carnage."

"I'd liefer stay wi' ye," the boy said, stifling a sob as he stepped cautiously around the body on the ground, eyeing it as if he distrusted its continued stillness.

"I cannot take you with me," his rescuer replied firmly. "We still have much fighting to do to win this battle. So, get along home with you now."

"I canna . . . I darena go through them woods." He glanced up the hill and then at his former tormentor. "Rab's dead, is he no?"

"Aye, you need fear him no longer."

"But they'll blame me! They'll say it were my fault, and they'll kill me."

"Who are 'they'?"

The boy, trembling, fiercely shook his head. "I dinna ken!"

"Come now, you must know them. You called the man Rab."

"Aye, sure, 'cause that other coof did," the boy said. "I were in the woods when they found me, and they made me fetch and carry for them. I dinna ken who they be." He glanced up the hill again, still trembling. "That other 'un . . . he's sure tae tell his lot that this were my fault, though. Then they'll kill me the minute they clap keekers on me again. I . . . I ha' nae one. All me own lot be dead."

Recognizing true terror, the warrior said calmly, "Can you climb a tree?"

"Aye," the child muttered doubtfully. "But even an I do . . ."

"I'll put you up high enough to climb that one." He pointed to a tall, thickly canopied beech in the midst of nearby evergreens. "No one will see you there if you lie on your belly atop a thick branch. Also, your backside will soon stop aching."

"'Haps it will, but I'll break me neck a-climbing down."

"The King's army will win this battle before day's end. After we do, I shall return this way. You may come with me then, if you like."

"What if they dinna win?"

An ominous shiver shot up the warrior's spine at the unacceptable thought of failure, but he said firmly, "I will come for you even so."

The boy eyed him shrewdly. "There be dunamany fighting men," he said. "And I ha' seen nae King. What if they kill ye?"

"They won't." Nodding toward the beech, he said, "I cannot tarry, lad. You have my word as the King's warrior that I *will* come for you."

Absently rubbing his backside again, the boy gazed into his eyes. But when sounds of fighting erupted a short distance east of them, he said hastily, "Aye, then, put me up."

After seeing the lad vanish into the beech tree's dense canopy, and despite a bone-deep weariness beyond any he had known, the young warrior set off again at a long-legged lope. The lingering din of clashing swords, shouts, and screams from the opposite river-bank accompanied him.

The steepest part of the river behind him, he crossed to the west bank of the Lochy by leaping to a massive boulder that divided its frothy flow and then to the shore beyond it to the west. Having made the treacherous crossing with more ease than expected, he waved down the leader of the approaching men, whose helmet bore the two eagle feathers of a clan chieftain.

Raising a hand to halt his followers, the older man strode to meet him.

Both men wore similar arming doublets of mail under their plaids. The younger one—with tension surging through him—raised the faceplate of his helmet and met the older man's stern gaze.

"So it be yourself, eh," the older one snapped, pulling off his own steel helmet and shoving his other hand through unbound dark hair streaked with gray. "What brings ye here then?"

"The King and his army have joined the battle, sir," the warrior said.

"D'ye mean to say that Jamie himself leads the royal forces now?"

"He does, aye, and the Earl of Mar has defeated Alexander's army north of us. Also," he added, "the Mackintoshes of Clan Chattan still hold Inverness Castle despite Alexander's having besieged it and burned down the town round it."

The older man said grimly, "He *is* the Lord of the Isles. So, ye canna blame him for burning Inverness, not after Jamie humiliated him *and* other west Highland chiefs who supported him at Jamie's Parliament and Justice Court three years ago.

"Then he took Alexander to St. John's Town of Perth, scolded him in the kirk like a schoolboy, and imprisoned him. So Jamie canna be surprised that Alexander spent his wrath on the site of his humiliation. Aye, and dinna forget that he hovers nearer than the King does to all of us *west* of the Great Glen, my lad. Perforce, we ha' accepted Alexander as our liege lord. We *must* fight for him."

"Nevertheless, James *is* King of Scots," the younger man said. "So you would be wiser now to set yourself apart from Alexander. Despite his boast that he led ten thousand men, thousands died at Inverness, and more died when we trapped them in the bogs. James's forces now outnumber his."

"Ye did say that Jamie leads them himself?"

"I did. He may be as unscrupulous as many men say he is, sir. But he is prompt to act when aroused, and he holds his crown tenaciously. He utterly rejects Alexander's notion that, as Lord of the Isles and James's cousin, he is equal to the King and need not submit to him. Moreover," he added, "James *will* win this battle. So, if you *are* wise, you will persuade as many leaders in the Confederation as you can to support him *before* then."

"I dinna like your tone, lad," the Cameron chieftain said grimly. "But your words do have sense to them. Mayhap ye should come with me."

"With respect, sir, I ally with the Mackintoshes of Clan Chattan as you ken fine, having abandoned me to them long ago. I am as loyal to his grace as they are."

"Why did ye come to me then, like this?"

The younger warrior shrugged as he pulled his faceplate back down.

Then, bleakly, he said, "You *are* still my father, sir."

Holyrood Abbey, Edinburgh, 28 August 1430

The sun was hot that St. Augustine's Day, so after a mile-long walk downhill from Edinburgh Castle and the length of the Canongate to Holyrood Abbey, the King and Queen of Scots and members of their royal court had welcomed the cool interior of the magnificent abbey kirk, where they had assembled for High Mass.

Nobles and other citizens of the town having joined the procession, the congregation was unusually large.

After a three-hundred-year renovation, the lofty kirk boasted a six-bay choir, three-bay transepts with a central tower, and an eight-bay, aisled nave with twin towers at its west front. Rounded arcading north of the nave, kept from the earlier kirk, contrasted starkly with the pointed architecture of the south side.

Plump, gray-haired Bishop Henry Wardlaw of St. Andrews had already spoken longer from his pulpit than many thought necessary.

Some of his young listeners, notably two seventeen-year-old maids of honor in the front row, facing the Queen, shifted uncomfortably on their prayer stools.

When the bishop paused, Lady Fiona Ormiston turned to her neighbor, Malvina Geddes, to express her discomfort.

A quick headshake from Lady Sutherland, the Queen's mistress of robes, kneeling just beyond Malvina, stilled the whisper on Fiona's tongue. With a sigh, she straightened and stared fixedly at the bishop, wishing she could will him to silence.

She had already learned *much* more about St. Augustine of Hippo than any sensible person wanted to know. Sakes, the man had lived a thousand years ago!

But he'd deemed his sins significant enough to confess them all. Wardlaw said men learned much from Augustine's writing. Too much, Fiona decided, fearing that the bishop might describe the saint's every sin before he was done.

Usually, she liked learning about other people. But real people, not men who had lived so long ago that one's imagination boggled at such a distance of time. Nor did she know aught of Augustine's Italy or Africa, or care about such faraway places. She was more curious about places and events nearer at hand.

Although she had served the Queen for four months, including the previous fortnight here in Edinburgh, she had seen only the part of town that lay on the road from Stirling and from Edinburgh's hilltop castle to the abbey. She knew Stirling better. They had stayed in its castle for six weeks, and the village below was small.

The royal household, being numerous, moved often so that overfilled garderobes could be thoroughly refreshed before their graces' return.

Noting that his grace watched the bishop, Lady Fiona suspected that he also had an eye on the Queen beside him. She sat in a two-elbow chair like his own, and everyone knew they were deeply in love, even after six years of marriage.

James was not the only one who loved Joanna. Everyone loved her.

Had she not brought peace with England and shown from the first how kind she was? Although born and raised an Englishwoman, she had said that she wanted to be considered as rightfully Scottish as the King, who had married her and brought her home with him at the end of his long English captivity.

She had even changed her name from English Joan to Scottish Joanna to show how much she loved her new country.

A sudden disturbance at the other end of the nave's long aisle, at Fiona's left, diverted her thoughts and silenced Bishop Wardlaw midsentence. Turning to peer down the center aisle, Fiona beheld an extraordinary sight.

Striding barefoot toward the altar was a tall, muscular, bare-legged man with shoulder-length, unkempt, tawny hair and an equally shaggy beard and mustache.

He wore only a midthigh-length, saffron-dyed shirt, and he carried a long, wicked-looking sword, pointed upward and bared.

Gasping at the sight, Fiona heard echoing gasps and hastily stifled cries from the congregation. Turning to look from a gaping Joanna to the King beside her, she saw James calmly stand and look at Bishop Wardlaw, now silent in the pulpit.

Three weeks past his thirty-sixth birthday, the dark-eyed King retained his boyish features and tousled auburn hair, but Fiona saw no hint now of the childlike look that so many described when they spoke of him.

King and bishop gazed at each other for a long moment. When the bishop raised his flyaway gray eyebrows, James grimaced and shook his head.

Then, facing the congregation and the man striding toward him, the King looked calm again, even speculative, leading Fiona to decide that he knew the fierce-looking man and felt no fear of him.

When the Queen seemed about to rise, a vague gesture from his grace stilled her in her chair. She clasped her hands together. Her face was unnaturally pale.

James had been King of Scots for over six years. He stood, patiently waiting, and watched the intruder without a trace of unease.

In contrast, Fiona easily detected Bishop Wardlaw's disquiet. As she watched, he opened his mouth and then pressed his lips firmly together again.

Looking back down the aisle, she found the newcomer much closer. Despite his proud bearing, he was clearly a barbarian. He was also inches taller and looser of limb than the square-built, heavy-shouldered King. The closer the man came, the larger his sword appeared to be.

A shiver shot up Fiona's spine.

The King was unarmed. Doubtless, every other man in the kirk was, too.

When the barbarian stopped just a few feet away from her, she winced at his rank odor. She also noted that his saffron tunic was bulkier than she had thought, and it was quilted. It concealed less than half of his long, muscular thighs.

Looking up, she saw that he stared unblinkingly at James.

The King stood a step above him, but the barbarian looked to be the taller of the two. His sword seemed enormous now, making her fear that *she* was too close.

His bearded chin jutted. He locked his gaze with the King's.

Then, deftly, he flipped the sword to grasp it by its blade point. He held that obviously weighty weapon long enough to drop to a knee.

Then, briefly bowing his head, he proffered the sword hilt-first to James.

Grasping the hilt but making no move yet to take the weapon, James was silent for a long, unnerving moment.

Then, his voice carrying throughout the dead-silent kirk, he said, "Ye'll recall, Cousin Alexander, that when we met over a year ago after the battle at Lochaber, I commanded your unconditional surrender. Ye were disinclined then to obey that command. D'ye agree now to submit to me . . . completely?"

Realizing only then that the barbaric-looking creature was James's cousin, Alexander, Lord of the Isles, Fiona gazed more curiously at him. The congregation was so quiet that she heard him draw a deep breath and let it out.

"Unhappily, Jamie-lad, I do submit," he said in heavily accented Scots. "Else, I'd ha' tae be a rare fool tae stand before ye as defenseless as I be the noo. By my troth, though, had them traitorous Camerons no shifted their allegiance tae ye that day, I'd ha' won that battle."

"But I did win," James said flatly. "I heard ye'd fled to Ireland."

"I did *visit* me cousin Donal Balloch there. But I dislike this strife betwixt *us*, Jamie. Also, that last time ye imprisoned me, after your Justice Court in Inverness, ye didna make me bide long in St. John's Town o' Perth."

James said, "*This* time, cousin, ye'll retire to Tantallon Castle, where ye'll bide at my pleasure as a royal prisoner. Afore ye leave, ye will concede that ye be my vassal and that, whilst ye may be *Lord* of the Isles, ye're no the *king* of them."

"I hear that Tantallon boasts fine views o' the Firth o' Forth and the German Sea," the Lord of the Isles retorted. "Am I tae find me own way there?"

"You will have a royal escort, well-armed," James said dryly.

"*Moran taing*, but first I must break me fast. I've no eaten since yesternoon."

"I have nae will to starve ye," James said, signaling to someone at the far end of the nave. "But henceforth ye'll take your meals at Tantallon. Also . . ."

He paused, for Alexander was apparently oblivious, looking around the nave as if he sought supporters among the congregation.

Fiona recalled then that he had supposedly had ten thousand followers at Lochaber. What if some of those men were in the congregation now?

Glancing down the aisle, she saw six men-at-arms striding toward him.

Alexander turned back to the King. "Aye, Jamie, ye had more tae say t' me?"

"Only that ye'll behave yourself at Tantallon, cousin, or I'll make ye shorter by a head. That would end *all* o' your mischief."

Then, as Fiona and the rest of the congregation watched—some in astonishment and others, including Fiona, with relief—the King's men-at-arms escorted the Lord of the Isles out of the kirk, to imprison him in the great stronghold atop a barren sea cliff on the southeasternmost edge of the Firth of Forth.

Hearing the tall abbey doors close behind them, Fiona fervently hoped that James could *keep* his barbaric kinsman locked up and well guarded.

CHAPTER I

—————⦿⦿⦿—————

The North Inch of Perth, 25 June 1431

The night had been nearly starless before the clouds moved on.

Now, a pale golden glow edged distant hills to the east, which told twenty-three-year-old Sir Àdham MacFinlagh, riding south on the west bank of the river Tay, that the moon—full tonight—was rising.

Sir Àdham's night vision was excellent, and his shaggy black-and-white dog, Sirius, ranging ahead on the undulating, shrub-lined path, would alert him to any disturbing movement, scent, or noise nearby.

The King's annual Parliament was meeting in the royal burgh of St. John's Town of Perth, so the road from Blair Castle, where he had spent the previous night, was safe enough to travel even at that late hour. Nevertheless, as Àdham neared the town, he welcomed the increasing moonlight.

Starlight had already revealed black heights of the town wall a half mile ahead, beyond a rise in the landscape. He could even make out the tall, pointed spire of what he suspected was the Kirk of St. John the Baptist, for whom the town was named. Then, the bridge crossing from the village of Bridgend to St. John's Town's High Street gate came into view.

At that hour, even the broad expanse of water to his left had hushed, looking black and bottomless as it flowed toward the Firth of Tay and the sea. He knew the Tay was a powerful river, but now, it seemed calm and contained, reminding him that sea tides influenced its current. It was low, too, flowing some ten feet below its banks. So the tide was also low but on the turn. The breeze wafting toward him from across the water stirred no more than an occasional ripple.

His path lay between the river and a wide field to his right that, despite big patches of shrubbery and scattered trees, he believed was the infamous North Inch of Perth. The current King's father, Robert III, had ordered a trial by combat there between the two great Highland confederations, Clan Chattan and the Camerons.

The full result of that great clan battle depended on who told the tale, and Àdham knew little more than that the two sides had had to provide thirty champions each and that the Camerons had lost all but one of theirs. It had happened before his birth, and although a truce had resulted, no one on either side had been eager to discuss the battle with him.

All was quiet on the Inch, too, unnaturally so. Not even a night bird's call.

His instinctive wariness of new places, augmented by years as a warrior, stirred strong then, as did his Highlander's mistrust of any town's dark environs.

His mount was tired after a long day's ride, and enough of the moon peeked above the hills to light the river and its surrounding landscape, so he dismounted to lead the horse. Absently shifting stray hairs of his beard from his mouth with a finger of his free hand and smoothing them, he scanned the nearby field.

He had not visited St. John's Town before, but his foster grandfather had explained exactly how he could find their clansmen by following the High Street into the town from its north gate.

He could see the top parts now of a massive dark tower rising above the end of the town wall near the riverbank. Moonlight also revealed that the rise ahead was a low, rocky hillock extending into the water.

A short distance ahead, to his right, orange light revealed two high windows of an otherwise shadowed building inside a wall of its own. Torch-glow suggested that its east-facing wall had a gateway, but the rise hid all save its twin towers.

Rustling shrubbery near the field's center sharpened the wariness awakened by its hitherto unnatural silence. His skin prickled, too, making him wonder if someone watched him from the Inch or from one of those lighted windows.

The dog's ears rose at the rustling sound, but when they relaxed almost immediately, Àdham relaxed, too, deciding that he had let his imagination turn a wakeful badger or fox seeking its supper into a bairn's boggart.

"Whisst now, ye dafty!" the older of the two watchers hissed to the one creeping toward him with what the fool apparently mistook for extreme stealth. "'Tis like a herd o' kine, ye be, a-pushing through them shrubs!"

"Whisst yourself!" his cousin hissed back. "Some'un's coming, Hew. A chap on horseback with a dog, and a great sword on his back. D'ye see our quarry yet?"

"Nae," Hew whispered. "Three men walked over from the town, though, and I saw one go into yon monastery. From here, I couldna be sure if them others went wi' him or stayed outside. I'm thinking we may ha' tae wait till they leave, though."

"Who were they?"

"Sakes, how would I know? But the one as went inside, by his bearing, were a nobleman sure."

"Deevil's curse on all three o' them. We canna bide here much longer! I did think this would be the night. But what if that dog senses us?"

"It'll hear nowt if ye say nowt," Hew muttered savagely. "It canna smell us, Dae, because wi' this breeze a-blowin' at us from yon river, the dog be upwind of us. This may be our chance tae win freedom for Alexander. So just hush your gob."

Instead, his cousin Dae hissed, "Look now, Hew. Some'un's a-hieing down tae the river from yon hedged garden!"

Àdham had seen no sign yet of his squire and the two other lads who followed him more slowly on foot, leading sturdy Highland garrons laden with bundles of the extra clothing and gear that they might need in town.

His sense of watchers had vanished when Sirius remained undisturbed, and he had heard no more himself beyond leaves hushing in the gentle breeze.

Increasing moonlight now turned the river into a wide silver-gilt ribbon. He began watching his steps as the path steepened and grew more rugged. But when he reached the top, he beheld a sight so unexpected that it stopped him in his tracks.

The dog stopped, too, and glanced at him uncertainly. Behind him, the horse whuffled, its sound no more than the fluttering wings of a nervous grouse.

Halfway down the rough slope, watching the moon, transfixed and unaware of her audience, stood a slender figure in a thin white nightdress or smock. The garment's long sleeves and gathered neckline hid most of her. But it stopped at her knees, revealing bare calves, ankles, and small feet below.

Àdham's breath caught in his throat, although anyone watching—had there been such a watcher—would have noted no change in his expression because he had habitually concealed his feelings since childhood. Emotions, after all, were private, not for sharing in the world of men that he customarily inhabited.

The lass, who looked only fifteen or sixteen, stood as still as sculpted marble, as if she focused every ounce of her being moonward.

Dropping the reins, hoping the horse would stay put, as the Blair Castle man who had provided it that morning had promised, Àdham stood still, too, unwilling to break whatever spell the moon goddess or unknown river nymph had cast on her.

Her dark hair, gilded by moonlight, fell past her hips in soft, shimmering waves. The white garment revealed little more than the slenderness of her figure, although his experienced eye detected the soft outline of a generous bosom.

As he watched, he heard only the murmuring river. Then, an owl hooted softly in the distance and Sirius made a petulant sound as if questioning his master's stillness or his judgment.

Àdham's wariness stirred again, but the lass did not react. Her gaze remained fixed, eastward, across the river on the rising moon.

To be sure, the moon, looking larger than life, was a splendid sight. More than half of it showed now above the dark mass of hills to the east. It seemed to have come nearer and grown bigger since the night before. Were he a fanciful man—which, decidedly, he was not—he might have called it magical.

Movement drew his gaze back to the lass as she raised her arms out from her sides. Then, to his amazement, she continued to hold them so as she stepped down into the water. She moved slowly and with more grace than one might expect on such a steep, uneven slope. Keeping her balance with outstretched arms, she eased forward until the flowing water reached her knees, her thighs, and then her hips.

Àdham shivered, watching her. Although the late-spring air was temperate, the hour was nearly midnight. The water had to be much colder than the air.

Evidently, though, its chill did not deter her. She took another step, then leaned forward and glided into the water, stroking gently from the shore, her head up, her hair spreading behind her on the water's surface. Still gazing at the moon, she let the current carry her southward, away from him, toward the town and the sea. Then, in an eddying swirl, she vanished beneath the sparkling dark surface.

He watched expectantly, but she did not come up. Suddenly fearful, he dashed after her. Heedless of rocks, the uneven terrain, and other such minor obstacles, he cast off his baldric, belt, and heavy wool plaid as he ran.

Lady Fiona Ormiston savored the rare sense of freedom she felt deep beneath the surface, as her arms swept her forward and her legs kicked hard against the Tay's strong current, heading back the way she had come. She was smugly pleased that she could hold her breath long enough now to count nearly to two hundred.

She knew that someone had been nearby, for her senses, especially on such moonlit ventures as this one, remained keenly attuned to her surroundings, and as she had waded into the water, she'd heard barely audible sounds of approach on the path northward and had given thanks that she wore her least revealing shift.

Peripherally, just before submerging, she had glimpsed a large, apparently cloaked figure cresting the rise and decided it must be one of the friars or a guard who, despite her caution, had seen her push through the monastery's garden hedge and followed her. Such a man might watch her, even report her presence to others, but he would not harm her. She hoped whoever it was would be kind enough to return from whence he came without disturbing her or telling anyone else at the monastery that she had come down to the river.

In any event, although it was unusual to see anyone on that path at so late an hour, she would be safe enough in the water even if he was a late-night traveler.

A niggling discomfort stirred then at the intrusive memory of her first secret moonlight swim, years before at her home, Ormiston Mains, which was nearly four days' distant from St. John's Town. That night, she had emerged naked from the Teviot to find Davy, the youngest of her brothers, waiting on the riverbank. Eight years older, then sixteen, Davy had disapproved of her nudity and scolded her in that maddeningly calm but cutting manner he had.

Emboldened by her successful escape from Ormiston House and the bracing swim, she had dared to inform him that she *liked* to swim by moonlight.

When he'd smacked her bare backside hard and warned her to behave, she had demanded to know why she should *not* swim—having done so for two whole years, since she was six—especially late at night when everyone else was asleep.

His reply was that *he* had been awake, so others might be as well. When she had tried to argue that now obviously logical point by insisting that she'd have seen anyone else before she went into the water, Davy had ended the argument by tossing her back in the river. By the time she swam out again, he'd collected her cloak from the damp grass and held it ready to wrap around her.

She smiled at that memory, because Davy was her favorite brother and lived only a day's journey now from their childhood home. Also, despite his displeasure with her that night, Davy had *not* betrayed her to their father.

That thought barely entered her mind before an unexpected surge in the water behind her startled her so that she almost gasped. Certain that someone was now in the river with her, she surfaced to see if it was the man from the path.

He faced away from her, snapping his head frantically back and forth in an obvious search of the silent water downstream. Other than his unfashionably long and visibly tangled dark hair, only his arms, moving on the surface, and his broad shoulders—oddly golden in the moonlight—rose above the water.

Aware now that he likely feared the river had swept her away, she used the same sweeping strokes she employed underwater to swim swiftly and silently back toward shore, moving perforce with the current, but diagonally, so the water would not carry her right to him, and with her head well up to keep an eye on him.

When she could touch bottom with her toes, using her arms and hands to steady herself, she said just loudly enough for him to hear her, "I'm over here."

He turned toward her, his movements powerful yet unhurried, revealing that, as she had suspected, he was a skillful swimmer, too. She had therefore been wise not to try to swim away from him against the current. Nor could she have scrambled back up the steep slope and run away without drawing his attention.

Although only her head was above the water, he saw her straightaway and snapped, "What the dev—?"

When he fell silent rather than finish the likely curse, she said warily, "Why did you jump in? Did you fear the river had swept me away?"

He did not reply. Moonlight lit his face, revealing a prominent, even beaklike nose, as well as dark and deep-set eyes with a gaze both penetrating and piercingly intense, as if he would peer right through her skull to examine her thoughts.

His dark beard was thick and as unruly as his hair. He pushed a few long, wet strands of hair away from his face and took a stroke toward her.

Hastily, she said, "Pray, sir, just swim ashore. I do not need any help, for I learned to swim before I could walk. Also, the firth's tide is on the turn, so the current is not as strong now as it is at other hours."

He stopped where he was and remained so steady that she knew he must be touching bottom and was strong enough to disregard the remaining current.

"Does anyone else know you are swimming here?" he asked. His voice was deep and so vibrant that it seemed to hum through her, strumming unusually pleasant chords in her body and instilling an unexpected calmness there, as well.

Those feelings did naught to help her identify him, though, nor did she trust her own calm. Doubtless, he was good with animals. But she was no dumb beast.

She had also detected an odd, vaguely familiar accent. In fact, there was something oddly familiar about *him*, although she knew they had not met before.

As for his question, she was uncertain of what to say.

He was certainly at home in the water. His shoulders were broad and muscular under what was evidently saffron-dyed cloth. She knew she could not outswim him, and she certainly could not outrun him even if she *could* manage to scramble up the slope to the riverbank before he caught her.

Such thoughts made her aware again of how vulnerable she was, and he was closer now, making her wish that he *had* been one of the friars or a guard.

"Are you going to answer my question?" he asked her. "'Tis the least you can do after pretending to drown."

"Sakes, I just swam underwater. Did you truly think I was drowning?"

"I thought you might be *trying* to drown."

"So you jumped in to save me?"

"This water is cold, and I've had a long day," he said. "Also, you have not answered my question, making me sure that you *did* slip away without permission."

She could hardly say that she had had permission, because she had told no one any more than that she meant to walk in the garden to enjoy the moonlight.

Although she could climb up the slope to the riverbank from where she was, she knew that her shift would reveal too much as she did and that the air would now feel colder than the water did.

So she stayed where she was, watching him, as she said, "I merely came out to enjoy the moonlight and swim in a well-guarded stretch of the river. And *you* interrupted my solitude. I am not cold, and I do not mean to return yet. But I am perfectly safe. If I whistle or scream, men will come."

"Then whistle," he said lightly.

Fiona grimaced, wishing the irritating man would just go away.

The expression on her face stirred Àdham's sense of humor, although he hoped he had concealed it. Clearly, she did not want to whistle and likely would not scream either, and he did not blame her. She would not want to draw such attention. Her air of confidence and gentle speech told him she was wellborn.

But if her people let her think she could safely sneak out at such an hour, they were fools. He had seen no guards. Doubtless, her father owned a house in town or had taken one there for the duration of the King's Parliament, although his foster grandfather had said naught of any nobleman's residence near the north gate.

In fact, he had described only one residence of note at the north end of town. That was a monastery of Dominican Blackfriars *outside* the north wall. Likely, it was the walled area that contained the large, shadowy building with its two lighted windows, and which Àdham could see more clearly now.

He was wet and cold, and the lass had neither whistled nor spoken since suggesting that she could whistle for help. She had taken a step or two up the slope, far enough to reveal her slim shoulders, but she still eyed him cautiously. Her eyes were unusual. Their pupils were so large and their whites so clear in the moonlight that if she had irises, they were either too light or too dark for him to discern them.

"You are gey quiet for one who needs only to whistle," he said gently, with perhaps just a touch of mockery.

"I think I have somehow amused you," she said. "I could hear it in your voice before, and with the moonlight on your face now, I saw your lips twitch."

Her voice was lower than most women's and so softly musical that it was as if it caressed his ears. Pushing that foolish notion from his mind, he said bluntly, "The plain fact is that *you* are not whistling, my lady. Nor have I seen any guards along this stretch of the river."

"I wonder if you doubt that when I do whistle, help will come."

"I believe someone might come," he said, certain now that she was noble, because she had not blinked at "my lady." "But I doubt that you *want* anyone else to see you clad as you are now. Will not your lord father be displeased with you?"

"So you think you know who I am, do you?"

"Only that you are noble," he replied honestly. "I dinna ken your name or even your age, come to that."

"My name is Fiona, and I shall turn eighteen on the last day of this month."

"What is your family name?"

She hesitated and then said with a sigh, "You will find out easily enough that my father is Lord Ormiston of Ormiston Mains, in Lothian."

Frowning, Àdham said, "So he is one of his grace's tame Lothian lairds, is he not? I do not know precisely where Lothian is . . ."

"The noblemen his grace calls his Lothian lairds all own lands between the south shore of the Firth of Forth and Scotland's southeastern border."

"Have you then, perhaps, a warrior knight amongst your kinfolk, a man of uncertain temper that men call Devil Ormiston?"

She smiled then, and her eyes twinkled mischievously, sending a physical jolt to parts of him that had lain dormant for months. "Aye, my brother Davy," she said. "But to say that Davy's temper is uncertain is gravely to understate the matter. In troth, I was recalling earlier *how* uncertain it can be."

He had no doubt that his amusement showed this time, but he said, "I expect he would disapprove of you being here with me. I have ken of him only because two of my kinsmen have spoken of his valor in battle and tourney. But we should get out of this water and warm ourselves whilst you tell me more about yourself."

"I don't suppose that I *will* tell you more," she retorted. "You may know who I am, but I do *not* know you."

"I am Àdham MacFinlagh of Strathnairn."

"Well, Àdham MacFinlagh of Strathnairn," she said, pronouncing the name nearly as he had, "I agree that we should not continue this discourse in the water. So if you will turn your back whilst I fetch my cloak, I shall get out. I suspect that this shift may become rather transparent whilst it remains wet."

"If you did not want anyone to look, you should not have come out in it," he said, unable to resist teasing her.

"You have already made your opinion clear, so you need not belabor it," she said, remaining as she was. "I shan't get out until you turn away. But you *could* just get out yourself, instead, and leave me to finish my swim."

"Nae, m'lady, I cannot do that," he said, although he did turn his back to her. "I'd be ill-serving your kinsmen if I left you here alone. Moreover, three of my men follow me and will soon be upon us if we stay here."

"Why are they not with you now?"

"Because they are afoot, and I was not. But, if we miss one another, I expect they will ask for me at the north gate, and the guard will direct them to the alehouse where we are to be staying."

Her eyebrows shot upward. "There is no guard for them to ask. All of the town gates, which people here call 'ports,' stay open to everyone, especially whilst the King holds his Parliament here. Have you not visited St. John's Town before?"

"I have not." He glanced toward her as he spoke and saw that she was scrambling onto the bank. She had been right about the thin smock, so he turned away before she could catch him appreciating her shapely backside and added, "I do know that St. John's Town is our Scottish capital, though. So why even *have* a wall around it, and fortified gates . . . ports . . . if no one guards them?"

"'Tis because of the Parliament," she replied. "Anyone who wishes to attend must be allowed to attend. So all the gates stay open. Sakes, St. John's Town has been a royal burgh *and* our capital since the early twelfth century."

"I did not know it was as long as that," he admitted. "Or that it was walled."

"Sithee, when England's first Edward invaded one hundred and fifty years ago, St. John's Town had only a ditch to defend against his assault. He built stronger fortifications, including a wall to pro-tect against our barbaric Highlanders. Decades later, Robert the Bruce recaptured Perth, and it remained peaceful until England's *third* Edward invaded a hundred years ago. Meaning to finish what his grandfather started and make his permanent base here, he forced the monasteries to rebuild the wall. St. John's Town thereby became Scotland's strongest town, more fortified than even Edin-burgh or Stirling. It remains so to this day."

"How do you know so much of St. John's Town's history?" he asked, as he made his way up the slick, rocky slope.

She bent to pick up a dark cloak from the grassy riverbank. As she did, her wet smock hugged her body enticingly enough to stir a brief wish that he could forget having vowed to behave honor-ably toward those weaker than himself.

"I *like* to know things," she said, looking back at him.

He was soaked through, and when a foot slipped, he realized that in his concern for her safety he had spared none for the leather breeks and snug-fitting rawhide boots he had worn to ride. The boots were getting little traction, and he did not want to embarrass himself by falling back in.

Covering herself as she straightened and turned back toward him, she added, "When I meet someone who might have answers to my questions, I ask many."

"But you fail to answer questions when others ask them of you."

"Look here," she demanded, "do you mean to betray me?"

"So you did sneak out," he said, looking for his warm woolen plaid.

"Think what you like about that," she said. "Are you coming now or not?"

"I am," he said. Putting fingers to his lips to give two quick, sharp whistles, he stepped onto the grassy slope and then to the path, where he picked up his cap.

Deftly braiding her wet hair into a long, tight plait over her left shoulder that would not instantly reveal to anyone who saw her that she had been in the river, Fiona glowered as the man made his way toward her.

His saffron-colored shirt looked almost thin enough to see through, certainly thin enough to reveal his muscular chest. To her relief, she saw as he emerged that he had kept his breeks on . . . and his rawhide boots.

They squished as he walked, so he was doubtless unhappy about those boots.

He was tall, taller than Davy, and broader, especially across his shoulders.

"Why did *you* whistle?" she asked when he came nearer, refusing to let his size intimidate her. The humming sensation inside her began again as he got closer. Striving to ignore it, she added, "Are you *trying* to wake everyone?"

He gestured toward the river path north of them. "I whistled for my horse. I left him just beyond that rise. Also, somewhere in that direction, my plaid, my bonnet, and my weapons lie where I flung them."

She cocked her head. "Your 'plaid'?"

"'Tis a garment that you might regard as a sort of bulky cloak or cape."

"Do you mean to *stay* in St. John's Town?" she asked, remembering that her glimpse of him had revealed a man heavily cloaked and trying to ignore a twinge of guilt at hearing that he'd cast aside his cloak *and* his weapons to rescue her.

He did not answer immediately, so she added, "Would you not liefer go into town as if you had never met me? Truly, sir, I did not need your help. No one here has forbidden me to swim by moonlight, although you are likely right about my father's reaction if he should learn of it."

Hearing hoofbeats then, she turned toward the sound and saw a handsome, dark horse with four white stockings and a white blaze on its forehead trotting toward them. A shaggy black-and-white dog loped awkwardly at its heels, dragging an unwieldy length of cloth and a wide leather strap from its mouth.

"Is your dog friendly?" Fiona asked.

"He is, aye, unless someone threatens me. His name is Sirius."

"Like the dog that follows the hunter Orion across the night sky?"

"Aye," he said, giving her another searching look. "And unless I'm mistaken, Sirius carries my belt and my plaid."

The dog approached him, its upper teeth bared as if it were smiling.

"*Moran taing*," he muttered, taking the cloth and draping the wide leather belt over one shoulder. Stretching the long cloth out and shaking a few dead leaves and some of the path's dust and gravel from it, he proceeded to wrap it deftly around his thighs, hips, and lower torso. "Fetch my sword, lad," he said as he adjusted the garment's folds and reached for his belt.

To Fiona's amazement, the dog trotted back the way it had come, and before MacFinlagh had fastened his belt, it returned, dragging a leather baldric and sword.

"You have trained him and your horse well," she said, watching in fascination as the man flung the remaining length of cloth over his left shoulder.

"I cannot take credit for the horse," he said as he reached down for the baldric and sword. "A friend trained it."

She nodded. Taking in his full image as he straightened and slung baldric and sword into place, then stood with his feet planted apart, gazing confidently at her, she felt a tremor of dismay and realized why he had seemed familiar to her earlier. His shirt; long, tousled hair; and unkempt beard had reminded her of the Lord of the Isles when he had submitted to the King at Holyrood.

Their accents, even the two strange words he had said to the dog, sounded similar. She had also seen northern lords and the men in their retinues in town wearing the odd garment he called a plaid.

He cocked his head. "What is it?"

"Why, you're a . . ." Hesitating, she fought to think of a tactful word.

His lips twisted wryly. "Aye," he said. "I'm one of those infernal, barbaric Highlanders that you mentioned earlier."

CHAPTER 2

Fiona stared at the man, wondering if he was mocking her again. He sounded educated rather than barbaric. But she recalled, too, that he had called her father one of the King's "tame" Lothian lairds.

"Faith," she exclaimed, "do you oppose his grace? Because, if you do—"

"I do not oppose James Stewart nor do I fully agree with all that he wants to do," he replied. "However, I *did* fight for him at Lochaber, and he is my liege lord."

"So, how is it that you speak Scots? I thought that all Highlanders spo—"

"All barbaric Highlanders," he interjected provocatively.

"Aye, then," she retorted. "I thought that all such persons spoke a language they call the Gaelic. But you speak Scots as if you had always done so."

"Two of my kinsmen studied at St. Andrews with Bishop Traill shortly before Bishop Wardlaw founded the university there. They taught me and some of my cousins to speak Scots, believing the language might help us communicate better with men we meet in battle or who lead us *into* battle. One such is a cousin of his grace's, once known as the Lord of the North but now called Mar."

"I have met Alexander Stewart, Earl of Mar," Fiona murmured.

"I, too," he said, shifting his attention to the dog still standing patiently before him. Patting it on the head, he said, "Good lad." Straightening again, he said, "That cloak must be damp now, my lady, so come along. I'll take you home."

To avoid debate, albeit certain that he would object to leaving her at the garden hedge, she said as they began walking, "Why did you look at me as you did whilst we were talking about your dog having the same name as Orion's dog?"

"I was surprised that you knew the name Sirius. My foster mother names her dogs after legendary creatures, so I did, too. But I know few others who do."

"My father's chaplain educated my brothers," she explained. "And Father is fond of retelling his favorite ancient myths. But, pray go on into town now, sir," she added firmly. "I *will* go back in, I promise. But you need not escort me."

"Nevertheless, I will do so," he said with an audible edge to his voice. "I cannot leave you here, because I doubt I can trust you to go home if I do."

Straightening her shoulders, she gave him look for look, meeting his calm but still intense gaze with more ease than she had expected. "I believe your motives are honorable," she said. "But others may think that I made a tryst with you. Talk of such behavior would do us both harm, so I must return on my own."

Although his expression revealed only a twitch of his dark eyebrows, she felt the strengthening undercurrent of his irritation as easily as she could sense the river's current, no matter how calm its surface looked.

When he sighed, she felt a prickle of unease but had time for no more before he picked her up as if she had been a sack of oatmeal and slung her, face down, over his left shoulder. Despite the woolen cloth over that shoulder, it was bone hard, and landing on it hurt her ribs and snatched her breath away.

Then, clicking his tongue loudly, he began to stride toward the town. She saw that both the dog and the horse followed obediently.

"Put me *down*," she muttered when she could talk. "You have no *right* to treat me so! Faith, sir, stop! You *cannot* parade me through the town like this!"

"I'll put you down when you agree to behave and go with me peacefully."

Her response, although she did her best to stifle it, was a half-shriek, half-growl of pure fury. She tried to kick him, but he'd clamped his left arm tightly over her cloak and across her knees, so her efforts only made her ribs ache more.

Even so, she could not let him take her into town. "I pray you, sir, *listen* to me. We must not create such a scene as this in town! I do not *go* that way!"

Àdham allowed himself a smile. He did not mind carrying the saucy wench, nor was she much of a burden. The way she had so swiftly stifled her outrage assured him that her father would thank him rather than rebuke him for refusing to leave her on the river-bank alone.

A snarl from nearby shrubbery erased his smile. But, before he could collect his wits to identify its source, a furry missile shot to his wet tunic-clad upper right arm and four sharp-clawed paws dug painfully into it.

Awkwardly reaching his right hand toward the wee cat—for such it was—he tried to slap it away, only to have sharp teeth catch hold of his hand. Still snarling, the cat dug its claws deeper.

Beside him, Sirius growled and shot Àdham a worried look.

Snatching his hand free, Àdham reached again for the cat.

"Don't hurt her!" the lady Fiona cried out. "She is protecting me. Prithee, put me down, sir," she added more calmly. "I'll take her. And I'll behave, I swear."

Believing her, he set her on her feet and watched her gently unhook the cat from his arm. That wee black beast, white-tipped ears flattened against its head and its tail atwitch, continued to growl at him even as she cradled it in her arms. In truth, though, the little cat had reminded him that he had no right to treat the lass so.

Irked by her insistence upon having her own way, he had briefly forgotten that she was a noblewoman, a lady, and he a knight sworn to behave honorably. Instead, he had behaved as he might toward one of his saucier younger cousins.

"There, there, Donsie-lass," she murmured. "I'm safe. Hush now."

Àdham saw spots of blood oozing from his injured hand. Sucking it, he was sure that more oozed from his arm to his tunic sleeve. "Donsie's a good name for that wee harpy," he said. "She's as hot-skinned as any demon."

"I have never seen her go for someone like that before," Lady Fiona said ruefully. "I apologize, sir. Had I known she was there, or that she might attack . . ."

When her words trailed to silence, Àdham said with a wry smile, "Do not say that you would have warned me. I would *not* believe you."

To his surprise, the mischievous look he'd seen earlier lit her eyes, and she grinned. "I reclaim my apology," she said. "It serves you right for treating me so."

That mischievous grin was too contagious. He allowed himself a more natural smile but shook his head at her. Although he could not approve of her behavior, she was certainly beginning to intrigue him.

She set the cat down and seemed as astonished as he was when it strode up to Sirius, who was many times its size, and hissed. When the dog cocked its head, the little cat humped its back and spat.

At that, with no more protest than a low, throaty moan, Sirius moved out of Donsie's way and watched warily as she stalked past him, tail high and straight, and went on her way across the field.

Patting the dog, Àdham said, "I dinna blame ye, lad. 'Tis a fierce one, that."

Lady Fiona chuckled. "Perhaps I should have used *my* claws."

Her chuckle was even more contagious than her grin, but he forced what he hoped was credible sternness into his tone and said, "D'ye think so?"

Evidently the tone failed, because she grinned again, unchastened.

Then, sobering, she said, "If you are determined to escort me, sir, I'll allow it. But we can*not* go into town."

"Faith, how did you come here if not through the town gate?"

"I walked across the Inch, of course." She pointed the way the cat had gone.

"Then this *is* the famous North Inch where the great clan battle took place." He looked around with deeper interest, the moonlight making the area brighter than ever. "So, the north gate . . . that is, the north port . . . lies yonder, aye? I am supposed to find my people in the High Street."

"The north port lies at this end of the west-facing wall. But this path will take you a shorter way through a narrow port by that old tower ahead. 'Tis called the red port because of the wee bridge across the mill lade there. Long ago, the bridge was red, so townsfolk still call *it* the red bridge to distinguish it from others. Thus did the narrow port become the 'red port.' From there, you go—"

"I'll not *go* until I've seen you safely inside," he reminded her.

"But I shall *be* inside by then," she said, her eyes still twinkling. "I reside at the House of the Blackfriars. And Blackfriars Wynd leads to the red port."

"Don't prate such blethers to me," he said grimly. "The Blackfriars are monks, *men*. I did hear that his grace stays with them when he visits Perth. But—"

"They are not monks but mendicant friars," she interjected. "At present, her grace, Queen Joanna, is with the King, their retinues likewise. And I have the honor to serve her grace as a maid of honor."

"So, if you *had* whistled, who would have come?" he asked curiously.

"There are royal guards, of course," she said, glancing at him, her eyes still alight. "Several of them would have heard me whistle or scream."

"I see," he said. "Even so, my lady, your behavior was unwise."

She sobered then. "Perhaps, but you must also see that as Father Prior and his people are our hosts, if Brother Porter sees you escort me to the entrance . . ."

"He will suspect a tryst, aye," Àdham said with a sigh when she paused. He realized then that he had been unwise not to give more heed to her earlier warning. "Very well, then. I'll stop where I can see you go in, though."

"You have not said if you mean to betray me," she said anxiously.

"I'd not do so a-purpose," he replied. "But neither will I lie for you."

"Then do not let him see you. If I'm quick, he won't catch sight of us together," she added. "As it is, I fear I've been out longer than I said I would be."

He shook his head at what was certainly an understatement but kept silent.

As they continued across the field, Àdham led the horse, and Sirius walked beside him. To keep his thoughts off her ladyship's shapely backside, fine bosom, lovely face, and intriguingly plump lips, he fixed his gaze on the monastery ahead.

It certainly looked grander than any other religious house he had seen.

The open gate between its two towers provided a fine view of the residence beyond. A broad, torchlit, flagstone courtyard led to a column-framed entry, its peaked portico topped by a weather vane that moonlight had turned silvery. The place more nearly suited Àdham's notion of a royal palace than a monastery.

That thought no sooner occurred to him than, hearing her sharply indrawn breath, he saw her hesitate, mouth agape. She was staring straight ahead.

Following her startled gaze, he saw that the monastery's front door had opened and a man filled the doorway, arms akimbo. Flickering torchlight distorted his features, but his pose and stiffened body made his feelings plain.

With a sudden if hastily stifled impulse to remove himself as far from the lass as he could go, Àdham said, "Who is that?"

"My lord father," she said, confirming the wisdom of his instincts.

Overcoming her own impulse to avoid the inevitable confrontation, Fiona drew a breath, let it out, and forced herself to keep walking. Even so, she felt relief when Ormiston pulled the door shut behind him before he strode to meet them.

She did not want Brother Porter to witness whatever was to come, not that she knew what that might be. Although Ormiston rarely lost his temper, he could be coldly cutting when he was displeased. Without looking at MacFinlagh, she said, "If you want to escape, sir, you should go now."

"I am not leaving," he replied grimly.

Oddly reassured but unable to bear the silence while one angry man crossed the entry court toward her and another radiated displeasure beside her, she looked at her companion and tried to think of something sensible to say.

"How angry will he be?" MacFinlagh murmured.

"He looks furious. But this has never happened before, so I do not know."

"Might he beat you?"

A shiver shot through her at the thought, but she dismissed it. "I hope not," she said. Then, hastily, she added, "Hush now. His hearing is most acute."

She could hear Ormiston's footsteps, soft whispers on the flagstones, and she could see his features clearly. His eyebrows were closer together than usual, his expression set. He was definitely angry and likely, before long, to be furious.

She prayed that Brother Porter had not betrayed her—and would not. He had not done so the one previous time she had come out to walk by the river.

Then her father was upon them, and she faced him silently.

His frown had deepened, making her feel as if she ought to curtsy as low before him as she did before Jamie Stewart.

When he did not speak, she said nervously, "I bid you good even, sir. I expect you were with his grace, and you must think—"

A slight shake of his head silenced her. His gaze shifted to her companion as he said with what she suspected was forced calm, "You can know naught of what I am thinking, daughter. Prithee, present your escort to me . . . if you can."

Heat flooded her cheeks at the proviso. But she managed to retain composure enough to say, "I beg your pardon, my lord. This is Àdham MacFinlagh of . . ."

"Of Strathnairn, your lordship," MacFinlagh said helpfully when Fiona's memory refused to produce the unfamiliar place name.

"MacFinlagh, eh? You belong to the Clan Chattan Confederation then, aye?"

"I do have that honor," MacFinlagh agreed.

"I have heard his grace speak of one MacFinlagh of Strath-nairn," Ormiston said in the chilly, cutting way that sent icicles up Fiona's spine and made her wonder what *that* MacFinlagh had done to displease him so.

The man beside her remained silent long enough to make her look up at him, sensing that her father expected him to say more.

"It is *Sir* Àdham, is it not?" Ormiston prompted with an enigmatic, even more chilling note in his voice.

Apparently undaunted by that tone but eluding Fiona's astonished gaze, MacFinlagh said, "I am that MacFinlagh, aye, sir."

Nodding, Ormiston said, "We will see you safely inside now, daughter, but you and I *will* talk more at the house tomorrow. After you see to your morning duties, and when it is convenient for her grace to dispense with you for a time, you will beg her mistress of robes to dispatch a page to inform me. I shall be with the King then, wherever he might be. At present, you will go straight to bed."

"Aye, sir," she said, knowing he would accept no other reply. As it was, she was grateful that he had not immediately taken her to task, as Davy or one of her other two older brothers or her sister would have done, audience or none.

As she walked with the two silent men toward the gateway, she stole a look up at Sir Àdham MacFinlagh's set face and wished fervently that she knew of a way to protect him from her father's wrath.

As one of Scotland's most powerful and influential men, and one who had the ear of the King, Ormiston could be more dangerous when he remained calm than when he did lose his temper. Although he would likely blame her as much as, or more than, Sir Àdham for what he suspected of them, he could certainly make Sir Àdham's life most unpleasant if he decided to do so.

Ormiston's words and stern tone stirred a twinge of sympathy in Àdham that under other circumstances might have led him to speak for her ladyship, but he resisted the impulse. Any sister, cousin, or, in due time, any daughter of his who slipped away from her protectors as her ladyship had done would deserve strict censure. By what he read in Ormiston's tone and expression, his lordship agreed with him. Lady Fiona would suffer a severe scolding, or worse, come morning.

After she was safely inside, Àdham expected to receive his share of that censure and wondered if Ormiston would believe aught he said to him. The man's scornful emphasis on "*Sir Àdham*," had surely stemmed from an outraged belief that he had arranged a tryst with the lady Fiona, thereby breaking his code of honor.

Both men were silent as they followed the wynd outside the monastery toward the town gate until Ormiston said grimly, "I do want answers from you, sir, and my house lies just inside the wall. I expect that *you* have lodgings in town, too, aye?"

"I arrived at the Inch from the north less than a half hour ago, your lordship," Àdham replied. "Moreover, I can assure you that I did naught to harm—"

"We will not pursue *that* topic in the street at such a quiet hour," Ormiston interjected curtly. "Do you mean to say that you do *not* have lodgings in town?"

"In a manner of speaking, I do. But, with respect, sir," Àdham added hastily, keeping his voice low, "I believe that you are harboring a misconception."

"Lad, I have advised the King for seven years now, since his return from his English captivity. That means that I often must make judgment of men who want something from him or seek to sway him one way or another. Therefore, I try not to form opinions until I acquire as much information as I can gather. I did think you were but *returning* to town now. So, prithee, just answer my question plainly."

"By my troth, sir, I have journeyed for four days from the north-central Highlands. I traveled from Blair Castle this morning, a daylong journey of over thirty miles, and arrived at the North Inch shortly before you and I met. I expect I do have lodgings in town, though," he added honestly. "I am to meet my clansmen at a High Street alehouse. They were to have acquired bedchambers there."

"That alehouse lies at the end of this road," Ormiston said. "Sir Ivor Mackintosh and Gillichallum Roy are there now with other Mackintosh men."

"I thought Gilli Roy would bide with the Mackintosh—his father."

"Malcolm hired a house not far from mine own in Curfew Row, just inside yon port," Ormiston said. "He thought Gilli would be happier at the alehouse with Sir Ivor and the others. But the hour is late, and since you seem to speak our Lowland tongue well, I would hear more about this incident tonight, ere we part."

Unaware until then that Ormiston knew Malcolm, "the Mackintosh," hereditary Captain of the Clan Chattan Confederation, *and* Sir Ivor Mackintosh, not only Clan Chattan's war leader but also Àdham's foster uncle, Àdham knew he'd be wise to explain matters before Ormiston saw either kinsman again.

In fact, although the man had been furious to find him with his errant daughter and firm about discussing the matter, he did seem more amenable now.

As Àdham was trying to imagine what he could honestly say about what had happened without revealing just *how* he and her ladyship had met, Ormiston said mildly, "In troth, I think we might both be grateful for some wine, aye?"

"I do want to explain matters, sir," Àdham said. "But my squire, my equerry, and another lad, who follow me with our baggage, will soon be seeking me."

"Your men can find the alehouse by asking anyone," Ormiston said. "And you need only follow this road until it ends at the Mercat Cross in the High Street. But I'll have one of my lads show you the way after we have talked."

"Then you leave me naught to say, sir, save thank you," Àdham said.

They had reached the little arched bridge, and the narrow port stood open beyond it, so he gestured for Ormiston to precede him. Only as he followed with the horse did it occur to him that his lordship was unlikely to walk the streets of any town unattended.

Glancing back to see two men quietly following, some twenty yards back, he murmured, "Are the two men behind us yours, sir?"

"They are. Neither his grace nor Father Prior likes the idea of armed men visibly guarding the monastery. So, although James has protection, the royal guards keep themselves and their weapons hidden. My two men awaited me in the shadows of those trees by the portico. When I saw you two tonight, I told them to stay there. Then, when we left the monastery, I signaled them to follow at a distance."

"I was certain you would want my head, sir."

"That remains to be seen, does it not?"

Unable to find reassurance in that response, Àdham wondered if he had misread Ormiston and had a fleeting wish that he'd not left his own men behind.

That thought fled the moment it formed, though. Had he not ridden on ahead, he'd have missed meeting the lady Fiona, who—whether she would ever admit it or not—might well have found herself in worse trouble than she faced now.

"What do we do the noo, Hew?" Dae asked his cousin when their quarry had gone inside. "Must we try again? We ha' lain here four nights, as it be, since ye heard she had come outside the wall, and then only tae *walk* by yon river."

"I doubt the lass will come out alone again," Hew muttered in a near growl. "If I dinna mistake the matter, that man wha' met them were Ormiston hisself."

"And the younger one? Who were he?"

"How d'ye think I'd ken him, Dae?" Hew muttered. "He's a big, braw lad, and dresses as we Highlanders all do. But I couldna see his features any more than ye could. Sakes, I dinna ken if that thick beard o' his be black or brown."

"Then what'll we do?" Dae repeated. "I ken fine that Sir Ro—"

"Whisst now," Hew interjected harshly. "We name nae names."

"But ye said the lass be our key tae open Tantallon and free Alexander, aye?"

"Aye, sure, for when we capture her, her da will do aught that we tell him tae do. This be but a wee hindrance, Dae. If nae opportunity arises afore this Parliament be done, most o' them lairds will go home. We'll likely find another chance then."

"How long will that be?"

"I dinna ken. But I ha' other notions, too. I'm thinking tae get m'self shaved and dress like a Lowlander. But dinna be prating about this tae any save me."

Wide-eyed, Dae gaped at him. "I wouldna, Hew!"

"See that ye don't."

Giving thanks to the Fates that her father had not noticed her wet hair or that her cloak concealed a wet shift, Fiona had bidden Brother Porter good night and hurried up two narrow flights of stairs to the tiny bedchamber she had cordially disliked until learning that she would have it all to herself.

Entering and shutting the door, she was glad that she had left the stone cresset burning. Its golden light made the tiny chamber seem warm and inviting.

The thought that Ormiston might order her henceforth to share a room with another of the Queen's attendants struck her then with unwelcome force.

Hearing an indignant meow outside the door, she opened it to let Donsie in. As she shut it, a calmer second thought suggested that her father was unlikely to call such attention to what he clearly viewed as her misbehavior.

"He will more likely make me feel small and irritating whilst he scolds me, Donsie," she murmured as she moved the lute she had practiced playing earlier from her bed into the woven-willow case where it belonged. She knew she had disappointed her father, but he would not endanger her position with the Queen.

She was nearly certain that, as long as he remained one of the King's closest and most trusted advisers, he would want her to be near him, albeit perhaps more closely guarded than before. Her service to Queen Joanna usually assured that she would be near Ormiston, because the King kept his beloved wife and their four wee daughters with him unless he had to be away with the royal army.

Drying herself with a towel, Fiona shifted Donsie aside and got into the narrow bed, wriggling under its covers to get warm. Then, listening to the cat purr as it nestled close to her, but certain the night's adventure would keep her awake, she tried to imagine how Sir Àdham was faring with her father.

To think that he was a *knight* and she had as good as called him a barbarian!

He was educated, even somewhat civilized if one discounted the odd clothing that Highlanders wore. At least, he had worn breeks and boots and had not complained about getting them wet. He had a nice smile, too. His teeth were white and strong looking, unlike those of many men she had met.

Thinking about him and her father, she felt a new stab of guilt.

Sir Àdham had tried only to rescue her, and for his effort, had to defend himself to a powerful lord. That was likely a new experience for him and, sadly, one for which he would not easily, if ever, forgive her. Still wide awake, she came just as sadly to realize that her father might be more than disappointed in her.

If Ormiston truly believed that she had slipped out into the moonlight a-purpose to meet Sir Àdham, he would also believe that she had betrayed his trust.

That Joanna or Lady Sutherland, her grace's mistress of robes, might believe the same thing caused less concern. Joanna was kind, and although the rules for her ladies were strict, she understood that some needed more freedom than others. She knew, too, that even at Blackfriars and other such residences, the large retinues and other residents made finding solitude with any sense of space nearly impossible.

Lady Sutherland was less understanding. But Fiona's adventure would cause ructions only if others had seen her with Sir Àdham before Ormiston joined them.

She would have little defense then, because no matter how many times she had assured herself that naught could happen because she had never seen anyone walking on or near the Inch so late at night, Sir Àdham had done so.

A mere hint of scandal could prove her undoing. But, even if Joanna dismissed her, Fiona doubted that Ormiston would send her home. Nor would the King demand it, because he depended on Ormiston. The trust between the two was strong, and James had reason to distrust many other members of his court.

Again, she wondered how much Sir Àdham would believe it necessary to tell her father. Could she trust a man—a knight, aye, but a semibarbaric one—who had said that although he would not willingly betray her, he would also not lie for her?

CHAPTER 3

The wynd that Àdham and Ormiston followed forked almost immediately after the red port, one branch leading into town, the other rounding a garden wall to their right. Large houses lined the row, and Ormiston led him to the second one on the right, its gardens visibly extending from the house to the town wall behind it.

It was smaller than some of its neighbors, but Curfew Row's residents were clearly wealthy. Not that Àdham had expected otherwise, for if the Mackintosh had taken a house nearby, he would likely have demanded even finer accommodations.

"My men will see to your horse," Ormiston said, gesturing to the two following them. "The stables lie behind the house."

"Thank you, sir, but they need do naught save tether him. I'll be on my way soon after we have talked."

"In troth, lad, I've been thinking, and I am strongly inclined to suspect now that I may be beholden to you," Ormiston said. "If that should prove true, you are welcome to sleep here tonight and rejoin your clansmen in the morning."

The invitation was tempting, but Àdham shook his head. "'Tis kind of you, sir," he said. "But you owe me naught, and if I fail to reach the alehouse, men there will raise a hue and cry for me."

"Not if I send someone to tell them that you're with me," Ormiston said. "But, if you would feel discomfited . . ." He paused, then added dulcetly, "That alehouse is said to be a gey noisy place."

"'Tis true that I'd welcome a quiet bed," Àdham admitted. "If your man will take a message for my squire and equerry that will bring them to me in the morning, I'd be fain to accept your invitation . . . if you still hold by it after we talk."

Having given the necessary orders to his two men, Ormiston led the way inside and through the house to a cozy chamber in the rear, where a fire burned cheerfully on the hearth. Taking a jug and two pewter goblets from a shelf, he poured what appeared to be claret into each and handed one to Àdham.

Then, gesturing to a table near the hearth where a pair of back-stools faced each other, he said, "Take that nearer seat, lad."

As Àdham obeyed the command, Ormiston stepped past him. Shifting the other back-stool a few inches closer, he sat and looked directly into Àdham's eyes, goblet in hand, for a long, silent moment, before saying gently, "Perhaps now, you will tell me exactly how you came to be in company with my daughter at such a late hour."

Taking a moment just as long and silent to gather his thoughts but seeing no way to describe their meeting without laying blame on her ladyship, and having no wish to do that, Àdham realized he had only one course to take.

"With respect, sir," he said, "you must ask her ladyship about that."

His jaw visibly clenching, Ormiston gazed sternly at Àdham, but Àdham met his gaze with long-practiced calm and sipped his wine.

"I believe," Ormiston said, "that you *owe* me an explanation if only to maintain your knightly sense of honor."

"My honor is in no danger, sir. I would willingly explain aught of mine own behavior were there aught more of import to explain. However, I cannot speak for her ladyship. I have told you where I was this morning and that I reached the North Inch shortly before you saw us together. She took no harm from me."

"Your hair, tunic, and breeks are still wet, lad," Ormiston observed quietly.

My boots, too, Àdham thought unhappily. Thankful that they had stopped squishing as he walked, he said only, "Aye, sir, I did enjoy a brief swim."

Ormiston sipped his wine, observing Àdham over the rim of the goblet.

To Àdham's astonishment, the man's hazel-gray eyes began to twinkle. "Your goblet must be empty or nearly so, lad, and I doubt I'll sleep yet a while," he said. "Moreover, his grace will not convene tomorrow's session until an hour or so before midday. Would you like more of this excellent claret before we retire?"

"I would," Àdham agreed, "if I may take your offer as a suggestion that you need ask me no more about what happened tonight."

"Aye, for the present," Ormiston said. "Sithee, I know my daughter well."

Deciding to let that statement stand without comment, Àdham said, "I ken little of what may be happening in the Parliament, sir. I do know that you serve as one of his grace's advisers. I've also heard that ructions may arise, so if you'd liefer not discuss such things with me, I'll understand. But if you can tell me aught of value, I would be grateful."

"Naught of much importance has occurred yet, although ructions *have* arisen. However, his grace by custom lets his lord chamberlain deal with such discontent until a particular issue is formally introduced for discussion," Ormiston said. "The issue stirring the most fractiousness so far concerns landowners' heritable rights."

"I do ken something about that," Àdham said. "Such rights are of concern to all Highland chiefs. They believe that his grace, in desiring to institute one rule of law throughout Scotland, means to trample on ancient, established jurisdictional rights that historically have been theirs, such as our lairds' courts and rights of the pit and gallows."

"And any other rights that pertain to inherited lands," Ormiston said. "Many lords in the Lowlands and Borders likewise object to losing such rights, believing that lawlessness, and thus chaos, will result."

"I tend to agree with that," Àdham said. "'Tis our chiefs and chieftains who maintain order in the Highlands. So, why does his grace *dis*agree?"

"Because power-hungry men can manipulate our current system to serve their own wicked goals, rather than the good of their people or their country," Ormiston said. "His grace points out that we have seen what happens when an evil man inherits or otherwise contrives to seize vast power. His unscrupulous uncle, the Duke of Albany, did just that and ruled Scotland for nearly four decades without ever being King of Scots, first as Regent for his aged father, then for his older brother, and then—as James and many others believe—by arranging for the English to capture James."

"I had not heard that," Àdham admitted. "Only that he had *been* a captive."

"The English held him for nineteen years, until Albany died," Ormiston said. "But tell me more about yourself now, lad. If you are with Clan Chattan, you must be kin to the Mackintosh."

"Malcolm is my liege lord. I live with my uncle, Fin of the Battles, at Castle Finlagh above Strathnairn, which is the valley of the river and town of Nairn."

"If you fostered with Fin of the Battles, then who is your father?"

"I'm the youngest son of Ewan MacGillony Cameron of Tor Castle, which lies a mile or so beyond the western edge of Glen Mòr, not far from Loch Lochy."

"I'm not as well-acquainted with the Highlands as I should be," Ormiston admitted. "I do know that what we Lowlanders call the Great Glen divides them from Inverness in the north to the sea in the southwest, but I have not visited the area. Even so, just as I knew of your knighthood, I also know that you acquired it by persuading a host of Camerons to support his grace at Lochaber two years ago."

"Just one Cameron, sir," Àdham said. "I chanced to see my father as the tide of battle was turning and I recognized his banner. I urged him to support the King and he persuaded others. See you, the Cameron Confederation, like Clan Chattan, has many factions. Clan Chattan controls most of the area east of the Great Glen, whilst the Camerons bide mostly west of it as far as the coast. So, the Lord of the Isles is nearly always a greater threat to them than his grace is. I do count Castle Finlagh as my home, though, so the Mackintosh is my liege, and our loyalty is and long has been to his grace. But this is the first time I have come to the Lowlands."

"I see," Ormiston said. "I know that Clan Chattan has kept loyal to James, but Alexander must have expected *all* Camerons to remain loyal to him."

"In troth, sir, he expected all Highland clans to welcome him and therefore believed that no Cameron or Mackintosh would side with his grace. He might also have thought that even if one confederation did, the other would not, because they had long been enemies. But Malcolm has been Constable of Inverness Castle for five years, and the confederations have kept a much longer, albeit uneasy, truce."

"I like Malcolm," Ormiston said. "He is a fine and venerable leader, so I am pleased to make the acquaintance of another Clan Chattan man."

Àdham nodded, wondering if Ormiston was aware that many people more likely believed that his having been *born* a Cameron meant that he must always be a Cameron and not, in their view, a true man of Clan Chattan at all.

Fiona awoke the next morning at dawn to hear the monastery bells ringing the hour of Prime. Her door opened moments later, and quick footsteps crossed to the narrow window near the foot of her bed.

"Good morrow, m'lady," her maidservant, Leah Nisbet, said cheerfully as she turned from the window to push back the bed curtain and tie it in place. "Lady Sutherland said her grace will no attend the Parliament this morning wi' his grace but will attend Lady Mass here at the monastery instead. Since she will have Lady Sutherland and Lady Huntly tae attend her, ye need see only tae your own prayers and morning duties till they return."

"They have not left already, have they?" Fiona asked, sitting up. She knew she must not go into town, even the short way to Ormiston House, without proper permission and a gillie to attend her.

"Sakes, m'lady, her grace ha' no left her bed yet, as ye should ken fine," Leah said. "She will say her morning prayers and break her fast afore she walks round tae the monastery chapel."

"I would speak with Lady Sutherland before then, Leah. Prithee, go and ask her woman if her ladyship will be kind enough to see me before I break my fast. I shall wear the emerald green gown with my horned headdress and the ruched white veil," she added, knowing that the green dress was Ormiston's favorite. "I shall also want my fur-lined cloak, because I must visit my lord father this morning."

"This smock be damp, m'lady," the maid said, lifting the garment from the low stool onto which Fiona had cast it the night before.

"I would not wear that one in any event, Leah," Fiona said, hoping that her cloak, which she had hung on its hook, was not also still damp. "I'll wear my white silk shift with the embroidered edging round its neckline."

Quickly washing her face and hands, she donned the silk shift and gown, waiting only for Leah to lace up the back of the gown before shooing her out to find Lady Sutherland and relay her request.

"But your hair, mistress! Ye canna do it by yourself."

"I can brush it whilst I await your return," Fiona said. "I must speak with her ladyship *before* she goes downstairs."

First, Fiona straightened her bed. Lady Sutherland had served the Queen since her grace's arrival in Scotland and was a kind-hearted woman. So, if Joanna still lay abed, her ladyship might deign to come to Fiona's bedchamber. If not, Fiona would have to go to the Queen's chamber and make her request there.

That thought brought a grimace to her lips.

She loved and admired the Queen, who despite being the mother of four small daughters and expecting a fifth child in the fall, had just turned six-and-twenty and was therefore only eight years older than Fiona. What gave her pause was the thought of having to make her request in front of Lady Huntly, who stood next to Lady Sutherland in rank but was older and less charitable.

Several other older ladies and three other maids of honor attended her grace. Most were fiercely ambitious for themselves or because their fathers or husbands hoped to use their positions with the Queen to curry favor with the King.

Pushing such thoughts from her head, Fiona had barely shaken out her skirts when the door opened and Margaret, Countess of

Sutherland, entered in a cloud of the earthy-sweet ambergris-scented perfume she favored.

Wife of one of Scotland's most powerful earls, Lady Sutherland was a handsome woman just a few years older than her grace. Willow slim, wearing a lavender ermine-trimmed silk gown and a boxlike lavender-and-white headdress surmounted with a gold circlet, she held her long, rustling skirts off the floor with delicate, beringed fingers. A silent, modestly attired attendant, having opened the door for her, entered in her wake and turned to shut it again.

"I ha' less than two minutes afore I must hie m'self back tae her grace, Fiona-lass," her ladyship said with a warm smile. "What would ye ask o' me?"

"My lord father desires me to visit him this morning at Ormiston House, madam. I would beg leave to do so after we tidy her grace's chamber."

"Aye, sure," Lady Sutherland said, nodding. "I ken fine that Ormiston will attend the proceedings today. Doubtless, he seeks a quiet hour wi' his daughter, away from all the men who would plague him tae speak for them, so ye dinna want tae keep him waiting. Forbye, ye'll take a lad wi' ye as an escort."

"I will, m'lady," Fiona said, making her curtsy. "Thank you."

Leah, entering seconds after her ladyship's departure, deftly plaited and arranged her mistress's hair and pinned the formal horned caul and veil in place. Afterward, Fiona donned her gloves and descended to the refectory where a table had been set aside behind screens for the maids of honor to take their meals.

Due to the advanced hour at which Àdham and his host had retired, the two men were breaking their fast much later than Àdham usually did.

Fortunately, the previous night's hearth fire had dried his breeks. His rawhide boots were still damp, but Sir Ivor had warned him that Lowland nobles protected their feet in town. So, despite their dampness, Àdham wore the boots.

When he'd entered the room, Ormiston had greeted him cheerfully but had kept his silence since, and Àdham felt no need to break it. He did wonder if his host, having had time to ponder his daughter's activities the previous night, might have more to say to him on that subject or more answers to demand.

A gillie entered with a full jug of ale to replace the empty one on the table.

Acknowledging the order with a quiet, "M'lord," the manservant left with the empty jug, shutting the door firmly behind him.

"We talked much of politics last night," Ormiston said then to Àdham. "I fear that I may have said more to confuse you than to aid you."

"'Tis likely your claret that addled my mind," Àdham said. "But I admit that I still know little of matters unrelated to those Highland clans nearest to me."

"You seem to have a good head on your shoulders, lad. So, as the sessions proceed, if you are interested, you will soon grasp the difficulties his grace faces. But I would ken more about the circumstances leading to your knighthood, from your own view of them. My youngest son is likewise a knight of the realm."

"Aye, sir, I know of 'Devil' Ormiston," Àdham said with a wry smile. "As to my knighthood, the battle that led to it was a painful experience. . . ."

When he paused, Ormiston nodded. "I see. Even so, his grace is not a man easily impressed by other men's skills, and he told me that yours impressed him."

Meeting his gaze, Àdham said, "I do have some repute as an archer and swordsman, having learned from Sir Ivor Mackintosh and his father, who are two of the best. His grace would have it, though, that by persuading Ewan MacGillony to support him, I did save his grace's life and those of many others. I'm not as certain of that as he is, but I did acquire a minion of sorts who insists that his grace must be right. He offers as proof that I did save *him*, too."

Raising his eyebrows, Ormiston said, "A minion *of sorts*?"

The image of young Rory rose instantly to mind, making Àdham smile.

He was glad, too, to change the subject, because when men spoke of his heroism in battle or in making the effort to recruit Ewan to aid the King, he felt obliged to explain that he had done only what seemed right and necessary at the time. Some scoffed at that statement. Others seemed to suspect him of inviting more praise, so he eluded such discussions when he could.

"If the laddie numbers more than ten years now, I'll be astonished," he said, and went on to explain how they had met.

"But he claims to have no ties of his own and has firmly attached himself to me," Àdham added after he had described Rory's relief at seeing him return to the tree. "He even, now and now, manages to make himself useful."

Ormiston's eyes twinkled then in the same way that the lady Fiona's did, but he said, "Surely, you do not let that laddie accompany you wherever you go."

"Nae, for my squire serves me well at home and in battle, and my equerry travels with me when we have horses to tend. I thought we had left Rory at home, but he followed on his own, so he aids my equerry and looks after my dog."

Ormiston smiled again, and their conversation continued amiably.

The next hour passed swiftly for Fiona in a hasty breakfast and attendance to her grace's chambers. As one of the youngest of her grace's attendants, she worked silently, knowing better than to put herself forward or encourage gossip from others.

However, she saw no reason to shut her ears to the other maids' gossip, because her curiosity nearly always defeated thought of restraint. Family members had declared that her chief fault was that when she knew that others had secrets, her curiosity became an insurmountable force, driving her to winkle them out.

Her brother Davy had once accused her of storing up such information to use against people who had irked her. But Fiona was sure she did no such thing.

When Davy pointed out that just letting someone know she had uncovered his secret might silence him as to her own misdeeds, the accusation did give her pause to reflect. Davy had been referring to himself and their two older brothers, though, so she decided he was mistaken. It was only fair, she had explained to him loftily, that having learned something to someone else's discredit, one should make the person aware that his secret had escaped his control. Also, she reminded herself now, if her brothers were daft enough to think she would betray them to anyone else, that was their own misfortune.

Finished at last with her duties and knowing that further delay would irk Ormiston, she fetched her cloak from her chamber. Leaving Donsie curled on her bed and shutting the door so she could not follow, Fiona hurried downstairs.

At the porter's chair, she found Tam, a tall, towheaded gillie in a pale gray tunic, awaiting her with Brother Porter, who wore the cream-colored wool tunic and scapular that men of his order customarily wore indoors. They saved the black-hooded capes that had given the Blackfriars their name for outdoor wear.

"Tam will await ye, to attend your return," Brother Porter said to her.

Smiling, she said, "I do thank you for sending him with me. But my lord father will likely escort me back here before he goes to Parliament House."

"Then his lordship will so inform our Tam," Brother Porter said gently. "Parliament willna convene for an hour or two yet, m'lady. So his lordship may ha' formed other plans for his morning."

Knowing debate would be useless, Fiona left for Ormiston House with her young guardian and reached the house ten minutes later. Leaving Tam and her cloak with her father's porter, she denied any need for that worthy to announce her and went briskly to meet her fate.

Hesitating at the closed door to Ormiston's sanctum to assure herself that whatever Sir Àdham had told him, her father would do no more than scold her, she drew a breath, let it out, opened the door, and went in.

Ormiston looked up from the document before him, his expression as enigmatic as it could be. Seeing her, he set the document aside and rose to his feet.

"Good morrow, sir," she said. "Mayhap I ought to have rapped. But—"

"Nae, lass," he said reassuringly. "You ken fine that my doors are always open to you. Sit now, and tell me about last night."

Although she yearned to demand that he first tell her all that Sir Àdham had said to him, she knew that would be unwise. She also knew that Ormiston would be more than displeased if she revealed the exact truth. So, to give herself time to think, she moved the back-stool that sat opposite him a bit farther from the table, sat gracefully, and carefully arranged her skirts.

Still silent, Ormiston took his seat again, but she felt him watching her and knew she had to speak. At last, meeting his now stern gaze, she said hastily, "I fear that you must be gey displeased with me, sir. But, by my troth, I did not sneak out of the monastery. Brother Porter knew I had gone for a walk."

There being no immediate reply, she added, "You know I cannot resist a full moon, and the monastery grounds and gardens are guarded and safe."

"Are they?" Ormiston asked. "Then, prithee, tell me just how you chanced to meet Sir Àdham MacFinlagh whilst walking through those gardens."

Unwilling to admit pushing through the gap in the hedge, she sighed and said simply, "I walked down to the river, sir."

Finding it nearly impossible then to go on meeting his hard stare, she felt only relief when, instead of demanding to know why she had not stayed in the gardens, he said, "So you arrived at the riverbank. What did you do then?"

Looking down at the table but finding no solace there, she looked obliquely at him and said, "I think you know what I did, sir."

"Sakes, Fiona, never tell me that you left Blackfriars in only your smock and your cloak —or less than that—and crossed the North Inch to the river to swim!"

Since she could say nothing without lying or admitting he was right, she kept silent, only to hear Sir Àdham's voice in her head, wondering if Ormiston would beat her. A shard of ice slid up her spine, and she eyed her father more warily.

His expression offered no comfort. Softly, much too softly, he said, "Where was Sir Àdham whilst you stood on that riverbank in your smock, or less?"

Catching her lower lip briefly between her teeth, she said, "I did wear . . . That is, he was on the path. But I don't think he saw me until

I'd waded into the water. He did see me go under, though. You know how I like to practice holding my breath and swimming underwater at home. That's what I was doing, swimming underwater against the current. When I felt the water surge round me and rose to the surface, he was looking frantically downriver, as if . . ."

Noting the increasing color in her father's face, she paused to pray that God would have mercy on her if Ormiston did not.

"As if he feared that you were drowning?"

"Yes, sir. He . . . He said afterward that he feared I might be *trying* to drown myself. But, of course, I was doing no such thing. I was just—"

"Enough!" Ormiston snapped. "I begin to believe, Fiona, that your brother Kenneth is right to say that I indulge you too much. Mayhap you do need a stronger hand . . . a strict husband, in fact. It is one thing, my lass, to do such things at home, where our people and I know about them and can keep you safe. To commit such folly here on Perth's North Inch, where anyone might come upon you and take advantage of your innocence . . . By my troth, I do not know what to say to you! I did believe that I could trust you to guard your reputation whilst you serve the Queen. But if this is how you repay that trust . . ." He paused to draw a breath.

Stunned, realizing that she had overstepped by a much larger degree than she had imagined, Fiona exclaimed, "I didn't think! Oh, prithee, Father, believe me! It was the first truly spring day we'd had, and I grow so weary of the constant chatter of the others and so rarely find any solitude beyond my tiny chamber! But I would not . . . I could not . . . truly betray your trust. Brother Porter did know that I might go down to walk by the river, although I-I'll admit that I failed to tell him I meant to swim. In troth, I did not mean—" Cutting off her own words when she read the derision in his expression, she grimaced. "No, sir, I shan't say that I did not mean to swim, for I did." She fought for calm before she added, "What will you do?"

"I ken fine what I ought to do," he retorted grimly. Then, as if he could not bear to sit there, looking at her, he stood and turned just enough to look down at the hearth, where the morning fire had reduced itself to glowing embers.

While he stared silently into them, she dared not speak. It was just as well, too, for she knew that not a single word she could say would mend matters.

Ormiston drew an audible breath, let it out, and turned back to face her.

Every nerve in her already tense body seemed to stand on end and twitch as she wondered what he meant to do.

She opened her mouth to apologize, but he spoke before she could. "I understand now why Sir Àdham refused to tell me how you had met."

"You talked with him, then."

"Aye, sure. As it happened, we talked late, so he spent the night here. But he said I would have to ask you about how you came to be together when I met you."

"I fear that he was as irked with me as you are, sir. Perhaps you think I ought to have feared him, but I'd seen at once that he feared *for* me. Sakes, no man would leap fully clothed into that river to take advantage of me. I did ask him to go on into town and let me return to the monastery alone. But he insisted on escorting me."

"By my faith, Fiona, if you tell me that you wish he had not—"

"I don't," she interjected hastily. "It just surprised me that he reacted in so much the same way that Davy would have."

Her father's lips twitched, and Fiona felt herself begin to relax.

"I doubt that he *acted* as David would have," he said, forming his words so carefully that she knew he was struggling to suppress any sign of amusement.

She had no trouble controlling her own sense of humor and felt only relief that Ormiston seemed slightly less likely now to treat her as Davy would have. "I did think that all Highlanders were barbaric," she said. "But, although Sir Àdham was stern and unwilling to believe that I can look after myself—"

"Don't spout such foolishness to me, not today," Ormiston warned her. "Had Sir Àdham been another sort of chap . . ." The color drained from his face.

Quickly, she said, "You are right about him, though. His sense of honor is strong, for he even *said* he would not lie for me. I am thankful it was not someone truly horrid who saw me go into the river. In troth, I failed to think about anything except being entirely by myself for a short time and enjoying a moonlight swim."

"You are still too impulsive," he said. "Moreover, you have shown that I cannot trust you to behave sensibly. If her grace should hear of this escapade . . ."

Fiona waited out the pause by biting her lip to avoid assuring him that if Brother Porter had noted her wet hair or clothing the night before, he'd likely keep her secret as he had done the only other time she'd gone alone to the Tay. On that occasion, she had waded in only to her hips, which surely still counted as walking.

"If her grace *should* learn of it," Ormiston went on, "she will have to dismiss you from her service. You must know that, Fiona."

"I do," she admitted. "But I promise you, sir, I won't do it again."

"You had better not," he said. "If I hear so much as a whisper about this in town, or from anyone else at all, I will remove you from her grace's service myself and deal much more harshly with you than I have yet. Do you understand me?"

"Yes, my lord," she said when she could speak past the knot in her throat. "The only other person who knows is Sir Àdham. And he won't—"

Realizing that she had no reason to trust him other than the initial instinct she had had that she could, she broke off.

Ormiston nodded as if he had followed her thoughts. "You had better hope that you *can* trust that young man. He scarcely knows either of us. And with matters likely to erupt during his grace's Parliament, setting clan against clan all over the country, Sir Àdham might find more cause to speak, or threaten to speak, than to keep this to himself."

Swallowing hard but unable to leave things as they were and knowing she would gain naught by telling him Sir Àdham had promised he would not *willingly* betray her, she said, "Will you ever forgive me, Father?"

"Stand up," he said, moving around the table toward her.

Trembling, she obeyed, aware that tears had welled into her eyes. Putting his hands on her shoulders, he looked down at her and said gently, "You need never ask such a thing of me again, my dearling. I know of naught you could do that I would not forgive. 'Tis true that your actions last night angered and disappointed me. But you need never fear more than well-merited punishment from me for any misdeed. It is my duty as your father to correct you when your behavior goes amiss. But that is all. What I do then I do out of love, never anger."

"I love you, too, so much," she said, leaning into him and giving him a fierce hug. "I'm sorry that I'm such a disappointment."

Holding her close, he said, "'Twas only your behavior, not you, that disappointed me. And behavior is easy to mend, Fiona. I expect you to see to that."

"I will, sir, I swear."

"Good, then. I trust that you brought an escort with you today."

Surprised by the abrupt change of subject and thus his hint that the interview was nearing its end, she said, "Aye, Brother Porter sent Tam, one of the gillies, with me. He told him to await me here. I did hope you would go back with . . ."

He was already shaking his head and setting her back on her heels. "Nae," he said when she paused. "Cousin Buccleuch's party arrived yestereve, and he sent me word that the lady Rosalie Percy has accompanied him. I mean to call on them before today's proceedings begin. Likely, though, we will attend whatever festivities follow the sessions tonight. I hope to see you there."

Fiona's spirits sagged. Sir Walter Scott of Buccleuch, though only a dozen years older than herself, was a powerful Border lord, a friend of Ormiston's, and she liked him. But his grandaunt, the lady Rosalie Percy, was a handsome widow.

Having married an English lord and returned to Scotland after his demise, Lady Rosalie now stayed with one branch of her family after another throughout the year. Ormiston had met her at Davy's wedding and several times since. His eyes glowed whenever he spoke of her, which had warned Fiona months ago that he'd formed a fondness for the woman. As Lady Ormiston had died when Fiona was seven, she strongly suspected that her father had thoughts now of remarrying.

Although she enjoyed Rosalie's company, she knew instinctively that such a change in Ormiston's life would cause a difficult upheaval in her own.

She and Rosalie—or anyone who tried to take her mother's place—would likely rub uncomfortably together at Ormiston Mains. And Fiona knew who would bear the blame for any strife that resulted from such conflict.

CHAPTER 4

Having taken leave of Ormiston after breakfast, Àdham had gone out to the stables, where he found his burly, dark-haired equerry, Duff, and his young helper busy with chores. The equerry was briskly currying the horse Àdham had ridden from Blair Castle. Nearby, flaxen-haired Rory gently groomed Sirius.

Beyond thumping its tail, the dog made no move to greet its master.

Àdham greeted Duff in the Gaelic. "Good morrow to ye, too, lad," he added in the same tongue to Rory. The boy still insisted that he knew naught of his clan or clansmen, which Àdham suspected was untrue, because few in the Highlands or Isles remained ignorant of their antecedents after learning to talk. However, aware that the Islesmen had committed many atrocities during their invasion and that the lad might have seen more than any child should see, he had let the matter drop.

Returning his greeting, Rory looked up from his task, his bright blue eyes atwinkle as he added, "'Tis good ye sent last night tae tell the Mackintosh and them where ye'd be sleeping. Else they'd ha' sent men out in search o' ye."

"Get on with your task, lad," Duff said. "We'd liefer ha' your silence."

"Aye, sure," Rory said, returning his attention to the dog and getting a cheek licked in approval.

"Have they room enough enough at yon alehouse stable for the horse?" Àdham asked Duff. "His lordship offered to keep it here if need be."

"There be stabling enough, sir," Duff said. "Whether ye'll think much of it be another matter. The lads there be a sorry lot. Since this horse belongs to—"

"Wheesht," Àdham interjected. "Whilst we bide in town, I'd not want anyone at yon alehouse to deem it valuable enough to steal. So, for now, it is mine."

"Aye, sure," Duff agreed with a nod. Then, his eyes widened and his jaw dropped. "Hoots, sir, look what be a-coming yonder. Be that the Queen?"

Àdham straightened when he saw the lady Fiona striding toward them, her emerald-green skirt swirling sensually enough around her slim legs to be pure silk. She did look regal, and elegant, but her presence in the stable unsettled him. Not just because of her beauty but also because, if she spoke to him as a familiar, Ormiston's men and his would all wonder how they had come to know each other.

He knew of no acceptable way to keep her out of the stable or silence her, though. She was heading straight for him and looked determined to speak to him.

"Finish up here, Duff," he said quietly, "and keep the lad with you. Keep him silent, too. That is Ormiston's daughter, the lady Fiona, so I'd liefer talk with her outside, whilst we walk in plain view."

"Aye, sir," Duff said, quirking an eyebrow. "She's a rare beauty, that 'un."

Àdham could feel curiosity radiating from him and from the ever-watchful Rory, too. But naught that he could say would satisfy or suppress their interest.

Without another word, he went to meet her ladyship.

"You should not have come to me alone like this, my lady," he said quietly in Scots when she was near enough to hear him.

"Good sakes," she said, raising her eyebrows, "I am perfectly safe here. And I wanted to thank you for letting me explain last night's events to my father."

"If that is all . . ."

"Prithee, sir, don't be rude," she said. "It would look much odder if we were to turn and walk away from each other."

"I apologize for my rudeness," he replied, smiling. "However, if you have more to say, perhaps we might walk back toward the house whilst we talk."

He gestured toward the stable's open doorway.

"Walking in the garden is a better idea," she said, turning toward the exit. "I do have a watcher who will escort me back to Blackfriars. But he'll see us in the garden and be content to wait patiently."

"Did you tell your father the truth?" Àdham asked as he opened the garden's picket gate for her. He caught her gaze then, and in the sunlight, saw that her irises were the light blue-gray of water flowing over pale gray stones. Her lashes were long, dark, and thick, and her skin looked so soft that he wanted to stroke it.

"Did you think I would be untruthful?" she asked archly, passing him. She paused then until he had shut the gate and rejoined her.

"What I think," he said, "is that you would be unwise to lie to him."

"I rarely lie, and never to him," she retorted. "Did he reproach you, too?"

"Nae, but I think I displeased him when I said that he would have to ask you for the details of our meeting. Did you tell him the *whole* truth?"

"I answered his questions, and he knows I went swimming, if that is what you mean. What he said to me is not your affair, though. He also knows that I often go outside alone at home when the moon is full."

"I'll wager that he did *not* expect you to take such a moonlight walk, let alone a swim, whilst you were staying at Blackfriars and attending her grace, the Queen."

She caught her lower lip between her teeth and held it so for a moment before she released it and looked up at him with her eyes glinting. "Are you trying to divert me so that you need not confess that he was displeased with you, too?"

"Nae, for he was not." Àdham smiled. "After I explained that

I arrived only minutes before you and I met him, he did agree to seek other details from you. We talked then about my family and kinsmen, and less personal things such as his grace's Parliament and some new laws that his grace wants to pass."

"Tedious topics," she said. "The women of the court also talk of such matters when they have no interesting gossip to share. I pay little heed to political talk."

"Do you pay more heed to the gossip?" he asked.

"Aye, sure, because people are more interesting than politics," she said. "My brothers say that men never gossip. But that's blethers, for how can they learn about other people if they never discuss them?"

"But gossip is just what people *think* of other people and the things they do. And most such talk is speculative, even imaginary. Men talk about real things."

"Important things," she murmured.

"Aye," he said, grinning. "I'm glad you understand that, m'lady."

"Faith, you are *just* like my brothers! You all think that you know everything worth knowing and that women know naught at all."

"I did not say that." When she remained silent but her eyes danced, he looked right at her. "Why are *you* smiling?"

"Because when I said that—that you are just like my brothers—I recalled saying the same thing earlier to my father. I told him you had reacted to my swim just as Davy would have. I think Father nearly smiled then, despite his anger, because he knew that you had *not* acted as Davy would."

"You imply that he might have reacted more violently, aye?"

She nodded. "He might have, but we must not tarry, sir. Tam *will* begin to wonder if I stay too long with you. He might even mention it to one of the friars. And whether men gossip or not, I must not stir talk about myself. Father warned me of dire consequences if I create a scandal. But I did want to thank you, and I see no risk in coming out here to bid a guest farewell."

"Do you not?" he asked soberly, holding her gaze.

Calmly accepting that look, from which any of his men might

have shrunk, she said, "Sakes, sir, do you fear that *your* people will talk about us?"

He had a sudden urge either to kiss her or to shake her. But he knew that either act would put them both in more danger than any action of hers might.

With strong effort, he held his tongue and kept his hands to himself.

Fiona continued to stare into Sir Àdham's eyes, startled to discover that they were an intriguing sea-green but determined to conceal her reaction, especially since, this time, his unpredictable behavior had stirred odd tremors within her.

Blessed—or cursed—with three domineering, volatile older brothers and one temperamental, much older sister, she easily recognized the earliest signs of incipient eruption. However, she had much practice at controlling, even stifling, her reactions to such signs. That he had quickly recollected himself impressed her, but there had been something more to it than that.

He said gently, "My lads will say naught. But you should take greater care, your ladyship, or others *will* talk."

"Our people won't. Nor will the men at Blackfriars."

"But those 'others' may as easily be enemies as friends."

"I must go now," she said, trying to ignore the odd sensations that his vibrant voice stirred in her. Before she could stop herself, she added, "Will you attend the festivities tonight after the parliamentary session?"

"I ken naught of festivities," he said. "Moreover, I doubt—"

"They hold them in the assembly hall in Parliament Close," she interjected. "'Tis the low building you will see next to Parliament House. Nearly everyone goes to the assembly hall. Men fear to offend his grace if they do not, and the powerful ones bring chieftains and others of note. Surely, your chief will include his knights."

Putting a hand to her shoulder and feeling her warmth beneath the thin fabric, he urged her back toward the gate. "I will go if I am told to go," he said, and he knew as soon as he said it that he hoped that would be the case.

"I doubt that your lord father will want to see us there together, though," he added. "Come to that, I think he would dislike seeing us like this now."

"And *I* think that if you *do* go, you should first trim your beard or have someone shave you," she said, raising her chin as if she did not a care a whit if Ormiston saw them. "Shaggy beards have gone out of fashion, sir—if ever they *were* fashionable," she added when he frowned. "Nowadays, fashionable men curl their hair, too. And they *rarely* let it grow past their collars."

"Aye, perhaps, but no one would take me for a fashionable man, no matter how I dress or how my hair looks," he said, shaking his head. "I'm a warrior, so I must keep it long enough to tie back, or it would interfere with my vision in battle."

"You will hardly engage in battle here."

"Your escort awaits you, m'lady," he replied, opening the gate and urging her on with a light hand. "You will not want to give him more food for chatter."

Rolling her eyes at him, Fiona sobered dramatically, bade him good day with a regal nod, and turned away to meet Tam. She knew that Ormiston had likely gone to visit Buccleuch and Lady Rosalie, but she was nonetheless thankful not to run into him or see anyone who might gossip about her private talk with Sir Àdham.

She could feel where his hand had touched her shoulder, and she felt other sensations when she thought about him. For reasons she could neither describe nor understand, he had a strong effect on her. She wanted to know more about him.

Doubtless, that desire was no more than simple curiosity about a Highland barbarian. In fact, though, and if one discounted his untidy appearance and odd garments, the man seemed no more barbaric than Davy was.

Admittedly, it was unusual for her to think about any man as much as she had thought about Sir Àdham, whom she had known for less than a day.

She liked talking with him, even—or perhaps especially—when he disagreed with her. The only other person with whom she talked so freely was Davy. And that was safe only if she did not let an argument carry her past what Davy would tolerate before losing his temper.

As she crossed the red bridge ahead of Tam, it occurred to her that she might dislike Sir Àdham's temper, if he lost it, just as much as she disliked Davy's. When that thought stirred an impishly curious desire to see what one must do to *make* Sir Àdham lose his, she called herself sharply to order.

If she were naive enough to speak such thoughts to any other lady attending the Queen, she knew exactly how that person would react. If one even spoke of a man who was not her brother, father, uncle, or grandfather, the others would accuse her of wanting to marry that man.

That was *not* the case with Sir Àdham, because she had decided long ago that she would marry no one who remotely resembled her brothers or her father. Such men believed that the rest of the world, especially its females, should obey their every command without question or pause.

Learning that nearly all Scotsmen believed such things and that many of their wives agreed with them—and warned their daughters that husbands expected such submission—Fiona had decided that she would have naught of such men.

If she failed to find one who was content to let his wife decide things for herself or was at least willing to discuss his decisions with her, she would not simply submit. Instead, she would work to persuade him to agree with her while encouraging him to believe that she was submitting. Just how she would do that, she did not know, but she was confident she would find a way.

At present, she felt no urgency about the matter, having not yet met any man with whom she could imagine spending a week, let alone the rest of her life.

Moreover, the man she did marry would not be one who lived so far from her home that she had never even heard of his. Nevertheless, Sir Àdham was intriguing, and she *would* learn much more about him.

There could be no danger in that.

Leaving his borrowed horse, Duff, and Rory with Ormiston's stable master, Àdham found the alehouse in the High Street and went right into its taproom, where members of Clan Chattan had gathered at a table and were imbibing whisky or ale.

"Ho, look at our ram returned to the fold," one chap shouted, adding, "Did ye find comfort wi' a skirt, me lad?" Several others quickly chimed in.

Deducing that they, too, had enjoyed a good night's rest, he grinned at their imaginative descriptions of his supposed overnight activities and moved to talk with his foster uncle and war leader, Sir Ivor Mackintosh. Sir Ivor was of uncertain age, and his golden-brown hair had acquired streaks of gray, but his broad-shouldered, well-muscled body remained powerful and lithe, and his hazel-green eyes were as sharp as ever. His accuracy with a bow and arrow, Àdham knew, was nearly flawless.

Having deep respect for his wisdom, Àdham often sought his advice.

At his approach, Ivor caught his gaze and, with a gesture, dismissed the man beside him from the table. "Ale, lad?" he asked in the Gaelic, shoving the jug toward Àdham with one hand and gesturing with the other to the vacated stool.

"None yet for me," Àdham replied in the same language as he pulled out the stool and straddled it. "Do you know where I am to sleep?"

"Aye, first chamber on the right when ye go upstairs," Ivor said. "Gilli Roy sleeps there, too," he added. "Nae one else wanted him."

"I don't mind the lad," Àdham said. "He has some odd notions, but we both know full-grown, more educated men who are just as daft. I did hear of some festivities this evening after the session, in an assembly hall, and that nearly everyone attends them. Does that include me?"

"Likely, it does," Ivor said, eyeing him shrewdly. "Gilli Roy will go, and Malcolm expects us and other knights and nobles amongst our lot to go. That hall sits in Parliament House Close, on the north side of the High Street."

"I need not attend the parliamentary session, though, aye?"

"Anyone *may* attend to watch," Ivor said. "But only barons, bishops, town leaders, and men invited by his grace take part in the sessions. Keep your ears open to what news ye may hear in town about what goes on there, though. I want to hear aught that interests ye, and so, I know, will Malcolm. Come to that, lad, d'ye mean to explain how ye came to spend last night in Ormiston's house?"

Wanting to think more before he confided details of the previous night to anyone, Àdham said only, "I met his lordship late last night on the North Inch. He invited me to take wine with him, warned me that this alehouse is a noisy place for sleeping, and invited me to bide overnight in Curfew Row."

Sir Ivor's graying eyebrows rose. "Ormiston's a gey powerful man. I'm thinking he may have told you much of interest."

"We did talk some about this Parliament," Àdham admitted. "I ken little about any involved in it, so we talked more about the King's wishes and his opponents' reasons for opposing him over such as heritable rights and other things that you and I and Uncle Fin have discussed with Malcolm."

Ivor nodded. "Ormiston's a canny one. Will ye see more of him?"

Without hesitation, Àdham said, "I expect he means to attend the festivities tonight. See you, his daughter, the lady Fiona, is a maid of honor to her grace. I believe the Queen and her attendants do mean to attend."

Realizing that he might have given Sir Ivor, a canny man himself, more information than wisdom might advise, Àdham reached for the jug and poured ale into a clean mug from the assortment on the table.

Sir Ivor said, "Methinks we should attend this affair together, lad. I would be fain to meet Ormiston, myself."

His light tone made Àdham look more closely at him. But Ivor's expression revealed only innocent interest in meeting his lordship.

A stranger in a green tunic and breeks entered the alehouse then, declaring in Scots, "I be a-looking for one Àdham MacFinlagh. Be any man here called so?"

"Aye," Àdham replied, raising an arm. "What is it you want of me?"

"I've a message for ye, sir. But I'm tae deliver it privily."

Sir Ivor's eyebrows rose, but he nodded when Àdham excused himself.

Immediately upon her return to Blackfriars, Fiona learned that the mistress of robes wanted to see her. Quickly returning her cloak to her chamber and straightening her caul, she found the countess and Lady Huntly with the other three maids of honor in the ladies' solar, redolent now of Lady Sutherland's sweet, earthy ambergris.

The maidens sat together in a cushioned window embrasure, attending to their needlework, while the countess laid out pieces of red woolen fabric on a square work table for a quilted doublet she was making.

Her serving woman, seated on a nearby stool, sorted threads for her.

Lady Sutherland looked up with a smile as Fiona curtsied, and said, "'Tis glad I am ye've returned, Fiona-lass. Her grace has decided tae attend the afternoon proceedings at Parliament House, so we will go down tae the refectory anon."

"Should I change from this dress to another, my lady?" Fiona asked.

"Nae, for that green silk becomes ye and 'tis also suitable for this evening. Ye need only don a fresh pair o' gloves. Her grace will want tae rest after the session and afore taking her supper. So, mayhap we might enjoy a stroll through the Gilten Herbar then. Meantime, ye might play your lute for us till we go downstairs."

"I will, with pleasure, my lady," Fiona said, making another curtsy. Stepping away, she retrieved her lute from its case nearby and seated herself on a stool by the embrasure. Testing strings until their notes were as they should be, she began softly playing and let her thoughts drift. If they drifted toward Sir Àdham, she told herself, it was only because the man was unlike anyone else she knew.

The summons to the refectory came a half hour later.

After the ladies finished eating, they tidied themselves and then, two by two, followed her grace's litter to Parliament Close.

Situated at the end of that narrow passage, Parliament House was a modest-looking building, but the lofty hall where the sessions took place was a fine square room. Wood lined the walls halfway up all the way around with light brown stucco above. In the northeast corner, a turnpike stair led to a loft from which visitors could observe the proceedings.

The lord chamberlain, having called the meeting to order before the ladies' arrival, hastily declared a brief recess when they entered.

While the Queen, Lady Sutherland, and Lady Huntly walked to the dais at the front of the hall, where his grace sat in a thronelike chair, Fiona and the other ladies went upstairs to the loft. Perched in a row along the front bench reserved for their use, they had a clear view of the hall below.

A few townspeople, all of them men, sat on two benches behind them.

The first time Fiona had attended such a session, she had given it her full attention. However, today, she soon began to wish that her grace had declined the King's invitation to attend.

The Queen's chair stood beside the King's, while her two chief ladies sat on a cushioned stone bench against the wall nearby. While they all settled themselves, four of the King's men moved through the chamber, responding to waves from men who wished to communicate with an official or another member.

When the proceedings resumed, a new official, introduced as "the dempster," began reading what proved to be a list of judicial deems, verdicts of the King's council from the previous day. Sighing, Fiona shifted restlessly and began to imagine lives for people she noticed while trying not to look as bored as she felt.

On the walkway outside the High Street alehouse, the messenger looked around warily until Àdham said impatiently, "Who the devil are you? And what is it you must say here that you could not say within?"

"I come from your uncle, Sir Àdham. He participates in the proceedings at Parliament Hall the noo. But if ye'll oblige him, he would speak wi' ye afterward."

"Which uncle? I have many." Àdham suspected he knew the answer but was uncertain of how he might react if he was right.

Lowering his voice, the man said, "Ha' ye more than one in this part o' the country, sir? I'd liefer no be speaking his name in the street, even do I whisper it."

"Methinks you make much of little, sirrah. Art from Kinpont, then?"

"Aye," the man whispered. Then, exhaling harshly, he added in a tone that barely reached Àdham's sharp ears, "He'd liefer *meet* ye at Kinpont, too. But 'tis far, and he said ye'd liefer meet on yon track by the river, near the old tower, when they ring the monastery bell for Vespers. D'ye ken where I mean?"

"I do," Àdham said, visualizing Lady Fiona clambering up the slope to the riverbank. "I answer to others, but I'll meet him if I can. If I cannot, mayhap he will attend festivities in the assembly hall later. We could find someplace there to talk."

"'Haps ye could. But I'll tell ye, sir, as one wha' kens the man weel; I'd meet him when and where he's set the time and place if ye can."

Nodding, Àdham turned away, wondering what to say if Ivor demanded to know who'd sent him the message. The family all knew that Sir Robert Graham of Kinpont, his late mother's brother, was no friend to the King. But Ivor would want to know if the man was up to mischief. Deciding to avoid any questions until he had some answers, Àdham went on upstairs. The first room to his right was empty, but he found his squire, Bruce MacNab, tidying a smaller chamber next to it for himself.

"I want you, Bruce," Àdham said. "I must change these clothes."

"Aye, sure, sir," the lanky, dark-haired young squire said with a nod. "Ye be sleeping in the next room and sharing it with Gillichallum Roy, aye?"

"So Sir Ivor told me. Prithee, see to these boots first," he added. "They got wet last night, my breeks, too. I mean to wear Highland gear whilst we're in town, but Sir Ivor did say that I should wear shoes or boots even so."

"Aye, sir," MacNab said. "God kens what filth bare feet will find in yon streets. The kennels soon be overflowing, though men do say they drain the cess well away from the river. Sir Ivor told me ye'd be attending festivities tonight," he added. "Will ye want tae change again afore ye do?"

"Nae, I'll wear a clean tunic and the boots with this plaid,"

Àdham said firmly. "I'll watch where I step until then, but see to my boots before Vespers."

The discourse of the Parliament that day concerned something called barratry, which, as Fiona understood it, had set the King of Scots in opposition to the Pope in Rome. It had also set him at odds with Bishop Henry Wardlaw of St. Andrews, Primate of Scotland.

The Queen had explained to her ladies that James thought Scotland sent too much money to Rome to pay for the innumerable supplications, appeals, and suits and countersuits by clergy against clergy, as well as requests for dispensations to marry within forbidden degrees or papal permission to annul other marriages.

Such activities provided the lifeblood of Holy Kirk, because money changed hands at every stage. So, as a result, good Scots money that James wanted to keep in Scotland left the country daily and traveled to the pockets of the Curia in Rome.

The King's intent was clear. All barratry must stop or its costs be minimized.

Opposition from the papacy and Scotland's own clergy—according to Joanna—had incurred his grace's deep displeasure.

Midway through the afternoon, the chamberlain announced that two men, Sir Robert Graham of Kinpont and Bishop Wardlaw of St. Andrews, desired to make themselves heard before the members.

Dark-haired Sir Robert, wearing a dark-red velvet robe and matching cap, declared that the King and Parliament had no more business interfering in the income of Holy Kirk than they had trying to pass laws that undermined the heritable rights of his grace's most loyal Scottish nobles.

"Landowners must retain their rights to punish trespassers and leave their estates to their rightful heirs without interference from the Crown. His grace's notion of forcing everyone to act in the same manner throughout the kingdom, without regard to local custom, undermines all Scottish law, to wit . . ."

Fiona decided that although Sir Robert spoke eloquently, had a memorably mellifluous voice, and doubtless possessed a solid grasp of Scottish law—for he cited laws and policies to prove each of his too-many points—the man talked too long, was too adamant and generally tedious, and was visibly irking the King.

When Bishop Wardlaw began by reverting to Sir Robert's first point, the state's right, or lack of such, to interfere with the Kirk and the Kirk's need to collect the barratry funds, James abruptly stood, silencing him.

Tersely, the King said, "If the good bishop is so bereft of funds that his kirk cannot continue without taking vast amounts in taxes and tithes from our citizens' pockets, mayhap we should relieve him of that costly university he founded two decades ago. We can easily reestablish it here in Perth."

A hush fell over the hall. Even Fiona had heard of St. Andrew's University, which men declared equal to, if not better, than English universities at Cambridge and Oxford, and another nearly as famous one in Paris.

Into the hush, Wardlaw said diplomatically, "I believe that, if we put our heads together, your grace, we may come to agreement about how to manage the difficulties plaguing this matter."

Fiona could see that his grace was in an *un*diplomatic mood. But the Queen stood then and said, "If your grace will excuse me and my ladies, I believe that I might enjoy much benefit from a stroll in the Gilten Herbar."

Since most people in St. John's Town were aware, although her grace showed no sign yet, that she was expecting another child in a few months, no one was surprised when James smiled and said gently, "Ye must do as ye please, my love. Mayhap ye'd liefer rest than tire yourself tonight with the evening activities."

Fiona hardly dared to breathe for fear that Joanna might agree with him. That would mean that her grace's attendants must also miss the festivities.

But Joanna returned his smile, shaking her head. "I am not as frail as that, my liege. I will enjoy the music and may even dance with my husband. However, vital as I know these proceedings to be, my presence does naught to improve them."

"Ye're wrong about that," James said evenly, looking only at her. "I'd warrant that every man here is glad ye be with us, even those who, afore our discussion o' barratry, may have said that your presence *was* unnecessary."

A chuckle, hastily stifled, drew smiles from others in the chamber. But Fiona breathed easily again, and the ladies all began getting to their feet.

Whatever anyone else thought of the Queen's decisions, Fiona told herself that *she* yearned only to breathe the fresh scents of the Gilten Herbar and leave all tedious parliamentary discord behind. She would attend the festivities, of course, because others expected it of her, and not for any *other* reason.

CHAPTER 5

The bell for Vespers tolled as Àdham went through the red port and past the ruined tower that was all that remained of the ancient castle. The tower formed part of the town wall, jutting northward from it and blocking his view until he crossed the bridge. So, he did not immediately see the man he had come to meet.

People strolled on the North Inch and along the riverbank. Others went to or from the monastery or walked alongside a thick wall of hedges that extended from the monastery's stone wall to a gated archway.

That archway revealed more of the grounds, including a garden. Doubtless, her grace's ladies walked there unless the garden was part of the brothers' cloister, reserved for meditation and prayer.

Realizing that he'd let his gaze linger, watching for a particular figure, he turned to see his uncle striding toward him with a frown on his long face.

Sir Robert Graham looked much as he had a decade or more before, when Àdham had last seen him. For, despite their kinship, they had met only two or three times in his youth. He had heard much about Sir Robert from his Highland kinsmen, though, and knew that the powerful Grahams held large estates in the Lowlands.

Sir Robert's long red gown was that of a wealthy nobleman. Visibly silk-lined and trimmed with dark fur, its skirt had slits at the sides, front, and doubtless the back to facilitate riding. However, he also wore purple-and-gold, pointy-toed silk shoes, so he was unlikely to ride anywhere without first changing into boots.

The long red-velvet cap that covered his hair, and thus kept Àdham from seeing if he curled it, boasted a flowing, soft, pointed tail.

Despite Lady Fiona's assertion that men of fashion shaved off their beards, Sir Robert still sported the dark, pointed, two-inch-long one that Àdham recalled. It was neatly styled, and the hair on his uncle's upper lip looked freshly trimmed.

Such sartorial splendor failed to impress Àdham, who believed that a knight worthy of the title went well armed. To be sure, he wore only his dirk in its leather sheath, himself, but as far as he could tell, Sir Robert was weaponless.

"Let us stroll by the river," Sir Robert said in credible Gaelic without preamble. "Few will heed us there or understand what we say."

"Have we reason to be privy, then?"

"Aye, perhaps, because I do recall how ye came by your knighthood two years ago," Graham said bluntly. "Ye did yourself nae good thereby, my lad."

Tempted to point out that he was *not* his lad since they scarcely knew each other, but put off by Graham's latter statement, Àdham said, "Why is that?"

"Don't act the dolt with me," his uncle retorted. "Ye ken fine that the Camerons and Clan Chattan were duty bound to support Alexander in Inverness and at Lochaber. He believes now that both confederations betrayed his Lordship of the Isles. So, since James himself told me that ye'd persuaded your Cameron kinsmen to change sides when they did, ye must now persuade them to change back to their true liege."

"The Mackintosh was Constable of Inverness Castle then, so of course he defended it, and I talked only with Ewan MacGillony. Since Ewan is your good-brother, you must know him well enough to know he makes his own decisions."

"Aye, but ye *persuaded* the traitorous man, and *why* ye took the trouble lies beyond my ken. Ewan's done naught for ye since your mother left ye bereft o' her care and advice. Amabel was my own sister, I'd remind ye."

"I am the youngest of her sons by six years," Àdham reminded him. "When Mam died, Da had no women left to whom he could entrust my care. He remarried at the urging of his clan chief, but his new wife wanted her own bairns and naught of me. So, when Uncle Fin offered to take me, Da agreed. I am content at Castle Finlagh and think of it as my home. But I hold naught against my father."

"I see. Nevertheless, ye'd be wise to voice support for Alexander's release as soon as ye can—here, at Finlagh, and elsewhere. The North rightfully belongs to Alexander, so his Islesmen will not suffer his imprisonment much longer without taking vengeance. Then, all who failed him at Lochaber *will* suffer. That includes all Camerons, including ye, my lad, as well as your foster Mackintosh kinsmen."

"Be plain with me, sir. Is such an attack imminent?"

Graham shrugged and said, "I have nae ken of such. Although one does hear whispers that Alexander's young cousin, Donal Balloch, Chief of Clan Donald of Dunyvaig, has returned to the Isles and sends messages to him. Because of their kinship, Balloch takes affronts to the Lordship of the Isles personally. He declares Jamie's imprisonment of the rightful Lord of the Isles unlawful and unwarranted.

"The fact is, lad," he added grimly, "that siding with James and the foolish notion he adopted during his English captivity of leaving all lawmaking to the King and his Parliament, as the bloody English do, is most unwise."

"I'll reflect on all that you say," Àdham said. "But you should know that by laying waste to Inverness merely to spite the King, Alexander enraged nearly all Highlanders. As for trying to destroy Inverness Castle, which, as we all know, the King had refurbished and strengthened after three Lords of the Isles had added to its ruin, many consider that act alone to have been lunacy."

"Aye, perhaps, but Alexander *is* Lord of the Isles and *equal* to the King."

"Other than his Islesmen, few agree with that," Àdham said. "Alexander Stewart, Earl of Mar, who is also rightful Lord of the North, has declared that for Lords of the North and Lords of the Isles to claim equal status to the King ill-serves all Scots. Not only would three equal monarchs stir confusion throughout the land, but they are the King's own cousins, after all, and should support the Stewart claim to the throne. My father made arguments like yours. But when he learned that the King might win, he decided that he *should* win. Other Camerons agreed with him."

"Every man of them should hang," Sir Robert said. "And soon, they will."

Àdham said, gently, "Do you realize that you speak of the two largest clan confederations? Do you recall how many men Clan Chattan alone can raise? Would you really hang half of the Camerons and expect the other half to help you do it?"

Graham was silent, and movement near the monastery drew Àdham's eye.

A line of ladies, two by two, emerged from the hedged garden through the open iron gate of the hedge-flanked archway and headed toward the monastery's main gate. He wondered if they would all attend the night's festivities.

"Did ye enjoy your visit to Blair Castle?" Sir Robert asked, abruptly reclaiming Àdham's attention.

Although he managed to suppress his astonishment, he knew Sir Robert had meant to surprise him and likely knew he'd succeeded. Evenly, Àdham said, "Since you informed me over a decade ago that we are kinsmen by marriage to the Earl of Atholl, his younger son, Caithness, has become a friend and visits at Finlagh. But I did *not* know that you keep so keen an eye on Blair as to know all who stop there."

Graham's mouth quirked smugly. "Atholl's people keep me apprised of such. So I ken fine that ye bided overnight and someone lent ye the horse ye rode here yestereve."

"As Atholl's countess, Elizabeth is as much my kinswoman as yours, so I did take the opportunity to pay my respects," Àdham said, wondering *how* close his uncle was to Atholl and how he knew that messages had reached the Lord of the Isles at Tantallon.

Since Sir Robert supported Alexander and opposed James, Àdham suspected that Sir Ivor and Malcolm would recommend that he keep his distance from the man. As for Atholl, the King's sole surviving Stewart uncle, everyone knew that he and James disagreed more often than not.

"We should turn back now," Sir Robert said. "I expect ye mean to attend the entertainment tonight in Parliament Close."

Àdham murmured acquiescence but made no further comment.

Fiona, strolling behind Joanna and Lady Sutherland in a fog of ambergris sweetness that even their stroll through the Gilten Herbar failed to dispel, looked longingly toward the river Tay. As her thoughts drifted to the previous night, she wondered if the moon would be as full when it rose again that night.

It ought to be, she decided, although it would likely rise long after they returned from the festivities and thus too late for her to enjoy.

She would definitely not venture outside again to watch for it.

Just then, she caught sight of two men standing near the ancient tower, one in what looked like a blue-green plaid and the other in a long red robe and cornet cap.

"Why do you sigh, Fiona?" plump, golden-haired Lady Malvina Geddes, walking beside her, asked. "Surely, you look forward to tonight's festivities."

"'Tis naught," Fiona replied vaguely. She believed that the man in the plaid was Sir Àdham. Even at that distance, she recognized his long, unkempt hair and beard and the way he stood with his arms folded across his chest.

The other man resembled her father in height and breadth of shoulder but was definitely not Ormiston. She would recognize *him* or any of her three brothers with ease, just by the way each held himself and moved.

The man she believed was Sir Àdham glanced briefly toward her.

Immediately, she faced forward, glad that the two ladies ahead of her were setting a brisk pace. Had they not, with her thoughts dwelling on moons and men as they had, she might have walked right into her grace.

Aware that Malvina was likely feeling snubbed, Fiona apologized for her reverie and assured her that she was eager to enjoy the evening ahead.

Before adjourning to the assembly hall, the ladies attended Vespers in the monastery chapel and ate a light supper. Then, they returned to Parliament Close in the same manner as before but to a more festive chamber.

Long trestle tables covered in white cloths stretched much of the length of the chamber from below the dais and its high table toward the entryway. A clear central space remained for the entertainment and, perhaps, for dancing. When the Queen and her ladies entered, musicians began to play.

The four maids of honor took places at the front end of the trestle nearest the ladies' end of the dais, while the Queen and her chief ladies ascended to their places at the high table and stood facing the lower hall. The King and his most trusted advisers entered without fanfare shortly afterward and went straight to the dais.

Ormiston was with them, and catching Fiona's eye, he nodded toward the rear of the hall. Turning, she saw Sir Walter Scott of Buccleuch with the lady Rosalie, who was stylishly attired in a vermilion silk gown embroidered with white flowers.

Easily comprehending that paternal nod, Fiona excused herself to the others at her table and crossed the hall toward Buccleuch and Lady Rosalie, only to stop when a stranger, foppishly garbed in particolored hose and a plumed cap, stepped into her path, swept her a bow, and said, "Lady Fiona Ormiston, aye?"

"Pray, sir, let me pass. I do not know you."

"But I do ken who ye be, lassie, and I would ken ye better," he said brashly. "A wee beauty like yerself shouldna walk about unattended if she doesna want appreciative gentlemen tae speak tae her."

"One who speaks to me without proper introduction is no gentleman," she retorted, raising her chin. "Moreover, my lord father is watching us from the dais. I assure you that if you do not step aside, I have only to glance at him . . ."

When she paused, letting him fill in the rest for himself, he said curtly, "Ye dinna ken who ye be snubbing, lass. Ye'd be wise tae take better heed."

Making no effort to reply, she looked to the high table and saw Ormiston frowning as he watched them. The irritating fop evidently saw the frown, too, for he snapped, "Och, aye, then. But ye'll likely meet wi' yer sorrows anon."

"Mercy, Fiona," Lady Rosalie said when Fiona joined her and Buccleuch. "Who was that impertinent young man?"

"I do not know, madam. But he has churlish manners."

Shaking her head so that the gauzy veil over her horned headdress fluttered, Lady Rosalie smiled as mischievously as if she were fifteen instead of fifty. "I thought you might walk right over him," she said, her dark eyes dancing. "You looked as if you wanted to."

Beside her, Buccleuch said quietly, "We must find seats at one of the tables, madam. His grace stands at his place, so the beef cart will soon enter through that doorway yonder. You are welcome to sit with us, Fiona."

"Thank you, my lord, but I must return to our table. Her grace will not ask much of us this evening, for she told us to enjoy ourselves, but I must not tarry. I came only to welcome you and to make my greetings to Lady Rosalie." Smiling, knowing that Ormiston would expect her to make her ladyship welcome, she added, "We do have room at our table, madam, if you would like to sit with us."

"Is that allowed?" Rosalie asked her.

"Aye, sure, at such an informal event as this one is," Fiona said. "Her grace encourages us to welcome guests. Sithee," she added with a wry look, "some of the younger ladies' families expect them to find husbands whilst they serve Joanna."

"Is Ormiston amongst them?" Buccleuch asked with a teasing grin.

She had known him all her life, so she grinned back and said lightly, "No, sir. He just likes to keep me near him."

Lady Rosalie said, "Would you mind dreadfully, Wat, if I accept Fiona's invitation? I have never conversed with a queen's ladies before."

"You must do as you please, madam," he replied. "In any event, his grace is looking my way, and I do want a word with Douglas of Dalkeith, who sits near him. Just don't let any ill-deeded huggermugger carry you off without shouting for me."

"I'll watch where you sit so I shout in the right direction," she assured him. "But, despite the fop who accosted Fiona, this seems an unlikely place for huggery-muggery." When Wat shook his head at her, she smiled. "Shall we go, Fiona?"

Fiona had just seen Sir Àdham enter with the man in the long red robe and realized that she had seen that man before. Even so, it took a moment to recognize him as the nobleman with the mellifluous voice who had spoken against the King earlier at Parliament House. Brief thought returned Sir Robert Graham's name to her memory, and she wondered how Sir Àdham could know such a tedious person.

"Fiona?"

Vaguely aware that it was the second time Lady Rosalie had spoken her name, she flushed and swiftly begged her pardon. "I fear that I let my thoughts run away with me, madam. But we had better make haste. His grace is gesturing now for the Bishop of St. Andrews to say the grace-before-meat."

Despite a quizzical look suggesting that she might have more questions, Rosalie said, "Then let us go quickly."

"I willna ask ye to sit with me, Àdham," Sir Robert said as they crossed the assembly hall. "Others expect me. So, since ye're no of a mind with us . . ."

Realizing that Graham expected him to fill the pause, Àdham said firmly, "I am to sit with Sir Ivor Mackintosh tonight, sir. I must bid you farewell now."

"We will see more of each other anon," Graham said as firmly.

Not here, not tonight, and never if I can avoid it, Àdham thought.

As he did, he saw the lady Fiona walking with an older, elegantly garbed noblewoman across the wide central opening between the trestle tables.

Then, as the two turned toward the ladies' end of the dais, he saw a tall popinjay in blue-and-purple particolored hose and a dagged jacket that barely covered his buttocks hurry after them. The fop must have spoken, for both ladies paused and turned toward him. Another, slightly shorter, popinjay caught the first one by an arm, whereupon the first grimaced but turned obediently and moved toward the far side of the hall with the second. Àdham had seen neither man's face.

Lady Fiona and her companion continued toward one of the trestles.

Now what was that about? Àdham wondered. Assuring himself that it was naught, that the larger man was just a clunch-witted lout and the other a kinsman of the older woman or of Fiona herself, he glanced toward the high table, where he had seen Ormiston eyeing him when he'd arrived with Sir Robert.

Not only was his lordship still there, but he was also watching Lady Fiona and her companion. And he was frowning.

Locating the two fops again by their clothing, Àdham noted the shorter one's orange-red, smartly curled hair, clean-shaven cheek, and jutting nose and chin but still could not see his whole face. Both men's attire looked costly. The taller one's manners wanted mending.

The smaller man turned at last to scan the chamber, and Àdham recognized him as Gillichallum Roy Mackintosh, Malcolm's youngest son.

"What an annoying man that was, dearling," Lady Rosalie said. "He is the same one who accosted you earlier, is he not? I could not be sure."

"He is," Fiona said.

"He is gey persistent for someone you do not know. Art sure you do not?"

"I had never seen him, or the man who stopped him, before," Fiona assured her, striving to keep her voice free of her irritation at being cross-questioned.

"I ken fine that I have no right to press you in such a way," Rosalie said. "But your lord father also took note of him. I glanced that way just as that younger man stepped in, and Ormiston was staring right at us, frowning."

"If you fear that he will be annoyed with us, madam, you need not be."

"Oh, no," Rosalie said. "He knows we would never encourage such a menseless creature. But he is likely to keep a more protective eye on us now."

Knowing she was right, Fiona led her to the table assigned to the maids of honor, where they both enjoyed their supper and lively conversation with the others.

Ormiston stayed with the King.

The Queen also kept her seat, and—perhaps due to her delicate condition and his grace's desire for a healthy son—did not dance. Thus, Fiona felt obliged to stay with Lady Rosalie and politely declined several invitations to join the dancers.

Other entertainment included tumblers and fools in their motley garb and tinkling bells. The jugglers were deft and the royal minstrels exceptionally skilled.

When the musicians began to play for a second round of dancing, Joanna stood with her chief ladies, signaling her intent to retire.

"Must you go with her, dearling?" Rosalie asked Fiona.

"Aye, madam," Fiona said, suppressing a sigh of disappointment. "But I see that my lord father has excused himself and is coming this way. We should wait here for him. Some of these men have taken more drink than they should."

Rosalie bristled. "Sakes, Fiona, if you imagine that I am not as skilled as you are at deterring such nuisances, you need have no further concern. I have looked after myself quite capably these many years past."

"I am sure you have, madam, and I meant no offense. Her grace has seen that you are with me and has paused to wait for me. Moreover, Father is nearly upon us now. So I shall bid you good night and will doubtless see you again tomorrow."

By then, Ormiston was with them, so she bade him good night, too, and returned to the monastery with the Queen and the other ladies. As they walked, she noted with wistful delight that the still-full moon was rising.

The mild regret she felt then had naught to do with lost opportunity for a stroll or a swim but with the fact that she had not seen Sir Àdham since he had entered the hall. He had not even bidden her a courteous good evening.

Àdham, having pleased Sir Ivor by presenting him to Ormiston at the assembly, spent much of the next day avoiding Sir Robert Graham.

While Ivor and Malcolm attended the sessions, Àdham and other clansmen practiced combat skills on the North Inch or explored the surrounding territory.

As Àdham cultivated new acquaintances and kept his ears aprick for news, he noticed that Malcolm's son, Gillichallum Roy, had grown unusually restive.

Reluctant to reveal his acquaintance with the lady Fiona, Àdham had said nothing yet to Gilli Roy about the stranger's attempt to accost her at the festivities the previous night. However, since Gilli shared his bedchamber, Àdham knew the lad's sleep had been restless and fraught with dreams, so that night, he asked Gilli what was wrong.

Avoiding his gaze, Gilli said plaintively, "I dinna like it here. This alehouse and the street outside be too noisy. In troth, I dinna sleep well unless I lie in mine own bed."

"You seemed to enjoy the festivities last night in the assembly hall," Àdham said. When Gilli shrugged, he added bluntly, "The chap you were with, the one who seemed to be a friend of yours, accosted a young lady in a most uncivil way."

Gilli stiffened. "I ken fine what ye must have seen, Àdham. But he is nae more than an acquaintance who has been friendly to me. As tae the lass—"

"That *lady*," Àdham said grimly, "is a maid of honor to the Queen."

"I didna ken that. But if ye saw what he did, ye also saw me stop him."

"Who is he?"

"His friends call him Hew," Gilli Roy said. "All I can tell ye is that he speaks the Gaelic like a Highlander. Leave me be now. I want tae sleep."

Whether he slept or not, Àdham insisted that Gilli Roy accompany him and the others both the next day and Friday for training. The lad's sulky attitude irked him, but he felt obliged to keep an eye on him. For the Mackintosh's son to fall into bad company or create a scandal in St. John's Town would *not* be good.

The responsibility distracted him, but even so, he noticed that the Queen had stopped attending the festivities. Her ladies had also vanished from sight.

Not that Àdham shirked his duties to think about the ladies—one in particular—for duty did come first. Nevertheless, by Friday afternoon, he knew that during every respite the men took on the North Inch, he looked more often toward the monastery than in any other direction.

Only then did it occur to him that with more than a score of men practicing warrior's skills on the Inch, any likelihood of the young ladies' superiors letting them walk nearby was nonexistent.

Surely, even the intrepid lady Fiona, despite her moonlight adventure, would hesitate to expose herself so at such a time. However, she had not attended the evening festivities for the past two days, either.

Perhaps she was sick.

If not, perhaps she would be there tonight.

The Queen, tiring now more easily than expected, had decided to attend only such sessions of Parliament as the King asked her to attend. For that respite, Fiona felt only relief at not having to endure the tedious speeches.

However, Joanna had next declared the evening festivities too much for her, making her younger ladies and maids of honor fear that she would forbid them to attend. But when Lady Sutherland and Lady Huntly offered to accompany any of the young ladies that her grace might spare from evening duties, Joanna agreed.

As the youngest two, the ladies Fiona and Malvina were the last spared, so Fiona had not clapped eyes on Sir Àdham for days. She *had* tried to catch sight of him among the men honing their skills on the Inch, unsuccessfully, through the garden gate. At last, though, Friday night after Vespers, she and Lady Malvina accompanied Ladies Sutherland and Huntly to the assembly hall, to take supper.

The four of them found places at the trestle near the ladies' end of the dais, where Fiona and the other maids of honor had sat before. Choosing a place from which she could see most of the lower hall, Fiona looked around while they awaited the grace-before-meat. Disappointed not to see Sir Àdham, she reminded herself that no matter how well spoken or intriguing the man was, his absence, not to mention its cause, was no business of hers.

Had he not ignored her suggestion that, before attending that first assembly, he furbish himself up a trifle by trimming his beard and arranging his unruly hair more stylishly? To be fair, he had explained that, as a warrior, he must keep his hair long enough to tie back, but he could at least have curled the ends a bit.

When she tried to imagine what he might look like so, she realized that without his untidy hair and beard, she had no idea *how* the man might look.

Her sense of humor stirred at the thought.

"Would you like to share what amuses you, Fiona?" Lady Huntly asked.

"I am merely pleased to be here, madam. I enjoy the music and look forward to seeing the dancing." Her foot tapped in time to the music.

"We must hope to witness *only* such diversions tonight," her ladyship said grimly. "Her grace sent two of us to attend today's session, and a near-insurrection occurred there. Horrid men rushed in, shouting for release of the Lord of the Isles. When others tried to put them out, chaos ensued."

A frisson of fear shot through Fiona. She had not seen Sir Àdham or Ormiston for days. Rational thought swiftly reassured her that Àdham was unlikely to attend Parliament. But she knew that her father *had* been there.

Lady Sutherland said ruefully, "Lady Huntly didna mean tae give ye a fright, Fiona-lass. She should ha' told ye nae one were harmed. 'Twas but a nuisance, his grace did say, and worse that two men tried tae get a message tae Alexander. James ordered them all arrested and thrown into the Tolbooth."

Having heard that many western Highlanders supported the Lord of the Isles and demanded an end to his year-long imprisonment, and recalling Sir Àdham's allegiance to the King, Fiona's alarm for him surged.

Moments later, with deep relief, she saw her father enter with Buccleuch, only to feel new alarm sweep in at the sight of Lady Rosalie walking proudly between them, her right hand resting on

Ormiston's left forearm. The two of them, she decided with a sigh, might as well have had a royal herald preceding them, announcing his lordship's intention to marry her.

When Buccleuch turned as if to speak to one or both of them, his gaze met Fiona's. He smiled, but only as if he were glad to see her, not as if he wondered how she might feel about the couple beside him. Politely, she returned his smile while she tried to decide how she did feel about them *as* a couple.

She had often thought that her widowed father ought to remarry. But . . .

Deciding to think about that later, she turned her attention to her supper.

She had barely finished eating when Lady Malvina said lightly, "I see my Geddes cousins yonder, Fiona. Mayhap you would like to walk over and greet them with me. Lay brothers are clearing the center area for the entertainment, so we should go now, or we shall have to walk all the way round it."

"Aye, sure, I'll go . . . if you will excuse us, my ladies."

Lady Sutherland assured them that they were to enjoy themselves and that she and Lady Huntly would await them as long as necessary. "Although not past midnight, me dearlings. Ye must attend tae your morning duties, as usual."

"We know, madam," Malvina said. "Come, Fiona. My cousin Hamish is talking with a gey handsome young man, whom I do not yet know."

Chuckling, Fiona said, "You see every handsome man as a future husband, Malvina. But the value of a husband depends on more than his looks, you know."

Grimacing, Malvina said, "If ye think I want tae spend the rest of my life with a man who makes me think of an ogre or a toadstool rather than a charming gentleman, ye're much mistaken. Only imagine having tae break fast every morning with such a man, let alone tae sleep with him."

"Mercy, hush," Fiona said on a gurgle of laughter. "You do *not* want to hear someone repeating *that* declaration tomorrow to all and sundry."

Blushing, Malvina agreed that she would not like that, and they hurried on to her kinsmen. The handsome young man speaking to Hamish proved to be another cousin who showed more interest in Fiona than in Malvina. But Fiona, finding the discussion tiresome, let her gaze drift to other parts of the room.

The young man said, "I fear that you find my remarks tedious, my lady."

"I beg your pardon, sir," she replied, flushing hotly. "I was thinking that we should return to our table before Lady Sutherland sends someone to fetch us."

"Go ahead, Fiona," Malvina said. "Say that I'll return afore midnight and that one o' my kinsmen will escort me tae the residence if they have retired."

Believing that Lady Sutherland was more likely to send her back to insist that Malvina return at once, Fiona nearly said so. But aware that that might make them persuade her to stay longer, she bade them good night and began to wend her way amid entertainers and spectators, trying to do so without irking anyone.

She had nearly reached the halfway point when someone grasped her elbow from behind and a cheerful masculine voice said, "One moment, my lady. Are you not Ormiston's daughter, the lady Fiona?"

Turning abruptly and with annoyance, she saw blue-and-purple particolored hose; a short, dagged, matching cote-hardie hugging a narrow waist; a broad chest, and broader shoulders before the upper part of that body jerked back and spun away as a fist flashed hard to its chin. The unknown man collapsed at her feet.

Looking with amazement at Sir Àdham MacFinlagh's equally astonished profile, she was about to demand what he thought he was doing, knocking people down, when she realized that his astonishment had focused wholly on his victim.

Leaning down, he grabbed the other man by both arms and hauled him to his feet. "Caithness!" he exclaimed, giving him an angry shake. "What the devil do you mean by dressing yourself up like a popinjay and accosting her ladyship in such a churlish way?"

CHAPTER 6

Shocked by his own actions and tone of voice, Àdham released thirty-three-year-old Alan, Earl of Caithness, but he continued to hold his gaze as he waited to discover how Caithness would react. That nearly everyone around them was staring at them did not trouble him. He was concerned only about Caithness.

To his relief, Caithness turned to Lady Fiona and said ruefully, "I beg your pardon, your ladyship. I should not have put my hand on ye, but ye slipped away just as I was coming to tell ye that your lord father has left for the evening."

Without so much as acknowledging Àdham's presence, he added, "Ormiston asked me to tell ye that the lady Rosalie is longing for her bed. So, he and Buccleuch are escorting her to the house Buccleuch has taken in South Street."

"Thank you, sir," Fiona said. "I confess, I do not know who you are." Turning to Sir Àdham, she said, "Perhaps you will present him to me properly, sir."

Grimacing, as rueful now as Caithness was, Àdham said, "I wish I could claim that I do so with pleasure, my lady. However, since he likely wants my head for clouting him just now, I will say as politely as possible that this *gentleman* is Alan, Earl of Caithness. He is also, I am even sorrier to say, his grace's close cousin and the younger son of Walter Stewart, Earl of Atholl and Strathearn."

"Mercy!" Fiona exclaimed as she swept the handsome earl a deep curtsy. "But, surely, you do not mean to demand Sir Àdham's head, my lord."

"I do not," Caithness said, laughing as he rubbed his jaw. "I'm only glad he recognized me soon enough to slow his punch, Lady Fiona, or I'd be seeking my teeth on the floor. As for the aspersions he cast on my apparel . . ." He glowered at Àdham. "I'd wager my hose, jacket, and cap cost more than your entire wardrobe."

"Then you wasted your gelt," Àdham retorted. "Moreover, that clothing makes you resemble the lout who accosted her ladyship here three nights ago. Had I known you were in town, I might have recognized you. I cannot say that even then I'd have been certain. When did you acquire such curly hair?"

"Sakes, Àdham, ye must have seen that it has become the fashion. Ye look as if ye've just come in from the wild, though. We must polish ye up, I think."

Well aware that she was part of a scene that both Lady Sutherland and Lady Huntly were sure to condemn, and grateful that her father had left the hall, Fiona was nonetheless, albeit secretly, pleased that Sir Àdham had leaped so swiftly and vigorously to her defense. Watching him hastily straighten the blue-green plaid he still wore, wondering how he might react to Caithness's suggestion that he needed polish, she discerned a surprising glint of amusement when he began shaking his head at his friend.

Then Sir Àdham looked at her and smiled. The smile was still a bit rueful, but it reminded her of how reassuring it could be and how white and even his teeth were. He was definitely of finer character than many of the men she had met with the court. So far, he seemed to be a man of his word, too. Just then, his smile widened, alerting her to the fact that she was staring at him.

With a flutter of unease, she looked to see if anyone else had taken notice and realized that, although any number of people had seen Sir Àdham knock Caithness down, most of them had returned their attention to the entertainers. The crowd around them was so thick that she could not see the ladies' table, let alone Lady Sutherland or Lady Huntly.

However, from the raised dais, the King of Scots was looking right at her.

Beside him, Douglas of Dalkeith, another of the King's trusted advisers and a close friend of Ormiston's and Buccleuch's, also watched them.

Clearing her throat, Fiona said as calmly as she could to Sir Àdham, "We have drawn his grace's eye, sir. I must return to Lady Sutherland and Lady Huntly."

Sir Àdham and Caithness stared at her and then at each other.

"If Jamie witnessed that scene, he'll be gey wroth with both of us if we tell him the truth of it," Caithness said. "We must concoct a nobler tale."

Astonished and without thinking, Fiona said, "You would lie to the *King*?"

"Aye, sure," Caithness said. "Jamie is nobbut three years older than I am, after all. And truth is but one man's view of an event, nae matter how many have seen it. None of these others watches us now, so we can forget them. What d'ye say, Àdham? I expect we must escort her ladyship back to her table afore we conspire."

Sir Àdham said evenly, "We will see her ladyship restored to her table, Alan, but we will *not* make up a tale to tell his grace. If he demands an explanation, we'll tell him the truth. Since he is deep in conversation with Dalkeith, I think we would be wise to await such a summons and not interrupt him now."

"Art afeard that our Jamie will rebuke ye, Àdham? Ye've likely never met him, but I ken him fine. Dinna fear that I'll abandon ye."

"Your lordship is mistaken on all points," Àdham said in the same even tone. "I fear naught, for it was his grace himself who knighted me after Lochaber."

"Mayhap ye told me that, but I wasna even there, m'self," Caithness said with a sigh as he gestured for two men ahead of them to stand aside. Then, moving past Fiona and Àdham to clear the way, he added over his shoulder, "I was fain to go, but my lord father forbade it. I think he resigned the Caithness earldom to me as his apology for keeping me from taking part in that splendid victory."

Àdham touched Fiona's shoulder, urging her forward through the now courteously parting crowd, as he said to Caithness, "It was not so splendid, sir. More accurately, it resulted in vile and bloody carnage."

"Perhaps," Caithness replied over Fiona's head. "But I'm nae feardie. And I must prove myself if I'm ever to win *my* knighthood. An earldom that one's blood-royal father resigns to one out of his many titles is as nowt to winning one's spurs."

"I am sure that you will win yours, my lord," Fiona said with a smile, deciding that she liked the charming young earl.

Àdham noted with amusement the sudden blush in Caithness's cheeks but said naught to suggest his belief that her ladyship was just being polite.

The crowd parted enough to reveal that two of her grace's older ladies sat alone at the ladies' table. Àdham was relieved to see them, but Caithness said abruptly, "If I'm not to tell tales, Àdham, I must leave ye here. The younger of those two is Lady Sutherland, Joanna's mistress of robes, and I do *not* want to hear what she'll say if she saw me accost Lady Fiona afore ye knocked me down."

"I doubt that she was able to see that, my lord," Lady Fiona said.

"I agree with that, Alan," Àdham said. "Moreover, I should tell you that I borrowed your horse to come here from Blair, but I've kept it safe."

"I ken fine that ye've got him, and welcome," Caithness said, casting another look around. "But, I'm away. I willna give Lady Sutherland my head for washing."

"What a thing to say!" Fiona said to Àdham with a chuckle as Caithness melted into the crowd. "*I* think he is perfectly charming, though, *and* gey handsome. Would Lady Sutherland *dare* to scold him?"

"She would more likely warn you that he does not always behave himself, even with powerful noblemen's daughters," he replied with a wry smile and a barely discernible edge to his voice.

Cocking her head slightly, she raised her eyebrows and said, "Indeed, sir? Methinks that my noting his lordship's charms has irked you. But, prithee, do not frown at me, for I do know that I owe you my thanks for coming so swiftly and chivalrously to my rescue. You have done so now twice, and although I did not require your aid either time, I— Faith," she added when he began slowly shaking his head, "do you dispute my word?"

"You know I do not," he said, extending an arm to her. "Would you like me to restore you to your guardian ladies now, or—"

"Mercy," Fiona interjected, "I can see Lady Huntly, and she is irked. I must go at once, sir. I do thank you, but I still think Caithness is charming."

Looking over her shoulder as Lady Huntly whisked her away, she saw that Sir Àdham still watched her, looking a bit dazed. She grinned at him.

Having no further interest in the evening's festivities, Àdham decided to return to the alehouse. Emerging from Parliament Close into the High Street, he nearly bumped into Gilli Roy, who was apparently also heading that way. He wore his particolored hose and linen shirt again, along with a plumed, light-colored hat atop his smartly curled red hair.

"I want a word with you, lad," Àdham said.

"I saw you talking with Ormiston's daughter," Gilli retorted. "I hoped you might sleep again at Ormiston House."

Feeling his temper stir, Àdham tamped it down and said quietly, "How do you come to recognize Ormiston's daughter?"

Even in the dim light of the flambeaux that lit the walkway, he saw color suffuse Gilli Roy's cheeks. But the lad shrugged again, saying, "She is pretty. Also, you told me yourself that she serves her grace, so men do talk about her."

"And accost her," Àdham said, giving him a stern look. "What more can you tell me about that churl who approached her so rudely Tuesday night?"

"I told you all that I know! His name is Hew and he speaks the Gaelic and Scots." Before Àdham could reply, he added, "You must care about that lass, aye?"

"That *lady's* father is one of the King's close advisers, so I suggest that you speak respectfully of her or not at all."

"Aye, Ormiston of Ormiston. Did he present her to *you*?"

"I met him the night I arrived, on the Inch near town," Àdham said glibly. "When I told him I was meeting kinsmen here at the alehouse, he invited me to take wine with him first at his house. Later, he told me that the alehouse was noisy and invited me to spend the night. It was a kindness. What else did you see tonight?"

"I saw you hit Caithness, if that's what you mean."

"I mistook him for your uncivil friend," Àdham said, mentally cursing that act again. "Caithness will expect you to keep the incident to yourself, and so do I."

Staring upward, Gilli said, "I heard people cry out when they saw it, so I expect the whole town will know of it by morning."

"Perhaps," Àdham said, although he did not recall any outcry. His attention had fixed first on the hand gripping Lady Fiona's arm and then on his having floored Caithness instead of the lout from Tuesday night. "You had better hope that I don't hear about it from anyone *you* have told."

Gilli shrugged. "I just want to go home."

Accustomed to his uncertain moods, Àdham changed the subject, but Gilli's comment about people crying out when he'd floored Caithness echoed disturbingly.

Having experience enough with the royal court to know that everything occurring within or near it fueled hearsay, rumor, and gossip that spread fast, Fiona had slept fitfully. Awaking reluctantly Saturday morning to the sound of her door shutting and quick steps to the bed, she blinked.

"Were there a fight over ye yestereve, m'lady, during the entertainment?"

"Good sakes," Fiona murmured, blinking again, as the last remnants of sleep fled and she saw Leah hovering over her, awaiting an answer.

Irritated but scarcely astonished, Fiona drew a breath to cool her temper, then sat up, saying, "There was no fight, Leah. If you heard such a thing, someone has evidently tried to build a trifling incident into a shocking event. That is all."

"Then, will ye tell me what did happen, so I can tell folks the truth of it?"

"I'll tell you only that a man I did not know put his hand on me and another man dissuaded him. But I forbid you to talk of this,

Leah. If anyone asks you about it, you can honestly say that I was in no danger and that naught of import occurred."

With a nod, but nonetheless persistently, Leah added, "They did say that the man what got knocked down were the Earl o' Caithness *and* that he spoke your name."

Suppressing a sigh, Fiona said, "I will not discuss this further, Leah. There was no fight, and I was not in danger. Prithee, say no more and do *not* encourage others to discuss it. If I hear that you have behaved otherwise, I shall be most dis—"

"Nae, then, m'lady, I won't," Leah assured her hastily.

Leah had served her for years, and Fiona had enough faith in her to believe she would obey her. However, if Leah had heard about the incident, little hope remained that Lady Sutherland had not.

Dressing carefully, Fiona went downstairs and learned straightaway that Lady Sutherland wanted to see her and would send for her when she had broken her fast.

Finding Malvina and Sarah Douglas, one of the other two maids of honor, alone at the refectory table reserved for them, Fiona greeted them as she took her place and reached for a manchet loaf in one basket and then an apple from another.

As she did, Sarah quietly excused herself.

Using her eating knife, Fiona began to slice the apple into quarters, but Sarah's skirts had barely cleared the nearest doorway when Malvina leaned closer and said breathlessly, "Is it true, Fiona? Did a giant Highlander really knock the Earl of Caithness on his backside last night because Caithness accosted you after you left me? Oh, prithee, tell me everything, for I saw none of it."

Sighing, Fiona repeated what she had told Leah, but she had lost her appetite. Her father would be furious when he heard what had happened, which he surely would now, and heaven knew what consequences would follow. Malvina continued to plead for details, so Fiona nearly thanked the lay brother who entered then and told her that the mistress of robes would speak with her now.

Rapping on Lady Sutherland's sitting-room door a few minutes later and hearing her ladyship bid her enter, Fiona obeyed, shutting the door behind her.

Lady Sutherland sat on a back-stool near the small, sparely furnished room's window embrasure. She gestured to her stool's twin a short distance away.

"Sit ye doon, Fiona-lass," she said. "A matter has come tae me attention that requires explanation. I thought we should discuss it afore ye attend tae your duties."

"Aye, sure, madam," Fiona said, sitting obediently and folding her hands in her lap. She hoped her ladyship would thus fail to see that her nerves were on edge.

Knowing only what Leah and Malvina had told her, she was uncertain of how harmful the incident between Caithness and Sir Àdham might be to her.

Lady Sutherland smiled warmly. "I dinna think ye did wrong. But I did hear wild tales of summat occurring yestereve whilst ye were returning tae our table."

"An incident did occur, madam, but naught that endangered anyone or that I would be unwilling to explain."

"Good, then simply tell me what happened."

Simply? Fiona wondered. *Could a knight of the realm striking a noble member of the royal family ever be considered a simple occurrence?*

Keeping that thought to herself, she explained briefly what had happened and why. She took care to include the apology that Caithness had so promptly and sincerely offered her and her willing acceptance of it.

When she finished, Lady Sutherland smiled as warmly as she had before.

Fiona felt her tension ease.

Then her ladyship said cheerfully, "I see exactly how it was, me dearling. We must hope now that I shall describe it just as plainly tae her grace."

That same morning, after breaking his fast, Àdham walked with his squire to the Ormiston House stable. As they turned into Curfew Row, MacNab said, "There be some grand houses in this town, aye, sir?"

"It *is* a royal burgh and the capital of the country," Àdham reminded him, although he did agree that few, if any, houses in

Inverness—also a royal burgh—would compare to those along Curfew Row. None was palatial, but all were built of stone, and many possessed glazed windows.

St. John's Town itself was no larger than Inverness or Nairn, although neither—nor any other Highland town—boasted a wall. St. John's Town even smelled much the same as the others, since all three towns sat near the sea.

When they reached Ormiston House, they went straight into the stable, where two of its occupants greeted Àdham with near delirium. He dissuaded the dog from propping its dirty forepaws against his thighs only by catching the paws.

"Down, sir," Àdham said in a tone that received instant obedience. "As for you," he said to young Rory, who was fairly dancing in his eagerness to impart news of evident import, "Stand properly before you speak to me."

"Aye, sure," the boy said as he planted his feet together on the ground and stood rigidly straight. "But I've taught Sirius a trick, and I did think ye'd want tae see it. I fetched this old cap o' yours, tae teach him."

"Show me, then."

"First, ye ha' tae go out and hide. I'll keep Sirius here till ye're hid."

Looking at Duff, who grinned and nodded, Àdham said, "Very well." He went quietly to the garden where he had walked with Fiona, shut the picket gate after himself, and crouched behind one of the hedges. Through its branches, the next thing he saw was Sirius leaping over the gate. The dog ran straight to him.

Rory followed, shouting, "The lad is grand, is he no? I taught him tae seek ye oot, but I wasna sure he'd fetch ye as easy as he fetched yer old cap."

"Very clever," Àdham said. "Are you behaving yourself?"

"I think so, aye," he said, shooting an anxious look over a shoulder at Duff.

The equerry said, "I'm pleased enough, sir. He's made hisself useful to Lord Ormiston's people, too."

"MacNab and I are going onto the Inch for target practice. If anyone comes looking for us, that is where we'll be."

They left at once, and as they crossed the red bridge on their way to the archery butts at the far end of the Inch, Sir Robert Graham's image rose in Àdham's mind. Aware, as he was now, of where his uncle's sympathies lay, Àdham wondered if the man had taken any part in the parliamentary ructions.

Meantime, Sir Robert's evident belief that he could command his nephew's behavior had irked him. Furthering their kinship, he decided, would be unwise.

In any event, he and MacNab could pass a few hours honing their skills with their weapons. Afterward, they might wander along the riverbank to explore more of the nearby landscape than either had yet seen.

For a time, they alternated rounds of a friendly archery contest with fierce, albeit ever-heedful, swordplay. Then, shortly after midday, as MacNab was returning with the arrows they had just shot, he shouted, "Yonder, sir! I think that's our laddie a-coming!"

Turning, Àdham saw Rory running full pelt the length of the Inch toward them. Accepting his own arrows from MacNab and slipping them into his quiver, he unstrung his bow as he strode to meet the boy.

"What is it, lad?" he asked.

"His lordship," the boy gasped out before pausing to snatch a breath.

"Ormiston?"

"Aye, he sent me tae tell ye he would speak wi' ye straightaway."

Suspecting that the boy might have committed a mischief, Àdham said, "Do you know *why* he wants to speak with me?"

Shaking his head fiercely, Rory said, "Nae, and ye needna look at me so, neither. I've done nowt save what Duff or them others tell me tae do."

"Then I beg your pardon if I looked as if I suspected you'd been up to mischief. I cannot think how such a notion entered my head."

Grinning, the boy said, "Me neither. But his lordship does want ye. Mayhap ye're the one what's been up tae mischief, aye?"

"Mind your tongue, lad," Àdham said. As he said it, he grimaced, realizing that Ormiston had likely heard about the incident with Caithness.

Rory's eyebrows flew upward. "Sakes, what *did* ye do then?"

Giving him a stern look, Àdham said, "I did naught that could shame me. Moreover, if I had, it would be nae concern of yours, would it?"

Rory gazed thoughtfully, even skeptically, at him until Àdham said softly, "Do you want to debate the point until you irk me?"

"I do not," the boy said firmly. "But ye shouldna look so if ye havena been up tae summat, 'less ye want folks tae *think* ye have."

"Enough," Àdham said firmly.

Rory nodded. "Should I go wi' ye or stay here wi' MacNab?"

"We'll all go," Àdham said, waving for his squire to join them.

When they reached Ormiston House, Àdham sent the other two to the stable. "I'll send for you, MacNab, when I'm ready to return to the alehouse," he added.

"Best slick your hair doon afore ye go in," Rory said. "It be all a-tangle."

When MacNab hid a grin, Àdham said curtly, "The pair of you would do well to seek shelter in yon stable now."

Watching them walk away, Àdham tugged off the string he used to tie back his hair and ran his fingers through the tangles, wondering bleakly if everyone in St. John's Town considered himself, or herself, an authority on men's hair.

Hoping that, if Ormiston *had* heard about his striking Caithness, he'd heard at least a semblance of the truth, Àdham drew a breath to restore his calm and retied his string as he approached the house. The door opened just as he reached it.

A man he'd not seen before said, "Sir Àdham, I am his lordship's steward. His lordship awaits you in the rear chamber. He said you know your way."

"I do, aye," Àdham replied, whereupon the man stood aside to let him pass.

Pausing at the closed door of Ormiston's room, Àdham heard his host's invitation to enter before his knuckles touched wood to rap.

Inside, he found his lordship coming to his feet.

"We need no ceremony, sir," Àdham said. "You told my lad to hie himself, so just tell me how I may serve you."

"The summons was not solely mine," Ormiston said with a rueful smile. "His grace awaits us at Blackfriars. 'Tis he who would speak with you."

"Is this about last night, sir? Because if it is . . ." He let the sentence die when Ormiston shook his head.

"You need explain naught, Àdham. I ken fine how it was."

"But one does not go about knocking cousins of his grace on their backsides . . . not with impunity, at all events."

"There may be consequences, aye," Ormiston admitted. "But his grace awaits us. Shall we go?"

There being only one answer to that question, Àdham accompanied him to the monastery chapel.

CHAPTER 7

Fiona loved the Gilten Herbar, named for the arched and gilded arbors under which its paths wended past beds of aromatic herbs, flowers, shrubbery, and fruit trees. Wherever sunbeams broke through the canopy of vines, they danced on those golden frames and many other gilded decorations. The only sounds were bird-songs and the crunch of gravel under their feet. Any Blackfriars currently residing there, rather than traveling as mendicants, were at their prayers or reciting their rosaries.

The Herbar served as the monastery's kitchen garden, but Fiona loved the flowers, their scents and colors, the noisy birds, the squirrels' chatter, and the changing light on the gilded arches and ornaments. As she and Malvina wandered along a path, her imagination danced with the sunbeams and peopled the flow-erbeds with fairies and other wee folk. Realizing that Holy Kirk would likely frown on thoughts of fairies capering through a mon-astery garden, she smiled.

"I just wondered, that's all," Malvina said rather abruptly.

"Wondered what?" Fiona asked, glancing at her.

"Faith, were you not listening to me?" Malvina demanded indignantly.

Guiltily, Fiona said, "I fear I was lost in thought, comparing our gardens at home with this one." Her mind raced, seeking a way to sound sensible without encouraging discussion of imaginary wee folk. "So, prithee, forgive me and I shall listen most intently to you. What did you wonder?"

With an injured little sigh, Malvina said, "Art sure you want to know?"

"You have been my best friend since I joined her grace's court," Fiona assured her. "Aye, sure, I want to know."

"Very well, then," Malvina said, brightening. "Do you recall meeting my two cousins last night, before the incident with Caithness? You left so hastily after that that I could not be sure you would."

"I do, though. I talked to the one you deemed handsome."

"A tedious prattler, I thought, and *not* wealthy," Malvina said with a dismissive wave. "In troth, I was irked when he talked to you instead of to me, because I had to talk to Hamish, whom I have often thought rude and disagreeable. But now, I think I might marry him, Fiona. What do you think of that?"

Fiona gaped at her. "Why would you *want* to marry a rudesby you dislike?"

Grinning, Malvina said, "Because, although he teases me in a most uncivil way, he is no longer so horrid. Sithee, I learned last night that he is to inherit his grandfather's estates. Hamish will be wealthy, Fiona. I shall have a household steward and more servants than my mother has. We will even have a house in Edinburgh's Canongate. I shall command every elegancy of life!"

Dryly, Fiona said, "Only if he *asks* you to marry him."

"But he has . . . that is, my father and his have talked for some time of such a match and have settled the arrangements. Hamish told me as much last night. I said then that I was not certain that I *wanted* to marry him, but of course, I will."

"Then, I think Hamish is a lucky man and you will be very happy," Fiona said sincerely. She had been aware for some time that Ormiston was seeking an acceptable match for her. She knew, too, that *he* would not simply present someone and tell her that he and the young man's father had already made the arrangements.

What he *had* told her was that, in Scotland, a woman could refuse *any* man.

❖   ❖   ❖

Inside the towering, empty monastery chapel, James, King of Scots, stood at the center of the transept in front of the high altar.

"I recall ye well, Sir Àdham," the King said. "Sakes, I recall every man I have knighted. I even recall your clan war leader, Sir Ivor Mackintosh, although I was but a bairn when he won his knighthood."

Gazing in awe at a kirk more magnificent than any other he had seen, Àdham said, "Sir Ivor is Shaw Mòr Mackintosh's son, your grace. He is also my foster mother's brother. So Ivor is as an uncle to me." Collecting his wits and facing James directly, he added, "Mayhap you also know my paternal uncle and foster father. Men call him 'Fin of the Battles.'"

The King smiled reminiscently. "I do remember Sir Fin, aye, for that is what *I* called him. Nearly three decades have passed since last I saw him, but I owe my thanks to him and to Sir Ivor. As I do to ye, lad. However, whilst I ken fine that the Mackintosh is a good friend to me, yon Clan Chattan Confederation has got so big that I do wonder if all of its members remain as loyal to me as your captain does."

Àdham was silent. It was no business of his to speak for other members of the confederation.

James added gently, "I have heard rumors of ructions within your own confederation. Likewise do I hear tales of fractious factions within Clan Cameron. If I recall correctly, your father is Ewan MacGillony Cameron, aye?"

"Aye, your grace," Àdham said.

"Yet ye call yourself MacFinlagh," James said.

"I fostered with Uncle Fin. So I have associated myself for years now with Fin and Castle Finlagh."

"Yet Ewan MacGillony Cameron—if what I hear be true—has at times spoken against my policies."

Àdham met the King's quizzical gaze and said, "I speak for no man save myself, my liege, not even for Ewan MacGillony. I am your man and will remain so. But I would remind you, with deep respect, that Ewan did lead the MacGillony Camerons at Lochaber against Alexander of the Isles. He has not taken up arms against your grace since that day. Nor, to my knowledge, has he spoken against you since then."

"Aye, he fought for me, and I ken that other Cameron factions followed his lead. But others under Lochiel, the Cameron Captain, fought for Alexander, aye?"

"I was in the thick of battle, my liege, so I cannot answer your question of mine own knowledge. But I did hear that Lochiel supported Alexander."

"There is also the matter of mine own uncle, Atholl," James said softly.

A ripple of unease stirred in Àdham. If James knew that Atholl's second wife, the lady Elizabeth Graham, was Àdham's grandaunt, would he assume . . . ?

Accepting Àdham's silence with the same ease he had the first time, James said, "Ye must ken fine that I dinna trust my uncle Atholl or *some* of his kinsmen, including *your* uncle, the so-eloquent scoundrel of Kinpont. He and Atholl make plain their antipathy for my belief in a rule of law for all, and Blair Castle overlooks the main route from here into the Highlands. If Atholl decides to keep the next royal army from passing that way, he could make a damned nuisance of himself."

"So I have heard," Àdham said. "But I have met Sir Robert only a few times and have never spoken to the Earl of Atholl. Nor do I ken aught to Atholl's discredit unless it is discreditable now merely to speak against potential royal policies."

Aware of Ormiston shifting his feet, Àdham wondered if he'd said too much.

"Ye do speak your mind, sir," James said, his lips quirking into a slight smile. "Methinks such candor may be a long-held Highland habit. I'll own, though, that many of my Borderers and trusted Lothian lairds do oft show a like tendency.

"Sithee," he added, "I recall times past when speaking truth to one's ruler could lead to one's death. I pray that I never become such a ruler. Mentors of my youth, here and in England, taught me a few maxims that nearly all of them held in common. Two that I have never forgotten are to listen to mine enemies as if they were my friends and to keep them as close as I can whilst still keeping safe."

Àdham nearly asked if that was why he had imprisoned the Lord of the Isles at Tantallon, which was less than a day's journey from Edinburgh Castle. He held his tongue, though, because Fin had said more than once that although he had oft regretted his speech, he had never regretted his silence.

"My intent," James went on, "is for our Parliament to become the primary source of laws for Scotland. To accomplish that, I must reduce the powers of a few stubborn noblemen who prefer to create their own laws—not just Alexander of the Isles, who claims title to all Scotland north of the Forth and insists he will seize every stick and stone of it—but Atholl, too, and others. I do welcome opposing views, but I will suppress active resistance wherever I find it."

"I've heard that many Scottish noblemen believe that Parliament should not assume such great powers, your grace. They suggest that you are merely trying to undermine *their* inherited and heritable rights."

James exchanged a look with Ormiston, who raised his eyebrows ironically, as if, Àdham thought, he had expected such an exchange. Then, turning, he looked down the length of the nave as if tacitly removing himself from the conversation.

"I do know that such qualms exist," James said. "'Tis why I need your help."

"I am yours to command, sir," Àdham said warily. "What am I to do?"

"First, I'd have ye keep your eyes and ears open whilst ye visit certain areas of the Highlands in my stead to learn where troubles *may* arise. Sithee, if I know of discontent before it spurs rebellion, we might ease such tensions before they erupt."

"Do you mean that I am to spy for you, your grace?"

James, looking surprised, said, "Ye may be unaware that I had my early schooling at St. Andrews with the bishops and was likewise well-schooled during my English captivity. In neither country does one gentleman spy on another. I learned, as doubtless ye did yourself, that such behavior is unacceptable. In either country, the penalty would be death. And no landowner would suffer for hanging a man or a woman who pried into his personal affairs."

"In a town, someone might get away with such prying," Àdham said. "But a clan controls an entire area, so strangers are ever suspect. If one were too nosy . . ."

"I do not expect ye to sneak about, lad, let alone in another clan's territory. But contact between your central Highlands and Edinburgh, Stirling, or even Perth is slow, difficult, and often non-existent. However, your affinity with the two great clan confederations provides ye with a vast and scattered kindred, which makes ye ideally suited to serve as a distant set of eyes and ears. If ye'll aid me so, I'll be less blind and deaf to aught that threatens the peace of my realm from that part of it."

After brief consideration, Àdham nodded. "I'll do what I can, my liege. The Mackintosh and Sir Ivor will likely have duties for me, too, as you may suppose."

"I expect so," James said, glancing at Ormiston, who was still apparently fascinated by the long aisle of the nave. "There is another matter I would put to ye," James added. "I believe ye be neither married yet nor promised, aye?"

"Aye, sir," Àdham admitted uneasily.

"Excellent," James said, flashing his charming smile. "The best way I know to build friendships where enemies have existed is through tactical marriages. I hear that ye've met Ormiston's daughter, the lovely lady Fiona, and likely ken her better than any other lass hereabouts. Come to that, I also heard ye were moved to intervene last night when a close cousin of mine accosted her ladyship."

Stunned by the obvious suggestion that he should consider marrying Lady Fiona, and suddenly aware that he would not reject that notion out of hand, Àdham wondered nonetheless if the King had mentioned the incident with Caithness as a subtle threat of consequence if he should reject it.

Àdham said, "'Twas but a natural impulse to aid her ladyship, my liege. I failed to recognize Caithness from behind when he grabbed her arm, startling her. Such behavior at a court festivity being . . ."

"Utterly unacceptable," James said with a smile when Àdham paused to seek the most diplomatic word. "Such an impulse speaks well o' ye, lad. In any event, ye should ken that I'd be pleased to bless a union betwixt yourself and her ladyship. Not only did ye serve me well at Lochaber, but mine own lass is gey fond of Fiona. Also," he added firmly, "her lord father does favor such a match."

A certain portion of Àdham's body, certainly the least cognitive part, stirred with delight at the thought of having the lady Fiona as his wife. However . . .

Glancing at Ormiston to find his lordship looking at him with the same sternly enigmatic stare he had encountered on the Inch soon after meeting the lass, he felt an inexplicable, nervous urge to clear his throat.

Reminding himself that his lordship did not intimidate him, Àdham said, "Is that true, sir? You would approve such a marriage?"

Ormiston's hazel eyes narrowed and his lips pressed together before he said evenly, "Wouldst accuse his grace of a lie, sir?"

"You ken fine that I do no such thing," Àdham replied in the same tone. "I'd wager, though, that her ladyship will be loath to accept me as a husband."

"You will leave Fiona to me," Ormiston said.

"Nae, then. I want no wife who must be forced to accept me."

"And I would not force my dearling lass to marry," Ormiston said with an edge to his voice. "I meant only that I know her well and will talk with her. Sakes, lad, I favor the match chiefly because, although I have never seen her show interest in any man before, I saw straightaway that you have piqued her curiosity. In troth, I doubt that she would reject this notion of his grace's outright. However, she *may* claim to agree only because it is proffered at his grace's behest."

"I cannot say that I'd like that any better," Àdham said. "She thinks all Highlanders are barbarians."

"Then persuade her otherwise. Give her cause to agree. . . . Unless *you* are unwilling. Are you opposed to the match, Àdham? Do you favor someone else? If you do, I'll not press you further. Nor will I allow his grace to do so."

Wondering at the word *allow* in reference to James, Àdham squelched an impulse to question it. In fact, he believed that Ormiston would do as he said and without a qualm. Even so, Àdham was sure Fiona would refuse to marry him and realized, to his own surprise, that he hoped she would *not* refuse. Yet . . .

"Her ladyship does not speak the Gaelic," he said, looking from Ormiston to the King and back again. "I fear, too, that she would become gey lonely in Strathnairn and yearn for her home, her family, and familiar surroundings."

James said, "Or she may be fain to learn your language, visit new places, and meet new people. My beloved lady had no qualms about moving to Scotland, and Fiona has seemed curious about everything she has seen these two years past."

"She does expect to marry someday," Ormiston said. "Whilst I'll admit that I never imagined her living at such a distance from us, if you do this, our family will not abandon her. I would not impose my company on your journey home, lad, but I would expect to visit you there, if possible, before the snows fly."

"I am willing," Àdham said, although he found it hard to picture the wealthy Ormiston at rustic Finlagh, let alone to picture the lady Fiona there after living with the Queen's court.

Exiting the monastery chapel with the King and Ormiston, who had asked a lay brother to summon Fiona to the parlor, Àdham stood silently in the courtyard with his lordship and watched James go inside.

Ormiston said mildly, "Art sure of this, lad?"

Although he was anything but sure, Àdham said, "I said I am willing, and I keep my word, sir. By my troth, I'll be gey pleased if her ladyship does agree. I'm thinking, though, that I'd be wise to put the matter to my people first. If they have strong objection to the union, to pursue it further could lead to trouble."

"His grace did discuss it with the Mackintosh," Ormiston said. "Malcolm approves, so no one else should object. However, if *you* have concerns that someone might, you must relieve them if you can. Find Sir Ivor and talk with him.

"Meantime," he added, "I will talk with Fiona. If you will meet me at the house when you hear the bell for Vespers, I will give you her answer."

"Aye, sure, sir," Àdham said. "But the decision *must* lie with Lady Fiona."

❖   ❖   ❖

Fiona and Lady Malvina were returning from the Gilten Herbar when they perceived Fiona's maidservant, Leah, hurrying toward them.

"Your lord father be a-waiting in the parlor, m'lady," Leah said. "He would speak wi' ye straightaway, Brother Porter said."

Hoping that Ormiston had not come to scold her for the small part she had played when Sir Àdham hit Caithness, Fiona hastily straightened her caul and veil. Then, pinching more color into her cheeks, she headed for the wee parlor where maids of honor and other attendants could meet and talk with their visitors.

Her father, standing by a window that overlooked the monastery's orchard and his grace's new tennis court, turned toward her when she entered.

"Should I shut the door?" she asked him.

"Aye, I'd like this conversation to stay between the two of us for now."

"Have I displeased you, sir?"

"Nae, lassie. I fear the boot is on the other foot, or soon may be."

She raised her eyebrows, stifling an urge to smile at the absurd suggestion that he might fear angering her.

"I can see that my comment amuses you," he said. "I'd best spit out what I've come to say, then, so we can discuss it. I hope your amusement won't turn to ire when I tell you that his grace and I have come to an understanding that significantly affects your future."

"Am I no longer to serve Joanna then?"

Looking surprised at the question, he said, "You've done naught to displease her grace, my dearling. I believe she loves you nearly as much as I do. But you cannot act forever as a maid of honor. You have your own life to live, after all."

A sense of foreboding shot through her. Not true fear but wary anticipation . . . of what, she knew not. Surely, her father would not say she had to leave Joanna and go home simply because he had offered for Lady Rosalie's hand in marriage.

"Does it have to do with what happened last night, sir?"

"In a way, I suppose it does. However, his grace has asked a boon of me and suspects that his notion will not discomfit you. I am not certain of that, though. I ken fine that you have enjoyed a comfortable life at Ormiston Mains and have also enjoyed your service with her grace."

"I love Joanna dearly, so my service is a pleasure for me. Does his grace want me to live elsewhere?" A chill shot up her spine at the next thought that occurred to her. "Do I truly have a say in this matter, sir, or have you and his grace made up your heads that I must do as you have decided?"

"You have every right to refuse what we propose. But I hope you will give it due consideration first. I have seen for myself that you are friendly with Sir Àdham MacFinlagh and that he cares enough about you to act as your protector."

A place deep inside her warmed at hearing that Sir Àdham cared about her. However, trepidation followed. How was it that, just when one began to find life interesting, Fate should threaten to upend all that one had come to take for granted?

"Faith, sir, you *cannot* mean— That is," she amended hastily, when his eyebrows knitted together, "surely, Sir Àdham has not *offered* for me. Sakes, I was thinking only seconds ago that mayhap *you* had offered for Lady Rosalie."

To her surprise, Ormiston, looking like a boy caught in mischief, shifted his gaze from hers to a portrait on the wall beside them of St. Dominic, wearing the cream-colored tunic, scapular, and black-hooded cape of a Dominican friar. Drawing a breath, he looked at her and said, "Would you dislike it if I had?"

Every fiber of her body stilled at that question, but she would not disappoint him again. "How could I dislike Lady Rosalie when she has always been so kind to me and to everyone else who meets her?"

"She is kind, and she is merry," Ormiston said. "I'll admit that she attracted me the first time I met her. Moreover, I doubt that she will do aught to alter our life at Ormiston Mains. And you will soon become fast friends with her."

Realizing that he *was* contemplating marriage for himself, Fiona wondered if she dared ask him the question that leaped next to her mind.

"What is it, lassie?"

"I have heard that it is difficult for any woman to take the reins of a new household if she must also get along with an unmarried daughter experienced at running it. Is that why you want me to marry?"

"I have already said that you can reject his grace's suggestion," Ormiston reminded her. "I meant that."

"Have you also discussed this with Sir Àdham? I doubt that he would be content to live at Ormiston Mains."

"You would live with him at his home, Fiona, but we would visit you. And, naturally, the two of you would be welcome to pay long visits to us."

"I'd have to live in the Highlands?" Her voice ended on a squeak.

"Aye, sure. A woman lives with her husband. And Àdham *is* a Highlander."

A barbarian, her inner self whispered, sending a quiver up her spine. "I . . . I don't know. The Highlands seem dreadfully frightful and wild, sir. They speak another language there, too, the Gaelic. I ken naught of it."

"You would learn quickly, I think. Moreover, Àdham speaks Scots, as do a number of his kinsmen, I believe."

"Faith, I need time to think," she said desperately. "When must I decide?"

"We did talk to Àdham. Also, his grace has invited us—the three of us—to sit at the high table this evening with him and the Queen."

"Father! How can I possibly think if you need an answer by suppertime?" she demanded, her voice rising. "Moreover, if we sit with the King and Queen at the high table, every member of the court will assume that our wedding date is settled."

"Doucely, lass. You may have all the time you require. I will tell his grace that you want to give our suggestion more thought before making your decision, and that you would liefer not accept such an honor with Sir Àdham before then."

"But why do *you* think I should marry him?"

"He is a man of good character and a skillful, courageous warrior. Moreover, his grace has many enemies, so anything we can do to help him make more friends where he has few will aid him and thereby make our country stronger. Also, just as you perceive Highlanders as barbarians, so do Highlanders perceive Borderers. Border reivers oft steal cattle from Highlanders north and west of Loch Lomond, and you know as well as I do how vicious they can be. You can aid Sir Àdham *and* his grace just by being yourself and letting Àdham's people come to know you."

Since she could hardly say that she did not care a whit about what was good for Scotland, only about what might be good or bad for her, she held her tongue.

"You must also talk with Sir Àdham, I think," Ormiston said. "The two of you should discuss all of the concerns you have about this notion."

"Has he agreed to it then?"

"He has not refused." His lips twitched into a near smile. "In troth, I think he expects you to reject him outright. But I hope you will not do that. I want you to give careful thought to his grace's request before you decide what is best for you."

Which, Fiona's inner voice muttered, *means he expects you to oblige the King and himself and, thereby, also resolve any issue that might stand betwixt him and Lady Rosalie. Because, whatever he might say, her ladyship will surely have qualms about sharing Ormiston Mains with a well-loved good-daughter.*

"How do you suggest that I approach Sir Àdham to suggest such a talk?" she asked, forcing calm into her voice, determined not to reveal how horrified she felt about having to discuss their so-likely marriage with Sir Àdham.

"If we are not to dine on the dais this evening, I shall invite Àdham to take supper with me at the house, and to walk with you in the Gilten Herbar afterward," he said lightly. "I ken fine that you will enjoy watching the moonrise, at least."

Clearly, he had not given thought to how late the moon was likely to rise that night. *You see*, her inner voice muttered irritably, *they* have *decided this matter*.

CHAPTER 8

The rest of the afternoon passed quickly—too quickly—for Fiona. She saw to her usual duties, and since she rarely conversed with others while doing so, she had hoped she would be able to think. However, she soon realized that she was thinking only of *being* married to Àdham, not of whether she wanted to be or not.

His image filled her mind, pushing out more emotional thoughts, because, although he attracted her and spoke like a gentleman, his shaggy beard and too-long, unruly hair still made him look like a barbarian. That image strongly reinforced her belief that he would live more like a barbarian than any gentleman—or lady—should.

Life in the Highlands would surely bear no resemblance to life with the royal court. Nor, she suspected, would it be as comfortable as life at Ormiston Mains. Or at any of the other great houses she knew in the Borders.

Memory of her earlier talk with Malvina intruded then. She could easily imagine Malvina surrounded by luxury, enjoying a wealthy husband and all the trappings of a life of ease. But Malvina was marrying Hamish Geddes, who was nearly as dull a man as her handsomer cousin, whose name Fiona had forgotten.

Sir Àdham would never be dull. Nor, despite his frequently unkempt appearance, did he fit her earlier image of a true barbarian. He had also proven that he would protect her from any danger or rougher men they might meet.

She could not imagine dull Hamish lifting a finger to protect Malvina. He would doubtless hire bodyguards to do so; but Malvina had always shown interest in handsomer men, which could lead to danger of another sort.

Fiona realized that she did not know if Sir Àdham was what she or others would call handsome, because she had seen only part of his face. He was powerful looking and a warrior. She had always felt safe when she was with him, and he had intrigued her and piqued her curiosity from the first night of their acquaintance.

She had only to see him coming toward her to feel warm inside. So, perhaps she did not care as much about his appearance as she had thought. Still . . .

With suppertime approaching and no decision presenting itself, she went to her chamber and dismissed Leah, saying she would wear what she had on. In truth, Fiona wanted time to calm herself before seeing Àdham. Minutes later, though, with no more ceremony than a light *rap-rap*, the door opened and a cloud of ambergris wafted in, announcing her visitor as clearly as any royal steward might.

Fiona was making her curtsy when Lady Sutherland swept in and shut the door behind her. "Arise, me dearling," she murmured. "I would speak wi' ye."

Obeying, Fiona eyed her ladyship warily. "Is aught amiss, madam?"

"I ken fine that ye've only just come up, because I asked Malvina tae tell me when ye did," her ladyship said. "Sithee, her grace sent me tae see . . . That is . . ." She grimaced. "Ay-de-mi, I'm making hard work o' this. So I'll speak plainly. She heard that ye'd likely received an offer tae wed and would ken if it please ye or no."

Despite Fiona's own concerns, her sense of humor stirred. She knew that the walls and halls of every royal residence had ears, so rumors spread swiftly. Lady Sutherland might have relayed the news to Joanna herself, if the King had not. But he might well have discussed his wishes with her earlier.

"I have received no offer yet, my lady," Fiona said. "But my lord father did tell me to expect one."

"Then it will likely come after supper," Lady Sutherland said, nodding. "That dress becomes ye well, but ye must tidy your hair. Where is your Leah?"

"I . . . I wanted to think," Fiona said.

"So ye told Leah ye'd look after yourself, aye?" When Fiona nodded, Lady Sutherland added, "Did Ormiston tell ye tae expect the offer this evening?"

Suppressing a sigh, Fiona said, "He will arrange for me to walk with Sir Àdham in the Gilten Herbar after supper."

"Good, then," Lady Sutherland said, clapping her hands. "Guide him toward the far end, dearling, and I shall see that nae one disturbs ye. Ye needna come doonstairs for supper, either. Ye willna want tae be wonderin' who may ha' ken o' this, so I'll have your Leah bring ye up a tray. But now, let us see what we can do wi' your hair. Ye should wear it in a net, I think. Nae need for a formal caul tae stroll amidst the monks' flowerbeds."

Feeling as she suspected anyone might feel who was approaching a possibly grim fate, Fiona submitted herself to Lady Sutherland's capable skills.

Having learned that Sir Ivor approved of the union as strongly as Malcolm did and was certain that Fin would, too, Àdham went back to Ormiston House.

Although he had diplomatically told Ormiston that he'd be pleased if Lady Fiona agreed to marry him, he realized that *not* wanting her to reject him was hardly the same thing as being pleased. Just thinking about her sent his imagination down pleasurable pathways, though, and stirred responses in him that had surprised him.

He had felt protective of her from the start, in the same way he felt toward the female members of his foster family. She amused him in similar ways, too. But she also challenged him at times and made him see things in different ways.

She was beautiful, charming, and easy to like. On the other hand, she was too fond of having her own way and prone to ignoring the wishes, even commands, of those in authority over her. Surely, even in the Lowlands, where men curled hair that God had made straight and wore absurd clothing, wives obeyed their husbands.

So she would have to change some of her ways. But she must know that life in the Highlands would be different from the life she had hitherto enjoyed.

Admitted to the house by Ormiston's steward, Àdham went straight to the room at the rear of the hall. There, after describing Sir Ivor's reaction for his host, he added, "Ivor did say that he wants to talk with you himself, sir."

"About the settlements, aye," Ormiston said amiably. "Fiona has agreed to talk with you, so you should know that her tocher includes a small estate of mine on the river Teviot north of Ormiston Mains. I have settled gelt on her, too, heritable to her daughters."

Àdham nodded. "I have land in Strathnairn, which currently lacks a home. So, we'd live with my uncle at Finlagh in the north-central Highlands for a time, but I do expect to acquire more land with my sword in battle, or otherwise."

Over supper, they discussed other matters, including how Àdham's party might travel to the Highlands, until Ormiston said, "We must not keep Fiona waiting any longer."

Accordingly, they returned to the monastery, and when Brother Porter admitted them, Ormiston explained briefly why they had come.

The porter nodded. "I'll just show the pair o' ye into the parlor, m'lord. Then I'll hie a maidservant upstairs tae tell her ladyship ye be here."

"I have agreed to let them walk alone in the Gilten Herbar," Ormiston said.

"As ye wish, m'lord. I will do all I may to provide privacy for them. The brothers do also walk there of an evening. Her grace and her ladies do, too. But," he added with a smile, "I expect everyone will ken their need and leave them be."

The notion that "everyone" knew why he was there annoyed Àdham, but he reminded himself that he had made his decision and must see it through.

Ormiston was silent after Brother Porter left the room, and both men remained standing. Although Àdham welcomed the silence, he was listening for Fiona's footsteps. Despite his sharp ears, though, the click of the latch was the only warning he had before the door opened and she stepped into the doorway.

She wore a gray, fur-lined mantle over a light-green kirtle with buttoned sleeves extending to her knuckles. Its neckline plunged to reveal the soft swell of her breasts, and a dark green belt embroidered with pink, yellow, and blue flowers nipped it in below her bosom. Dark netting loosely confined her hair. Her mantle hood covered the back half of her head, framing her lovely face with soft gray folds that enhanced the otherwise pale bluish gray of her irises.

When her gaze met his, she gave him a long, appraising look. Then she turned to her father. "You said that Sir Àdham and I might walk alone, aye?"

"I did, and you will. I lingered only so that Brother Porter could see that I do approve. He sent someone, too, to ensure that you will have some privacy."

"I want to ask *you* something privately before you leave," she said.

"Then we will excuse Sir Àdham for a short while and talk here."

"I'll wait with Brother Porter in the entryway," Àdham said.

She stood aside, and as he passed her, her light floral perfume wafted gently to him. Her skin looked pale and smooth, especially what he could see of her breasts, outlined as their plump, bare upper parts were in the silken vee.

His body stirred eagerly, and he increased his pace, slowing only after he had shut the door behind him and heard its latch click into place.

"What is it, lass?" Ormiston asked when the door had shut behind Àdham.

"I do not want a husband whose face I have not seen, sir," Fiona said bluntly. "I suggested as tactfully as possible that Àdham . . . that is, *Sir* Àdham . . . would be wise to adopt at least some of the town fashions. But as you have seen . . ."

Seeing her father's lips tighten, she wondered if her comments had irked him. But then she noted the twinkle in his eyes. "I wonder," he said gently, "if you will be as willing to change your ways to accommodate his people's notions of fashion as you desire him to change his to suit yours."

"Surely, Highland ladies do not wear only their shifts and a long length of woolen cloth wrapped round them," she said with a sense of shock.

"In troth, lassie, I have met few Highlanders of either sex, so I have no ken of what Highland women wear. However, I do know that Sir Àdham's war leader, Sir Ivor Mackintosh, married Lady Marsaili Drummond-Cargill, niece to his grace's late mother, Queen Annabella Drummond. They dwell at Rothiemurchus not far from where you will be. Lady Marsaili is visiting kinsmen a few miles from here and means to ride back with you. Sir Àdham told me that you and your party will bide overnight at Rothiemurchus."

"Faith, sir, I never gave a thought to traveling!" Fiona exclaimed. "I am certain that Leah will *not* want to live in the Highlands."

Giving her shoulder a gentle squeeze, he said, "We'll sort all that out after you and Àdham decide whether you can both agree to this marriage. But I'll speak to him about his beard and hair if you cannot be certain of doing so without flying out at him if he refuses. As to Leah, I agree that she is unlikely to welcome such a move. But Lady Marsaili will have servants traveling with her. She may help you find a new maidservant, or Àdham's foster mother will."

"He mentioned his foster mother to me the night we met," Fiona said. "But I know naught of his family or where we will live."

"Then you must ask him whilst you walk," Ormiston said. "This decision is yours to make, dearling, but I do hope you will base it on what you already know and like about this young man and not on your uncertainty of the unknown."

To inform him that her uncertainties had only increased would avail her little, so Fiona decided just to inform Àdham that she could not marry him. Feeling oddly uneasy about that decision, she nevertheless agreed with Ormiston to talk with Lady Marsaili, too, and he escorted her to the door.

When Ormiston opened the parlor door, he stayed only long enough to say, "I'll want to know what the pair of you decide, Àdham. I will be at the house."

"I'll stop in on my way back to the alehouse," Àdham promised.

When Ormiston had gone, Àdham and Fiona followed the porter to a narrow door in the north wall of the main house, which opened into the Herbar.

Pausing there, Brother Porter said, "You may return by this same route, Sir Àdham. That way, you may escort her ladyship to the foot of her stairway."

He shut the door then, leaving them alone on the graveled path.

"Am I to know what you discussed with your father, or do you mean to keep that to yourself?" Àdham asked as they walked toward the first of the many arbors. The rhythmic crunch of gravel underfoot accompanied them.

Feeling heat well into her cheeks, and aware that the remaining daylight would let him see her blushes as easily as she felt them, she said, "If you must know, I told him I cannot marry a man whose face I have never seen."

Looking up then, she saw a muscle twitch near his mouth. But whether it was a near smile or irritation, she could not tell.

He said, "I'll shave if it means that much to you. In troth, I rarely do so, because a beard helps keep me warm whilst I'm traveling or sleeping outside. Also, having so rarely wielded a razor, I lack deftness with one, and my squire shares that lack. So, I'd liefer let a barber trim my beard. Would that be enough to please you?"

Surprised that he would submit so easily, she nearly said yes before she remembered his hair. "If you would also have that barber trim your hair, so that it is tidier and more pleasing to the eye. *That* would satisfy me."

He was silent, making her wonder if she had asked too much. If she had, she decided, so be it. Her right to refuse him remained as an option.

Àdham, watching her, saw her rounded chin come up and could almost hear her thoughts. She meant to have her way, and some demon within him urged him to deny it to her. But, in truth, he admired her willingness to speak her mind to him.

Most Highland women he knew *did* speak their minds, and he had often wished he had authority enough over one or another of them to command silence. Often, since childhood, he had promised himself that when he married, his wife would obey him without question or debate. That thought, now, made him smile.

"What are you thinking?" she demanded. "Does it amuse you that I'd liefer have a husband I can see than one as shaggy as an unkempt hedgehog?"

"Aye, perhaps," he said with a chuckle. "But, in troth, I was thinking that I've long been mistaken in the sort of wife I *thought* I'd prefer."

"By my faith, sir—"

"Nae, do not bristle at me now, lass. I'll trim and tidy myself all you want, so tell me what else puzzles or concerns you. You must have questions."

She was looking at the path ahead, and when his gaze followed hers, he watched in fascination as the breeze and the angle of the setting sun conspired to make the gilding on the arbor frames dance and sparkle.

The two of them passed into the shadows of the next arbor before Fiona said, "I do have questions, sir. So many that I know not where to begin."

"What comes into your head if I ask which one is most important to you?"

"Why, a score of questions about *you*, of course. I want to know all about your family, how old you are, and how you came to be knighted."

"I turn four-and-twenty in November," he said. "And the King knighted me."

"Then you are three years younger than Davy," she said. "So, tell me *why* his grace knighted you."

"I won my spurs in battle," Àdham said. "I doubt that you want to hear the details any more than I want to relate them to you."

"You killed people then."

"'Tis the nature of battle that warriors kill other warriors or the others kill them. I'd wager that Sir David won his spurs in much the same way."

"In part, but also because of his many victories in the lists," she said. "He told me that his knighthood was as much a matter of luck and pleasing the right people as aught else. But, prithee, tell me about your family now."

"My sire is a Cameron chieftain who supported James at the Battle of Lochaber. When my mam died whilst I was still small, my da sent me to my uncle, whom men call Fin of the Battles. I fostered with him and his wife, the lady Catriona Mackintosh. I have lived at Castle Finlagh ever since then, so I have pledged my fealty to Clan Chattan."

"You mentioned your foster mother the night we met but not that your father is a Cameron and she a Mackintosh," she said. "'Tis a gey good thing that you were born *after* the Great Clan Battle of Perth and were not a Cameron knight then. Even I know that that battle was meant to end the long feud between those two powerful clans and that the Camerons lost. The two seem peaceful now, but were such a thing to happen again . . ."

"I have sworn to support the Mackintosh *and* his grace," he said firmly when she paused. "I will do so forever, despite what the Camerons may ask of me."

She nodded thoughtfully and then said quietly, "My mother died when I was seven. If my father had sent me away then . . ." She shuddered.

"It was hard, aye," he admitted. "Have you any more concerns about me, lass? Any that might make you refuse to participate in a wedding?"

"I have heard that many Highlanders plot against the King," she said. "Might any of your people do so . . . Camerons or Mackintoshes?"

"Nae, lass," he assured her. But as the words left his tongue, it occurred to him that the Camerons of Lochiel might well involve themselves in such a plot.

"What?" she demanded. "You look as if you would say more about that."

It was not the first time she had seemed to know his thoughts; however, in fairness, he had several times felt as if he could hear hers. Moreover, he knew she had the right to hear the truth from him.

"Well?" she said.

Smiling ruefully, he said, "I just remembered that one of my Cameron kinsmen is not as fond of Jamie as he might be."

"Just one?"

"Aye, but he has many followers. I am loyal to James, though."

When she still hesitated, slightly frowning, he had that sense again of being able to understand her thoughts. Gently, he said, "What is it, my lady? Do you dislike me so much that you mean to refuse?"

Without looking at him, she said, "I did think I might . . . Refuse you, that is."

Stunned by her words and his own immediate, overwhelming desire to reject them outright, he realized that he had wanted her to *want* him. If she did not . . .

She stopped walking then and looked up at him. Being more than a head shorter, she had to tilt her lovely face up to do so. With a wry smile, she said, "How can I refuse what you have not yet offered, sir? *Are* you offering for me?"

Relief surged through him. He wanted to kiss her.

Realizing that it still might be his only chance to do so, he caught hold of her chin, put a hand to the back of her head, and gently kissed her soft, rosy lips.

Her beautiful eyes widened, but she made no objection, so he did it again.

Fiona's senses reeled. What had she done, and when had an impulse ever felt so right? The disappointment she had seen in his sharply indrawn breath, opened mouth, and briefly shut eyes when she had admitted thinking of refusing him had struck her hard. So, too, had the fact that they shared a similar, grievous childhood loss. Together, those factors had expelled any lingering thought of refusal.

Such were her thoughts with that first gentle kiss. In truth, despite her body's reaction to it, it resembled kisses she had oft received from kinsmen and her father's close friends. The second one, though, was naught of the sort.

There was no betrothal yet! Sakes, he had not even offered for her, so he had no more right to kiss her than Caithness or the loutish fop in the purple-and-blue hose had. But he was *still* kissing her. And the sensations he stirred were not remotely like any she'd experienced when other men had kissed her. Moreover, she was wantonly enjoying every tingle and thrill that he stirred within her, pressing her body closer to his and moving her lips against his. Her heart pounded so hard that she could almost hear it.

His beard troubled her not a whit. In truth, it felt velvety where it touched her face, and she wanted to stroke it. But, like a dafty, she stood as she was, silent and compliant when she ought to be demanding fiercely that he release her.

Her breasts tingled and felt as if they were swelling. Other feelings, ones she had never felt before, deep within her, made her forget all of her reservations.

He drew her nearer, stroking a hand down her back to her waist, pressing her closer against him and kissing her much more thoroughly.

Her lips moved urgently now, feeling his and tasting him. But when he tried to press his tongue between them, she pulled back. "What are you *doing*?"

Still holding her, he looked into her eyes, his own eyes twinkling.

"I am taking delightful liberties," he said with a grin. "You would entice a man made of stone, my lady. In troth, I have wanted to do that from almost the first moment I saw you. But you have not answered my question."

"Nor you mine," she retorted. "You cannot expect me to answer yours if you are *not* offering for me."

"I think that your lord father explained how matters stand," he said. "So, aye, I *am* offering for you. Do you still have concerns enough to make you refuse?"

"You know that I do have that right."

"I do, but the better I come to know you, the more I hope you will not."

"And not merely because his grace and my father *want* you to marry me?"

"Primarily his grace," Àdham said unexpectedly. "But others besides your father agree that ours would be a desirable union. I'm certain now that I agree."

"I do not even speak your language."

"Neither did I learn to speak yours until I went to live with my uncle, who insisted that I speak only Scots with him. If I could learn Scots, you can learn the Gaelic. So, now, lass, do you think you can stomach me as your husband?"

She hesitated, wondering how she had ever imagined she could refuse him. Still, there was one lingering, vital question. "Do Highlanders beat their wives?"

He seemed taken aback by her question. "Do men of Lothian beat theirs?"

Grimacing, she said, "I expect that many do if their wives displease them enough. However, it is *not* a common thing at home for any man to hit a woman."

"That is true in the Highlands, too. Clachans and clans alike take umbrage if a man strikes his wife or children without good cause."

"What is a clachan?"

"A village," he said. "But answer me, lass. If you mean to say nae, say it."

"I will say aye, sir, although I fear that I may regret it."

Grinning, he said, "Doubtless, we both will have *some* regrets. We do seem able to talk to each other without speaking in riddles or thinking things we do not say aloud. So, when one of us irks the other, mayhap we'll be able see it through."

She smiled, feeling warm all over. "I *like* you, Sir Àdham MacFinlagh."

"'Tis a good start," he said. "You fascinate me, lass."

Her breath caught in her throat then and it seemed long before she breathed normally again. No one had ever said such a thing to her before.

She was staring at him, her mouth partway open, as if, Àdham thought, he had surprised her with his honesty. He put a hand on her shoulder, urging her on, and they walked past fragrant herb gardens and flowers to a hedged, grassy area with a long net strung across its center.

"What is that place yonder?" he asked.

"'Tis called a tennis court," she said. "Men wear gloves and hit a ball over that net. My father and other men play the game with James."

The Herbar provided wonderful privacy, and Àdham was grateful for it. He had spared no thought for a possible audience before kissing her.

At last, he said, "I wish we could stay here until the moon comes up."

"Aye, but it will soon be dark; and as it is, even Brother Porter may decide we have tarried too long and come to prod us along," she said. "Father must be impatient, too, to hear what we have decided. In any event, we'll have plenty of time to become better acquainted before the wedding."

He stopped then and turned her to face him. "My people are already talking of going home."

"But you arrived only a sennight ago!"

"Aye, but I was the last to arrive because of other duties I had. The others have been here for a fortnight, and what remains of the Parliament apparently has more to do with the King's Council than with the Highlands."

"I don't even have a maidservant to go with me," she said. "Mine will not want to travel so far from home. Father said that a lady will travel with you, but—"

"Lady Marsaili, our war leader's wife," he interjected. "I think you will like her. But will you not trust me to keep you safe and see to your needs?"

She gazed at him for a long moment and then seemed to relax. "I am sure you will try, sir. Doubtless you think me a feardie, but I'm not. I will own, though, that my first reaction to all of this about marriage and leaving here was pure panic."

"I would think less of your intelligence had it not been," he said softly. "I think you are gey brave in your willingness to go through with this with me. So, I will make you a promise. If you find that you cannot tolerate the Highlands—"

"Prithee, say no more," she said. "I will marry you without such a condition if you promise *not* to set me aside if I displease you. Men do set wives aside in the Lowlands if they think they have cause, even banish them from the clan to starve."

Smiling, he said, "Surely not noble wives. But I do promise that willingly, Fiona, and I keep my word. I'm beginning to think we'll deal well together."

"I hope so. Nevertheless, sir, we must go in now."

She seemed thoughtful again. But she was clearly more at ease with him, so he escorted her back to the residence. After wending their way to Brother Porter, Àdham saw her to the stairway leading to the royal chambers.

He waited then only to see her skirts vanish around the next landing before letting Brother Porter show him out. Then, he strode briskly to Ormiston House, where he found his lordship in his rear chamber but not alone.

His grace, the King, sat comfortably across the table from him with a pewter goblet of what looked like Ormiston's excellent claret in hand. "I trust that all went well, lad," he said, raising his goblet.

"As well as one might expect, sir." Looking from the King to his lordship and back, he added, "Lady Fiona did think we'd have time before wedding to know each other better. I warned her that my people may be nearly ready to go home."

"Aye, good, because the Mackintosh and his clansmen mean to leave Wednesday morning," James said lightly. "Likely, ye'll go with them."

"I did expect to return when they do, but—"

"Excellent," James said. "Then, unless someone strongly objects, we'll arrange for ye to be wedded and bedded on Tuesday. Ormiston will so inform Fiona."

Having just taken a sip of his wine, Àdham nearly choked on it. He loathed having his future so abruptly decided for him. But, with effort, he held his tongue, for he believed in avoiding futile conflict with those in authority over him.

If the King of Scots did not count as such, no one did.

James set down his goblet. "I must go now, but my lass will be gey pleased when I tell her about this."

When he'd gone, Ormiston said, "You were wise to accept his decision that you wed on Tuesday, lad. But I could see that you had qualms about marrying so soon."

"None for myself," Àdham replied. "I was thinking, though, that her ladyship may feel rushed, even forced, into this marriage."

"I'd not blame you if *you* felt that way, too," Ormiston said. "But you have not answered my question. *Do* you feel as if we've forced you into this marriage?"

"By my troth, sir, the lady Fiona will suit me fine," Àdham said frankly. "But if she feels forced, the outset of our marriage may be unnecessarily thorny."

Ormiston grinned. "No matter how well-suited you are, lad, you *will* fall out. But you will find that Fiona does not quarrel. She goes silent and often fails to speak her mind when she should, because she fears upsetting others. You should know, too, that while she may forgive you, she never forgets a serious wrong."

"Neither do I," Àdham said evenly. "So, I *will* understand that trait in her."

"Will you?" Ormiston said, his eyes twinkling. "I do look forward to visiting the pair of you as soon as possible and meeting the rest of your family."

CHAPTER 9

Awakening Sunday morning to the sound of her bedchamber door closing and the sweet smell of ambergris filling the air, Fiona blinked at the sight of Lady Sutherland, garbed in scarlet and blue, beaming at her from her bedside.

"I ha' kept your Leah waiting on yon landing," her ladyship said. "Sithee, your lord father be wi' his grace now, but he entrusted me wi' a message tae give ye."

"W-What is it?" Fiona asked, sitting up and clutching the coverlet to her chest.

"Tae put it plain, his grace has asked Bishop Wardlaw tae wed ye tae Sir Àdham on Tuesday, here in the Blackfriars' chapel."

"Tuesday!" Fiona stared at her in shock. "*This* Tuesday?"

"Aye, Fiona-lass. Sithee, the Captain o' Clan Chattan and the rest of Sir Àdham's party will leave St. John's Town Wednesday morning. The two o' ye must go wi' them."

Stunned, recalling that Àdham had said his people might go soon but yearning to cry out at such *unseemly* haste, Fiona managed nonetheless to stifle her outrage, knowing that Lady Sutherland had no power to mend the situation.

Realizing that her mouth was agape, she shut it.

Lady Sutherland put a warm hand on her shoulder, saying, "I ken fine that ye were no expecting this. But ye must get up the noo. We'll attend the Lady Mass today, and her grace would like tae see ye afore we break our fast. I'll send Leah in tae assist ye."

Minutes later, Fiona was nearly ready to depart.

"I do not need a formal caul for a Lady Mass, Leah," she said as she twitched a fold of her lavender gown into place and slipped her feet into matching slippers. "Prithee, just a plain white veil. I must go straightaway to her grace."

With the veil neatly pinned in place, she hurried to the Queen's antechamber, where Lady Sutherland awaited her.

"I'll take ye straight in, child," she said with a fond smile. "Her grace was delighted tae hear o' your wedding. For the nonce, we just want tae be sure ye'll have all that a bride requires tae be comfortable and confident."

Having no idea what to say to that, Fiona kept silent.

Signing to a maidservant at her grace's door to open it, Lady Sutherland swept Fiona before her as if she were shepherding a lost sheep back to its fold.

When they entered, Joanna, her honey-blond hair plaited into a knot at her nape, was standing on a low stool while her attire woman arranged the gold-brocaded, dark green silk overdress, or houpland, that her grace wore. Its black velvet belt nipped the dress in below her breasts, just above the open vee where the houpland's skirt split to reveal her rose-velvet underdress. When she stepped off the stool, her skirts puddled on the floor and the belt's trailing ends lost themselves in the folds.

Then, the attire woman and her minions were gone, and Fiona was alone with the Queen and her mistress of robes.

"Have you decided what you want to wear, dearling?" Joanna asked her.

Stunned by the question, Fiona said the first thing that came to mind. "My blue silk gown is *my* favorite, but Father prefers the emerald-green, so I'll likely wear one of those."

"I thought so," Joanna said. "However, love, every bride deserves a *new* gown for her wedding. I ken fine that you have not had anything new for an age. I have, though, and we were much the same size before I began increasing."

Fiona glanced at Lady Sutherland. Then, lest she seem

ungrateful, she said, "'Tis most generous, your grace. But I must not impose—"

"Prithee, do not deny me this pleasure. I have some lovely new gowns I shall never wear, because they'll be unfashionable before I fit into them. 'Tis all Jamie's fault, of course," she added with a chuckle. "It is also his fault that you are in this position. I know he has cause for what he has done, but I also know how you must feel. I was in much the same position, after all, when he asked me to marry him."

"You had just two days to prepare?" Fiona exclaimed.

"A few more than two," Joanna admitted. "But when one knows how long parleys for most royal marriages last and how long the wedding planning takes after the betrothal, I vow, it felt as if it all happened in a flash. Then, overnight, I was on a horse riding to Scotland beside your King, with a train of courtiers following us."

She related some amusing tales about that journey, and by the time they set out to attend the Lady Mass, Fiona's qualms about accepting her help had fled.

As they walked, Fiona realized that the Queen's other ladies all knew of her odd betrothal. "We know you had no time for a formal betrothing," Lady Malvina confided cheerfully as they walked together. "Moreover, if his grace says one is betrothed, then one *is* betrothed. Are you excited, Fee? I must say Sir Àdham is not the sort of man I want to marry, but he knocked Caithness down to protect you, so he must be hard-smitten. My father says it is unnecessary to like one's husband. I do *like* Hamish, I suppose, but I feel no passion for him. If he were not so wealthy . . ."

"I do like Sir Àdham, Vina," Fiona confessed when she paused. "I do not know if I will like living in the Highlands, though."

Malvina gaped. "The Highlands! Why, I thought you would live near Ormiston Mains. My father said that you have an estate there. Is that not so?"

"That estate is part of my tocher," Fiona said. "But a woman lives with her husband, Vina, not the other way round."

"I suppose you must, then. But in the Highlands? Mab Gordon told me that newly wed Highlanders spend their first night in a dreadful shack whilst their neighbors crowd round and shriek or sing at them and horrid pipers pipe all night long. They cannot move into their own house until the second day, Mab said."

"Have mercy, Vina!" Fiona begged. "I'm nervous enough about this as it is."

"Is he wealthy?"

"I don't know," Fiona said, smothering a sigh. "I still have much to learn about him, but I doubt it. I will have my tocher, though."

"I, too, when I wed," Malvina said, frowning. "Hamish said he will look after it for me." More confidently, she added, "But Sir Àdham will take good care of *you*, Fee. Thanks to Caithness, we know that much."

Fiona heard more such talk throughout the day. She heard, too, that Lady Sutherland had arranged for some of the ladies to take flowers from the gardens into the kirk. Father Prior had even assigned two lay brothers to aid their arrangement.

Sunday afternoon, Ormiston visited and the two of them drew up a list of what he should bring her when he visited Castle Finlagh.

"I fear that a Highland castle will be a barren place, sir," she said after listing the things she most desired. "Mayhap you should also bring the furnishings from my bedchamber, so I can have something that will make me feel at home."

"You must ask your husband about that, lass," Ormiston said with a fond smile. "The distance from Ormiston to Perth is a three- to four-day journey. It must be a five or six days' journey from Perth to the coast of the Moray Firth, which is where Nairn lies. I will arrange to stop with friends along the way, but I'm afraid I can bring only those personal things you said you would miss most."

She had suspected as much. In fact, she had known she would be far from home, but she had had no idea how far. She hoped he was wrong about the distance.

Later, the Queen's ladies made much of measuring her to be sure that her wedding dress would fit. Tradition forbade a bride to try on her dress and ordained that its laces be untied, a fact that Fiona recalled from Davy's marriage to his wife, Robina. However, there were other traditions of which she knew less or nothing.

Shortly before supper, when she begged leave to refresh herself, Lady Sutherland said, "I'll go wi' ye, child. I would talk more wi' ye."

"Aye, sure, my lady," Fiona said, wondering what she had done now.

When they reached her chamber, Lady Sutherland looked it over as if she had never seen it before. Staring at the bed, she said, "'Tis just as I thought."

"What is, madam?"

"Even were this wee chamber no on the ladies' side o' the residence, it could never serve for proper bridal bedding. That bed be *much* too sma.'"

Unable to think of an acceptable response to such a statement, Fiona finally said, "It is a bit narrow. But I have found it comfortable."

Lady Sutherland gave her the same speculative look she had given the bed. "Your mother died when ye were but a bairn, did she no, dearling?"

"Aye, when I was seven," Fiona said.

"And your sister Gellis married dunamany years ago, aye?"

"Aye, madam, before I was born, for she is the eldest."

"You are not close then, I think."

"Gellis and her family live in Galloway, so I rarely see any of them." *Not*, Fiona added mentally, *that I miss her.*

"Then, unless ye've talked o' such matters with young women whose ken be greater than yours, I expect ye ken little o' what a man expects of his lady wife."

"I can run a household," Fiona said. "I like children, and they like me."

"But d'ye ken how bairns come tae be born?"

"I think so, although the exact manner is not clear in my mind," Fiona said. "Robina, my brother Davy's wife, explained much to me. But hearing is one thing, the doing is often altogether different, I think."

"Then, let us talk a wee bit longer, child."

"*Getting married?* What the deevil d'ye mean, *married?*" Hew Comyn demanded of his cousin that evening. They had met at the sole alehouse in the village of Bridgend, where Dae's family lived, across the bridge from St. John's Town. Since it was well before suppertime, and a Sunday, the place was much quieter than it might be on another day.

Even so, Hew lowered his voice when he said, "We canna let that lass marry anyone. What if he takes her away someplace? How will we capture her, then?"

"But he will take her away, won't he?" Dae replied. Swilling a deep draft of his ale, he wiped his lips on his sleeve before adding, "They say it be a Highlander a-marrying her. So, he'll take her home wi' him, aye?"

"Who is he?"

"I dinna ken, but I'm thinkin' it may be the same chappie we saw whilst we waited on the Inch that night. Some'un pointed him out at yon alehouse in the High Street, and he's big and brawny like that 'un we saw. I didna get a close look at either one o' them, but they did say she's tae marry a knight o' the realm, knighted by Jamie hisself. I dinna think we dare irk such a man."

Hew agreed that it might be dangerous but knew better than to say so. If he did, his nervous cousin might demand that they abandon the plan altogether.

"I'll tell ye who the man is," a grim, gravelly voice behind Hew said, startling him to his feet.

"Sir!" he exclaimed as he turned to face his father, Comyn of Raitt.

Eyes narrowed, Raitt was plainly unhappy with him. "'Tis twice now ye've failed tae follow directions," Raitt said. Glowering at his nephew, he added, "Ye've done nowt tae aid him, Dae, but ye might get tae your feet when I speak tae ye." When Dae hastily obeyed, Raitt added, "We'll move tae yon corner. I dinna want tae make a gift o' this discussion tae anyone else wha' comes in."

When they had seated themselves at a table there, Raitt leaned across it toward his son and muttered, "First, ye bungled getting Donal Balloch's message tae Alexander that we carried here from the west. Now, ye two ha' failed tae capture the lass. So ye've likely spoiled what chance we had tae force Ormiston tae back us against James."

"Only because some chap came along and foiled our first

attempt," Hew said. "Dae said he's heard the chap be a Highlander, so—"

"That *chap* is Sir Àdham MacFinlagh, foster son o' me irksome neighbor, Fin o' the Battles. And, just as Dae told ye, James knighted him . . . at Lochaber."

"Sakes, I wouldna recognize him if I'd seen him, for I've scarce clapped eyes on the man since he were a bairn," Hew said. "Moreover, I ha' lived wi' Dae's kinsmen here since our Rab died, as ye ken fine, since ye sent me tae them then. I dinna ken what ye—"

"Hush yer gob, and I'll tell ye what ye're going tae do!" Raitt snapped.

Àdham had also discovered that news of his intentions had swept through the royal court. Some people expressed less pleasure than his grace and Ormiston had, though.

Caithness was the first to congratulate him, Monday morning, while Àdham was breaking his fast in the alehouse taproom. "So ye've snatched that lovely lass from everyone else's grasp, have ye?" the young earl said with a broad grin. "Ye're nobbut a heathenish thief, cousin!"

"Don't tell me that *you* wanted her," Àdham retorted. "You told me when we first met that you intend *never* to wed."

"I did not say I wanted to *marry* her," Caithness said with a cheeky grin.

"Have a care," Àdham said. "Thanks to his grace and her lord father, her *ladyship* and I are as good as betrothed now, so—"

"Not unless ye've bedded her," Caithness said, raising his brows. "That *is* the custom in this shire, and I thought 'twas likewise in the Highlands."

When Àdham moved to stand, Caithness said hastily, "I cry pardon, cousin. My tongue ran away with my good sense. I make you my deepest apologies."

"Her ladyship is unlikely to look twice at a rogue like you in any event," Àdham said with a grin. "And, as the wedding takes place tomorrow morning, and his grace would take umbrage if I knocked you on your backside again . . ."

"I beg ye'll do nae such thing," Caithness said, ruefully rubbing his jaw. "I'm still sore from the last time. Besides, I came to tell ye that I mean to ride as far as Blair Castle with your party on Wednesday. I've had my fill of my father and a number of his kinsmen."

"Has Atholl offended you, then?"

"Every day, aye. My lord father despises my friends, my clothing, my taste in wine, and most of all my politics. Sithee, I *like* Jamie, and so did Atholl when Jamie returned from England. Sakes, he hied himself off to greet him. But now he and"—he shot a hasty, speculative look at Àdham—"and others who oppose Jamie talk of matters that sound to me distressingly like treason."

Àdham said, "You speak of my uncle, Sir Robert Graham, I think."

"I do. If it offends ye to hear me say such things of him . . ."

"Nae, Alan, but take care *where* you say them." He shot a meaningful look toward the tapster wiping off a nearby table. "You are welcome to ride with us," he added. "I know not what plans Sir Ivor has made for each day's travel, but I doubt the ladies will want to ride farther than Moulin."

"Dinna be daft, Àdham, Wednesday night ye'll stay at Blair, all o' ye. My father *said* he'll stay in town till the end of the month. Even my stepmother is away now, so I can house your entire party."

"I doubt Atholl will approve of your housing a party of Mackintoshes, though."

"Perhaps not, but I do often house my friends. Moreover, your bride will be more comfortable at Blair. I'd wager the lady Fiona has *never* slept on the ground."

Since Àdham had not spared a thought for her ladyship's past travel habits, he said, "I'll talk to Ivor. You're certain that you will be the only Stewart at Blair Castle?"

"Aye, as certain as we can be that ye'll be the only one kin to a Graham."

CHAPTER 10

The morning of Fiona's wedding day dawned bleakly under cloudy skies. But the air was warm, and Lady Sutherland assured her that all was in train to see her properly wedded and bedded before she left for her future home.

Although Fiona remained uncertain about the bedding, she told herself that if every other bride had survived it, she would, too.

Concerns lingered about her future husband and her own ability to adapt to a way of life about which she knew almost nothing. Even so, the strongest emotion she felt was anticipation, even eagerness, to see what lay ahead.

The other maids of honor and their seniors, including the Queen, were eager to aid in her preparations. Joanna, Lady Sutherland, and Lady Malvina were the only ones, however, whose insistence that they would miss her seemed sincere.

Others, including Lady Huntly, seemed more interested in discussing who might take Fiona's place when she left. Such positions were highly prized, and noblemen and women of all ranks schemed and competed fiercely to place their sons and daughters as close to the royal couple as possible.

Political maneuvering was the least of Fiona's worries, albeit a primary cause of her increasing eagerness to enter the new phase of her life. Even so, some fears remained strong. Several had an irritating tendency to interject themselves just as she was growing eager to learn what marriage was all about.

While those helping her bathe and perfume her body chattered with one another, her thoughts drifted to the man who was about to take her away from the life she knew.

Would his people like her? She had not met any of them, unless one counted his friend Caithness. He and Sir Àdham seemed to treat each other more as kinsmen than fellow warriors or casual friends. Moreover, Àdham said he had not been to Perth before, so the two had not met in St. John's Town. She had no notion where the Earldom of Caithness was, though. Perhaps it neighbored Àdham's Strathnairn.

Although her first impression of Caithness had been startling, she had quickly come to like the young earl's cheeky smile and his charm.

Àdham did not fit her image of charming or courtly. Kind, yes, and untidy, but she would try to persuade him to furbish himself up after they married.

She had never seen him angry. How, she wondered, would he behave then? Although they had briefly discussed men who beat their wives, and he had admitted that Highlanders sometimes did, she did not recall his saying that he would not.

She would simply have to learn to read him and understand his moods.

Doubtful now, she grimaced into her looking glass, because although she could read her brothers and her father, she had oft managed to anger them, even so.

She would be so far from home and all that she knew. Faith, she was far from home now, but by suppertime tomorrow she would be miles farther away.

Feeling salty tears prick her eyes, she dashed them away and got up to make sure that Leah was packing her clothes carefully.

She had pictured her husband and their wedding quite differently.

In her imaginings, her husband had been a strong, handsome warrior, much like her brother Davy—or Àdham, come to that— lanky and agile, but refined and lacking every vestige of Davy's devilish temperament. If *that* husband had sported a beard, it would be stylish, not so shaggy that one could see naught of his face save his hawklike nose and his intriguingly green eyes under their thick, dark brows.

Her imagined husband would have been somewhat smaller, too, and less overwhelming. At over six feet, Àdham was too big. His frame was also too powerful-looking and muscular to suit her notion of perfection. Everything about the man, including his hands and feet, was large.

"Fiona-lass, it be time tae don your dress," Lady Sutherland said. "We ha' less than an hour now, wi' the wedding tae take place afore midday High Mass."

"Aye, my lady," she said quietly. Leah helped her take off her robe, under which she wore only a new white kirtlelike silk shift that she had had made to wear with her court dresses but not yet worn. It felt soft and clingy against her skin.

The gown Joanna had chosen was a yellow houpland, its sleeves and hem trimmed with ermine. Royal seamstresses had made it for her grace, and those same seamstresses had altered it to fit Fiona's slimmer figure. The houpland's wide sash, gaily embroidered with colorful wildflowers, nipped it in loosely below her breasts.

Her head was bare, her hair unbound, and the lacings of her houpland and shift untied, all as tradition demanded. But Joanna had assured her that people at what amounted to a royal wedding, attended by both the King and Queen of Scots, would never so far forget themselves as to snatch the laces from the bride's gown, let alone from her shift, as often happened at less stellar weddings.

"It is time to go," Joanna said quietly a short time later. "Art sure this marriage is to your liking, Fiona?"

Fiona looked directly at her and smiled. "I am content, your grace. Faith, even were I not, I would lack the courage to say so to his grace."

"If you want to say nae, you need say it only to me," Joanna replied calmly. "James believes strongly in the rule of law. He particularly believes that our laws must be clear and apply to every citizen, including himself. The laws of Holy Kirk and those of Scotland agree that a woman can reject marriage to any man, regardless of who demands that marriage. Now, what do you say, my dearling?"

Fiona hesitated but only because she realized that her curiosity about Sir Àdham had long since overwhelmed any fear she might have had of marrying him.

"By my troth, your grace," she said, "although I am more grateful than I can say for your concern and your kindness, I am content."

"So be it, then," Joanna said, indicating that the others should precede them.

Àdham stood in the transept of the monastery chapel, near its high altar, flanked by his grace on one side and the Mackintosh and Sir Ivor on the other. The King had informed him on his arrival that he would aid him in his dressing and meant to stand up with him. So, Àdham, unhappily clean shaven, constrained, and uncomfortable, now stood between his grace and the burly Malcolm.

The monastery chapel's soaring nave teemed with townspeople and most of the nobles who had come to St. John's Town for the King's Parliament.

Barefaced, in a fashionably tight-laced, tight-fitting doublet, to which James's own manservant had attached a pair of too-snug woolen hose with thongs, their thread-wrapped tips passing through brass-wire-lined eyelets, Àdham felt more exposed than when he was naked. Worst of all was the baglike thing called a codpiece. Trussed with similar thongs to both doublet and hose, it confined his genitals snugly, too snugly. The whole process of dressing had taken too long, and how the devil he was to untangle himself from the lot later, he knew not.

"Stop twitching," the Mackintosh growled. A thickset man, the top of whose head barely reached Àdham's shoulder, Malcolm's voice carried nonetheless easily over the liturgical chanting of friars in their choir stalls. "And dinna scratch!" he added. "Ye be behaving more like a gallous heathen than a knight o' the realm."

A man who knew his own worth and capabilities, Malcolm often boasted that, built lower to the ground than most Highland men, he was better able to endure extremities of weather, scarcity, or want of rest. Although unpolished with letters, he had been fortunate in war and had accomplished most of his goals in life.

"I note, sir, that you do not wear such garb as this," Àdham muttered. "Nor have you shaved off *your* beard."

"I wear what I choose tae wear, as always. And I'm fond o' me beard."

James said, "Ye're wearing Lowland garb to please your lady bride, sir."

"As ye agreed, yourself, to do, Àdham, the shaving likewise," Sir Ivor added sternly from beyond Malcolm, ignoring the fact that Àdham's agreement was to trim, not shave, his beard. "So snick up, and leave that fool hat be, too. If ye knock it off to the floor, I'll give ye a clout."

The clarion blast of a trumpet from the west entrance silenced them, and the friars' chanting faded when minstrels with a harp and lutes began to play.

At the far end of the center aisle, the women of her grace's court had gathered in readiness to approach the transept.

The congregation rose to its feet from collective prayer stools and everyone turned to watch the procession, led by the Bishop of St. Andrews and two acolytes.

Her grace's three remaining maids of honor followed the bishop, one by one, and four of her senior ladies came next, two by two. The Queen walked serenely behind them, alone. When the bishop stopped at the foot of the altar dais, his acolytes continued up two steps to stand, one on each side of the high altar.

The Queen's ladies turned toward the empty choir stalls left of the transept and took their places facing the friars and lay brothers in *their* stalls on the right.

Àdham saw Ormiston then, beyond her grace, at the nave's entrance. He did not yet see Fiona but assumed that she stood beside her father.

When the last two maids of honor stepped from the aisle into the ladies' choir stalls, Joanna entered the transept, moved to the left, and turned with her hands folded at her waist to look back toward the nave entrance.

Àdham had his first full view of Fiona then and realized from her stunned expression that it was also the first time she had been able to see him or, perhaps, recognize him in his fashionable and damnably uncomfortable splendor.

She was beautiful. Her yellow gown opened from just beneath her bosom to the floor, revealing shimmering white silk beneath it. The hem of that white garment, edged with a band of pink, yellow, and green embroidery, skimmed the tops of pale yellow slippers. The slim fingers of her right hand rested on Ormiston's left forearm, those of her left hand gripped a small bouquet of pink and yellow flowers, doubtless plucked from the Gilten Herbar.

Her dark hair, crowned with a circlet of similar flowers, flowed unbound, unnetted, and unveiled down her back, reminding him of his first view of her. When she turned to hand the bouquet to her grace, he saw that her hair gleamed in midday sunbeams from the clerestory windows and reached well past her hips.

He smiled ruefully as she approached, and saw her eyes widen. He decided then that her earlier shock did stem from belatedly recognizing him, so he grinned.

To his delight, she grinned back, raised her chin, and left her father standing at the transept, while she walked with head high to join Àdham before the bishop.

"Who gives this woman to be wedded to this man?" the bishop demanded.

Stepping forward a pace, Ormiston said, "I do, your eminence. I am her ladyship's father, Ormiston of Ormiston."

"Then," said the bishop solemnly, "as we ha' gathered here in the sight o' God to join together this man and this woman in the honorable estate o' holy matrimony, if any man can show just cause why they may not lawfully be joined together by God's law and the laws o' this realm, let him now speak or else hereafter and forever hold his peace."

Àdham held his breath. At this point, he'd strangle anyone who spoke.

Hearing movement and whispers from the audience behind her, Fiona knew from other weddings she had attended that such sounds were common during the silence that followed those words in the wedding service. Even so, she nervously dampened her lips, fearing that someone might object to the marriage, although she could not imagine what "just cause or impediment" he or she might offer.

When the bishop raised his hands, the whispers stopped.

Looking from Àdham to Fiona, Bishop Wardlaw said, "I require and charge ye both, as ye will answer at the dreadful day o' judgment when the secrets of all hearts shall be disclosed, that if either o' ye knows any impediment, why ye may not be lawfully joined together in matrimony, that ye do now confess it. For be ye well assured that anyone coupled together otherwise than God's Word doth allow be *not* joined together by God. Neither is their matrimony lawful."

Fiona glanced at Àdham and saw that he was gazing at her.

The bishop turned with a smile then to Àdham, and Fiona listened while he repeated his vows to take her for his wife until death parted them.

She continued to watch him, thinking how handsome he was without his beard and scarcely heeding the words until the bishop said, "D'ye have a ring, sir?"

"Aye." Àdham took it from Sir Ivor's hand and gave it to the bishop.

Intoning, "By the Father, the Son, and the Holy Spirit," as he touched the ring to Fiona's left thumb and first two fingers, Bishop Wardlaw slid it onto her ring finger.

Her vows followed next, and she repeated them, promising to be meek and obedient in bed and at board. Then, at last, the bishop bade them face the congregation while he pronounced them husband and wife and introduced them formally as Sir Àdham and Lady MacFinlagh.

"Ye may kiss your bride, sir."

Àdham put warm hands on Fiona's shoulders and gently kissed her lips. His lips were firm and warm against hers, but quick, and the moment was gone.

She felt as if she were standing beside herself watching her life change irretrievably. But the lingering warmth of Àdham's lips on hers was real. And when he smiled as he stepped back, she felt the warmth of that kiss spread through her body.

High Mass followed, but although Fiona stood and knelt automatically when Àdham did, she heard not a word of it. Kneeling on her prayer stool beside him on his, she was conscious only of his warmth and strength and the sound of his deep, rich voice when he made such responses as the mass required of the congregation.

Everything had happened so quickly that, despite her father's assurances, and her grace's, she felt a surge of panic, as if her life had fled beyond her control.

By the time they adjourned through the crowd of guests to the refectory, which lay brothers had turned into a regal chamber for the wedding feast, her sense of being a bystander at someone else's wedding had swept back. When anyone spoke to her, she replied politely but scarcely heeded her own words. She hugged her father and let Lady Sutherland and Malvina hug her. But, if she had one sensible thought of her own before she and Àdham made their way onto the dais and sought their places at the high table, she had no memory of it later.

When they stood at their places, Àdham murmured, "Do you like your ring?"

She looked carefully at the gold band on her finger. Finely engraved with tiny, exquisite curlicues and flowers, it gleamed and sparkled, reflecting candlelight from the hall. "It is beautiful," she said sincerely. "How did you come by it?"

His cheeks reddened but he answered frankly, "His grace gave it to me. He said I should tell you that it is a gift for us both from her grace, the Queen."

"I will cherish it forever, for she has always been kind to me. I shall miss serving her, too. Does it trouble you that someone else provided it?"

"Nae, lass. It pleases you, and I am not so selfish. Moreover, 'tis the symbol that binds us together, so I am content to see it there. You are to sit now," he added, standing behind one of the two central chairs and indicating the one to his left.

Still stunned to know that her ring had come from Joanna, Fiona obediently moved to her place but kept gazing at her ring, watching the light play on it. Only when she realized that the person who stood next to her was Joanna did she collect her wits. "Your grace, forgive me! I should not be standing in your place."

"Every new-married bride has the right to act as hostess at her wedding feast, my love," Joanna said firmly. "You will sit there, and I shall sit beside you."

"Àdham told me about the ring," Fiona said. "I will treasure it always."

Joanna touched the back of Fiona's left hand. "I will miss you, dearling."

Feeling tears well in her eyes, Fiona was grateful that the King gestured then for the bishop to say the grace-before-meat, so she could blink her tears away. When everyone had taken his seat, James signaled the minstrels to begin playing.

Àdham kept his gaze on his trencher but his attention fixed firmly on the lady beside him. Her nearness radiated allure. Her concern for how he might feel about her ring had touched him. But her proximity provided more cause to curse the garments into which his clansmen and King had so ruthlessly stuffed him.

Whenever she looked his way, certain parts of him squirmed uncomfortably. *What the devil possessed men ever to confine themselves so?* he asked himself.

A bagpipe sounded from the kitchen end of the refectory, and he saw a piper taking slow steps down a cleared path toward the room's center. Behind him came a wheeled cart bearing a tall pyramid of what looked to Àdham like round rolls stuck together with honey and jam. He had never seen anything like it.

He looked to his right to find James grinning at him. "'Tis a fine creation, that, lad. It was popular in London, especially for weddings. A French chef visiting there called it a *croquembouche*, and when it appears at a wedding, the object is for the chef to pile the rolls as high as he can without toppling the pyramid. A bride and groom standing opposite each other must kiss over the *croquembouche* without toppling it. If it falls apart, they say the marriage will, too, so ye must take good care."

"It is a custom in the Borders, too," Fiona said. "The rolls are fried, so they are crunchy, and they often contain a custard." Smiling at Àdham, she added, "Shall we attempt the feat, sir, and see if our marriage will prosper?"

Grinning, Àdham said, "For another chance to kiss my bride, aye, I'll do it."

When the rectangular cart stopped a few feet from the dais, perpendicular to the high table, its attendants stepped back. Àdham took Fiona's hand and, cheered on by clapping, stomping feet, and delighted cheers, led her to stand on one long side of the cart and took his own place opposite her.

Noting that the top of Fiona's head appeared barely higher then the pyramid of rolls, he could not be surprised when general laughter broke out, along with a few ribald shouts of doom for their marriage.

Then, to his surprise, Gilli Roy Mackintosh stepped forward with a stool. Stopping at the end of the cart, he flicked a conspiratorial glance at the high table, waited for the laughter to stop, and then said confidently, "His grace said her ladyship would require this, Àdham. But he said I must first ask if ye'll permit it."

"Aye, sure, lad, and right gratefully," Àdham declared, grinning again. The stool provided all the aid he needed to avoid the *croquembouche* and kiss his bride without toppling it, and he took full advantage to the general merriment of his onlookers.

The festivities included music and ring dancing, and lasted until late afternoon when the King stood at last to announce a final toast to the newlyweds. As he did, Joanna leaned near Fiona and said loudly enough for Àdham to hear over the cheers from below the dais, "'Tis time for us to go, love. We must prepare you for the marriage bed."

Àdham groaned then, painfully. But when Fiona looked back in concern, he said, "Just go, lass. All of this flummery will soon be over."

Hoping he was right and that the King and the other men would not keep him long, he watched until she was out of sight.

Every moment after that seemed twice as long as the one preceding it, until at last, Caithness shouted, "We must prepare the man for his bedding, lads!"

The result was wholly unmonastic chaos, making him yearn for rescue from Father Prior or Brother Porter. But most of the friars still in attendance just laughed and raised goblets to toast his departure.

Àdham put up little resistance, knowing that the sooner his *friends* got him out of his clothing and upstairs, the sooner he could claim his bride. That goal and at last ridding himself of the loathsome, constrictive garments were all that mattered.

By the time they reached the landing outside the allotted chamber, he was praying that his captors would quickly leave him to his duty and that he would be able to find his customary garments after he claimed his bride.

Someone opened the chamber door. Then, before anyone else moved, a stentorian voice above them on the stairway bellowed, "Hold there, men! Ye'll recall that ye be in a religious house—*my* house, since I be prior here. Ye'll stay outside o' that chamber if ye please, or even if ye dinna please. I will bless the bed wi' the pair o' them in it. Then I shall leave them to their duty, and so, by heaven, will ye!"

A few groans and daringly ribald comments followed his stricture as the men shoved the now-naked Àdham into the chamber. The men of his escort parted then to make a path and stood quietly while Father Prior followed him inside.

The chamber was small, containing only a pair of sumpter baskets against the nearest wall, a washstand, a bed, and one narrow, east-facing window.

The men on the landing stood in near silence, peering in.

"Get along now, the lot o' ye," the prior said, shutting the door.

Àdham, staring at the bed, where his bride awaited him with the coverlet drawn up to her chin, glanced at Father Prior.

"What be ye waiting for, lad? Get ye in, get ye in!"

Smiling reassuringly at his bride, Àdham obeyed, cautiously turning back the covers to avoid exposing her to the prior's gaze. *That*, he felt certain, would disconcert all three of them.

As soon as he was in the bed, the prior made the sign of the cross over it and spoke a brief blessing. Then, he left, shut the door, and they were alone.

❖   ❖   ❖

Able to think only of her own nakedness and Àdham's beside her, Fiona lay stiffly as near to the wall as she could get. The cupboard bed had walls on three sides and a curtain to pull for privacy. It was not a wide or a long bed, although it would likely have seemed wide to one who slept in it alone.

Àdham was too big for it, she was sure. His muscular legs were so long that his feet would hang over the side.

"Art frightened, lass?"

"I . . . I don't think so," she murmured. "In troth, I do not know *what* I feel. Everything today has seemed as if it were happening to someone else, not me."

"I know," he said, surprising her. "I have felt much the same."

"But, surely, *you* do not fear what the future may bring you." Realizing what she had blurted out, she added hastily, "I do not mean for you to think that I do. . . ."

"You don't?" He turned his head toward her and smiled. "I would fear for your sanity, Fiona, if you did *not* have fears. You cannot know much about how we live in the Highlands, and I know that you worry about being far from your family and unable to speak with some of my people at Rothiemurchus and Finlagh."

"Rothiemurchus?"

"Aye, where Sir Ivor and his family live, including my foster grandfather, Shaw Mòr. It lies on our way, so we will bide at least one night with them."

"Where else will we bide on our journey?"

His smile widened as he said, "We can discuss that later, or tomorrow as we ride. For now, we should get on with this duty of ours."

"Tell me what I must do."

"I'll show you and teach you as we go," he said. "This first time, the doing itself should not take long. But I mean to take my time preparing you, both to ease our way and so that you may know how pleasurable certain parts of it can be."

She could not imagine such an act as Lady Sutherland had described to her being pleasurable. But Àdham, doing no more than turning onto his side and stroking her body, soon proved that he knew what he talked about.

Before long, he had her squirming yet hoping he would not stop what he was doing. Hearing a moan escape from deep in her own throat, she told herself that she should not make so much noise. But she could not seem to stop moaning until he touched her between her legs where no man had touched her before.

Next, most daringly, he eased a finger to her opening there.

A squeak of protest escaped her lips.

"Don't stiffen up now, Fiona-lass," he murmured. "This won't take long, but we must complete our duty."

"That hurts," she said a moment later, indignantly.

"I believe you," he replied. "I'm told that it does hurt the first time but only then. We'll see tomorrow if that is true or not."

"Tomorrow?"

"Aye, for we'll be in a proper bed tomorrow night. We'll likely sleep on the ground the night after that."

"On the *ground*?"

He chuckled. "Caithness doubted that you'd ever slept on the ground before. I expect he was right."

"He certainly was," she said, aware that his finger was well inside her and moving around. The sensation was not exactly unpleasant, but it was unlike anything she had felt before. "H-How can anyone sleep on hard ground?"

"One sleeps where and when one needs to sleep," he said. "A warrior must sometimes sleep sitting up against a tree or a rock with one eye and both ears open. Highlanders oft sleep on the ground when they travel. Sakes, many of our clansmen sleep on the ground, albeit on straw pallets, even in their homes."

"Aye, Borderers sleep on pallets, too," she said, reassured to hear something familiar. "I slept on one when I was a bairn. So did my brothers and sister, I think."

"We do not carry pallets when we travel," he said. "I am going to change my position now, lass. Do not be alarmed."

"If you are going to insert something larger than your finger . . ."

"I am," he said as he positioned himself over her. "But it will fit, too."

She did not believe him, but she had promised to be meek, and if it hurt, it hurt. It did, too, more than he had said it would. He seemed to fill her completely and to expand the part of her that was admitting him until she wondered what sort of consequences might result from such widening.

A sharper pain surprised her into another squeak.

"You're a woman now," he said with a warm smile. "And you are mine, lass. Never forget that."

The last three words disturbed her, because it sounded as if he thought that he owned her now, like a cow or a horse. She had heard men speak so of their women before, but Davy's wife did not act as if Davy owned her. Nor did Davy. Even Buccleuch's wife did not act so, although since Buccleuch owned much of Teviotdale, *he* might think of his wife and bairns as some of his chattel.

Those thoughts vanished in another burst of pain when Àdham began moving faster and deeper in and almost out of her. Then he stiffened for a long moment, gasped, eased in and out gently a few more times, and then fell to one side of her in such a way that she was glad he had not fallen atop her.

He lay at her side, breathing deeply, until she feared he had fallen asleep.

"Sir Àdham?"

"Just Àdham," he murmured.

"What did you mean when you said I was yours and never to forget it?"

He was quiet until she opened her mouth again to ask if he *had* fallen asleep. As the words were about to leave her tongue, he said, "Did that irk you?"

Before she could imagine how to answer him, he added, "I'm thinking now that if Uncle Fin had said those words in that same rather curt manner to our Catriona, she'd have had his head off his shoulders and into his lap."

Fiona laughed then. "Borderers say the same thing, that an angry woman might hand someone his head in his lap. But you should know, sir—"

"Àdham."

"You should know, Àdham, that I have an imagination that

flings up images of what people say to me. *No one* could imagine someone my size handing someone your size his head in his lap."

He rolled to his left side again, bent his elbow, and rested his chin on his palm, holding her gaze as he did. He was grinning, and she marveled as she had before at how nice his smile was and how strong and white his teeth looked.

"Fiona, mayhap I should not have said what I said in the way that I said it. In troth, I was feeling proud of you and pleased that you are *my* wife and not someone else's. I am not by nature a jealous man, but I do believe in loyalty, so it would irk me to see my wife flirting, or worse, with another man."

"But that is good," she said. "A man *should* feel so about his wife, just as a wife should feel so about her husband. Is that not also true, sir . . . Àdham?"

Grinning again, he bent and put his lips to hers. But that kiss grew to be nothing like the chaste one in the kirk or the one over the *croquembouche*. It began gently, his lips just touching hers, then firming as he moved closer and planted his right hand on the other side of her, shifting her hair out of its way. Her lips parted slightly, and his tongue took advantage, darting inside, making her gasp.

CHAPTER II

Adham knew he was rushing things. But his lady wife was so tempting that he did not want to stop. He teased her lips a little longer and stroked her smooth, full, firm breasts again to remind himself of what a treasure he had found in her. But he also knew that if he did not want to have to wait days to repeat their coupling, he would be wise to end such activities for the evening, at least.

He murmured, "We must get cleaned up. You likely feel some discomfort."

To his delight, she smiled warmly and said, "Just how do you know how a woman feels, Sir Àdham MacFinlagh?"

"I, too, have an imagination, Lady MacFinlagh," he retorted. "Now, up with you. The moon has been out all day, and now that darkness is falling, I thought you might like to walk down to the river with me and watch the stars come out."

Her eyes gleamed, but she said, "I wonder what they did with my clothes."

"Someone put two sumpter baskets against yon wall. I'd wager they hold our clothes—at least, something *other* than what we wore earlier. If our things are not in those baskets, I'll shout for my squire. He'll know where they are."

He rolled out of bed and stood beside it, waiting for her.

She stayed where she was. "Look and see if they're there."

Obediently, he opened the first of the two baskets and found, as he had expected, that it contained clothing, feminine clothing. "This one is yours," he said. "Come and choose what you want to wear."

Realizing that she was shy, he went to the second kist, opened it, and took out his tunic and a leaf-green plaid with fine red lines crisscrossing it. Putting on the tunic, he turned back to her. "Up, my lady. I have seen and felt every inch of your body, and I like it fine. So come out of that bed before I pluck you out."

Smiling, she inched out of the bed feet first, keeping herself covered as much as she could until she realized that her feet would not touch the floor.

"Prithee, sir, that looks like my shift on top. Will you hand it to me?"

"Nae, lass, come and fetch it yourself. If I fetch anything, it will be you."

Giving him a look that ought to have seared him, she slid down off the bed, visibly drew a deep breath, and let go of the sheet.

She was truly a gem. He wanted to ask her to turn around for him and let him gaze at her backside. But he did not want to anger her or make her more bashful than she was already. Given time, she would get used to him. So he turned to the washstand, where someone had thoughtfully poured water into the basin.

That person had also refilled the ewer and provided a slops jar.

They cleaned themselves quickly. Then, she donned a plain shift, a dark green kirtle, and her fur-lined cloak but left her feet bare. Àdham was glad to see that. It meant she was accustomed to going barefoot, as most Highland folk did.

As expected, MacNab sat on the stairway, dozing, but woke when Àdham spoke his name.

"Tidy up in there," Àdham said in the Gaelic. "But first, do you know how we can get outside without meeting anyone who's *hoping* we'll reappear tonight?"

"Aye, sir. Being certain that you knew naught of this place, I went round after you were safe in yon chamber to acquaint myself with the residence."

Aware that Fiona, behind him, did not understand them or know MacNab, Àdham said to her, "This is my squire, Bruce

MacNab, m'lady. He has learned Scots but fails to practice. I hope you will help him improve his skill."

"I'll try," she said, "if he will help me learn to speak the Gaelic."

"He will."

"I am pleased to meet you, Bruce MacNab," she said, smiling at the squire.

"I thank 'e, m'lady," he said in heavily accented Scots, nodding as he spoke.

Àdham, continuing to speak Scots, said, "Show us how to get outside now, and when you finish tidying our chamber, go to bed."

MacNab nodded and turned toward the stairway, "Doon here, sir," he said quietly, leading the way downstairs and through what Àdham deduced was the monastery kitchen. Then they were outside in the dusky night, near the monastery wall on the west or back side of the residence, not far from the chapel.

The Gilten Herbar lay north of them, the river Tay to the east. In the stillness, Àdham could hear the mill lade chuckling in its bed behind them, and discerned a path leading northward toward a narrow, open gate.

"We can reach the North Inch through the Herbar, aye?" he said to Fiona.

"Aye," she said. "Someone will be watching the archway gate, but the lay brothers and royal guards know me, so whoever is there will let us out. By the time we return, the brothers will all be abed. We can use the main entrance then."

Àdham thanked MacNab, adding in Scots, "Wake us early enough to break our fast without haste before we must leave."

"Aye, sir. Can ye find your way back tae your chamber?"

Giving him a look, Àdham said, "If that is your notion of a jest . . ."

"Nae, sir; I'm off, sir," MacNab said hastily. "I ken fine that ye can find your way back from nigh anywhere a body drops ye."

Fiona was glad they had switched to speaking Scots. Their Gaelic had sounded like gibberish. Surely, the sounds they made were not really words; nor did she think she could learn to make such sounds herself.

Although her fears had stirred again, the night was pleasantly cool. A breeze through the trees and across the flowerbeds wafted herbal scents to her, and beside her, Àdham kept silent, as if he respected her thoughts. They emerged from the garden with no more ceremony than the guard at the gate opening it for them.

As they neared the river, Àdham looked around the area. At last, he said, "Do many people wander here at this time of night?"

"It is light enough still for some, especially with a half-moon up," she said. "But once darkness falls, the Inch usually becomes deserted. If we walk by the river, no one will trouble us."

"I was not thinking of *walking*," he said with gentle emphasis.

Astonished, she looked up and saw his teeth flash in a smile. "What *are* you thinking?" she demanded, needing to be sure he meant what she hoped he meant.

"I believe the tide is incoming now," he said.

"And?"

"So the water must be as cold as it was a sennight ago."

"It will be, aye. But I'd wager that Highland waters are also cold, mayhap more so. Also, at night, water often feels warmer than the air above it."

"It does," he said, grinning. "But I would be displeased if my bride were to make a scene for others of her swimming, even if she retains her smock."

"Which she always does," Fiona said firmly.

"We'll see about that," he retorted. "But I think we will walk beyond that bend yonder, where there may be a more private place to swim than right here."

"It is not as late yet as it was that night," she reminded him, lest he think she had been foolish to swim where she had.

"Let us see what lies round that bend," he said, urging her forward with a light hand at the small of her back.

The site he chose was a short U-shaped bend, and although the water was not still, the incoming tide had slowed its course even more than it had the previous week.

Stripping off her cloak and kirtle, Fiona walked without hesitation down the steep bank and into the water. The water felt wonderfully cool and cleansing. No sooner did she dip herself in, though, than she looked back to see Àdham strip off his tunic and walk in stark naked.

Àdham stroked toward Fiona, watching how she swam. He decided that she had learned the art, as he had, by watching frogs or learning from someone else who had watched them. She moved more smoothly than any frog, though, and with her long hair still floating on the water behind her, she was much more beautiful.

That she was so much at home in the water removed another item from his mental list of things that might create hardship for her in the Highlands. Not that all Highlanders knew how to swim, heaven knew. Grown men had been known to step into what they thought was a shallow burn only to slip and be swept away and drown.

She was as graceful in the water as she was on land and appealing to watch.

He knew that Sir Ivor was pleased with what the King had wrought, as was Malcolm. What his uncle Fin and Shaw Mòr might think he would learn soon enough.

Meanwhile, he was content with his bride and eager to learn more about her.

She turned her head then and smiled at him.

Accepting the smile as an invitation, Àdham moved close and pulled her into water shallow enough for them both to touch bottom. Then, gently slipping an arm around her and his free hand beneath her shift, he stroked her bare body and breasts until she moaned and then smiled at him.

"The sensations you stir in my body astonish me," she murmured. "But I hope you don't expect to do this for long, because I'm growing cold standing here."

"I'll keep you warm," he said, pulling her closer to his body, letting her feel him against her. Not that there was much to feel just then, he realized. She was not the only entity in the river that disliked its chill.

With a backhanded movement, she splashed him, and he pushed her back into the deeper part so that she came up sputtering. Then, she waved an arm across the surface, dousing him again and making him laugh.

He was glad that she was playful and looked forward to taking her to his favorite pond near Finlagh, where the water was warm on sunny summer days. They could play there, and he would teach her other ways to enjoy warmer water.

Now, the waning half-moon to the west was nearing the distant dark hills, although its reflection continued to dance on ripples wherever they moved.

"I hate to leave here," he said. "But we must be up and away with the dawn."

"I hope someone told my father that that's when we must go," she said. "I did not know we were to leave so early."

"Ivor or Malcolm will have told him, and Ormiston will have asked one of them if they did not. He will be there to bid you farewell, never fear."

He helped her onto the bank and pulled her close so that she faced him. "Look at me," he said quietly. When she tilted her face up, he kissed her, weaving his hand through her wet hair so he could kiss her more thoroughly. "You taste good," he said as he freed her and reached for the clothing she had laid atop his plaid on a nearby rock. "I wish we could linger to watch the moon go down, but you'll catch an ague if we don't get you warm soon."

The door opened, and Brother Porter stared, clearly surprised to see them.

"We've been for a swim," Àdham said as if everyone swam in the dark. "Her ladyship's cloak is damp, and she will need it in the morning."

"Aye, sure, Sir Àdham," Brother Porter replied, "I'll see that it dries as it should, and a lad will take it up afore ye leave your chamber. I'll send someone now to fetch aught else ye may have as needs drying, too, sir."

They agreed, and soon after they reached their room, a lay brother rapped on the door and took away the damp clothing. Minutes later, they were back in bed.

Àdham gently pulled Fiona nearer, saying, "I want to hold

you close before we sleep, but we'll explore no more of coupling tonight. You have not complained of soreness . . ."

"I don't feel sore anymore," she said when he paused, finding it easier than she had expected to discuss the subject. "The chilly water eased the worst of it. I don't know how it will be whilst we ride tomorrow"—she had a horrid second thought—"We *will* ride, will we not? We shan't have to walk all the way."

He hugged her closer. "Nae, lass, we'll have horses. Your da said that you have your own horse in town, so I expect he'll bring it along tomorrow."

"My horse is in the Ormiston House stable," she said. "Your equerry is still there, so he likely knows which one is mine."

"Aye, he'll have it ready and will bring it along with mine."

"Don't you mean the Earl of Caithness's?" she asked with a teasing smile.

"I do, but whilst it was in your father's stable, it was believed to be mine. It seemed safer to keep quiet about its belonging to Caithness, or some thief might have been stupid enough to steal it. We brought several garrons with us, too, but Caithness said that I should ride what he calls a 'proper horse' into St. John's Town, and his man willingly provided that one for me when I stopped at Blair."

"What is a garron?"

Sounding amused now, he said, "A Highland pony. 'Tis a gey sturdy, sure-footed beast that can carry considerable weight, even mine own, for some distance. In troth, I'd rather walk than ride one, because my feet nearly touch the ground if I do. But Lowland horses find the Highland landscape difficult, even impassable at times."

"Is it dangerous for them?"

"I'm told that Border women are excellent riders," he said. "So I expect that you ride well. Our likely route along the river Garry is easier for Lowland horses than most other ways, so you should have no trouble. We don't travel fast, although we do hope to cover some thirty miles tomorrow."

"Mercy!" Fiona exclaimed. "Her grace rarely rides more than half as far in a day. When we came here from Stirling, which is less than forty miles, we stopped overnight twice, at two castles."

"Was one of them Auchterarder?"

"Nae, for her grace did not want to irk the King. At present, he is displeased with the Grahams . . . mostly with Sir Robert Graham of Kinpont."

Àdham did not reply, and she wished she could see his expression. The room was too dark, though. She could see myriad stars through the unshuttered window, but the sky was black around them. Evidently, the moon had gone to bed.

Remembering that their conversation had begun with Caithness and Blair Castle, she said, "I know that Caithness is Atholl's son, but, although James is currently displeased with Atholl, I think he does like Caithness."

"Because Caithness rarely agrees with his father," Àdham said lightly. "His allegiance is to James, and Caithness is an honorable man. That is all that matters."

"But surely his allegiance might change! That happens, does it not?"

"Aye, sure, but he and I have known each other for some years," he replied. "And, despite what happened the other night, we are friends. My lads and I bided a night at Blair Castle on our way to St. John's Town, and he has invited us all to do so again tomorrow."

"But Blair is *Atholl's* seat. What if James learns that we stayed there?"

"He kens fine that Highlanders seek hospitality where they must and that it must be granted when someone requests it. Also, James knows that you and Lady Marsaili will be with us. But we can talk all day tomorrow. We must sleep now."

To her surprise, his breathing slowed at once, and soon he was asleep.

Fiona, having never slept with anyone else in her bed before, lay wide awake beside him, fearing that if she moved she would wake him.

When Àdham opened the door the next morning, the wee black-and-white cat slipped past a neatly garbed young woman on the landing and darted inside.

"I'm Leah," she said. "I thought her ladyship might ha' need o' me."

"Aye, she does," Àdham said, opening the door wide. "Here's your Leah now, my lady. I'll take my kist down and see if our horses have come." Snatching up his plaid from the top of the sumpter basket, he donned it, fastened his belt, picked up his cap and the basketful of his belongings, and left the room.

Fiona, stroking Donsie, welcomed Leah with delight. "Faith," she said. "I feared I'd have to leave without bidding you farewell."

"I do wish I could go wi' ye, m'lady. But me da wouldna like it, and I dinna think I'd like living so far from home."

"I'm not sure about that myself," Fiona said with a wry smile. "But we'll see each other again. I mean to visit Ormiston Mains as often as I can."

They continued chatting while Fiona dressed.

When she was ready, she handed Leah the cat, bade them both farewell, and broke her fast with Àdham in the refectory. By then, others including Ormiston, Caithness, and an apparent sea of servants, men-at-arms, and horses were awaiting them on the Inch outside the monastery wall.

The blond boy she had seen briefly in her father's stable stood with them, and Àdham greeted him by tousling his curls and speaking to him in the Gaelic.

"Aye," the boy replied. He added something else and gestured to the dog, Sirius, which was already lapping Àdham's hand in greeting.

Seeing the dog evidently reminded him of Donsie's attack the night they met, because he turned to her and said, "Where is your cat, lass? I forgot about her."

"Donsie is not mine," Fiona said. "She belongs here at Blackfriars. She just seemed to adopt me upon my arrival and likes to follow me. She's gey friendly, though. She'll find someone else to protect," she added with a grin.

Parting with her father was much harder than parting with Leah or the cat.

Ormiston hugged her tightly. "I'll miss ye fierce, lassie," he muttered.

Tears welled in her eyes. "I am still uncertain about life in the Highlands, sir. Prithee, do not forget that you promised to visit us soon."

"I have no doubt that you have married a good man," he said gently. "You will enjoy your journey, make many new friends, and I *won't* forget my promise."

"When are you going to marry Lady Rosalie?"

He smiled. "I have not even asked her yet. I do mean to do so anon, though."

"I shall be gey sad to miss your wedding, but Rosalie must come with you when you visit us," she said.

Although Fiona was loath to leave him, they parted at last with a final hug.

As she turned away, she saw Àdham awaiting her with Donsie in his arms, apparently content there, despite her erstwhile attack on him.

"Evidently, she thinks more of you than you think of her, my lady," he said with a teasing smile. "Unless you want her to follow us all the way . . ."

"I don't, and she might try to do that," Fiona said. "If you truly do not object to having her with us, sir, I can wrap her in my shawl." Ormiston helped her mount her horse, and she saw Àdham's eyes widen as she did.

"You ride astride like a man?" he said with a slight frown.

"Aye, sure, sir, as most Border women do," she said. "You must also have seen that I use a man's flat saddle. Will Highlanders object to that?"

"I won't," he said firmly. "I wondered how you could cope with our rugged trails in one of those tipsy boxes I've seen that Lowland women call saddles."

After mounting her horse, she took the little cat from Àdham, wondering how Donsie would adapt to riding, but the cat purred and arranged itself by making something of a nest between Fiona's thighs.

Then, since they had said most of their farewells at the wedding feast, and everyone else was ready, they departed as the sun peeked above the eastern hills.

Their party was larger than she had expected, because Malcolm had a tail of a dozen men and Sir Ivor had nearly as many. As most of them walked, their pace was slow, but to Fiona's delight,

Àdham rode beside her. The morning was chilly but not cold, and she felt herself relaxing as they rode alongside the river.

"You said that Lady Marsaili would ride with us," she reminded Àdham.

"Aye, she will. We'll meet her in a few hours."

A short time later, Rory rode up to them on one of the garrons and spoke to Àdham in Gaelic. Thanking him, Àdham said with a grin to Fiona, "Sir Ivor wants me, and he apparently told our Rory here to look after you. Can you bear it?"

"I shall enjoy his company," she said, smiling at the boy.

When Àdham rode on ahead, Rory guided his smaller horse to ride beside her dappled gelding. Looking up at her, he said, "D'ye like t' be married, m'lady?"

"So far, I do," she said. "I did not know that you could speak Scots."

"Aye, sure," he said. "I keep me ears open tae learn new things. Also, at Finlagh, near everyone speaks Scots and the Gaelic, so I do, too. Can ye no speak the Gaelic?"

"No, I cannot, nor understand a word of it. Mayhap you can help me learn."

"Aye, I can do that. I'll do just what Sir Àdham and them did wi' me." He patted the garron. "*Gearran*," he said.

"That I did know. I did not know that the word was Gaelic, though."

"It is, aye, but ye dinna say it quite the same, though." With a gesture toward her horse, he added, "that be *each*. The cat be *caht*, yon oak tree be *darach*, and . . ."

"Enough!" Fiona exclaimed, laughing. "I'll never remember so many words at once."

"Aye, but ye'll learn if we keep a-doin' it, though," he assured her. "Ye must also learn how words go together and how they change now and now. But if a body can make hisself understood, he needna say it all just right."

Their pace remained a steady, brisk walk or a trot, but Fiona was astonished to see that only the leaders rode. Most of the men-at-arms lacked even garrons and walked or jogged along the road.

To Rory, she said, "I can see that those men all carry weapons of one sort or another, but none seems to be carrying extra clothing or food."

The boy shrugged. "Most o' such men do ha' extra tunics. So, if a man falls in a burn or damages his tunic past wearing, he can don another one. But we sleep wi' our plaids wrapped round us, and we carry oatcakes and such, so we dinna need aught else. I'm only a-riding this garron tae bear ye company."

They chatted desultorily then, the boy occasionally pointing to something and repeating the Gaelic word for her. Reaching the cathedral town of Dunkeld at midmorning, they found Lady Marsaili and her entourage awaiting them.

The entourage included six men-at-arms and a gray-haired woman somewhat older than her ladyship, whom Fiona supposed to be her attire woman. She was glad to see that both women rode, as did two of their men-at-arms. Lady Marsaili wore a stylish moss-green riding dress with a plaited circlet of matching fabric like a crown on her head. She appeared to be several years younger than Lady Rosalie.

Fiona saw Àdham then, riding toward the newcomers with Sir Ivor, Caithness, the Mackintosh—or Malcolm as he'd said to call him—and a young red-headed man. She recalled him as Gilli Roy Mackintosh, who had brought her the stool so Àdham could kiss her over their *croquembouche*. When they met, Sir Ivor kissed his lady, and Àdham turned his horse and gestured for Fiona to join them.

When she did, Lady Marsaili smiled upon seeing the cat but said without waiting for Àdham to introduce her formally, "Fiona, I am as good as Àdham's aunt, so prithee, call me Marsi as my other friends and family do."

"Then I will also do so, my lady, thank you," Fiona said, smiling. Up close, she could see lines at the corners of her ladyship's eyes and others near her mouth. But she was a beautiful woman all the same, with an irresistible smile.

"We shall ride together and grow acquainted as we go," Marsi said. "Where do we spend the night, Àdham? The others did not think to tell me, nor I to ask."

"Blair Castle," he said. "Caithness invited us and would not let me refuse. Also, he lent me this horse I'm riding, so I'm obliged to stop to return it."

She tilted her head, giving him a searching look. "We must talk, sir."

"It will be my pleasure," he said. "Malcolm is waving, though, so we had better be on our way. We still have nearly twenty miles to put behind us today."

"Then I shall ride with you first." Turning to Fiona, she added, "I shall leave my Kate with you now, my dear, but I will return shortly, I promise."

More than stunned, Fiona watched the pair of them ride away and could tell that Marsi seemed to be annoyed with Àdham. Her auburn hair, in coiled plaits over her ears, glinted with flaming highlights where sunlight touched it, stirring Fiona to wonder if Lady Marsi might have a temper to match those flames.

"Àdham, I must know what you have told Fiona about yourself so that I do not speak of aught that I should keep to myself," Marsi said, pushing a strand of hair that had escaped her net back into it.

"You may say anything you like to her," he said.

"Then, since you say we'll stay at Blair, she knows of your kinship to the Grahams and Atholl, and James does, too."

"The subject did not arise with James. He did mention Atholl along with Sir Robert Graham in much the same breath, though. So he likely knows of my connection to them. I have not explained the exact connections to Fiona, although she did meet Caithness."

"So I heard. But is it not unwise to let her think that you and he are just friends?"

"Sakes, madam, this marriage came as a surprise to us both. To try to explain the complexities of my more awkward, not to mention *distant*, kinships at once. . . ." He gave her a direct look. "Would that not also have been unwise?"

"Perhaps. You do plan to stay at Rothiemurchus, do you not?"

"Just overnight," he said, feeling his tension ease with the change in subject. "Malcolm and Gilli Roy want to get home, and I must reach Finlagh before anyone there learns about my wedding.

Catriona will want my head for it as it is. If she should hear about it from a mendicant friar or anyone else . . ."

"She will torture you first, and you'd deserve it," Marsi said with a laugh. "What demon possessed you to wed in such haste?"

"We were given little choice. But in troth, I am content," he said lightly.

"Then I am gey pleased for you, Àdham. But I must rejoin Fiona now, and you must be frank with her as soon as you can. You *do not* want her to learn that you are closer to Sir Robert or to Atholl than you have admitted. She will think you purposefully kept that from her, and that is never good in any marriage."

CHAPTER 12

On a hillside northwest of Dunkeld, two horsemen watched the converging parties below with differing degrees of dismay. "Sakes, there be too many o' them!" Dae Comyn exclaimed. "We canna do nowt agin so many."

"They willna all go tae Finlagh wi' Sir Àdham, 'cause he went alone tae St. John's Town," Hew said, suppressing his own concerns. Dae *must not* fear that he lacked confidence. "Them others be the Mackintosh's men and Sir Ivor's," he added. "They will soon part wi' Àdham and the lass tae go their own ways."

"Even so," Dae said, "he has men o' his own, does he no? If your da wants that lass so bad, he should ha' sent some o' his own men with us."

"He'll need them hisself when he returns from town, but he did tell us where tae get more. We Comyns have kin all over Scotland, after all."

Dae looked less than persuaded but nodded and turned his attention back to the long line of travelers below.

Fiona found Lady Marsi an edifying companion. More important, her stylish appearance revealed that Highland women were not all barbaric, even if some of their men likely were.

"Do you like living in the Highlands?" Fiona asked her bluntly.

"I would live wherever Ivor wanted to live," Marsi said with a warm smile. "I love Rothiemurchus, though. 'Tis gey beautiful there, as you will see."

"Is Castle Finlagh also beautiful?"

Marsi hesitated, looking thoughtful. "It is not as large as Rothiemurchus or Raitt, which was Fin and Catriona's first home together. But they have made Finlagh exceedingly comfortable, and its ramparts enjoy splendid views."

"Why did they move to a smaller place?"

"They did not do so by choice," Marsi said with a grimace. "Nearly twenty years ago, Alexander of the Isles quarreled with the Duke of Albany, who governed the kingdom in Jamie's stead whilst Jamie was captive in England. . . ."

"I know what happened then," Fiona said. "That was the Battle of Harlaw, which Alexander and his Islesmen lost and the Earl of Mar won—like Lochaber. But what had Harlaw to do with Sir Finlagh leaving Raitt Castle?"

"Harlaw is days away from where we live, and Fin rode with Clan Chattan. Whilst he was away, the Comyns seized Raitt. That is why Fin and my good-father stayed at home this time. The men leave now only if both castles are well guarded."

"Why did they not band together to storm Raitt and take it back?"

Marsi grimaced. "Because our cousin Alex Stewart, by then Earl of Mar and Lord of the North, decided that peace was more important and matters should stay as they were for a time. Then, Jamie came home, and he *craved* peace, especially in the Highlands, which are more difficult than other parts of the realm for any King to control. Hence, he left control to Alex where he could. But Alexander of the Isles, who, as you know, is also our cousin, does not *want* peace. He believes he is—"

"Equal to James, I know," Fiona said with a sigh. "I heard him say so at Holyrood when he submitted to his grace. He has often irked James since by sending and receiving messages plotting his escape from Tantallon. Someone usually intercepts them, but his grace cannot be sure that none travels as intended."

"Aye, and likely some do. But tell me about yourself now."

Fiona complied, and the time passed swiftly. Stopping only at midday for a meal of bread, cheese, and ale, they reached Blair Castle just before sundown.

Situated a half mile north of the road and the river Garry, the castle loomed amid flower-bedecked shrubbery and tall larch, beech, and fir trees. The area beyond its parklike setting was a wild and beautiful landscape of forest-clad hills and mountains.

Caithness had sent a man ahead to warn his people that they were coming, and he assured the others that supper would soon be ready.

As Àdham helped Fiona dismount, the young earl approached, saying, "I've told my people to put ye in my sister Elspeth's room. Her bed should hold ye both." Shouting for a lad to carry up whatever they might need overnight, he moved on to bid Malcolm, Sir Ivor, and Lady Marsi welcome and relay similar news to them.

Àdham handed Donsie to young Rory with orders to look after her carefully. "If you think you cannot," he added, "find a basket and leave her shut in our room."

"I'll tend tae her, aye, sir. And I'll keep her safe, too, m'lady," he added.

After supper in the great hall, Malcolm declared that the members of his party needed a good rest and should retire as soon as they had eaten.

Fiona, hoping to see more of Blair Castle, was reluctant to retire so early, but Àdham distracted her thoughts by teaching her more delights of the marriage bed.

He treated her gently, but she was still tender inside and was glad when he reached his culmination. Soon, his deep, even breathing told her that he slept.

Caithness had been wrong about one thing, though. The bed was *not* big enough for them both to sleep comfortably. Àdham had tucked his legs up to fit and lay on his side, facing away from her. His position put her against the wall, and it was cold despite a bed curtain that prevented direct contact. At last, she dozed, only to waken sometime later, sprawled across the otherwise empty bed, shivering.

Àdham was gone. But she heard a distant murmur of male voices.

❖ ❖ ❖

Uncomfortably confined in the too-small bed and fearful of rolling onto Fiona, Àdham dozed fitfully until frustration won. Then, cautiously, wary of waking her, he had slipped out of the room. Aided by lighted cressets at each end of the gallery overlooking a dark and apparently empty great hall, he found a nearby service stair, descended to the ground floor, and emerged in the castle scullery.

A door next to the sink led to a dark alley that opened onto the stableyard.

Everything was silent, telling him that the hour was well past midnight.

The chilly, fresh air was a relief after the stale, smoky interior of the castle, and the waning moon above shone brightly. Drawing a deep breath, he realized that such profound silence was unnatural and wondered if something had disturbed the night creatures.

A rattle of pebbles drew his eye to movement near the stables—two men, if his night vision was as reliable as usual. Both moved confidently. Deciding they must be Blair men, he turned quietly toward the grassy area where the Clan Chattan men slept. Approaching silently on turf, he heard whispers, then a contented purr, and then saw a small head pop up.

"It's me, Rory," Àdham murmured in the Gaelic. "Naught to trouble ye."

The boy kept silent. One of two larger figures beside him rose to its feet with the singular grace that told Àdham who it was before MacNab stepped toward him.

He murmured, "Caithness has unexpected visitors, sir."

Creeping to the bedchamber door, her ears aprick for Àdham's return, Fiona cautiously opened the door and tried to imagine where he had gone. The great hall, below the gallery rail, was dark. With her door open, the voices sounded louder and seemed to come from the castle's vast entry hall, at the foot of the main stairway.

Moving to that end of the gallery, trying to think of what she could say to Àdham if she met him on those stairs, she recognized one of the voices as Caithness. Another silkier, more honeyed voice seemed familiar, too.

On tiptoe, she moved to the spiral stone stairs and down to the small landing at the first turn. The voices were clearer. They were speaking Scots.

" . . . and it doesna concern ye, Alan." The speaker sounded as old as Malcolm, who had achieved his sixtieth year two or three years before, according to Àdham.

Caithness said, "Why do you cavil, sir? What brought you here like this?"

The silkier voice said, "Ye heard your da, lad. Take yourself off to bed now, afore ye hear summat as may cost ye dear."

It was the mellifluous voice of the "eloquent scoundrel," as she had heard his grace describe the man. So, what was Sir Robert Graham doing at Blair Castle? And why had he arrived at what had to be sometime between midnight and dawn?

Stepping down a stair, hoping she could see them without their seeing her, she dared to peek around the stair's central post.

A larger landing, ten or twelve feet square, separated the bottom portion of her stairs from the stretch of wider steps that swept to the floor below. Near the foot of those wider stairs, she saw what looked like Caithness's broad-shouldered back.

He said, "I can tell that ye're up to nae good, the pair o' ye." As he turned his head, jaw clenched, his profile revealed the effort he exerted to control his temper.

"I do not understand ye, sir," he added. "I ken that ye fear Jamie will weaken *your* authority whilst he tries to make Scottish laws fair for all. What I *don't* know is why ye now support our cousin Alexander, whom I've oft heard ye disparage."

"I've nae liking for Alexander, Alan," the elderly voice said. "But he is the rightful Lord o' the Isles, and Jamie has nae right tae keep him locked up at Tantallon! Aye, and come to that, what business did *ye* have tae be inviting the whole o' Clan Chattan here, as ye and your *cousin* Àdham seem tae ha' done?"

A noise on the stairs above Fiona sent shivers up her spine. But she could not have stopped listening to step back up and look even if her life had depended on it.

"They are returning to the Highlands, sir," Caithness said. "The Mackintosh is leading them. Surely, you would not have had me refuse them hospitality."

Loud coughing from above Fiona startled her into a near screech. She barely reclaimed wits enough to move up a step before Caithness could turn his head.

Above her, descending with silent speed that belied his age, Malcolm paused long enough to mutter in heavily accented but fluent Scots, "Get ye tae bed, lass, *now*, else I'll tell Àdham o' this." Without another word, he continued his rapid descent around the post, slowing only when he reached the wider steps to the hall.

Then she heard him say lightly, "Atholl, I heard yer voice, so I hied me doon tae thank ye for your generosity. I'll take a mug o' that whisky, an ye please."

Not daring to linger, Fiona fled back upstairs to her bedchamber and was reaching for the latch when Àdham opened the door from within.

His expression when he saw her was angry enough to make her knees quake and send a shiver up her spine.

He stepped aside with a curt gesture indicating that she should precede him back into their bedchamber. As soon as he had shut the door again, he said, "What the devil were you doing out there?"

Raising her chin, she said in much the same tone of voice as his, "I was looking for you. What else would I be doing? You left first. Where have *you* been?"

He said evenly, "I could not sleep, because Lady Elspeth's bed is too small for two of us. I needed to stretch my body. So, I went outside to be sure that my men were comfortable and asleep."

She raised her eyebrows. "And were they?"

"Not all of them," he said, eyeing her more narrowly. "You knew something had disturbed them before you asked that question. Since I heard voices from the entry when I crossed the gallery to this room, I expect you heard them, too, aye?"

She hesitated, weighing her answer. At last, she said, "Caithness has visitors. I heard his voice and others. Do you know who they are?"

"His father has returned," he said. "One cannot be surprised that Atholl should come home, but he did tell Caithness he meant to stay in town until the end of the month."

"Then 'tis strange that he has come just when we are here," she said. "Do you know who came with him?"

"He always travels with an entourage, but I don't know who his companions are. MacNab and Rory saw them arrive. I could hardly question Atholl's stable lads about him or his guests. Then, when I looked for Malcolm, he was not in his room, so rather than wander about, I came here. Did you hear aught of what they said?"

Fiona wondered how much to tell him. He had not behaved as if he might condemn her for listening to what others were saying. Surely, it was reasonable that most people, finding themselves in the same position, would listen just as she had.

Still, Atholl had called Àdham Caithness's "cousin," which must make Àdham kin to Atholl, too. If he was, why did he not say so? Could he be less loyal to James than he'd led her and her father to believe? Might he even be party to whatever Atholl was planning?

"Lass," he said with an edge to his voice, "I can tell by looking at you that you did hear something. What was it?"

"Voices," she muttered. Caithness had not sounded as if *he* were in it. Atholl's opposition to James clearly irked him. Surely, they were not plotting to—

"Fiona, I would like a sensible answer," he said curtly.

Startled, still lost in her thoughts, she stared at him for a moment before she could collect her wits. Then, noting his expression, she said hastily, "I heard men's voices when I awoke. When I realized you were not with me, I thought you must be with them. So I went to see if I could hear your voice."

"You did not hear it," he said tersely. "So what, or whom, *did* you hear?"

"I heard Caithness talking to someone, Atholl, I think," she said. "Yes, for someone else said, 'ye *heard* your da' to him. There were other voices. . . ."

"*Who* else?" he demanded when she paused.

Grimacing, she said, "A man Jamie calls the eloquent scoundrel . . . Sir Robert Graham, Laird of Kinpont. I heard him speak in Parliament. His voice is memorable."

The moonlight in the room was fading. Even so, she saw Àdham wince and look upward. She knew that his mood had changed again.

"Do you know Sir Robert?" she asked him.

"I do," he said. "See here, lass, I can tell when you try to decide how much or exactly what to tell me. Don't do that. Just answer me. This may be important."

"To whom?"

"I'll know more about that when you tell me what else you heard, all of it. Do you know if more than three men were there?"

"I heard only those three voices, and I did not hear all that they said."

"Fiona, don't quibble. Just tell me what you heard."

"The scoundrel—"

"Sir Robert."

"Aye, he told Caithness to go to bed." She described the rest as clearly as she could remember, adding, "Then Atholl asked Caithness what had impelled him to invite the whole of Clan Chattan to Blair."

Àdham's lips quirked into a near smile then. "What else did they say, lass?"

She wanted to ask about his kinship to Caithness. But his smile had vanished as quickly as it had appeared, so she decided it was not a good time and said instead, "Caithness told Atholl that the Mackintosh was here. Then Malcolm himself began coughing loudly on the stairway above me. I nearly screamed."

"But you did not."

"No, I was *more* terrified that they'd hear me below."

"What happened next?"

With a grimace, she said in a rush, "The Mackintosh told me to get to bed or he'd tell you where he'd found me. Then he went down and asked Atholl to pour him some of the whisky they were drinking. I came back up here and found you."

Àdham bit his lower lip then as if he were trying not to laugh.

"It was not funny," she said indignantly.

"I was imagining how you must have looked when Malcolm spoke. But you are right. It is not funny. I wonder if Caithness knows the danger he may be in."

"Caithness!" She stared at him. "I doubt they are plotting against *Caithness.*"

He gave her a fiercer look then than any he had yet given her. Very softly, he said, "You say that as if you believe they *are* plotting against someone. Do you believe that?"

She tried to swallow but could not. After all, Malcolm *had* sounded friendly with Atholl. Moreover, Jamie's policies had angered many Highland nobles, as well as some of the most powerful Lowland ones. What if Malcolm agreed with them?

"Answer me," Àdham said grimly.

Drawing breath, she met his stern gaze and said, "Aye, then, I do believe it."

"Who?"

"I think you know." When he just waited, she muttered, "The King. I think they are plotting *with* Alexander to free him. One thing I forgot is that Caithness accused them of being up to no good. Could Malcolm be involved? Are *you?*"

Àdham sighed, opened his arms, and when she looked wary, he said gently, "Come now, I want to hold you. Malcolm is *not* involved. He is Jamie's man to the bone, lass, just as I am."

She walked to him then, and he held her tightly as he murmured near her right ear. "Don't wander off like that again in a strange household, lassie. You might walk into danger, and I'd be most displeased if you came to harm."

She tilted her head up. "What would you do?"

"To you or to the villain who harmed you?"

"The villain," she said.

"We Highlanders believe in vengeance, and I take care of mine own."

She opened her mouth to ask what he'd do to her but changed her mind when he kissed the top of her head. She tilted her face up then so his lips could find hers.

To her surprise, relief, and ultimate delight, he scooped her into his arms, carried her to the bed, and taught her more about pleasuring. When she awoke hours later, the sun was up and he was gone. But he had laid out a fresh kirtle and smock for her, along with the boots and netherstocks she had worn the day before.

No matter how late Malcolm had returned to bed, Àdham knew that the old man would be up betimes to get an early start on the long day ahead.

Finding him at the high table in the hall, finishing a trencher of beef or mutton and eggs, Àdham said in the Gaelic, "May we talk, sir?"

"Aye," Malcolm replied, adding in the same tongue, "Take some bread and meat for yourself. We'll walk outside. Blair has impressive gardens."

Splitting a manchet loaf, Àdham speared juicy rare slices of beef from the platter with his eating knife. Piling them in the split loaf, he followed Malcolm from the hall.

When they were outside, Malcolm said quietly, "I'm thinking that your lass must have told you she saw me during the small hours."

"And that you threatened to tell me you'd seen her if she did not take herself straight back to bed, aye."

Malcolm smiled. "Did she tell ye all o' that on her own?"

Returning the smile, Àdham said, "I may have prodded some. See you, I'd wakened earlier and gone out to see to the men. When I learned that Atholl had come, I knew you'd want to know, but you weren't in your room, so I went to ours and found her gone. I came out as she was returning. You had gone downstairs."

"I see. And what d'ye make of it all?"

"Fiona thinks that our host and my irksome uncle are plotting against his grace, and I agree. Would it be a kinsman's betrayal to send a warning to James?"

"It would not," Malcolm replied firmly. "Does Fiona *know* Robert?"

"Nae, she recognized his voice, and she knows that Jamie dislikes him."

"Then ye must tell her of your close kinship with him afore anyone else does."

"So Marsi advised me," Àdham said. "I know I must, but I'd liefer wait until we know each other better. Sakes, sir, she asked me if you or I were involved in a plot with them. Learning that Robert is my uncle could make her think so again."

"Why should it? It is not as if ye *did* plot wi' the man or ever lived with him."

"Or liked him," Àdham agreed. "But when I met her, she believed all Highlanders were barbarians. She fears even the land itself, I think. Moreover, she has left her home, all of her family, and all of her friends. Her own maidservant refused to accompany her."

"Catriona will see that she'll be comfortable enough at Finlagh. 'Tis no as grand as what she kens, but Fin and Catriona have made a home for themselves and their bairns. They will warmly welcome Fiona."

"I should also tell you I heard that Alexander's cousin, Donal Balloch, has returned to the Isles. He's evidently been plotting vengeance since Lochaber."

"And where did ye come by *that* news?"

"From the one my lady calls 'the eloquent scoundrel.' *She* told me that men *have* tried to get messages to Alexander and that some may have succeeded."

"Sakes, men have tried to free him, too," Malcolm said, adding, "Your lady got that 'eloquent scoundrel' bit from Jamie, I'd wager." When Àdham agreed, he said, "When did your meeting with Robert take place?"

"He sent for me to meet him on the Inch the day after I arrived in town, to inform me of my disloyalty at Lochaber in supporting his grace against Alexander."

"I see," Malcolm said. "Did he alter your thinking about that?"

"He did not. When I pledge my loyalty, I honor my pledge, as you know."

"I do," Malcolm said, clapping him on the back. "We must hope that your lady's loyalty is as dependable. You see to it that she keeps happy at Finlagh."

"As to that, sir, I will have to be away at times. I promised his grace to find out what I can about the strength of other central Highland chiefs' loyalties to him."

"Whose does he fear may be swayed?"

"He named no names. I do not need to ask the Comyns if their loyalties have swayed *toward* him, but I suspect he does fear that my father's loyalty may swing back to agree with Cameron of Lochiel's."

"If Balloch *is* raising an army, you must learn how many of our leaders are aware of that. But keep your ears open, lad, for news of Jamie's other enemies. We know Atholl and Graham have been scheming to free Alexander. If they're conspiring with Balloch, they are more dangerous than we thought."

"So Balloch is the true danger, aye?"

"Aye, sure. The lad may be only eighteen, but he is Chief of Clan Donald of Dunyvaig and Alexander's own cousin. Moreover, he proved at Lochaber that he can gather a sizable army. He is young, angry, already a renowned champion and distinguished tactician, and he is therefore *gey* dangerous."

"Then we must get word to his grace of the meeting here tonight, aye?"

"Aye, but I'll attend tae that . . . after we leave here," Malcolm said. "I can send someone less likely to be known than your lads or Ivor's. I'm thinking, too, that the less notice we draw from Atholl, the better."

"Caithness knows I've married Fiona. I don't know if Atholl knows or not."

"He knows," Malcolm said. "Nowt happens within the royal court of what Atholl calls his 'thankless nephew' that Atholl does not hear. Moreover, your wedding was such that everyone in town knows about it. Don't be surprised if Atholl demands to know why ye neglected to invite him."

Àdham soon had cause to be grateful for Malcolm's warning, because when he entered the great hall, he saw his bride at the high table, sitting in the place of honor at the Earl of Atholl's left, chatting animatedly with him.

Fiona had been watching for Àdham and noticed his entrance to the hall but kept her attention on her host. Atholl had invited her to join him and Caithness on the dais when she had come downstairs in search of her husband.

Atholl said, "'Tis a pity ye be leaving us so soon, madam. We would be pleased tae ha' your company, all o' ye, for some days if ye change your mind."

Aware that Àdham did not look happy to see her on the dais with Atholl, and wishing she were almost anywhere else, Fiona drew on her experience with the royal court and smiled, saying earnestly, "I wish the decision were mine to make, my lord, because Blair Castle is one of the finest houses in Scotland. I did see your splendid gardens from our window. You are most fortunate in your gardeners."

"They are adequate," Atholl said. "I must say, I was surprised tae hear o' your so hasty wedding. I expect ye must ha' been surprised, too."

Blinking as Leah did whenever she was at a loss for words, Fiona said, "Surely, my lord, your daughters obey you just as I obeyed my lord father."

"So the wedding was *Ormiston's* doing?"

Taking refuge this time in feminine flutter, she said, "Why, I do not know how to answer that, sir. Do you discuss your decisions with your children?"

"He does not," Caithness said bluntly from beyond Atholl. "He demands obedience just as any father does. Do you not, sir?" he added with an innocent air.

"Has it become customary in your circles, sir, tae interrupt another conversation at table?" Atholl demanded.

"Och, aye, I fear that it has," Caithness said. "Sithee, sir, my friends rarely stand on such ceremony that one must keep silent until one is bidden to speak."

"This is my table, however," Atholl retorted.

"Aye, sure, it is," Caithness agreed. "Although I do confess that I had expected it to be my table whilst my guests were here. One does wonder why, after telling me that you meant to stay in town until the end of the month, you followed so hard upon our heels yestereve, instead."

"As I had nae notion that ye'd invited guests, I came here for reasons that do not concern ye. Nor do I mean tae discuss them wi' ye."

"But you had guests, too," Caithness said. "Or have they departed?"

"I dinna ken what ye mean, nor do I like your tone," Atholl said. "Nor do I answer tae ye for my actions or my friends. Ye, on the other hand, *do* answer tae me for yours."

"I answer first to his grace, the King, though," Caithness replied. "He said he might send me to Glen Mòr, to aid Mar at Inverlochy Castle, if the many Islesmen undaunted by his grace's imprisonment of their lord stir more trouble there."

"Ye'd do better tae aid your own father, me lad," Atholl retorted.

Fiona quaked inside, fearing that she had landed Caithness in the briars.

Fortunately, Àdham approached then to ask if she was ready to depart. Agreeing that she nearly was, she cast a rueful look past Atholl to Caithness.

He grinned at her and winked.

Àdham greeted Atholl politely, adding, "I must thank your lordship for your hospitality and your extraordinary courtesy to my lady wife."

"In troth, I was attempting tae learn just why your wedding took place wi' such unseemly haste," Atholl replied bluntly.

Stiffening, Àdham said in a coldly disbelieving tone that Fiona had not heard from him before, "*Unseemly?*"

Caithness muttered something, but Àdham ignored him. He continued to look the Earl of Atholl straight in the eye and to await a response from him.

Blandly, Atholl said, "Ye canna be amazed that ye've stirred curiosity, lad."

Feeling his jaw clench and noting that Malcolm had skirted the trestle tables in the lower hall and was approaching the far end of the dais, Àdham drew a breath.

Collecting his wits, he said evenly but loud enough for Malcolm to hear, "I do not know how his grace's suggestion that such a marriage could improve his relations with landowners in the Highlands and Lothian can have stirred curiosity in anyone who knows him as well as you do, your lordship. But mayhap you are unaware that it *was* his grace who arranged our wedding."

Noting a gleam of humor in Malcolm's eyes before he lowered them to the dais step, Àdham relaxed.

Atholl had composed himself, too, for he said, "Jamie may ha' said some such thing tae me. But the man be so full o' whimsical notions that one loses track o' them all. I didna mean tae offend ye, lad."

Feeling his teeth clamp together at the dismissive "lad," Àdham forced a smile and said, "Art ready to depart, my lady? Or must you finish packing things?"

"I do have some things—"

"Good morrow," Malcolm said in Scots behind them, silencing her. "I heard when I awoke that ye were here at table, Walter," he added when Atholl whipped around to face him. "So I hied me doon tae thank ye again for your hospitality. 'Tis a rare treat tae see how fine ye be keepin' yer place here."

"I expect ye must also ha' been party tae this marriage," Atholl said.

"Nae, then, I had nowt tae do with it. Jamie and Ormiston fixed it all up betwixt 'em. Then Sir Àdham agreed tae it and thereby won hisself a rare prize, as ye ha' seen for yourself, Walter."

"Aye, aye," Atholl said, patting Fiona's right hand, which she had rested on the table as she prepared to rise from it.

Àdham moved to stand beside her, ready to pull her back-stool out of her way as he extended a hand to assist her to her feet.

Slipping her right hand out from under Atholl's with a smile, she accepted Àdham's hand and arose with her usual fascinating grace.

The earl stood and smiled down at her from his loftier height. "Ye be always welcome, my lady," he said. "I dinna ken your father well, but if he decides tae visit ye in the Highlands, prithee tell him that he, too, should bide here on his way."

"Thank you, my lord," Fiona said, bobbing a slight curtsy and thereby irking her husband. "I shall send word to him of your invitation at my first opportunity."

The Mackintosh engaged Atholl in conversation then, allowing Àdham to whisk his wife off the dais and out of the hall.

CHAPTER 13

"You still look angry," Fiona said when they reached their bed-chamber. "Was it something that I said or did?"

"Nae, lass, although I did not like to see you curtsy to that churlish man. We Highlanders bend only to his grace the King or to a Lord of the Isles if we swear fealty to one. We do not bow to each other or to other men without good cause."

"I should think that *not* irking a man like Atholl would be cause enough."

His brow relaxed. "Doubtless, you have the right of it," he said. "Have you much more to do? Malcolm is eager to be away, and so am I."

"Do you think Atholl's invitation to my father was sincere?"

"Aye, sure, it was. He'd like naught better than to sit Ormiston at his table and try to wean him away from his grace."

"He would fail," she said. "I fear that he might harm Father, though. Joanna says Atholl is an evil man and *never* to be trusted."

"Not evil, precisely, just arrogant enough to think James owes him gratitude because Atholl helped bring him home from his English captivity. But Atholl's notion of gratitude is that James should behave as Atholl commands."

"You told me you had only just met Atholl," Fiona said from the washstand. "How do you know so much about him and how he thinks?"

"Malcolm knows him, and we hear of him from the few mendicant friars that visit Finlagh. Also, Caithness confides in me."

"How did you meet him?" she asked as she dried her hands.

"Sithee, the northeasternmost part of Scotland is the Earldom of Caithness. So, when Alan has had enough of his father, he travels to Nairn, where he keeps a boat, and sails on to Caithness. I met him in Nairn, and he visits us two or three times a year. But we're keeping the others waiting, lass. We must go."

They left soon afterward and followed the increasingly steep path westward along the river Garry.

Some distance behind Malcolm's party, six men followed, two on horseback and four afoot.

"Just *four* men tae aid us, Hew?" Dae Comyn said, shaking his head. "And nae more horses? Ye must be daft tae think four lads will be any use tae us."

"Ye Lowlanders all think a man needs a horse tae do aught," Hew replied quietly enough so that the men following on foot would not hear him. "Atholl's men will keep up, just as them following the Mackintosh do. Also, *that* lot will be less likely tae heed a party o' six than they would a score o' men or more."

"Even so—"

"Once we get intae the mountains," Hew interjected, "we'll likely ha' tae follow afoot ourselves if we're tae catch MacFinlagh off his guard. We'll ha' time enough afore then, though, tae see what's what. But we canna follow too close."

"What if they elude us?"

"There be only one way intae the Highlands from here as be safe for horses. Come tae that, I'm thinking we'd best slip past 'em when they stop for the night and seek out the best place tae wait ahead. I've a notion about that, too."

That afternoon, Àdham rode beside Fiona, giving her hope that she might learn more about his kinship to Atholl and Caithness. But with others close behind them, she was content for a time to let him point out sights and identify birds and flowers when he could. She saw no hint of his earlier annoyance.

He was evidently a man who could shed his anger and not let it simmer.

That night, they stopped at Loch Ericht, a long, slender body of water, where the men slept on the ground. Fiona and Donsie did not, because Lady Marsi knew a nearby laird's family and had arranged beforehand to bide the night with them. She insisted that Fiona stay with her and her woman, saying that even with Àdham to guard her, it was unseemly for a knight's lady to sleep on the ground with so many men.

Fiona did not object, and when Àdham looked as if he might do so, she gave him a look that told him what she would think of him if he did. He grinned at her then, which made her chuckle and blow him a kiss.

Early the next morning, they set out again, heading northward. Though the trail was no longer steep, it was still rugged, so Àdham kept an eye on Fiona. But she was a fine horsewoman and her mount was nimble and steady.

Midafternoon, they stopped to rest the horses at the head of Loch Insh. When they were ready to ride on, Fiona mounted and Àdham held the cat up to her, but the little beast surprised them both by darting up his arm to his shoulder instead.

Grinning, he said, "I'll keep her for a time if she'll stay put when I mount."

Donsie apparently liked riding high above the ground, for she settled on Àdham's shoulder with her head tucked against his neck and purred.

He said to Fiona, "We should reach Loch an Eilein by nightfall."

"We've seven or eight miles yet to go, Àdham-lad," Malcolm said in the Gaelic, looking back at them. "And we'll have nae moon tonight. I'll feel better an we get these womenfolk safely within-doors afore dark."

Urging his horse up beside Malcolm's, Àdham replied in the same tongue, "With as many armed men as we have, sir, I doubt we need worry about an attack."

Malcolm grimaced. "I'd not put one past the damnable Comyns, could they manage it in the midst of Mackintosh country. Besides, this road be treacherous after dark."

Àdham could not deny that statement. Moreover, a thick Scottish mist was ever likely to surprise unwary travelers in the darkness.

He glanced back at Fiona and saw that she was watching them closely and had taken young Rory up behind her. When Àdham's gaze met hers, she smiled but raised her eyebrows as if she thought he might have something to say.

Smiling back, he returned his attention to Malcolm.

"Could you hear what they were saying over the sound of the river?" Fiona asked the boy, who had accepted her invitation to climb up behind her on her horse.

"Aye, sure," he said. "The Mackintosh be worried about darkness coming on, 'cause he says there willna be a moon tonight. And he says this track be treacherous. He wants you womenfolk all safe inside afore dark."

Trepidation stirred strongly in her. "Does he fear an attack, Rory?"

"He's more worried that the road gets treacherous after dark," the boy said. "But he did say he wouldna put an attack past them damnable Comyns."

"You should not use that word to me, you know," Fiona said, hiding a smile.

"Why not? Ha' ye no heard it afore?"

"I have heard it, aye," she said, grinning. "I have also seen my brothers well skelped if my father heard them using it where I or another lady might hear them."

"Well, it be what the Mackintosh and them say when *they* talk o' the *thievin'* Comyns," the boy said grimly. "Nae one at Castle Finlagh trusts 'em."

"Have you not always lived at Castle Finlagh with Sir Fin and Sir Àdham?"

"Nae, for Sir Àdham plucked me out o' a fierce battle two years ago and brung me home tae Finlagh tae live wi' them."

"But what were you doing in a battle? You cannot be more than ten years old now."

"I dinna ken how old I be," he admitted. "But I were no *in* it. Two villains caught me in some woods and forced me tae fetch and carry for them."

"You poor bairn!"

"Nae, I'm no a bairn," he said grimly. "I ha' seen too much tae be still a bairn. D'ye want tae learn more words in the Gaelic the noo?"

Fiona agreed. For the next half hour, he pointed to things and told her the Gaelic word for each one, and Fiona did her best to repeat what he said.

The glen steepened and its walls grew higher, for as Rory explained, they now had the treacherous Cairngorms to the east and the equally dangerous Monadhliath Mountains to the west. The slopes were forested, with intervening spreads of boulders and scree, and she thought the area was beautiful. She had never seen anything like it before, certainly not in the rolling hills of the Scottish Borders, which held a different beauty all their own.

Here, rivulets, rills, and waterfalls rushed to join the Spey. Fiona's horse picked its way nervously, wary of the swift-flowing water below to their left.

Fiona felt wary, too, doubtful that anyone could survive long in such a river.

On the steep, forested east slope above the riders, with his other lads concealed in nearby foliage, Hew Comyn watched them through the trees, frowning. "D'ye see that bairn a-riding wi' her ladyship, Dae?"

"Aye, sure, I do," Dae said. "What of 'im?"

"I'm thinking I ken that bairn, is all. He's taller now 'n older. But if he be the one as went missing at Lochaber two years ago and he be a-travelin' wi' these folks now, I'm thinking that Sir Àdham MacFinlagh may ha' much more tae answer for than just a-snatching Ormiston's daughter away from us."

Reminding Malcolm that he was but newly wed, Àdham excused himself, reined in his horse, and waited for Fiona and Rory to catch up with him.

"I see that Donsie is keeping your neck warm now, sir," Fiona said lightly. The cat had stretched itself right around his nape and fallen asleep.

"She seems content," he said. "You may dismount now, Rory, and help Duff with the garrons. We'll reach Loch an Eilein in another hour, but the road to the stable lies this side of the loch, and Duff will need your help."

"I know that, I do, but I'm guessing ye want tae talk wi' your lady and dinna need me tae help ye do that," Rory said, slipping off Fiona's horse to the ground.

"You will keep such impudent comments to yourself if you are wise," Àdham told him sternly.

"Och, aye then, I'm mum," the boy said, as he turned and darted back down the line of men behind them to find Duff.

"I wish I could believe he'd stay mum," Àdham said as he urged his horse alongside Fiona's. "The pair of you seemed to be engaged in serious conversation."

"He is teaching me to speak the Gaelic," Fiona said with a too-innocent smile.

"He also has excellent hearing," Àdham said. "Was Rory kind enough to translate our conversation for you?"

"Only part of it. He told me that the Comyns are *damnable* men," she added, eyeing Àdham speculatively, as if to see how he would receive her use of such a word.

He chuckled.

She cocked her head. "I thought you would say I should not use that word."

"I expect you *know* that you should not. I would be displeased to hear you say it to anyone else, but you may say what you choose to me when we're alone."

Her smile widened. "I have felt as if I could do that almost from the moment we met. Do you not think that is strange?"

"It may be gey strange, lassie. But I have felt that way, too."

An hour later, they dismounted and left the horses and most of the men-at-arms—including MacNab, Duff, and Rory—at the path to the Rothiemurchus stables and walked. Carrying Donsie, Fiona soon saw Loch an Eilein and the castle that covered much of an otherwise wooded islet in the northwestern part of the loch.

Her breath stopped for a moment at the serene beauty of that scene.

The sun had dropped behind hills to their left, but its light still gleamed on the castle ramparts, as well as on the trees and water of the loch's opposite shore.

"So what think you of Rothiemurchus?" Àdham asked when he and Fiona stopped near the water's edge. The breeze stirred ripples on its surface.

She drew a deep breath and smiled. "'Tis as beautiful as Marsi said it was."

Marsi, Kate, Malcolm, Sir Ivor, and the other men, Fiona noted, had found boulders or logs to sit on while they waited for boats from the islet to fetch them.

"How will we collect our clothing and such?" she asked Àdham.

"Duff and the others will bring everything here," he said.

"'Tis a beautiful place," she said.

"Aye," he said. "Malcolm's father, William, and his wife lived here. So did his older brother Lachlan before he moved his family to Loch Moigh. After the great Clan Battle of Perth, Lachlan resigned the castle to Shaw Mòr for his fine leadership of Clan Chattan at the battle. It still belongs to Shaw and his family."

"We talked of that great battle before, and even I have heard of the legendary Shaw Mòr," Fiona said. "It all happened years before we were born, though."

"Aye, and few people hereabouts talk about it anymore," he said. "Clan Chattan and Clan Cameron have been friendlier for some time now."

"If your father is a Cameron chieftain, you must belong to both clans, aye?"

He was still for a moment, then looked away.

"What is it?" she asked.

"There, yonder," he said, pointing. "See the boats setting out?"

"Aye, but you looked as if you did not want to answer me. And, although you did tell me that you pledged your fealty to Clan

Chattan, you did not explain *why* you did when your own father is a Cameron."

As the words spilled out, she wished she had been more tactful and hoped he would not be irked. Despite his assurance that she could speak her mind to him, she realized that, on certain subjects, her courage lacked the strength of her curiosity.

Àdham grimaced, but he did not want to keep such matters to himself any longer, not from Fiona. She had a right to know how and where his roots had planted themselves.

Accordingly, he said, "My father is Ewan MacGillony, a Cameron chieftain, and I was born at Tor Castle, a half day's march above the south end of Glen Mòr on the western side. I did tell you that my mam died when I was small. I was eight then, the youngest of my mother's four sons by six years. My da soon remarried, and when his second wife began increasing, she wanted me out of her way."

"How horrid of her! How old were you then?"

"Nine years and some months."

In the dusky light, he saw tears well in her eyes. "Had your father naught to say about that?"

"I don't know, lass. By the time I learned what she had demanded, he'd agreed that I must go and live with Fin and Catriona."

She shook her head and wiped the dampness from her eyes with a sleeve.

"Da said I'd be happier with them," Àdham said. "I believe he was right."

"You told me that the lady Catriona is a Mackintosh, though. So, if Sir Finlagh is your uncle, he must be Sir Finlagh MacGillony Cameron."

"I've never heard anyone call him so. Ewan *does* identify himself as a Cameron now that he's a chieftain. But most people near Finlagh call Uncle Fin 'Sir Fin.' Men who come looking for him ask for 'Fin of the Battles.' He rarely speaks of his MacGillony or Cameron kinsmen, although he and my father are friendly. But here is our boat now."

As he strode forward to catch the boat's bow painter and help pull it ashore, he felt a lightness of spirit that he had not known for years and wondered if it had resulted from sharing a small part of his complicated heritage with Fiona or from her easy acceptance of it. Perhaps, he decided, it was both.

In the back of his mind another thought stirred. Perhaps her obvious anger at his father's allowing a second wife to banish his youngest son from their home had provided much of what had stirred that warm feeling.

Whatever it was, when others began getting into the first boat, Àdham gave her upper arm a gentle squeeze and urged her to join them. "Have you been in such boats on your own river, lass? Or will this be your first experience in one?"

"I have been in boats many times," she said. "I can row one, too."

Even when she smirked, she was beautiful, he thought, smiling at her.

The second boat arrived, and they all sorted themselves into the two of them. When they had settled, men remaining on shore shoved them off.

A short time later, walking uphill toward the open gateway in the castle's high, massive curtain wall, Fiona stared in wonder. The house at Ormiston Mains, where she was born, despite being just across the river Teviot from the oft-warlike Scottish Borders, possessed no curtain wall. Evidently, though, here in the Highlands, such added security was necessary even on an island in the middle of a loch that seemed to sit in the middle of nowhere. The thought made her shiver, and she began to wonder if their uneventful journey had been *unusually* uneventful.

She had seen from the boat that the fortress covered the nearer half of the island, leaving its northern end densely wooded. As they passed through the gateway to the courtyard, she saw the castle's four-story keep occupying the far southwest corner of the curtain wall. The fortress boasted two smaller towers, one at the north end near the gateway, the other at the southeast corner. Inside the wall, the bailey contained a number of outbuildings as well as the keep.

"Welcome to Rothiemurchus," Marsi said when she caught up with them. "You and Àdham must visit us often, Fiona. But let me introduce you to the two people hurrying toward us—Ivor's mother and father, Lady Ealga and Shaw Mòr."

Since Marsi had said she was the proud mother of four children, all of them married with bairns of their own, Fiona had expected to meet a crowd. However, the group joining them for supper included only other members of their party plus the graying, but nonetheless legendary, Shaw Mòr; Lady Ealga; and the castle servants and men-at-arms who slept on the island or would guard it through the night.

Fiona was tired enough by then to reject supper in favor of her bed. But civility demanded that she sup with her hosts and bear her part in the conversation. However, Lady Ealga's eyes were as keen as any archer's were, because as soon as gillies began clearing platters, she spoke to Marsi, who said, "Ealga suspects that you are aching for a bath and a soft bed, Fiona. My Kate will assist you."

Fiona accepted the decision with relief, had her bath, and was asleep before Àdham came to bed. She did not stir until he woke her the next morning with teasing kisses. As a result of what followed, she barely had time to break her fast and take polite leave of her new friends before they were on their way again.

CHAPTER 14

The Blair Castle horses stayed in the stables with their equerry to rest. So, with Malcolm, Malcolm's men-at-arms, Àdham's three lads, and Gilli Roy—who preferred to ride with the men-at-arms and seemed to Fiona to be avoiding both his father and Àdham—their traveling party was half the size it had been. The scenery continued to impress her, but she missed Lady Marsi and her Kate. She had enjoyed their company.

A short time later, the party reached a fork in the trail and bade farewell to Malcolm, Gilli Roy, and their men.

Before Malcolm turned away, he said in Scots, "I'll expect to hear from ye in good time, Àdham, so I'll no delay ye now. I ken fine that ye're eager to get home. Ye'll come see us anon, though, and bring your lady tae meet my Mora."

"I will, sir," Àdham said, shaking his hand.

"Will we be safe with just Duff, Rory, and MacNab?" Fiona asked nervously as they waved again and followed Sirius on a barely discernible path northward.

"We should be," Àdham said confidently, raising a hand to protect Donsie as she settled into her favored position, draped across the back of his neck. "We're in mostly Mackintosh country from here to Inverness. Lochindorb, some distance ahead, is a royal castle. Over a hundred years ago, before Robert the Bruce ended their occupancy there, Clan Comyn controlled it."

"The damnable Comyns," she murmured with a teasing smile.

"Aye, and they still talk as if the Bruce stole it from them. Now, Mar's people oversee it as part of his earldom. He was born there and lived there as Lord of the North before he married the Countess of Mar. As you likely know, he is also a close cousin to Jamie. We all address him as Mar these days, so you may not know that he was christened Alexander. With Jamie and Joanna as popular as they are with the common folk and a general enmity toward Alexander of the Isles . . ."

Fiona nodded. She liked listening to him. She had still not asked him about his kinship to Atholl, though, and hoped that the lack was due not to loss of courage but to the presence, and ears, of Duff and Rory—not to mention MacNab, whose taciturn silence she had begun to find a bit off-putting.

Eventually, turning west, away from the river Spey, they emerged onto a grassy plateau. Àdham reined in, and following his gaze to a loch three times the size of Loch an Eilein, many feet down a steep slope below them, Fiona saw a larger stronghold than Rothiemurchus on an island in the middle of the loch.

"Is it common here for men to build their castles on islands?"

"Many have, aye, because they are easy to defend," Àdham said. "That is Lochindorb. Castle Finlagh perches a good distance up a steep hillside, atop a knoll. On clear days, you can see the Moray Firth from its ramparts and upper windows"

"Will we stop at Lochindorb for the night?"

"Nae, for it lies too far off our path. I'd liefer keep going."

His confidence was contagious, and although Fiona was uneasy about sleeping on the ground, the bed he made for them that night atop leaves and pine branches in an alcove of boulders that sheltered them from a chilly wind was more comfortable than the one she had shared with Marsi two nights before.

MacNab and Duff tactfully bore young Rory and Sirius some distance away, giving Fiona and Àdham privacy enough for coupling. Due to the wind, she kept on her shift and he his tunic. Then, lying on their sides like spoons, he covered them with his plaid and her cloak. Soon, Donsie snuggled in with her warm back against Fiona's stomach. Lulled by purring and soft night bird calls, they slept.

In the midst of a pleasant dream of swimming and playing in the river Teviot with Àdham, Fiona abruptly awoke in darkness with a large hand clapped across her mouth and her hair twisted up in someone's fist. Àdham and Donsie had vanished.

Something hissed in the distance. But a nearby clang of steel overwhelmed the hissing as that fist and large hand dragged her clumsily—furious, terrified, and struggling madly if ineffectively—from her pine-bough bed.

Àdham, wakened minutes before to silence by a cold, wet nose urgently nudging his bare neck, had eased himself from the still-sleeping Fiona and risen to his feet. The silence and the still-quiet Sirius at his side, staring straight ahead, told him an enemy lurked there. Keeping low and making no sound, he slid his sword from its scabbard and stepped swiftly but silently away from the pine-bough bed, hoping to draw any enemy away from it.

Two shadows loomed before him, both bulkier than Duff and shorter than MacNab. As the first one leaped toward him and Àdham raised his sword to counter the coming blow, he heard clanging swords in the distance and knew that either Duff or MacNab was also fighting for his life.

With only starlight now, all he saw of his opponent was his shape, and it was just as hard to detect stones and shrubs on the ground around them. He had all he could do to keep an occasional eye on the second chap where he hovered nearby.

Someone to his right said quietly, "Loch Moigh," and he recognized Duff's voice just as two more swords engaged each other.

With his second, would-be opponent busy, Àdham dispatched the first, only to see a third man run toward him from the shadows with sword at the ready.

Just then, he heard a cry from Duff, off to his right.

Terrified, Fiona struggled fiercely, trying to free her hair from whoever had grabbed it and to bite the hand against her mouth so she could scream. To her surprise, as she fought, her terror became anger. Moments later, at the sounds of nearby clanging swords, it turned to fury. If someone was trying to kill Àdham . . . !

Digging all ten fingernails into the hand clamped over her mouth and squealing as loudly as she could against that hand, she heard with deep satisfaction a grunt of pain from her assailant. Then came a hiss and a snarl; whereupon, the attacker, crying out, abruptly let go of her and reeled away.

Fiona scrambled away in the opposite direction. But, having recognized Donsie's snarl, she stopped and turned, wishing that she had a real weapon.

"Dinna think ye'll get far, lass," her erstwhile assailant growled, moving toward her. "I ha' five men wi' me. Ye'll be ours in a trice. Aye, *and* a widow."

Keeping an eye on him as she stepped away, she noted the denser darkness of the boulders outlining their sleeping place. Hoping that Àdham had left a dirk or some other weapon buried in the pine boughs, she moved toward them.

Her attacker darted in front of her, stumbled on their bedding, but quickly recovered his balance and reached to grab her right arm.

As he did, a huge rock, seemingly launched from the starlit sky behind him, cracked him on the head. Collapsing at her feet, he took no further interest in her.

She could still hear the clanging swords.

"This way, m'lady," a voice hissed as one of the boulders in the pile rose up before her. "Nae one will see us back this-a-way, and we'll be out o' *their* way."

Recognizing Rory with astonishment, she said, "Where did *you* come from?"

"Yonder, where MacNab and me were. I sent Sirius tae find Sir Àdham. But I kent ye'd need me help more than MacNab or Duff would. Sithee, when I left MacNab, he were a-fighting two o' them bastards."

"What should we do with this one?" she asked, deciding that he could call their attackers anything he liked.

"Nowt," Rory said firmly. "Best we get away from him, lest I didna kill the . . . the man. Ye mustna let them see ye, though. Come intae these bushes wi' me."

"Did you recognize any of them?" she murmured.

"Nae more than ye did. I can see nowt save shadows, so mind your step."

Hurrying as fast as she safely could to follow him, she heard him add on a chuckle, "I ha' that wee, vicious cat here wi' me now. She's a one, she is."

"Hew, get up or we're sped!" Grabbing his cousin by the shoulders, Dae dragged him away from the boulders into the darkness beyond them. When Hew struggled to free himself, Dae breathed a sigh of relief. "Can ye get tae your feet?"

"Aye," Hew muttered. "But keep low. What of the others?"

"Two o' them four chaps that Atholl sent with us went for his squire and equerry," Dae hissed back. "T'other two went for Mac-Finlagh. He put his first one down quick, so I slid away when the second one went for 'im. I couldna tell which were which then, let alone take on the likes o' MacFinlagh wi' a sword. At home, I wield a Jedburgh axe. Be davers, Hew, I hope ye dinna try aught like *this* again."

"Where are the others now?"

"The one's likely dead, but yonder ye can still hear swords. How did he get ye, Hew, and where's the lass?"

"I had her till one o' them clouted me from behind. But we'll get her back."

"Aye, sure, but what do we do now? We canna stay here or they'll see us."

"We'll make for the loch below," Hew muttered. "I ken Lochindorb's lands like me own. They'll no try tae follow us down to the loch, either. I can tell ye that."

Fearing for Fiona's safety and realizing that his own would mean little to him if she were dead, molested, or badly terrified, Àdham felled his second attacker and turned to find Duff still fighting the third but gasping and stumbling as he did.

Stepping in to finish that battle, Àdham turned from the fallen attacker and said, "Art injured, Duff?"

"Aye, sir, he cut me left arm, and me sword grew gey heavy for one hand. I thank 'e for putting him doon. I've bound up me wound wi' a strip o' me plaid."

MacNab appeared out of the darkness then and said, "I have one dead, sir."

"Then we have four dead, and I do not want to waste time burying them, nor do we have tools to do so. Moreover, Duff is injured. We cannot leave their bodies out in the open like this, though. We'll cover them with rocks."

"There may be more of those louts about," MacNab said.

"Mayhap there are, but I must find my lady."

"I'm here, Àdham, with Rory," Fiona said, emerging from the dark shadows and into his open arms.

He held her tight, noting that the hair-thin vestige of a crescent moon rising now, belatedly, would aid them little in the gory task to come.

"There were two others," Fiona said. "Rory and I just heard them scuttling away down that very steep hill toward the loch."

"Did either of them hurt you?" he demanded.

"One of them woke me by grabbing me by the hair," she said. "He covered my mouth and dragged me from our bed. But he will have scars, I think, from my fingernails. Donsie attacked him, so I got away. He would have caught me, though, if Rory hadn't cracked him on the head with a rock from atop those boulders."

"You did well, both of you," he said. "I'm sorry about this, lass. I should have asked Ivor to send an escort with us."

"Do you know who they were, Àdham?"

"I could see little more than my opponents' shadows. But, this near Lochindorb, they might well have been Comyns."

"At least, we are all still alive," she said. "That is what matters. In troth, although I was terrified at first, the one that grabbed me angered me more than he frightened me. Then, it was over so fast that I scarcely had time to *stay* afraid. But might they not find reinforcements below and attack us again?"

"Nae," he said. "Recall that Lochindorb is now under the Earl of Mar's control. If the villains *were* Comyns, they likely know the landscape hereabouts, because Comyn of Raitt continues to assert that it rightfully belongs to them. That is why they support Alexander of the Isles, as they do. Raitt expects Alexander to return Lochindorb to him if Alexander can defeat the King."

"I do recall that Robert the Bruce killed the Red Comyn to keep him from seizing the throne, because Comyn would have submitted to the English King."

"Aye, but my point was that if our attackers *were* Comyns, they'll gain no aid from Mar's people. So I doubt they will trouble us again before we reach Finlagh. Most of the territory from here west to Glen Mòr is Clan Chattan land. Comyn of Raitt is the only rat in the nest."

"But you did say that Raitt Castle is near Finlagh, aye?"

"It is just a few miles away, aye. But a range of hills with two crags extends between us. We'll avoid the public road that crosses Raitt's land, though, in case Comyns did attack us. There is a pass of sorts, and we can walk the horses."

"How far is Finlagh from here?"

"About twenty miles, so two days with the horses."

"In the Borders, raiders can ride fifty miles in a night."

"Aye, perhaps, but the terrain hereabouts, even near the rivers, is often rugged, steep, and splashed with scree-filled moraines to traverse or circumvent. Our small garrons are sure-footed, but we walk horses more than we ride them."

She nodded but did not reply, so Àdham knew that she was still fearful.

Nevertheless, her behavior both surprised and pleased him.

He had expected her to be frantic if not beside herself with terror. But she had sounded much as Catriona might have after such an incident.

As he helped MacNab and Duff move the bodies together and bury them with rocks, he decided they would depart as soon as they had finished the task.

He wanted to get home, so that he could be sure that the increasingly intriguing lass he had married would be safe and he could begin the task of tracking down the bastards who had dared try to harm her. It occurred to him then that the task Jamie had given him might aid him in that endeavor.

It was good that Fiona would be with Fin and Catriona then, too, because Cat would show her how to go on and look after her when he had to be away.

He would make sure himself, though, that his sometimes too-daring wife understood that she was to enjoy no more solitary moonlight rambles.

CHAPTER 15

─────◆◆◆─────

Fiona's first view of Castle Finlagh was of a massive, grim-looking, four-story, gray stone tower atop a tall grassy knoll halfway down the steep slope below them. They had just crested a dip between two higher peaks north and south of them, and the landscape beyond spread for miles. Some of it was hilly, much of it forested, with somewhat higher hills to the south.

The knoll below them, its sides splashed with heather and bramble, jutted up from the contour of the forested hillside. It sat in a vee between what appeared to be two tumbling burns. The castle clearly dominated the landscape beyond it.

From the pass, some distance south of them now, Àdham had sent Duff, Rory, and MacNab on ahead with their horses, the garrons, and gear, so that he could show Fiona his favorite view of Finlagh.

Stroking the cat cradled in her arms and thinking that Castle Finlagh looked smaller than expected, she said, "It seems gey isolated here. But that tower looks much like our Border peel towers. Likely, it would be harder to approach, though, unless your enemy came, as we do, from above."

"Are Border castles so isolated, lass? Methinks that Border lords, like Highland lords, have tenants and other dependents living nearby."

"Aye, sure, but I have seen no tenants' homes here."

"Most of our dependents live in the forests, in cottages."

"Our forests are royal, controlled for his grace by rangers," she said. "Scott of Buccleuch, whom you met at our wedding feast, is Ranger of Ettrick Forest."

"Aye, well, our forests are clan properties, and clansmen live in them, including most of our servants. So, Finlagh is not isolated. It may look so from here, because it fills that knoll, but there is a path. The vale beyond," he added, "is Strathnairn, where the river Nairn flows. It is also Clan Chattan land, full of Mackintoshes and other member clansmen—Davidsons, MacGillivrays, and such. The hills to our right obscure our view, or you would also see the town of Nairn."

"Where is the castle entrance?"

"Overlooking Strathnairn," he said. "A hornwork protects it, and a portcullis. When we go onto the ramparts, the view will give you a more exact image of where we are. Come along now, and I'll show you," he added, urging her on down the hill.

As they approached the castle, they met a wide, deep ditch cut vertically into the slope of the knoll below the castle's base, forming an outer rampart, but soon they reached a pathway wending its way up around the knoll to the castle.

Finlagh was rectangular, its end walls half the length of its longer ones. The stonework looked solid, but Fiona's experience with the much larger fortresses at Edinburgh and Stirling made Finlagh look undersized and much less formidable.

Setting the now-wriggling cat down, knowing it would not let her get far before coming in search of her, Fiona said, "Is the castle impregnable?"

"As impregnable as a private castle can be," he said, giving her a reassuring hug. "As you'll see, the hornwork juts nearly to the cliff in front, so guards on the bastions can defend against any attackers approaching from north, south, or west."

"You must keep guards on the ramparts all the time then, too, aye?"

"Aye, sure," Àdham said. "You can see them, so they can see us here. Our position is strategically sound, lass. Fin believes an ancient fort once stood here."

"But what if someone besieges you? Is there a siege tunnel?"

He shook his head in the same way that her brothers did when she questioned such confident declarations of theirs. But he was smiling. "You will be safe here, Fiona. However, we do have enemies, as you have seen."

"The Comyns," she said, nodding. "If they *were* our attackers at Lochindorb, would they be the same ones who stole Raitt Castle? Lady Marsi said some Comyns did that. Rory said so, too."

"*If* our attackers were Comyns, then Comyn of Raitt would be responsible, although Malcolm said that Raitt was in St. John's Town when we left."

"You never lived at Raitt, though, did you?"

"Nae, I was but a bairn then and my two youngest cousins not yet born. But here we are," he added, waving at someone in the bastion tower window above the path.

The tall iron gates opened wide as they approached, and a pretty woman in her forties with long, thick, tawny hair and laughing eyes hurried across the small bailey and through the gateway to meet them.

"That is Catriona," Àdham said as he waved. "The big dark-haired fellow strolling in her wake is my uncle Fin."

"Faith, Àdham, who is this that you've brought to us?" Lady Catriona demanded in Scots with a wide, hopeful smile that warmed Fiona's heart. To her surprise, her ladyship spoke Scots as fluently as Àdham did, without the heavy, nearly unintelligible accent that she'd heard from MacNab and other Highlanders.

Àdham eyed his aunt narrowly. "Do you expect me to believe that you have not already heard all there is to know about us?" he demanded. "Especially when you greet me in Scots instead of the Gaelic?"

"Mind your tongue, lad," Fin said as they met, clapping him hard enough on the back to make him take a step to balance himself.

Catriona grinned. "We did hear a rumor or two about a wedding," she admitted. "We told each other it was blethers. But, since it clearly was not, prithee introduce your lady to us."

"Aye, Àdham, tell us about this lovely lass who stands so calmly whilst your aunt roasts you," Fin said. "Methinks I like her already."

"Where are the twins?" Àdham asked. "I'd liefer tell this tale only once."

Catriona gestured grandly toward the entrance, where he saw his twin cousins standing at the top of the timber stairway, waving.

"We'll go to meet them," Catriona said. "What have you done with Sirius?"

Àdham whistled for the dog, and when Sirius loped up the pathway with Donsie scurrying erratically after him, Catriona laughed.

"Where did he find the wee cat?" she asked, still chuckling.

"Fiona will tell you about that later," he said.

"So her name is Fiona, is it?" Catriona said, raising her eyebrows but casting another warm smile at Fiona.

"Aye, madam," Fiona said, smiling back.

"Her father is Ormiston of Ormiston, one of Jamie's Lothian lairds," Àdham said. "But I am nigh to starving, and it must be nearly time to eat. I trust you had warning enough to expect us for the midday meal."

"Even had we not, you ken fine that your aunt would not starve you," Fin said. "But, since you seem determined to ignore your manners, I shall introduce myself to your lady. Prithee, call me Fin, Lady Fiona."

"She is Lady MacFinlagh, if you please, sir," Àdham said.

"But you must call me Fiona, all of you," Fiona said, looking from Fin to Catriona and then including the twins, who were near enough now to hear her.

Smiling, Fin said, "I trust that, if you married her ladyship in town, you did so properly in a kirk, even if it was without your closest kinsmen to bear witness."

"Are you vexed, sir?" Àdham asked. Noting the sudden worried frown on Fiona's face, he added, "I'm teasing him, lass. You may trust me when I tell you that when Uncle Fin *is* angry, one does not have to *ask* if he is."

Her gaze still fixed on Fiona, Catriona said, "We must soon celebrate your marriage, so that you can meet everyone. Did you marry in your hair, Fiona?"

Àdham cocked his head. "How could she have married without it?"

Fiona was already nodding. She grinned at him and said, "It means that I wore my hair loose and unveiled, which I did. Joanna said it would please you."

"It did," he said, holding her gaze.

"Let me make our twins known to you, my dear," Catriona said. "The one striding ahead with the wee scar on her forehead and her mouth open to talk is our Katy. The one in the lovely blue dress that she made herself is our gentle Clydia."

Fiona looked from one wheaten-blond twin to the other. Had the day not still been sunny, she doubted that she would have noticed Katy's scar, but other than the scar and their clothing, she saw no way to tell them apart, especially as each wore her hair in thick plaits reaching almost to her waist.

With a smile that matched Catriona's, Katy exclaimed in equally fluent Scots as she neared them, "Why, how beautiful you are! Art sure, though, that you were wise to marry our homely Àdham? Had you taken a handsomer man, the two of you might have produced exceedingly beautiful bairns."

Àdham frowned, and Fin said quietly, "Enough, Katy."

Fiona saw that Fin's darkly tanned skin made the scar on the left side of *his* forehead more noticeable than Katy's. But his deep-set eyes drew more of her attention. Under thick, black lashes, their irises were an unusually clear gray.

Glancing back at the twins, she saw that each had inherited those eyes.

Katy, still smiling, silenced but undaunted, eyed Fiona critically.

Amused, Fiona said, "Do you often tease Sir Àdham so? I vow I should hesitate to do so, myself."

"Then I can deduce two things about you straightaway," Katy said. "You have already tasted his temper, and you failed to stand up to him. You will soon learn that, in our family, a woman who bends too easily will soon be a sad woman."

"I know one young woman who will hold her tongue now or forgo her dinner," Fin said. "That is no way to talk to a guest."

"But Fiona is hardly a guest, sir," Katy said, twinkling at him. "She is now my good-sister, is she not? And, since she is," she added without awaiting a reply, "is it not my duty to help her feel at home here?"

Fin said, "Look here . . ."

"Sister?" Fiona said at the same time, looking from Katy to Àdham. When Fin fell silent, she added, "I thought you said you were cousins, Àdham."

"I did," Àdham said, giving Katy a look of amused exasperation.

Returning his gaze steadily, Katy said, "Àdham has been more of a brother to me and Clydia than our own brothers have been. But mayhap you mean to live elsewhere and have come here now only to meet us and ride on. I do hope that is not so, because I think that we three *sisters* could become fast friends."

Fiona glanced again at Àdham, who seemed content to leave Katy to her. "I think Àdham means to stay for a time, at least," she said. "And I'd like to have two new sisters." Smiling at Clydia, who smiled shyly back, she added, "My own sister married before I was born, so I have known her only as one more adult in my family who orders me about."

"You three can talk whilst we eat," Catriona said. "Àdham, you'll share your chamber with Fiona, and I expect you both want to tidy yourselves before we dine. But don't dally. We want to hear more about your wedding and your journey."

"Much more," Fin said, giving Àdham a direct look.

Fiona noted that, as Àdham began to lead her away, Fin put a light hand on Katy's shoulder to keep her from following. Clydia stopped with her.

Catriona caught up with Àdham and Fiona. "Fiona, I did hear that you have no woman of your own with you. Is that right?"

"Aye, madam, it is. But I can look after myself."

"Nevertheless, my own Ailvie will attend you today, and mayhap her daughter Bridgett will suit you as an attire woman."

"Thank you, madam," Fiona said with true gratitude. She missed Leah Nisbet more than she had thought she would. In truth, she missed Leah's chatter almost as much as her skills as an attire woman.

"This way, lass," Àdham said, breaking into her reverie. "Our room lies near the top of the tower. You can see almost as far from there as from the ramparts."

"And you may come with me, Sirius," Catriona said to the dog, which had followed them inside. "Bring your new friend and introduce her to the others."

"Others?" Fiona said to Àdham as he followed her up the stairs. "Do you have many cats?"

"Nae," he replied with a chuckle. "But Catriona raises wolf dogs. We have just two now, Eos and Argus, who are likely lying by the hall fire. They are the 'others' to whom Sirius is to introduce your cat."

"I have never seen a wolf dog. They won't harm her, will they?"

"Eos and Argus are gentle creatures unless something or someone threatens one of us," Àdham replied, understanding her concern. "But, even if Donsie were to take it into her head to attack me again, I doubt that either dog would lift a paw."

He had not expected her to show fear of the dogs, but if she had never seen a wolf dog, he supposed the very name might make her wary. He and Cat would soon teach her how to manage them, though. What was more important to him was that Fiona seemed to like the twins and they liked her.

"Is Fin angry with Katy?" she asked quietly, as if her thoughts echoed his.

"We'll know the answer to that if she joins us for our midday dinner. Or if she does not," he added lightly, feeling little sympathy for Katy if Fin *was* scolding her. "That lassie too often lets her tongue run away with her good sense."

"I don't want her to be in trouble on my account," Fiona replied.

"Fin did not send Clydia away," Àdham pointed out. "So I expect that Katy will dine with us, but she does need to learn to think before she speaks. She often treads a narrow line between what he will accept and what he will not."

"I like her spirit," Fiona said. "I think she was right, too, that we will become friends. Is Clydia always so quiet?"

"They are usually together, and Katy has always talked more than enough for two. But if you want to learn about plants, trees, flowers, or forest creatures, or what will aid you if you fall ill or injure yourself, Clydia is the one to ask. Our room lies off the next landing," he added, gesturing upward.

A glimmer of hope stirred in Fiona's mind. He did not sound as if he meant to confine her within Castle Finlagh's walls, and she found herself more eager to explore the area around them than she had expected. She nearly asked if it would be safe for her to roam about. But she held her tongue when he reached the landing and opened the door to his chamber for her.

His bed was larger than hers at home and much larger than the narrow cot she'd had at Blackfriars. Both the bed and the chamber were typically masculine, though, tidy and Spartan. Their two sumpter baskets looked out of place.

Paying the baskets no heed, Àdham shut the door and went to the washstand.

Watching him pour water from the ewer to the basin, Fiona decided that rather than ask if she could do something that he might forbid, she would discuss her question first with Katy and Clydia.

Catriona's Ailvie, a neatly garbed, blue-eyed woman several years younger than her mistress, rapped on the door moments later. With her help, Fiona hurried through her ablutions. Then, leaving Ailvie to see to her unpacking, she followed Àdham downstairs to join the others in the great hall.

Scarcely noting two trestle tables flanked with people in the main portion of the high-ceilinged chamber, Fiona halted at the sight of the two enormous dogs lying with Sirius near a rather smoky hearth fire. Both were lean with rough, dark blue-gray coats, and they were the largest dogs she had ever seen, dwarfing Sirius.

The two rose and stretched, watching her as they did, with their large heads slightly cocked and their ears rising. The taller and larger one—likely Argus, the male—measured a yard at least from the floor to his withers. Eos was a bit smaller.

Feeling Àdham's hand on her shoulder, urging her forward, she looked up at him. "You did not tell me what giants they are. Art sure they are friendly?"

"I'm sure," he said, raising his free hand, palm outward toward the dogs.

They sat then, sweeping ashes off the hearth with their long, wagging tails.

Looking beyond the trestles to the high table on its dais, Fiona saw Lady Catriona watching them. As Àdham had predicted, Clydia and Katy were there, too, and Fiona saw that they had left a place between Katy and Lady Catriona for her.

Catching and holding her gaze, Catriona smiled and motioned her forward. To Fiona's relief, the dogs lay back down again.

When Àdham offered her his right forearm, she raised her chin, squared her shoulders, and walked confidently with him to her place on the dais, offering a smile to anyone who met her gaze along the way.

When Àdham had taken his place beside Fin, Fin said the grace-before-meat and signed to a pair of gillies to begin serving as everyone took their seats.

"I hope you don't fear dogs," Lady Catriona murmured to Fiona.

"Oh, no, madam. I had simply never seen such large ones before."

"They are most biddable," Catriona assured her. "If you like, we can take them into the woods this afternoon. I often walk outside the wall after our midday meal, and the twins like to go with me. However, Katy has chores to do, and Clydia will stay to help her unless you would like Clydia to go with us."

"I would like to know her better," Fiona said, inhaling the welcome aroma of roast lamb as a gillie paused behind her with a platter. "But, prithee, do not make her come if she would liefer stay with her sister. Mayhap, if I help them both, we all might go together, unless Àdham has other plans for me."

"Fin wants to hear all the news from Perth," Lady Catriona said, nodding to the gillie to serve her some lamb and remaining silent while he served Fiona. When he turned to serve Katy, she added quietly, "Katy needs no help with her chores, so I'll invite Clydia to come with us. We'll show you a few of our favorite places. The twins will show you others, too, so Clydia will want to see what you see. We'll take the dogs, too, so you can become acquainted with them and they with you."

Wide-eyed, Fiona said, "Could someone not shoot them from the hillside?"

"We have watchers on the hills, and people in our woods, so even an archer as skilled as Ivor or Àdham would have difficulty shooting anything through such foliage without someone catching sight of him. Moreover, the dogs would likely become aware of any intruder before the intruder would see the dogs."

Somewhat reassured, Fiona said, "I would ask you something else, madam, but I am unaccustomed to having a husband, so mayhap I should ask Àdham first."

Lady Catriona's hazel-gold eyes twinkled, and she leaned close to murmur, "Ask me anything you like, my dearling. But, prithee, stop calling me 'madam' and address me as Catriona or Cat. Nor need you fear that I'd tell Àdham aught that you say to me. If it is something that you *should* discuss with him first, I will say so."

Relaxing, Fiona said, "I have always been able to take time to myself, ma— That is," she added hastily, lowering her voice, "I enjoy occasional solitude, and I have rarely lived where I could not take long walks alone. But I do not know the Highlands, and much of what I have heard has seemed fearsome to me. Also, I expect that Àdham has already told Sir Fin that someone attacked us . . ."

"Aye, near Lochindorb," Catriona said. "Duff and Rory told him."

"Then you likely know all about it," Fiona said. "What I want to know is if you think it is too dangerous for me to go outside the wall."

Catriona tore a piece of meat into strips and dipped one strip into a nearby sauce bowl before she said, "Few people hereabouts stay indoors or within walls all day unless imminent conflict or a storm threatens. Most of our people live outside the wall, and I often walk alone to visit tenants or to amuse myself. I have done so since I was a child at Rothiemurchus, when I would row a boat across the loch and walk into the hills. Àdham *may* insist that you take someone with you until you know your way about, and I don't recommend defying him. He *is* your husband."

"I don't want to defy him. I just like to walk alone sometimes. If I had always to have someone with me, I would feel . . ."

"Caged here?" Catriona suggested when Fiona paused.

"Aye, although I do not want to be rude."

"'Tis how I would feel. However, I may have a solution to suggest to him if he is reluctant to let you go alone."

"What is it?"

"Take Eos and Argus," Catriona said. "I will teach you how to make them mind you. And, with them to guard you, you'll have no need to be fearsome."

Feeling a sudden, inexplicable urge to cry, Fiona caught her lower lip between her teeth and forced herself to inhale deeply and let the breath out slowly. Then, and only then, did she say with what she thought was commendable calm, "Thank you, Catriona. I would like that. I also like to swim," she added wistfully.

"So do I," Catriona replied with a grin. "I grew up swimming in Loch an Eilein, and I confess that I miss being able to walk outside our gate and straight into the water. We had the boats and a raft that we could paddle on the loch."

"I was in one of those boats. Have you any place here to swim?"

"Aye, sure we do," Catriona replied. "You must ask Àdham to take you to the pool that Fin created for us in the southernmost of our two burns.

"We must also teach you to speak the Gaelic," she added. "I had to learn Scots, so I know what a trial learning another tongue can be. But when I realized that Fin and my brother Ivor could keep secrets from me by speaking Scots together, I can tell you, I soon set my mind to learning to speak it, too."

"I do think Àdham may be keeping secrets from me," Fiona murmured.

"Tell me about your visit to Perth now and how you came so hastily to marry," Fin said quietly enough that his words would not carry beyond Àdham.

"I hope our so-hasty wedding truly has not irked you, sir."

"I know *you*, lad, and I'll wager that the marriage was not your idea or her ladyship's. So, tell me about it. Then, you can tell me of anything else I missed by staying here at Finlagh, including how you were attacked and Duff was injured."

After Àdham briefly described events leading to their wedding and what had happened near Lochindorb, Fin said, "I agree that they were likely Comyns, unless you made new enemies in Perth."

"I don't think I did," Àdham said. "But Malcolm said that Comyn of Raitt was there for the Parliament. Mayhap, he sent men after us."

"Who else attended Jamie's Parliament?"

Doing his best to relay what little he had learned about the sessions, Àdham made a glib reference to Sir Robert Graham.

"How fares your uncle?" Fin asked mildly.

"He supports Atholl at every turn and opposes his grace." Adham briefly explained what he'd learned during their overnight stay at Blair Castle.

"Jamie knows Graham is your uncle, aye?"

"Aye, for he said as much to me," Àdham said. He paused then as awareness that Fiona still did not know of that kinship loomed in his mind like a dark cloud.

As if sensing his line of thought, Fin said, "Have you described your kinships to Clan Cameron, Robert Graham, and the more distant one he provides to Atholl's lady wife to your own lady?"

Assuring himself that Fiona still chatted with Cat, Àdham said, "She knows that Ewan is my father, but I have not yet told her that Robert is my uncle."

"Tell her, lad. That is the exact sort of detail that, when revealed by someone other than the one involved, to a person experienced with the royal court, can turn an ordinary kinship—even one that is weak at best—into a possible conspiracy."

Adham nodded. "I'll see to it, sir."

"Do you mean to make your home here?" Fin asked. "You are welcome to do so for as long as you like, of course."

"I'd prefer a home of our own, but we'll stay here for now. James asked me to use my kinship with both confederations to learn who is prepared *now* to answer a royal call to arms and who will more likely support Alexander."

"Sakes, he must know that few minds have changed since Lochaber, unless Ewan or Cameron of Lochiel has changed his."

"Do you think my father could change *my* mind or would change his own? He is your brother, after all."

Fin met his gaze, saying calmly, "Nae, for if Ewan even thought of switching sides again, he'd warn us both. But, kinship or none, you do *not* want to go poking about west of the Great Glen, where Alexander's support is strong and will stay so."

"I agree," Àdham said. "Sir Robert himself told me that Alexander's cousin, Donal Balloch of Dunyvaig, is raising an army to take back what James calls 'every stick and stone on the mainland' that Alexander claims as his own."

"I've heard such rumors, too. But I doubt young Balloch can seize any land this side of Glen Mòr. After all, Mar defeated Alexander himself at Lochaber."

Àdham shook his head. "Despite Balloch's youth, I ken fine that you have also heard what a skilled tactician and warrior he is. Moreover, he has likely exchanged messages with Alexander at Tantallon, and Malcolm told me that men have even tried to free him. We—that is, Malcolm—sent word to his grace from Blair, warning him that they may be plotting another such attempt."

"Aye, your lady's account of what she overheard at Blair Castle may suggest that," Fin said, nodding. "You do realize that, if Jamie knows you are kin to Sir Robert and thus indirectly related to the nefarious Atholl as well, his faith in you must be strong."

"I don't mean to let him down, sir. I just hope he knows what he's doing."

"I, too, lad," Fin said dryly. "I met him when he was nae more than a bairn but have not clapped eyes on him since. At the time, he was wise beyond his years, and bold, albeit a mite too imperious and outspoken for his own safety. We must hope that the years and his trials have blessed him with more wisdom."

Àdham kept his less certain opinion of his grace's wisdom to himself.

CHAPTER 16

Aware that she had neglected Katy while she chatted with Catriona, Fiona turned to the girl with a smile and said, "Forgive me if I seemed to ignore you. Are you sure you cannot finish your chores soon enough to walk with us after we eat?"

Katy grimaced but quickly altered the expression to a rueful smile. "I ought not to have extra chores at all. But 'tis mine own fault, and 'twas kind of Mam not to tell you the whole. I am to forgo your companionship this afternoon because I spoke thoughtlessly earlier and must mind my tongue more carefully hereafter."

Fiona said sympathetically, "I do understand. My older sister brings out the worst in me, and I often found myself in just such a coil as a result. My father also takes umbrage at"—she searched for the right words—"speaking without due forethought. So do my brothers," she added with a sigh.

"You are cursed with brothers, too?"

"I am," Fiona said. "I have three of them, all years older than I am. Each one thinks he has every right to order my life even when Father is at hand."

"Sakes, we have just two elder brothers. We see them only three or four times a year, though, so they do not plague us as much as when we were small."

"When you were twin nuisances plaguing *them* dreadfully," Catriona said, speaking across Fiona. "Finish your meal now, dearling, and let Fiona eat hers."

"Aye, sure, Mam." With a wink for Fiona, she returned to her trencher.

Clearly, Fiona thought, although Katy fit Davy's notion of "saucy," her manners were as refined as Fiona's. Several noble-women she had known with the Queen's court displayed less assurance and far less poise than Katy did.

Katy's father, Fin of the Battles, was likewise different from what Fiona had expected. He was stern, but he was no barbar-ian. She was sure that she would like them all. She just wished she could feel as confident about what lay beyond Finlagh's walls.

An hour later, the lush green woods on the southwest slope below Castle Finlagh were alive with birdsong, and leaves whispered as Fiona, Catriona, and Clydia passed by. Ahead, the two wolf dogs ranged back and forth, sniffing the air and ground but ignoring squirrels and other beasts, moving silently through the shrubbery.

"They're so big," Fiona said quietly, loving the serenity of the woods but unable to resist satisfying her curiosity. "How did you learn to control them, madam?"

"Just Catriona or Cat, love," Catriona reminded her.

"Yes, ma— Faith, I am so accustomed to calling women older than myself 'madam' that it falls off my tongue despite your wishes!"

"We Highlanders are less formal," Catriona replied. "Lowland women, like English and French ones, are more submissive, I believe."

Fiona chuckled. "*Some* Lowland women may be, but 'tis rare to hear of such. My home is across a river from the true 'Borders.' But our roots there lie deep, and few would ever call Border women submissive. We have minds of our own."

Clydia's lips twitched. "But whilst serving in her grace's court, certes . . ."

"Aye, sure," Fiona said, "maids of honor must oft *behave* sub-missively. But about the dogs, Catriona . . ."

Smiling, Catriona said, "I'll teach you signs that Eos and Argus obey, and you'll learn more by spending time with them. Today, we'll visit some of our people nearby, to introduce you and to invite them to Finlagh for a *cèilidh*."

"What is a kaylee?" Fiona asked, hoping she was saying it correctly.

"It is a grand social gathering to help celebrate your wedding. And we must do it before Àdham has to leave again. But, as we go, watch how the dogs behave."

"We have sleuth hounds at home to hunt reivers who steal live-stock," Fiona said moments later. "Our dogs sniff only the ground, but yours sniff everything."

"Aye, they do, but Eos and Argus can sense lurking danger, too, and warn you of it," Catriona told her. "When they do, you must heed them." With a laugh, she added, "My first wolf dog intro-duced me so to Fin."

"Mercy, how could a dog do that?" Fiona asked.

"I dinna ken how, but he did," Catriona said. "'Tis a tale for another time, though. For the nonce, can you whistle?"

"Aye, sure," Fiona said, remembering how she had boasted of her ability to Àdham the night they met.

"Try doing it like this," Catriona said. She gave two sharp whis-tles, one high, the other lower pitched, similar to a bird's chirps.

Both dogs stopped where they were and looked over their shoulders at her.

Fiona watched in wonder as Catriona showed her other things the dogs could do simply by obeying short whistles, clicks, and silent hand and arm gestures.

"Why do you not speak your commands?" Fiona asked.

Clydia gave a gentle shake of her head.

Catriona said, "Our woods are safe enough if we stay west of our hills. But strangers going to Nairn or Inverness do sometimes pass through. So a woman walking alone is wise to avoid drawing attention to herself. The dogs will alert you when they sense others approaching. They'll also let you know if those who approach be friendly or not."

"Sakes, how can they tell the difference?"

Clydia said, "They know a person or they don't and they distrust strangers, just as we do. Katy and I usually walk together, but Mam said that you'd often want to walk alone, as she does. So you must heed what the dogs tell you, and never fear that you might fail to recognize such a warning. They will see that you do not."

"Look yonder, Fiona," Catriona said, pointing. "My Ailvie's mam's cottage sits in that clearing, so we'll visit her first. As auld Rosel is also Bridgett's granny, you may meet Bridgett there, so you can decide if she'll suit you as a maidservant."

Clydia said, "Granny Rosel kens much about herbs, and people say that she has experienced the Second Sight."

"I have heard of the Sight," Fiona said. "But to see something happening elsewhere or in the future sounds most unlikely to me."

"Granny Rosel will explain it to you," Clydia said.

Fiona could see the cottage now, framed by a thatched roof, the edges of which nearly touched the ground. Its upper front wall was wattle and turf, much like Border cottages, with a base of dry stonework. The wood door stood ajar. As they drew nearer, she saw that the cottage front boasted one narrow window.

Catriona called out a few words in Gaelic, heard a reply, and they went in.

The light came mostly from the open door and the glow of embers in a central fire ring. The sole occupant, a little gray-haired woman, greeted them in the Gaelic with visible and voluble delight. Although Fiona could not understand a word she said, Catriona and Clydia translated their exchange of greetings.

They stayed with Granny Rosel only long enough for Fiona to learn that, unlike rumors she had heard of the mysterious Sight, the rare incidents of it in the Highlands had occurred only while extreme violence such as a great battle was taking place a good distance away. Some women, Granny said, had been able to describe, at the time, exactly how and when a loved one died. But none had ever claimed to see into the future.

"How does she know that no one has?" Fiona asked as they were walking away.

Catriona said gently, "Granny Rosel saw her husband die at Harlaw, so it is a subject in which she has taken much interest."

By the time they returned to the castle, Fiona had met curvaceous, dark-haired Bridgett, welcomed as her maidservant, and had met at least a dozen other such friendly tenants. She had also grown accustomed to the giant wolf dogs.

Surely, she thought, Argus and Eos would intimidate any straying enemy.

Àdham and Fin had likewise taken their conversation outside.

As they headed uphill along one of the streams providing water for the castle, Fin said, "What did you think of his grace the King?"

"I think he creates problems for himself by pitting clergymen and nobles against each other, and ignores their ire in pursuit of his own goals."

"Kings behave so by nature," Fin said. "Sakes, most men of power will seek more of it. They ignore all who are powerless to stop them and act as they please whenever they can. You saw as much for yourself before you met James, aye?"

"Aye, but the men against whom his grace pits himself are *not* powerless."

"Art thinking of anyone in particular?"

"Atholl," Àdham replied flatly. "He would not be the first of his grace's uncles to think he should rule Scotland, and he does have supporters."

"So does Jamie," Fin pointed out. "And Jamie, whatever else he may have grown to be, is stout of heart and not a conniving snake like Atholl."

They fell silent then, and Àdham began to relax, feeling a surge of pleasure when the woods began to come alive again. He was home. He hoped he might stay long enough to help Fiona feel as much at home at Finlagh as he did.

When the castle hove into view again and Fin turned toward it, Àdham said, "I mean to walk farther, sir. 'Tis a fine day, and—" He stopped, because Fin was grinning. "What?"

"I'm thinking you heard that your beautiful wife meant to walk out with Cat and Clydia and hope to meet her or you mean to climb to the crag above Raitt to see what you can see. I'm hoping it is Fiona, lad. She is a good match for you."

Àdham smiled but decided not to admit that he *had* thought of climbing to the northern crag in the upthrust of hills between Finlagh and Raitt to see if there was activity at Raitt. But Fin's mentioning Fiona had stirred his body's interest, so he reminded himself that he had barely spoken to Cat or Clydia since his return.

"Remember to tell your lass about Robert Graham," Fin added gently.

Drawing a deep breath to cool his body's other notions, Àdham nodded.

The woodland music soon soothed him again, and he quickened his pace. His uncle was right, and since he had to talk to Fiona, it would be wise to do so at once.

When the women came into view at last, his gaze caught hers.

She smiled, warming him through again. He was reluctant to initiate such a conversation with others listening, but having heard her ask Cat earlier if Finlagh offered a place to swim, he knew exactly how they could find some privacy.

"Where are we going?" Fiona asked when Àdham, having informed Catriona and Clydia that he wanted time alone with her, turned back toward the castle.

"I have something that I must tell you," he said. "But, first, I want to show you the pool that Fin created."

"So, you heard us talking about swimming. But if you have something to say to me, sir, say it now and be done. Faith, if I have done aught to displease you—"

"Nae, lass, nae," he interjected swiftly. Then he hesitated, and had he not been so tall and broad, he would have looked like a bairn caught in mischief. The thought nearly made her smile, but she said, "What is it, Àdham? Just tell me."

"I have not been as forthright as I should have been," he replied bluntly.

"About what?" she asked, thinking instantly of Caithness and Atholl.

Instead, he said, "I fear that your 'eloquent scoundrel' is mine uncle."

Frowning, certain that she had misunderstood, she said, "Sir Robert Graham?" When he nodded, she put two fingers to her lips to avoid declaring her loathing for the man, and said instead, "So that is why you were talking to him on the Inch that day. Why did you not say so at once when I asked if you knew him?"

"I scarcely *know* him. He is my late mother's brother," Àdham said, guiding her up the steep incline with a hand to her waist. "He visited us at Tor Castle once or twice when I was small and again after Mam died. He took no interest in me then. But, learning that I was in St. John's Town, he sent for me and tried to persuade me to support Alexander and others who oppose his grace—and to convince my father to do likewise. I refused."

"Is that all you wanted to tell me?"

"Aye, sure. What else would there be? I have no liking for the man."

"Perhaps not, but that night at Blair, I heard Atholl call Caithness your cousin. I've been trying since then to think how to ask you about that. It never seemed the right time until now."

When he did not reply at once, she added softly, "I doubt that you would betray James, Àdham. But might not others who learn of such connections think such a thing? Come to that, why did you not admit your kinship to Caithness at once when you introduced him to me?"

Resisting an urge to grind his teeth but aware that, under the circumstances, her concern was reasonable, Àdham said with forced calm, "Because the connection is too slight for me to claim Alan as a cousin. Do not forget who his father is, lass. I am *not* a member of the royal family."

"But the lady Elizabeth Graham of your mother's family is the Earl of Atholl's wife. Does that not make you cousin to Caithness?"

"Lass, she is Atholl's second wife. His *first* was Alan's mother, so Alan and I have no blood kinship. He did laughingly name me 'cousin' when first *we* met, so if Atholl called me so that night, he was being derisive. Lady Elizabeth is my grandaunt, but she has no blood kinship to Caithness, so neither do I."

She regarded him silently for a long minute. Then, with a sigh, she said, "You should have told me about Robert Graham when I asked you."

"Aye," he agreed. "I should have." He waited, wondering if she had more surprises in store for him or expected a full apology.

Then they topped the slight rise beside Fin's weir, and he saw her smile as she gazed at the expanse of water beyond. "Is that Fin's pool?" she asked.

"It is," he said, relieved. "Would you like to swim?"

She hunkered down to test the water. "It may be colder than the Tay, but I think it is warm enough. Is it safe to do so without my shift?"

"People do wander about," he said. As he quickly folded his plaid and laid it atop one shrub, then tugged off his tunic and draped it over another, he added, "Also, we have men near the hilltops, watching for stray Comyns who might wander this way, so you might want to keep your smock on for now. But I'll help you doff your kirtle," he added, grinning as he reached to untie her laces.

Fiona welcomed his touch and marveled at his splendid body while he helped her find the easiest path into the water. As she submerged, using her hands to keep her full-skirted shift from rising to float on the surface as she sank, she looked at Àdham and was delighted to see him watching her closely.

Soon gathering knowledge of the pond's contours, she submerged and began to swim away from him. When he grabbed an ankle and tugged her back toward him, she reached out to him and let him pull her upright and into his arms. Moments later, her shift was gone, cast to the shore.

Laughing, she said, "Fiend, you're the one who said to keep it on!"

"I was recalling your shyness," he said, grinning back as he began to stroke her body from her shoulders to her hips and back to linger at her breasts. "As long as any lad who sees you is not daft enough to tell the world that he has, I'll feel only my pride and his envy at seeing what a treasure I have in you. Now, lass, kiss me."

She did, and matters progressed from playfulness in the water to passion ashore that might well have let such a lad see more of them both than Àdham had intended.

By then, though, thoroughly sated, Fiona did not much care if he had.

Having thoroughly enjoyed himself that afternoon, Àdham expected Fiona would reject other such activity for a day or so. To his surprise and delight, though, when he suggested retiring soon after supper, her reply was just a seductive smile.

"You won't need anyone to aid you tonight," he murmured against her right ear. "I want to do that, myself."

When she was naked, he swept her up and carried her to the bed. Eager for her, he undressed himself in record time and got in beside her, and she snuggled just as eagerly into his arms. Leaving the candle alight until it guttered on its stand, they explored each other's bodies thoroughly, and she enchanted him again with her passion. Now that his conscience was clear again, he looked forward to learning as much as he could about his lady wife.

However, he had no sooner left their bed the next morning than MacNàb informed him that Lady Catriona wanted to discuss the intended *cèilidh* with him, and he recalled that, upon their arrival, Cat had said that she planned to celebrate.

She would likely have to put it off for a time, though, since he intended to begin seeking the information James had requested as soon as possible.

But when he said as much to Cat, she said, "Blethers. I have told everyone to come for a *cèilidh* tomorrow night and to bring food and an instrument or a tale with which to entertain the company, just as we always do on such occasions. So, you will miss only a day's travel, my laddie. Even the King—nae, his grace especially, since he treasures his own lady wife as he does—would not expect you to abandon your bride on our doorstep the minute you return home."

"Nae one would accuse me of doing any such thing," Àdham protested.

"Aye, someone would, because I will accuse you, myself," she said flatly. "You may do all that you must do to plan your route and decide what you need to take with you and who else must go. Talk to Fin about that. But you *will* stay for your *cèilidh* if you want your handsome head to remain on your thick neck."

"Aye, sure, my lady," Àdham said, kissing her cheek. "But if aught delays this *cèilidh* or if Ivor comes for me—"

"Then my so-esteemed brother can either sing a song whilst Fiona plays her lute for him or strum one on his bowstring for someone else to sing," she retorted.

Knowing when he had lost a battle, Àdham grinned cheekily at her and went to find Fin, who likewise had no sympathy to offer him. "You would be wise to decide what entertainment you will provide for this celebration, my lad."

So Àdham, who secretly enjoyed singing, sought out his lady wife and explained that guests and hosts alike at a Highland *cèilidh* had to aid in the entertainment. "Cat said you play the lute, and I do recall that you brought one with you. So, mayhap you know a song that we can sing together. You need not fret if your singing does not match your skill on the lute," he added hastily when she looked stunned. "Everyone who knows the song will sing with us."

Fiona had no objection to playing her lute to aid the entertainment, and finding a song that they both knew proved easier than expected. But the following night, her jaw dropped in amazement at how large a party Catriona had managed to gather in so little time. "How can we possibly have enough food to feed them?" she asked.

"Sakes, Fiona," her hostess replied with a laugh. "Hereabouts, a man can be at home one minute and gone for weeks, even months, the next. All Highland social gatherings include an expectation that one may entertain a few guests or a host of them. 'Tis why everyone takes part, providing both food and entertainment."

The *cèilidh* proved to be a merry one, with pipers piping, fiddlers fiddling, jugglers juggling, whistlers with and without tin whistles, storytellers, poets, ring dances, and dances where men showed off their dexterity with swords or other weapons.

Although many social events that Fiona had experienced were more formal, she was beginning to believe that life in the

Highlands was less different from life in the Borders or even in Lowland towns than she had feared. This was fun!

However, the next morning, when MacNab rapped on their door, she quickly learned that it was not just to wake Àdham but also to inform him in the Gaelic that Sir Ivor had arrived with a retinue of men and desired to see him straightaway.

Recognizing Ivor's name, even in MacNab's Gaelic accents, and guessing the gist of his message from his urgency, she barely waited for the two men to leave before scrambling out of bed. Pulling on her kirtle over her shift, she hurried after them barefoot. When MacNab went on downstairs, she followed Àdham into the great hall, where they found Sir Ivor Mackintosh impatiently awaiting him.

Pausing at the threshold, Fiona waited to see if either man would try to send her away. But Ivor smiled when he saw her and said in Scots, "I'm for Lochindorb, Àdham. I want you to go with me, so you can tell Mar's people about that attack on you and see if they ken who it may have been. We can discuss chiefs or chieftains we think may be less willing to support his grace, too. Those are the ones with whom you'll need to talk privily *and* persuasively."

"I'll want to ask them if they've heard aught from Mar about Donal Balloch's progress, too," Àdham said.

"How long must you be away?" Fiona asked them.

"Only a night or two for Àdham, as it's just twenty miles," Ivor said. Turning back to Àdham, he added, "I'll head east from Lochindorb. I need the same information that James does from our chiefs in the Confederation."

"Member clans east of us are all loyal to James, are they not?"

"Aye, but as war leader, I need to know who is ready to *fight* at once if we need them. If Balloch means to win the north for Alexander, when Jamie does need us, I'll want everyone ready to ride as soon after our signal fires are lit as possible."

"I'll head west from here, then, when I return," Àdham said. "I can learn the same things from Confederation clans between here and Inverness, and along the west side of Glen Mòr. They may also ken more about Balloch's activities."

"Good, then," Ivor said. "How soon can we be away?"

"As soon as I can break my fast."

Following Àdham's departure, Fiona and cheerful, dark-eyed Bridgett spent some of the morning assessing the garments that Fiona had brought with her and the rest of it with the other women, doing much as Fiona had done at Ormiston or as a maid of honor. That morning, Fiona helped Bridgett and Katy take stock of supplies and check linens for damage, while Clydia tended her herbs in the kitchen garden.

That afternoon, Catriona, Fiona, and the twins visited two families who had missed the *cèilidh* to see if either needed aught that they could provide. After supper, until bedtime, they discussed ways that Fiona might simplify her garments.

Àdham returned two days later, as promised, but had time only to couple with his wife and sleep before he left again to talk with clansmen.

The next morning, the women attended to plain stitchery, for no household ever lacked mending to do. But they also began stripping fur, jewels, furbelows, and other such ornamentation from Fiona's court dresses.

Catriona soon arranged for a walk into Nairn, to purchase ribbons and other necessities. Bruce Lochan, the square-built captain of Finlagh's guard, sent an armed escort with them, because they would pass near Raitt Castle land.

"The laird is unreliable about the public road to Nairn," Catriona explained. "He harbors his right to pit and gallows as if he had inherited rather than stolen it."

The seamstress they visited asked if the rumors of possible war scared them.

"Not yet," Cat replied. Other townsfolk asked similar questions.

Fiona bought a trinket or two but longed for her favorite things from home. James and Joanna would remain at Blackfriars for some time longer, though, so it could be weeks before Ormiston returned to Ormiston Mains.

CHAPTER 17

---⚬⚬⚬---

Although Àdham got home as often as he could, for a day or two, July was nearly over before he was home long enough to relax any longer than that. Wanting time alone with Fiona and certain she would welcome it, he took her near the top of the shorter, southeastern crag, high enough above the castle on that cloudless, clear day to see a long stretch of the river Nairn, flowing north to the Moray coast.

In the distant southwest, snow-capped crags much higher than theirs were visible. Fiona stared at them, her jaw agape. She seemed to have stopped breathing.

Understanding her reaction, Àdham said quietly, "Beautiful, aye?"

She just nodded, still staring at the spectacular view. "We have *nothing* like that in the Borders. I have never seen . . ." She paused, shaking her head.

"The Cairngorms, miles behind us eastward, are similar. But those yonder are higher. Fin says they stand sixty miles from here. But afoot, due to rough terrain, 'tis nearer a hundred. The tallest one, Ben Nevis, is the highest peak in Scotland."

They sat quietly on a pair of boulders for a time before she looked around and said, "Raitt Castle lies somewhere beyond that higher hilltop yonder, aye?"

"On the northeast slope of a hill below that tor. But we're safe here, lass."

She looked at him. "I'm not as fearful as I was before. I've been out walking almost every day with Catriona and the twins, and even on my own, with the dogs."

"Art learning to speak the Gaelic yet?"

"*Tha, beagan,*" she said, still staring at the distant mountains.

"Aye, a little," he said, nodding. "What else can you say?"

"*Is mise Fiona.*"

He chuckled. "I know your name is Fiona. What more?"

"Don't ask me," she said with a grimace. "I am beginning to understand much more than I know how to say. Everyone is helping me learn, especially Rory and the twins, but I cannot form sensible sentences longer than three words."

"You will learn," he said confidently.

"I will," she agreed. "But how did so many at Finlagh and Rothiemurchus come to speak Scots?"

"Fin and Ivor learned at St. Andrews as students of the bishop, and Ivor's Marsi spoke both languages from birth, because her parents owned land in Perth and the Highlands. The twins and their brothers learned from Fin and Catriona, and others here learn from hearing phrases repeated at table and elsewhere."

Putting an arm around her shoulders, he urged her back the way they had come. "I know some other things you can learn when we get home, *mo bhilis.*"

"What does 'ma villus' mean?"

Realizing that the phrase had slipped out because he habitually used the term of endearment with the twins, he felt heat surge to his cheeks. "'Tis just a friendly endearment, akin to calling you a sweet lass."

"Oh."

"Shall we go?" he said, getting to his feet.

Fiona knew that *mo* meant "my," and suspected from his tone that the phrase was more personal than he had admitted. But when he suggested going back, she felt wary of asking if it meant "my sweet," lest she learn that it meant only "my wife." The way he'd said it had given her a warm feeling. The thought that he might call her merely "my wife" did not.

She had yet to spend much time with him, for she had learned that the Clan Chattan Confederation contained not only Mackintoshes but numerous other clans, some of which were themselves divided and distant from each other. When he was home, he usually spent his days with the men, ate meals with the family, coupled with her, and went right to sleep. Then, he rose early the next day without waking her, either to repeat that pattern or to leave again and continue his travels for James.

Despite her initial shyness, she had found their first few couplings interesting and mostly pleasant, even stimulating. Àdham had seemed to enjoy teaching her and revealing her body's secret sensitivities. After their first days at Castle Finlagh, however, she had scarcely seen him, let alone talked at any length with him.

Their walk today was a welcome exception, but the intimacy she had shared with him at Blackfriars and at Fin's pool was gone. He seemed distracted. He also seemed to assume that Fin, Catriona, and the twins had eased all of her fears about living in the Highlands. But thanks to the rumors of increasing enmity and possible renewal of war, with Islesmen threatening to reclaim territory the imprisoned Lord of the Isles apparently now insisted was an inheritance from his mother, she was not fully comfortable yet in her new home.

A twinge of guilt stirred, because she could almost hear her brother Davy saying, "Poor Fee, and what have you said or done to let him know how you feel?" Because that was Davy's way, and she suspected he would be right.

In truth, Àdham's casual belief that her fears had gone troubled her less than the proof she had recently received that her fear was reasonable.

Drawing a breath, she said, "Did Catriona or Fin tell you that we received a message at last from my father?"

"Nae, and neither did you until now. What was his message?"

"That he will likely not visit us for months yet," she said, swallowing the sudden lump in her throat that threatened to smother anything else she tried to say.

"Did his messenger relay his cause for the delay?"

"Aye," she muttered.

"What?"

"Good sakes, sir, because travel in the Highlands has become too dangerous! Many insist that we will soon be at war. Is that not the very reason that you have traveled hither and yon these past many weeks on his grace's behalf?"

"I have been doing so to ensure that if trouble does come, men will be ready to meet and defeat it. Moreover, if the Islesmen attack, they will do so nearly eighty miles southwest of here, at the lower end of Glen Mòr. And, *if* they do, the Earl of Mar will settle it from the royal castle of Inverlochy, which guards that end of the Glen. Trouble there should deter no one in the Lowlands from visiting Finlagh."

She gave him an exasperated look. "My father is no feardie. Yet he and Lady Rosalie have not even set a date for their wedding, because they hope to arrange matters so that we can attend. If *he* believes the Highlands are too dangerous to travel, it must be so. Perhaps he also thinks men might attack Tantallon to free Alexander."

"If men try that, they will fail," he said. "In any event, your father can surely arrange protection of his own for himself and his lady. I'd liefer be here when they do come, but things happen as they happen, Fiona. In any event, you said that you are not so fearful yourself, and you don't hesitate to walk out with only the dogs."

"I do that, aye," she said, wondering if he meant to take exception to those walks. "I have learned to trust Argus and Eos to keep me safe."

"They are worthy of such trust," he said. "Just take care not to go too far from the castle and to stay well south and southwest of it. I would dislike it if you heedlessly walked into danger by trying to get a closer look at Raitt Castle."

"I would not do such a foolish thing," she said flatly. In truth, she had long been curious about the place, but she was not such a dafty.

Although relieved that he had not forbidden her solitary walks, she would have liked to discuss further the possibility of war. But when they reached Finlagh, he left her with the women and talked only with Fin and MacNab at supper.

Later, when he joined her in bed and moved at once to couple with her, Fiona's temper flashed, and she surprised herself as much as she did him by pulling away and saying sharply, "No, Àdham! I don't want to. Not tonight."

Àdham could see that she was irked, because despite the hour, the shutters were open and the sky was still dusky. But he couldn't imagine why she should be.

He said quietly, "Art ill or in your courses, Fiona?"

"No, I am well. I . . . I just don't want to, not now."

"It is a wife's duty to couple with her husband," he reminded her.

She was silent, glowering. Her back was right against the wall.

"I may have to leave again as soon as tomorrow," he added.

She looked away toward the window.

"Fiona, what's wrong?"

"I told you. I don't *feel* like coupling tonight."

"But I do."

"And that is all that matters?" Before he could think of what to say to that, she added, "Despite our walk today, I feel as if you've abandoned me to the women here. You scarcely heed my presence unless you want to couple. And then you heed only your own wishes as if it does not matter a whit *what* woman is in your bed."

Stunned, Àdham's first reaction was fury, but he knew instinctively that he'd be wise to clamp a lid on that before things got out of hand. He wanted her, and she had vowed to obey him, but he wanted her to come to him willingly.

Although she had initially been shy about coupling, he had learned that she was avidly physical and reacted eagerly and sensitively to sex. Unconsciously, even innocently, she radiated sensuality in the very way she breathed. He liked to watch her, and when she submitted to him, she created an aura of mystery that fascinated him . . . not, he realized, that he had enjoyed that reaction for some time.

Perhaps he *had* been too hasty of late in their couplings.

She had looked away again, so he waited silently for her to look at him, forcing himself to be patient. At last, she turned and met his gaze . . . directly.

His body reacted with a near jolt, as if she were daring him to take her.

He knew she was doing nothing of the sort, but it *felt* like a challenge. He reached toward her. When she made no move to evade his touch and her lips parted softly, invitingly, he murmured, "Come to me, *mo bhilis*. We need do naught that you choose not to do. I did say this afternoon, though, that I would teach you more, and it occurs to me that I have not yet fulfilled my promise."

Fiona's breath caught as desire surged through her. Her earlier sense of isolation, even abandonment, vanished when her gaze collided with his. Moreover, his quiet words reminded her that he *had* spent the whole afternoon with her.

Perhaps she had been unfair.

When his fingertips touched her cheek, the expression of cool yet gentle impassiveness on Àdham's face fired responses throughout her body. She had sensed from the first time she'd seen that look that it was a mask concealing his deeper feelings. That she understood that about him without their ever speaking of such stirred something new in her, a sense of concern and compassion.

Why had she been so angry with him?

That mask was his true secret, not one she would boast of knowing to anyone, even Àdham himself. She could delight in her private knowledge, though, aware that his physical response to her was often equal to what she felt for him.

Good sakes, but the heat of his touch and the memories it stirred had banished that anger—nae, fury—that had erupted from the very core of her.

"What are you thinking?" he asked softly as his knuckles brushed her cheek, sending new waves of pleasure through her.

Since she did not want to tell him the truth, she continued to hold his gaze as she murmured, "I am thinking that I do want to learn more from you, much more."

"You were thinking something other than that," he said with a wry twist of his lips. "But that will do."

When he smiled, she smiled back but held her breath again when his hand moved from her cheek to her left shoulder and then to her left breast.

His fingertips gently brushed its nipple. Then, before she quite knew the manner of it, she was in his arms, his lips claiming hers, and his deft hands and fingers began inciting her to passion in ways he had not yet shown her.

By the time she had submitted utterly to him, she was hoping that he would not have to leave her again for weeks.

However, the next day, a running gillie arrived from Malcolm, summoning Àdham to Moigh to report all that he had learned in his travels.

Reluctant though Àdham was to leave Fiona so soon after their dispute, he knew that Malcolm would not accept a desire to spend another night or two with his bride as excuse for delay. Moreover, he suspected that if he did stay, he would find it harder to leave her the *next* morning.

It had never occurred to him that she might object to his lack of attention. After all, she understood that he was following royal orders, clearly a more important duty than dallying with his lady wife. He had an obligation to her, too, to be sure, but he had seen to that dutifully, nightly, whenever he was at home.

The truth was that he knew little about women in general. Before meeting Fiona, he had several times coupled with willing tavern wenches, rarely if ever with the same one twice. But he had no experience with *ladies* in such matters, let alone with lady wives, and Fiona's complaints had stirred conflicting emotions.

On one hand, her objections to his casual ways rather pleased, even flattered him. On the other, they had stirred his anger and a guilty awareness that he *had* left her to the care of others, while he saw to his more important duties.

Since he had no choice now but to leave, he lingered just long enough to bid her farewell.

He took only MacNab along for the two-day trek over rugged but well-protected Mackintosh country, so they were able to cover more than half the distance through the mountainous terrain southwest of Finlagh before dusk. When night began to fall, they found a grassy bank by a tumbling stream and ate their supper before true darkness came. Then, wrapped in their plaids, they slept until dawn light woke them, and despite steeper, more perilous terrain, reached Loch Moigh by midafternoon.

The castle on its island gleamed golden in the sunlight. Malcolm had set men to watch for them, so oarsmen rowed a boat out from the island to the timber landing on the southwest shore, arriving just as Àdham and MacNab reached it.

Malcolm led them into the great hall, where a fire crackled on the hearth.

"Gilli Roy be the only other one here, save my Mora," he said. "So choose any bedchamber. I'll want you to set out again at dawn, for I'm thinking that Mar must ken gey more of what Balloch be up to than we do. But I've heard nowt from the man. Ye'll also talk wi' our chieftains betwixt here and Glen Mòr, aye?"

"Aye, sir," Àdham said. "Should we then return here?"

"Aye, or send word wi' MacNab or someone else ye trust if ye must go elsewhere. Listen tae what anyone has heard from the west," Malcolm added. "If Balloch be raising as great an army as recent rumors say he is, ye'll have a better ear for what men may say than Gillichallum would. Nor would our Gilli be as much use to anyone if there be trouble afoot."

Realizing then that the likelihood of seeing his lady wife again in less than a fortnight was small, Àdham suppressed his disappointment and began to discuss other information that he had gleaned in his journeys.

Forcing herself to keep busy after Àdham's departure, Fiona tried to keep her mind on her chores but could not help feeling abandoned again.

The night before, she had been furious with him without truly understanding why. So, when he had pressed for a reason, she'd blurted out exactly what she had felt at that moment. Surely, if they had talked more . . . Though their activities had been most pleasurable. But he had fallen asleep directly afterward, as usual, so they had resolved nothing between them. And now he was gone again.

Recalling her angry words to him, Fiona felt heat rush to her cheeks. "I should not have spoken so to him," she muttered as she entered the scullery with a basket of fresh herbs she'd helped Clydia gather from the kitchen garden.

"You should not have spoken so to whom?" Catriona asked, putting her head around the wall of the nearby alcove containing the castle's bake-oven.

Startled, Fiona would have dropped her basket had Catriona not reached out to steady it. Drawing a breath, Fiona said, "'Twas naught, madam. I was thinking and must have spoken my thoughts aloud."

"'Twas *something* then," Catriona said with a smile. "So, I'll just give your herb basket to Cook and ask our Rory to keep the oven warm whilst you and I take a walk," she added in a tone that brooked no argument.

Moments later, the two of them were outside the wall, walking downhill alongside the largest and southernmost of the two burns while Argus and Eos ranged back and forth ahead on the well-worn path. Fiona inhaled deeply, exhaled, and felt herself relax. Until then, she had not realized she was tense.

"Art happy here with us, dearling?"

Surprised by the question, she looked at Catriona and said sincerely, "Everyone has been so kind that I should have to be daft to be unhappy."

"Then I'm gey curious to hear what has distressed you," Catriona said. "I ken fine that it was naught that our Clydia did."

"Oh, no," Fiona said, feeling wretched to have stirred such a thought. "She and Katy both behave as if they *were* my sisters. Faith," she added with a chuckle, "they are both much more pleasant company than my own sister has ever been."

"Then Àdham must be the one to whom you should not have spoken so," Catriona said. "Now, do not look at me like that, for whatever you said to him must remain betwixt the two

of you. But I will tell you that when I was your age, I was terrified that I'd have to marry a man who would take me to live
with his family, far away from mine own. I was certain I'd be
miserable."

"But Fin did not take you far from Rothiemurchus."

"He could have, but I doubt that it would have been as dreadful as I'd thought. If you do have aught that you'd like to talk over
with me, I'll keep your confidences and advise you as well as I can.
Sithee, mothers do that for their daughters, or they should. Àdham
is as much our son as our other two lads be, so I do feel like your
good-mother. I mean to be a grand one, too."

Fiona's throat ached, but she managed to say, "Thank you, Cat.
That means much to me. Àdham is lucky to have you. Did he realize
that when he was a child?"

Cat rolled her eyes upward. "He was an imp, nae, a wee devil."
Matter-of-factly, she added, "You lost your mam as a bairn, too, so
you may understand something of what troubled him. Not knowing just what he's told you . . ."

"That his father married again," Fiona said, "and his stepmother did not want him. So Ewan Cameron sent him to live with
you and Fin. I think that was a horrid thing to do. My father never
considered remarrying . . . not until recently."

"And you don't like it much now, I think," Cat said with a warm
smile.

"Not at first," Fiona admitted. "But I knew I was being selfish. I
do understand what you are telling me, though, about Àdham. I felt
my mother's loss most when we visited kinsmen. For years, I felt out
of place amongst them, because everyone except me seemed to have
a mother. It is one reason I loved being with Joanna, I think. She
treated all of us as if we were family. We had rules, of course, and
duties. And one of her chief ladies could be unkind, but never hor-
ribly or in her presence. Surely, Àdham came to feel at home here.
He certainly feels so now."

"Aye, because our sons were three and four years older and
were kind to him. Also, Fin and Ivor began to teach him the skills
of a warrior straightaway."

"When he was only nine?" Fiona was stunned.

"Aye, sure. When I was nine, my da taught me to use a bow," Catriona said, grinning. "So Ivor was willing to teach Àdham. And Fin is one of Scotland's finest swordsmen. Between them, they trained him well. Then the twins came along. He has doted on them since they were tiny, and is gey protective of them. But he is a bit mistrustful of women until he knows them. One cannot blame him for that, I think."

Fiona agreed. "I was furious with Mam for dying, furious with my father and brothers for letting her die. If Father had remarried then, I'd have wanted to murder her *and* him. Poor wee Àdham must have felt abandoned by both of his parents and utterly betrayed by his father for submitting to that dreadful woman's wishes."

"Aye, you do understand," Cat said, putting an arm around her and giving her a hug. "I'm thinking that your own mam likely looks down on you with great pride in the woman you've become, wishing she were in my place right now."

Unable to speak just then, Fiona returned Catriona's warm hug silently.

"Will ye look at that now!" Dae Comyn muttered. "We could ha' the two o' them straightaway back tae Raitt, were it no for them beastly dogs o' theirs."

He and his cousin Hew were north of the two crags and near the top of the ridge separating Finlagh's hilly lands from Raitt's. Lying concealed in shrubbery, they could see Castle Finlagh and the hillside below it.

"Ye're daft," Hew said, giving him a clout. "D'ye think them women would just let us snatch them up? They'd screech like banshees, and them guards on the ramparts can see them. If we was tae run down there, they'd see us, too."

"We could wait until the women get farther away and shoot the dogs."

"Neither one of us could hit one from here, even if them on the ramparts fail tae see us," Hew said. "If we get any closer, the dogs will smell us and then—"

"But Atholl and your da will be wroth wi' us for losing Atholl's men, so what *can* we do? And why d'ye want tae watch them if we canna capture the lass?"

"Ha' patience," Hew said. "Any lass that crept out o' Blackfriars Monastery tae swim in the Tay be one as defies orders. We'll just give her time tae decide that she's safe tae wander where she likes. Then we'll teach her why she should not."

By the end of the first week of their journey, Àdham and MacNab had learned little more than that the few travelers they met were heading for areas far from Glen Mòr. With a day and a half's walk to go, they topped a ridge above the Glen. Seeing five men coming up the hill toward them, Àdham called a halt.

"Those look like local tenants rather than fighting men," he said.

"Aye, but ye canna always tell a chap's business by his appearance," MacNab said, raising his eyebrows.

"We are merely mild, weary travelers seeking news of the area."

"And if they turn fractious, they are only five men."

Àdham agreed, so when the group drew near enough to hear him, he said in the Gaelic, "What news have ye had from Glen Mòr?"

"None save more rumors, sir," the leader replied. "Alexander's cousin Balloch be raising an army. But none do say just what he means tae do with it."

"God willing, the Earl of Mar will discourage him from entering Glen Mòr, so he will keep it in the Isles," Àdham said, standing and offering his hand.

"Sakes, sir, Mar has moved his headquarters to his grace's Castle Urquhart."

Dismayed, Àdham said, "How long ago did he leave Inverlochy?"

Looking upward, as if a drifting cloud might bellow the answer to that question, the spokesman said, "Must be nigh onto a fortnight now, methinks."

Thanking him, Àdham looked at MacNab.

"Sakes, sir," MacNab exclaimed in Scots, "whereabouts is Castle Urquhart?"

"On the west shore of Loch Ness three to four days from here," Àdham said grimly. "But it lies only a half-day south of Inverness, so we'll be much nearer home when we get there. Sithee, I served with the Mackintosh at Inverness Castle when Malcolm took over there as constable, so I do know how to get there."

"But instead of a day and a half, we have four to walk afore we find Mar."

"Aye, and when we do, I may put another Stewart on his backside. Why the devil did Mar move his headquarters without warning Malcolm? Unless he's left a strong force at Inverlochy, under a skilled commander, he's left the gateway from the sea into Glen Mòr wide open, just inviting Balloch and his Islesmen to return."

CHAPTER 18

Adham had been gone for nearly three weeks, and Fiona had begun to fear for his safety, but others were not as accepting of her fears as they might have been.

Fin told her bluntly *not* to worry, adding that Àdham knew what he was doing and had little control over where he might have to go next. And Catriona said just as bluntly one afternoon that women had worried forever about their fighting men without aiding their men or themselves by doing so.

"Go for a walk," she added. "You and I gain benefit from the peaceful woods."

Knowing that such solitary walks did raise her spirits, Fiona set out with Argus and Eos less than an hour later. Following the forested course of the burn southeast of the castle uphill, she soon came to Fin's pool nestled between the heather-clad slopes. For a time, she sat on a conveniently flat boulder and listened to songbirds and the music of the swift-moving water as it spilled over Fin's dam.

Eos and Argus snoozed nearby, the occasional twitch of an ear the only sign that neither was deeply asleep. She had visited the pool only twice since Àdham had brought her, once with the twins and again with Catriona. Each time, they had stayed only long enough to dabble their feet in the water before turning back.

Nearby woodland abloom with bluebells and other wildflowers invited exploration. Knowing that she was near Finlagh and had only to retrace her steps to return, she walked further up the hill to see what she could see from there. The woods were enchanting. A cool breeze wafted through them, making leaves whisper greetings as she meandered among the trees with her two furry companions.

At last, she came to a path she felt sure was one she'd followed before. Coming on an unexpected fork a short time later, where both paths led downhill, she chose the more inviting, narrower, and shadier one to her right because it offered more solitude. It was also less steep, providing fewer places where one might slip if one failed to pay close heed.

Hearing a distant trickling of water, she realized she must again be near the burn that tumbled down Finlagh's hillside and flowed northwestward for a time before turning due north to the Moray Firth. She was still going downhill and, thus, she assumed westward because the hill rose eastward behind the castle's knoll. To be sure, she had wandered up as well as down. But she had not topped any crest.

Sunlight still peeped through the thick canopy, its mischievous rays dancing through the shadowed greenery like streaks of playful lightning, making it hard in such dense woods to tell just where the sun was. The forest seemed darker than she remembered it and the path narrower. A squirrel chattered from a nearby evergreen tree. Tail atwitch, it scolded as if protesting her invasion of its territory.

Argus and Eos ignored the squirrel. But the little beast followed them, leaping from tree to tree, shrieking raucous threats and warnings as it did.

Amused, Fiona watched and followed until the squirrel disappeared.

The birds' chirps and other squirrels' chatter enhanced the peacefulness. Increasingly wary of where her chosen fork was taking her, she nonetheless savored the sense of privacy, so unusual for her in daylight hours. Before coming to Finlagh, serving the royal court or at Ormiston, she had rarely been beyond sight of others.

Only her nighttime rambles had provided such solitude.

She smiled then, recalling one particular evening by the river Tay that had proven otherwise. That memory, however, revived her concern for Àdham's safety.

A more noticeable rustling of leaves warned her of the dogs' return just before Argus's head poked through shrubbery ahead of her. She was nearly certain that his eyebrows lifted in query.

"I'm coming," she assured him, and grinned when the big dog turned back.

But she noticed then that the colors of the flowers had faded and realized that the sun had not merely passed behind a cloud. The sky was darkening.

"Mercy, I've walked into evening," she muttered. "I wonder how far I have come." Recalling that the days had begun to shorten, and where the sun had been when last she had seen it, she felt a quiver of unease.

She had done nothing yet to displease her new kinsmen. But she suspected that Fin would disapprove of today's so extensive, solitary ramble. She had clearly gone beyond view of the castle ramparts and had taken an unfamiliar turning.

At least no one was looking for her yet, because surely she would hear shouts if anyone were. Peering through the foliage, trying to identify a hill or rock formation as a landmark, she saw none. The woods were darker and denser here.

Nevertheless, she assured herself, she was *not* lost. She had only to tell the dogs that she wanted to go home.

Argus appeared as if she had summoned him, this time with Eos at his side.

"Let's go home, lad," she said, as Catriona had said that she should.

To her surprise, instead of heading back along the narrow path, Argus's head rose sharply, and he looked back over his shoulder. Eos did likewise. Then Argus nosed Eos out of his way and stepped past her with a barely audible growl.

Having never heard either dog growl before, Fiona froze where she stood.

Through the silence, she heard a feminine voice in the distance ahead. Her fear evaporated as rampant curiosity replaced it.

Unfortunately, the dogs stayed where they were, barring the path ahead.

Easing as calmly and silently as possible into the shrubbery then, she told herself she was just taking precaution, that if necessary, the bushes would conceal her. As she eased branches aside here and there, aware that the dogs' attention remained fixed on whatever or whoever approached, she sought an opening that might let her catch a glimpse of the female who had spoken.

A man's voice sounded then, a bit louder and carrying a note of familiarity that Fiona could not place. His voice was loud enough for her to tell that he spoke the Gaelic but not loud enough to discern his words. Not that it mattered, she decided, because she was unlikely to understand most of them at any volume.

She did detect a tone of command, though, with urgency in it.

Murmurs followed, then silence. The dogs were so quiet that she peeked out to make sure they were still there and alert.

Argus bristled, staring straight ahead. His growl sounded again, menacingly.

When that growl faded to silence, Fiona distinctly heard someone coming toward her through the shrubbery.

Àdham moved swiftly but silently through the woods, eager to reach Finlagh before the fast-fading daylight failed him. He knew exactly where he was and was aware of his deep fatigue but ignored it. He was determined to reach the castle and tell Fin all that he had learned. Having sent MacNab back to Moigh with messages for Malcolm from himself, Mar, and others, he had hoped to reach Finlagh earlier.

Meeting a chap with whom he had fought at Lochaber had delayed him so that he still had nearly a half hour's walk to go.

Fiona's nerves tautened nearly to snapping despite her stern attempt to persuade herself that she was safe with the two wolf dogs. The effort failed. So, when a lanky young man emerged from the shadows, it took her a moment to note his red hair and jutting nose and chin, and yet another moment to recognize him.

"Gillichallum Roy!"

Clearly taken aback, Gilli recovered swiftly enough to say in Scots, "Sakes, m'lady, what be ye doing here? Ye've nae cause tae stir so far from home."

"Have I come so far, then?" Fiona asked.

"Aye, ye must be a mile or more north o' Finlagh."

"North! I knew I'd taken a different path when it became flatter than the one I had followed up the hill. But I was sure that this one was taking me westward!"

"Ye'd be right only in that ye be skirting the west flank o' these hills," he said grimly. "But ye've turned northeastward the noo. Had ye gone much further"—he gestured behind him with a thumb—"ye'd be stepping nigh intae Comyn country."

"Then, what are *you* doing here? You are much farther from home than I am. And who was that woman whose voice I heard along with yours?"

"Just a woman," he said. "She were lost and looking for Cawdor land, so I told her she's but a half hour east of it from here and put her on her way. Sithee, I were in Nairn," he added glibly. "I go there now and now, for 'tis one o' the nearest towns tae Moigh. I'll bide a night or two at Finlagh afore I make me way home."

"Are you alone, then? Surely, you travel with an attendant or two."

"I *like* tae be alone. Ye must like it, too, since ye're on your own-some now."

Fiona frowned. "Àdham told me that Loch Moigh lies nearly twenty-five miles southwest of Finlagh, and that Nairn lies nearly four miles *north* of it. Surely, you do not walk thirty miles in a day across such rugged terrain as Àdham has described to me. Come to that, is not Moigh closer to Inverness than to Nairn?"

Shrugging as if such distances were naught to him, he said, "I like Nairn. Sakes, a man goes where he must and thinks nowt of a few hills in his path."

"But you carry only your plaid and your sword. What took you to Nairn?"

"I had errands tae do for me father," Gilli Roy said, taking a pouch from his belt. Untying it, he withdrew a rolled strip of pink fabric. "I got ribbons for me cousins and earbobs for me mam."

Glancing warily at Argus, who stood implacably between him and Fiona, he added, "I'll show ye the rest when we reach Finlagh."

"If you make the journey often, why did the dogs not know you as a friend?"

"I dinna ken why," he said, shrugging again. "They be friendly enough, though," he added, laying a hand gently on Argus's head.

The big dog stepped back and gave its head a shake.

Fiona chuckled. "I don't think I would deem his behavior welcoming. But he does seem willing to tolerate you. We must not tarry, though. It will soon be dark."

"We have time enough," he said, restoring the ribbon to the pouch and the pouch to his belt. "I'll lead, since I ken the way better that ye do."

"You must have walked dangerously near Comyn country, coming from Nairn," she said. "Were you not worried that you might meet some of them?"

"I was not. Nor did I meet any men."

"But is not traveling alone so near Comyn territory dangerous?"

"I be a peaceable man," Gilli Roy declared smugly. "Others, even Comyns, ken me as such and leave me be. 'Tis me own opinion that if more men behaved so, tae set the example, we might all soon live peaceably together."

"That may be true," Fiona said. "But, since—"

"Since others want war, I'm talking blethers," he interjected with a sigh. "I ken that fine. Have I no heard such from me brothers, me father, and most o' me male cousins? Sakes, the King hisself talks o' *forcing* men tae behave, declaring that there *shall* be peace, as if he thinks ordering it will make it so."

His frustration and sense of rectitude were clear. But although his opinions were such that her father and brothers might agree with some of them, his words and tone were those of an angry, discouraged young man.

Curious to see how he would react to frankness, she said, "You seem angry."

"Aye, well, 'tis nowt." He shrugged again. Likely, she decided, such shrugs had become habitual whenever someone questioned or challenged him.

More gently, she said, "I would be angry if my father or brothers told me that an opinion I'd shared in sincerity was blethers. Did they truly say that to you?"

"Aye, they did," he said, glancing back at her. "D'ye agree wi' me, then?"

Unable to bring herself to go that far but hoping to learn more about him, she said, "I do not know enough about such matters yet to form an opinion."

"Sakes, ye served the Queen! Ye should ken better than I do how the King treats his nobles. If he behaves so tae them, 'tis certain he mistreats everyone."

"But he does not," Fiona protested. "His grace expects much of his nobles, but he is kind to lesser folk. Why, when one of his sheriffs condemned a widow to have horseshoes nailed to her feet because she'd threatened to report his wickedness, the King ordered that sheriff made shorter by a head."

"I never heard that," Gilli Roy said. "But I tell ye, James goes too far when he tries tae deprive his rightful lairds and clan chiefs o' their heritable rights."

Feeling unequal to defending his grace's position on that or any other topic, Fiona felt only relief when Argus, ranging ahead now, stopped, raised his snout, and began wagging his tail. Behind him, Gilli Roy, perforce, also came to a halt.

"Someone must be in the woods ahead of us," Fiona said.

"Aye, likely," he said. "This path meets one just ahead that goes below Finlagh toward the Nairn. I expect ye thought ye were following that 'un and got off tae this one by mistake. Mayhap someone from Finlagh has come in search o' ye."

Argus uttered a sharp bark then and moved forward at a lope.

"'Tis a friend, at least," Gilli Roy added unnecessarily.

Fiona, silent, recalled that the intersection with the track Gilli Roy mentioned was not only farther north of the castle than any of her other solitary rambles had taken her but also well beyond the limits of what Àdham, and Fin, had set for her.

"I must have got turned around more than once," she muttered.

Argus had vanished around a bend in the trail.

As she noted that fact, a large figure replaced the dog, a heavily bearded one that gladdened her heart until her sense of self-preservation leaped sharply to life.

Àdham's gaze captured hers with a flash of delight swiftly followed by a scowl so menacing that her spine tingled and her breath caught in her throat.

"I think he be displeased tae see ye here," Gilli Roy said sagely.

Staring in shock at them, Àdham shifted his focus to his cousin and said grimly in Scots, "What the devil are the two of you doing here?"

Evidently, Argus sensed his emotions, because the dog stepped in front of him and turned as if to keep him from moving closer to Fiona.

Gilli had the temerity then to meet his gaze and say with a wry smile, "Cool your temper, cousin. I ha' just come from Nairn on me way back tae Loch Moigh."

"That does not explain what you are doing so far from Finlagh," Àdham snapped. "Or in these woods with *my* lady wife!"

Gilli looked at Fiona, clearly expecting her to dampen Àdham's anger.

"Well, madam?" Àdham said dourly.

Nervously, she licked her lips. The movement of her tongue stirred sensations that reminded him of how long he had been away and threatened to quench his anger. Grimly, he waited to hear what she would say.

Taking a breath deep enough to draw his attention from her lips to her bosom, she exhaled before she said, "It was such a fine day that I came out for a walk with the dogs. I did not mean to come so far from the castle. But I—"

"You shouldn't have come *this* way at all. How long ago did you meet *him*?"

"Just moments ago," she said, visibly wary. "He also said that I had come too far. We were on our way back when Argus caught your scent."

Shifting his gaze back to Gilli Roy, Àdham said, "Take yourself on ahead of us and warn them at the castle that I'll be there for supper."

To his astonishment, Gilli Roy held his ground, saying, "Mayhap her ladyship would liefer we all walk together."

With fists clamped now to his thighs, Àdham said with forced calm, "Do not irk me further, Gillichallum. I would be privy with my lady wife after a long and tiresome journey. You are much in our way."

Gilli eyed him long enough to make Àdham wonder if he would defy him further. Pressing his lips together, he narrowed his gaze until Gilli turned to Fiona.

"D'ye fear him, m'lady?" Gilli asked.

"No," she said firmly, looking at Àdham.

Although Àdham yearned to smack his cousin, he restrained himself and continued to hold his tongue until Gilli nodded and moved to pass Argus.

The dog glanced at Àdham, shifting as it did, so that Gilli could pass but also so that it kept itself between the two men. Eos stayed at Fiona's side.

Sakes, Àdham thought, the dogs were more leery of his temper than his hitherto foppish cousin was. Or his wife.

"I'll deliver your message, cousin," Gilli said quietly as he left them.

Torn between telling him to see that he *did* or just growling and continuing to hold Fiona's gaze with his own, Àdham missed his optimal moment to speak.

When the sounds of Gilli's footsteps faded in the distance and Argus moved to stand with Eos between Àdham and Fiona, Àdham said softly, and still without taking his eyes from his wife, "Argus, *suidh!*"

Argus sat.

Fiona stiffened and raised her chin.

She could feel Àdham's anger radiating from him. His rigid posture, heavier beard, sleeveless tunic, and weapons made him look fiercer than usual, too.

But she had not lied to Gilli Roy. She felt no fear of her husband—wariness, yes, but not fear that he might hurt her, even though she could tell from his rigidity, the red in what she could see of his cheeks, and his twitching hands that he was restraining his temper with near brute force.

When the silence lengthened beyond what she felt she should tolerate, she said, "When you told Argus to sit just now, why did you not use the hand sign?"

He inhaled deeply and exhaled hard, blowing air from his mouth. Then, speaking almost ruefully, he said, "I knew he would obey a spoken command."

"And you doubted that he would obey the silent gesture?"

He nodded.

"Because he was protecting me and thus Gillichallum, too—even from you?" When Àdham did not reply, she said, "You *told* Argus to guard me, did you not?"

Grimacing, he said, "I did, aye. But, to my knowledge, he has never taken such a command to mean that he should protect a person or an object from me."

"What you saw, sir, was *not* what you thought."

"I know that now. But had I known that you would come so far from the castle alone, I would never have agreed to your coming out alone at all."

"However, you do see now that Argus and Eos will protect me."

"I see naught of the sort, Fiona. What I see is my wife more than a mile and a half from Finlagh and less than a mile from Raitt Castle land."

"Surely, the dogs would protect me even from Comyns," she said, keeping her tone mild. Experience had taught her that if she could retain her composure and yet defend her position with facts and logic, she could often—albeit not always—prevail in a dispute, even with a man, even her father . . . sometimes, even Davy.

However, Àdham's eyes had widened, and his body stiffened again. So she felt little surprise when he said curtly, "Are you mad?"

"I do not believe so, no. I do remember the attack on us that night, and I have no doubt that our attackers had nefarious intent. But we did manage to defend ourselves, which did much to ease my fears. Are you saying that *that* is madness?"

"I am not," he said, crossing his arms over his broad chest, making the muscles in his bare forearms ripple when he did.

A chill went up her spine, more strongly than the first time. Other unusual sensations stirred, too, though, throughout her body.

"What I will tell you," he said, his voice hard again, "is that you are *never* to stray so far from the castle wall again. Nor are you to come this way at all without an armed escort. The Comyns might not murder you, although they have murdered many members of Clan Chattan before, including women and children, but they would certainly—given the least opportunity—take you hostage and make demands."

"Then I shall avoid giving them any chance to do so," she said, her tone still perfectly reasonable. "I think you are being overprotective, sir. I am accustomed—"

"You are *not* to come north of the castle."

"I did not think that I had," she protested. "I lost sight of its towers when I left Fin's pool. That route is circuitous, as you know. But I thought I had kept well south of Finlagh. I realized my mistake only when I saw that the sun was lowering to my left instead of to my right. You see, the woods here are so dense—"

"Enough, Fiona. You make my point for me. You do not know these paths yet. And evidently, you have not yet learned that all you need do is to tell Argus and Eos that you want to go home and then follow them. They will not fail you. But I want you to promise me that you will *never* come this way again."

Rather than admit she had been reluctant to return until she realized how late it was, she said, "I do think you are being unfair, expecting me to submit to such decrees without trusting me to use my own judgment as I have done for years."

"You forget that I have experience of your judgment, not only today but when first we met," he pointed out harshly. "Your *judgment* then led you to bathe at midnight in the river Tay with the nearby town packed as full of strangers as it could hold, any one of whom might have come upon you there with much more disastrous results than our meeting had. What do you say to that?"

Struggling to control her own anger, she pressed her lips together. Losing her temper had never aided her in a family of eruptible men and would not aid her now.

"Well?"

Looking heavenward, she heaved a sigh of exasperation.

"Don't do that," he snapped. "Answer me, or I swear I will shake you."

"Aye, sure, because that is what tyrants do, and you are behaving like a tyrant." When he stepped nearer, she said, "Are you *sorry* I went for that swim?"

"What I think about that *now* is not the issue. You will do as I bid you."

Grimacing, fighting the urge to shout, she said, "I had begun to think you more reasonable than most men, that you were different from my brothers and—"

"And your father?" he interjected coldly. "By heaven, if you consider him to be a strict parent, I take exception to that description. He is naught of the sort!"

Fisting her hands at her sides and narrowing her eyes, she said, "Don't you *dare* to criticize my father! *You* scarcely know him!"

"I know enough to be certain that he ought to have taken much sterner measures to teach you obedience to those in authority over you."

Squeezing her eyes shut, warning herself that he might be more violent than she had believed, she drew a breath. Trying to curb the urge to shriek at him or to remember how much she had missed him—

Her eyes flashed open then, and words flew off her tongue without thought: "Faith, and to think that I *missed* you, that I feared for your very life and have prayed every night for you to come home safely. What a fool I was to think you were different from other men! You still believe that I came out here to meet Gillichallum Roy, *don't* you?"

"I do not!"

"Aye, you do, too, Àdham. I could see that at once when you came upon us. If you think that I would *ever* do such a thing—"

"Enough!" he shouted. "If meeting Gilli Roy kept you from walking into Comyn country, I am much indebted to him. If my first thought when I saw the pair of you was—"

"Jealousy!" she snapped back. "That *is* what it was, is it not?"

He did not speak, but in the forest silence, she was certain that she heard his teeth grind together.

Drawing breath, she said, "Faith, but you have a suspicious mind, Àdham MacFinlagh. That's why you knocked Caithness down that night, too, is it not? You scarcely knew me then. You should be ashamed of yourself."

"By heaven," he growled, looming over her, "you go too far, madam."

"Oh, aye, I expect I do," she retorted, no longer caring what she said, how she said it, or what he might do. She wanted only to have her say, to try to make him understand how he was making her feel. "*You* told me that Highland women speak their minds, and I believed you. I foolishly thought that you would not object if I expressed *my* thoughts on this matter, which I tried to do in a reasonable way. But I see now that you are just another man who thinks all he must do is to issue an order and his womenfolk must obey it, whether they agree that it is sensible or not.

"Faith," she added when another thought struck her. "I suppose that when you said my father ought to have taken sterner measures, you *meant* that he should have beaten me into submission. So you are not only an unreasonably suspicious, jealous man but a brutal one. By heaven, I wish I could—"

The last word ended in a screech when he grabbed her by an arm, pulled her toward him, and then turned her and shoved her ahead of him.

"Argus," he muttered, "'*Dol dhachaigh!*'"

"Àdham, I—"

"It means, 'go home,'" he said in the same tone he'd used to Argus. "If you are wise, madam, you will go silently, because if you speak again before we reach the gates, I will *not* answer for the consequences. Moreover, I'll tell Fin where I found you and ask him to make sure that you do not leave the castle alone again."

Wishing she could shake *him*, Fiona remained obediently silent. But he had just confirmed her opinion that he not only had a suspicious nature but could become jealous and threaten violence without right or reason. Sir Àdham MacFinlagh, like most men, wanted to dominate everyone around him!

As he watched Fiona stride angrily ahead of him, Àdham tried to force his anger back under control but had little success. He felt as if he'd been traveling for weeks, debating with people much of that time—mostly men, to be sure—and fuming when he could not persuade them to his, and the King's, point of view.

It was blatantly unfair for him to return home and walk straight into a conflagration with his unbiddable wife, who ought to have stayed safely within the walls of Castle Finlagh. After all, if he could not trust her to protect herself . . .

Argus glanced back, as if to be sure that Fiona was still safe.

His sense of the dog's thinking stirred Àdham to recall how calm and reasonable she *had* been, even after he'd demanded to know if she were daft . . . in fact, right up until he had criticized Ormiston.

That, he knew, was ill-done of him. His displeasure was with her.

Now, remembering the explanation she had offered him, he realized that he should not have been amazed that she had gone astray. The same thing had happened to him the first time he had gone alone to that pool. The route *was* circuitous. It forked several times, too, and the terrain was deceptive.

He had been walking by himself then, too, still angry about his father's having sent him away. When Fin found him, Àdham had expected him to be furious, especially since Fin had warned him never to leave the castle alone. But Fin had hugged him and said that he was gey glad to find him safe.

He had forgotten that incident. Although he had been a child at the time and Fiona was an adult, the memory gave him food for thought.

They were still some distance from the castle, but he knew instinctively that any attempt to discuss the matter further now would be a mistake. She was most likely wondering just how angry he was and what he might do. However, such wondering would do her no harm and would give him more time to think.

After all, if he had reached home to find her missing . . . Or had Gilli Roy not turned her back and the damned Comyns had descended on her instead . . .

CHAPTER 19

"Men!" Fiona muttered to herself. *If only a woman could put one of them over her knee when he behaved unreasonably or threatened violence!*

Not that Àdham had exactly threatened violence. But "consequences" for which he would not be held answerable certainly sounded as if he had meant violence. With a sigh, she exerted herself to suppress such emotion-provoking thoughts and to strive for a return to calm thinking instead.

Argus kept looking back at her and likely at Àdham as well.

Eos had moved in behind her, so both dogs took their protective duties seriously even when they were protecting her from Àdham.

He did have cause to be upset with her for straying so near Comyn country. It was also reasonable that he had disliked finding her alone with Gillichallum Roy.

How, she wondered, would she have felt had he *not* been jealous?

More to the point, how would *she* feel if she were to come upon him alone in the woods with another young woman? That thought spurred her to wonder if the woman or girl whose voice she had heard really was a stranger. What if *she* had been expecting Àdham and had simply asked Gillichallum Roy if he had seen him?

That notion drew a wry smile to her face, and she mentally
shook her head at herself. Now, she could hardly blame Àdham for
asking if she were daft. He had shown no shred of interest in other
women, yet here *she* was, thinking thoughts exactly like those that
he had thought when he'd seen her with Gilli.

But then, after hearing their explanation of the meeting,
Àdham had clung to his jealousy. Her teeth threatened to grate
together again, and as she continued along the path, her thoughts
swayed from blame to understanding and back, again and again.
The castle on its knoll hove into view at last, and a quarter hour
later, they passed silently through the hornwork and inside.

Knowing supper awaited them, Fiona excused herself to
their bedchamber to wash and tidy herself. Àdham having said
naught to her in response, she decided she would ignore him
when he came upstairs, only he did not come up. When she
went back downstairs, she saw that he had gone straight into
the great hall.

He stood at the high table beside Fin with Gillichallum Roy
at his right. Everyone else was there, too, waiting. Passing Clydia,
Fiona hurried to her place between Catriona and Katy. Katy smiled
but made no comment, making Fiona wonder if Àdham had told
everyone where he had found her.

Catriona leaned near then and said quietly into her ear, "I hope
you had a pleasant afternoon, love. I also hope that you did not
expect to have Àdham all to yourself tonight. Fin has declared that
he wants to talk with him after supper and hear all that he has
learned these past weeks."

"I did have an agreeable afternoon," Fiona said, managing a
smile.

"Gilli said that you met him in the woods," Cat murmured.

"Aye, he was on his way here from Nairn."

"He was, and he brought us ribbons," Katy said, evidently over-
hearing them.

"*Shhh*," Catriona said. "Your father is about to say the grace-
before-meat."

They sat after the grace, and Fiona could hear Gilli Roy asking
Àdham about his journey, but she could not hear Àdham's brief

responses. Likely, she thought, if he had not yet reported to Fin, he was not telling Gilli Roy much of importance.

After supper, Fin took Àdham to his privy chamber as Catriona had predicted, and Fiona went with Cat and the twins to the solar. She soon realized that neither Àdham nor Gilli Roy had said more to the others than that the three of them had met in the woods north of the castle.

When Katy chuckled and said that Àdham had doubtless found Gilli too much in his way, that that was why Gilli had come ahead to tell them Àdham would be home for supper, Fiona managed a smile and changed the subject.

Àdham had not come to fetch her by the time her eyelids began drooping, so she took herself off to bed to await him there. She hoped she could stay awake but was nearly certain that she did not want to hear what he would say to her.

"Why the devil did Mar go to Urquhart Castle?" Fin demanded when Àdham reached that part of his tale. "Does he not take Donal Balloch seriously?"

They had spent much of the previous hour and a half discussing his journey.

Fin had listened carefully while Àdham described the men with whom he had spoken, relating their conversations as accurately, fairly, and faithfully as he could without inserting his own opinion of anyone or of anything said.

Now, though, faced with Fin's blunt question . . .

"Mar *said* he wanted to be sure Urquhart's constable had not got too friendly with Cameron of Lochiel," he said. "The castle sits near Lochiel's territory, but its constable is Mar's man, installed when he captured it two years ago. I think Mar got tired of sitting at Inverlochy, just waiting for things to happen, and visited Urquhart because it lies near Inverness. He was preparing to head south again when we left."

"So, how do you assess the situation now?" Fin asked.

"In troth, sir, any onset of war is uncertain," Àdham replied after some thought. "I agree with men west of us, most of whom believe Balloch is nearly ready to move. However, although Mar has heard the same rumors, a number of the chiefs and chieftains I met do fear that he is not yet much concerned. They say he insists that Balloch cannot have so much experience because he is too young."

"Mar is ever confident," Fin said. "I can tell you from my experience with him that he is a fine general, gey astute in battle. It is possible, though, that he has grown *over*confident. You say you sent MacNab to Malcolm. But we must get this news off to Ivor as well, because I suspect we'll get orders soon, ourselves."

"You'll stay here when we leave, though, and will have enough men to keep Finlagh's lands safe," Àdham said. He was confident that he was right, but for Fiona's sake and his own peace of mind, he needed to hear it again.

"I will," Fin said. "Shaw Mòr will look after Rothiemurchus, and Malcolm will lead the Clan Chattan men. Ivor, as war leader, will relay orders from Mar and Mar's lieutenants to our men. As we know, the Islesmen will likely approach again by sea, sailing up Loch Linnhe to Inverlochy by galley, as they did when Alexander attacked two years ago. Mar was in Inverness then, at the opposite end of Glen Mòr. This time, we must hope he can stop them at Inverlochy."

The two men talked for another hour, so by the time Àdham got to bed, Fiona was sound asleep, curled around her cat. He was tempted to wake her, but having no idea whether she remained angry or not, he decided he'd be wiser to get a good night's rest rather than risk fratching with her again.

Waking the next morning as early as usual, while she still slept, he arose cautiously, dressed silently, glanced out the window at a cloudy sky, and went downstairs to break his fast. Finding Fin awaiting him, he bade him good morning and made his usual request of the hovering gillie to fetch him a manchet loaf and two hard-boiled eggs.

Fin said, "Will you go to Rothiemurchus yourself?"

"Aye, I should," Àdham said.

"I agree," Fin said with a nod. "I know that you had to send MacNab to Malcolm. But MacNab had traveled with you and heard all that you heard. Ivor and Shaw Mòr will want to hear it from you. They will have questions, too, many of which a running gillie would be unable to answer."

"I mean to leave as soon as I've eaten."

"I'll order food for you to take along, then. You will stop on your way, as usual, but you must take a proper tail of eight men with you, because I'd like to know if you see any sign that Comyn of Raitt is preparing his men to travel. Whilst Gilli Roy may have got near Comyn land without incident, after your recent experience, whether your attackers were Comyns or not . . ."

When he paused, Àdham nodded. "I'll take no chances, sir. Likely, the Comyns ignore Gilli when they see him, despite his belief that he'd make a fine soldier if he were not so thoroughly a man of peace."

Fin said dryly, "He has failed to note that, whilst most folks hereabouts ken his beliefs fine, no one has offered to help spread them about. It occurs to me, though," he added, "that if you mean to leave right after you eat, you may have forgotten something . . . or some*one* . . . of some importance to you."

Àdham, famished and eyeing the gillie approaching with his breakfast, nearly asked Fin what he meant. Then, catching the older man's eye and detecting a quizzical, even humorous twinkle, he shut his own eyes to the sight. Opening them, he said, "I shan't leave without bidding my lady farewell, sir, if that is what you mean. She was sleeping when I left our chamber."

"I understand why you hesitated to disturb her then, lad. But if you do not want your head handed to you upon your return . . ." He paused, eyes still atwinkle.

Taking a breath and holding his tongue until the gillie had set his food before him and departed, Àdham said, "She is gey displeased with me, I fear."

"I did notice that," Fin said.

When Àdham grimaced, Fin added, "Sakes, lad, anyone of normal acumen must have noted the tension between you two at supper last night. Moreover, I doubt that she was still awake when you went to bed."

"She was not. Nor did I wake her."

"I won't ask what caused the strife between you. But personal experience has made it plain to me that a man is ever unwise to leave his lady without explaining his departure *and* giving her some notion of when he means to return. You would also do well to mend matters, if you can, before you leave."

"I don't know that I can," Àdham said bleakly. "Ormiston told me that she does not fratch, that she'll more likely stop speaking, and that she often fails to speak her mind when she should. He was wrong about that last part."

Fin was silent long enough that Àdham looked at him and saw that the twinkle had deepened. "I'd call that a good thing," Fin said at last. "If she flew out at you, she is comfortable enough to do so. But you need to talk with her before you go. To give yourself time to think, you might ask Lochan or my man to trim your beard for you. Your aunt Marsi will complain of it if Fiona does not."

Àdham nodded, reached for an egg, and knocked it too hard against the table, cracking the shell into such tiny pieces that it took longer than usual to peel.

Avoiding Fin's gaze, he focused on his breakfast.

Fiona had wakened to find Àdham gone, and Bridgett had entered shortly thereafter to help her dress in a simple blue kirtle. She was brushing Fiona's hair when Àdham entered the chamber without ceremony.

Donsie, curled on the bed, raised her head and lowered it when she saw him.

Someone had trimmed his beard, which nearly made Fiona smile.

Noting his frown, she said quietly instead, "Just twist my hair in a knot and stuff it into the blue net, Bridgett. I shan't wear a veil, so when you finish, you may go. You can attend to this chamber when Sir Àdham and I go downstairs."

"Aye, m'lady," Bridgett said, setting the brush on the dressing table. Taking a light blue woolen net from its box, she set it beside the hairbrush. Then, with a deft twist of her right wrist, she created a knot of Fiona's hair around her left hand, eased the knot into the netting, and tied the net with a matching blue ribbon threaded through it, at Fiona's nape.

When the bedchamber door shut silently behind Bridgett, Fiona felt too vulnerable on her stool while Àdham loomed over her, so she stood and faced him.

"Have you broken your fast?" she asked.

"I have," he said, meeting her gaze. "Art still angry with me this morning?"

Briefly catching her lower lip between her teeth, she let it go, shook her head, and gave him a wry smile. "I feared that you were still angry with me."

"Nae, lass, just trying to think how to make you understand how frightened I was to find you so near Comyn country after what happened near Lochindorb."

"You were furious," she said flatly.

"Aye, I was," he admitted. "'Tis how I oft react to such fear. But," he added firmly, as if he had thought she might protest, "I must also apologize for speaking as I did about your father. That was ill-done of me."

"Thank you," she said, still wary. "Did you tell Sir Finlagh that I am never to go outside the wall alone again?"

Àdham's eyes crinkled then at the corners, and his lips twitched almost to a smile. But his voice remained solemn as he said, "I did not. Sithee, lass, if the Islesmen attack, it will happen some four or five days' march from here. And, although some Comyns will stay at Raitt, many will go to aid the Islesmen. They are already on the move, so they likely have more news about Balloch than we do. I must go to Rothiemurchus today . . . a short journey only, I hope," he added when she frowned. "Ivor and Shaw Mòr will want the news I've gleaned these past weeks."

"I wish you were not leaving again so soon," she admitted. "Or that I could go with you," she added hopefully.

"I, too, lassie mine," he said, resting his hands lightly on her shoulders. "But you cannot go this time, because I must travel fast. I hope to be gone no more than three days, though. And I do want you to make me one promise before I go."

Grimacing, certain that he would tell her to stay inside the wall but not wanting to be at odds with him again so soon, she said only, "What?"

"That you will remember always to take both dogs when you walk out, and that you will take good care to stay both south and west of the castle knoll where our people will always be near enough to aid you if you shout for help."

Relaxing, Fiona said, "I do promise that. I know I let myself grow careless yesterday. I get curious and I like to explore. But truly, sir, I had no idea that I had wandered near Comyn land. Before you begin scolding again," she added, meeting his gaze, "I know that it was my own fault. It will *not* happen again."

Smiling, he gripped her shoulders as he said, "I am glad of that. But the fault does not lie only with you, *mo bhilis*. Although my duties took me hither and yon, I do have a duty to you as your husband, to aid you in learning to feel at home here."

"But everyone has made me feel so, not just the family but Granny Rosel and many others." She smiled. "Even that attack at Lochindorb helped in an odd way."

He frowned. "How can that be?"

"It was over so quickly, and I freed *myself* from that beast who grabbed me by the hair! Not that I was ungrateful for Rory's aid, or Donsie's," she added hastily when his frown deepened. "I am not so foolish as to think I needed *no* help or that I need *not* fear them. But it did ease my fears about the Highlands overall. Sithee, the Borders are gey dangerous, too. But one learns to adapt and *not* live in fear."

"I am glad of that, although I do not fully understand your thinking."

"Just call me *mo bhilis* again. Catriona told me that it means 'my sweet.'"

"Aye, it does, and you are, *mo bhilis*," he said softly. Pulling her closer, he put two fingers beneath her chin, tilted it up, and gently kissed her.

She could feel the silkiness of his beard against her chin and did not mind that it was still longer than she liked and already a bit unruly.

When a low moan escaped her throat, his lips softened against hers and his tongue pressed between them. His left hand cupped the back of her head as if he feared she might pull away. But he need not have worried about that.

Although she had only just got dressed, she made no objection when his other hand moved to her kirtle's lacing or when he stripped the garment and the shift beneath it from her body with a deftness that might have argued much practice.

By then, his clothing had somehow disappeared, too.

Her body aflame, she wanted only to feel him inside her and discover how long she could keep him with her before duty dragged him away again.

He picked her up and carried her to the bed, the skin of her body against the hardened muscles of his, and she marveled yet again at how strong he was and how light he made her feel, as if she were floating across the sunlit room. Her head rested against his shoulder, her cheek against his upper chest. Then he laid her gently on the bed and kissed her deeply, climbing onto it beside her as he did.

His hands stroked her body, arousing delicious tremors wherever they touched her, making her feel stirrings inside that she had never felt before. It was, she thought, as if he were playing a tune that thrilled its way delightfully into her blood, warming it as it flowed throughout her, until it threatened to burn beyond bearing.

Soon his lips followed where his hands led, until she was squirming, crying out, begging him to come into her.

"Aye, then," he groaned when she reached for him. "I had expected to take more time with you, but mine own eagerness is no match for yours."

With that, he claimed her swiftly at first but then more slowly, tantalizing her again. When, replete, they lay in each other's arms, he murmured, "I'll miss you."

"Three days is a long time, my dearling sir. You have become most essential to my happiness, so promise me that you will hurry back."

"I will," he said, eyes twinkling. "Else I'd fear to stir that temper of yours again." Even as he said it, he held her tight and murmured, "Ah, lassie mine . . ."

Later, she watched from the ramparts until he vanished into the distance.

Àdham and his men made good time to the ridge above Lochindorb. Noting that someone had removed the four bodies and scattered the rocks under which they had lain, he pressed on and made camp that night shortly after reaching the Spey.

Waking early, they arrived at Loch an Eilein by noon without incident.

No sooner had the boatmen delivered them to the islet, where Ivor awaited them, than Àdham saw two men waving from the distant loch shore. "Look yonder," he said to Ivor. "Is that taller chap not waving Caithness's banner?"

"He is, aye," Ivor agreed, gesturing for his boatmen to return and collect the newcomers. "We'll await them here."

"I doubt they bring good news," Àdham said. "I came to warn you that Donal Balloch has gathered his army faster than anyone thought possible."

Raising his eyebrows, Ivor turned and gestured for a man-at-arms who stood on the upper part of the slope between them and the castle wall to join them. When the man was near enough, Ivor said, "I want to hear what those two have to say, Tadhg. So take Sir Àdham's men to the hall and see them settled at a table. Tell Shaw Mòr and the lady Ealga that we will be along directly but no more than that."

"Aye, sir," Tadhg said, gesturing for Àdham's eight men to follow him.

The boat soon returned, and the man with the banner stepped out and strode toward them. "My Lord o' Caithness sends greetings, Sir Ivor," he said. "We left him at Loch Ericht early this morning, intending tae head on west with his men tae Inverlochy. See you, men in Edinburgh intercepted a messenger from Donal Balloch tae the imprisoned Lord of the Isles, claiming that Balloch will take back all land from this side o' the Great Glen tae the Irish Sea for him by mid-September. His grace desires all loyal Highland chiefs tae raise their clans and prepare tae stop Balloch where he makes landfall. Lord Caithness therefore asks that Clan Chattan make speed tae join him at Inverlochy but says *not* tae light fires. Opposing clans, he warns, may see your smoke, mayhap even the flames, and intercept your forces."

"What of the King?" Sir Ivor asked. "Will he lead his own army again?"

"Lowland chiefs who formed his royal army two years ago have sent their men into Perth and thence tae join Lord Caithness. However, her grace being close tae her time and wanting him near, his grace said that since a child of his could suddenly inherit the throne—in the event of his own death on the field—he would not risk the danger for the country that a battle over who should control a Regency would create."

Recalling the impact that the King's own presence on the field at Lochaber had made there, Àdham's heart sank, and he looked with dismay at Sir Ivor, but that gentleman's expression remained stoic.

Bruce MacNab returned to Finlagh the day after Àdham had left and said that Malcolm was ordering all clans of the Confederation to meet him at Inverlochy, prepared to fight with him under the Earl of Mar's standard for his grace, the King.

The next morning, a running gillie from Rothiemurchus arrived with a message to help spread the word. Terrified for Àdham, Fiona fled to Catriona.

"Prithee, what can we do? What can *I* do to stop thinking?" she demanded, fighting back tears. "I have barely had time to know him, Cat, and war terrifies me."

Catriona took her by the shoulders, looked straight into her eyes, and said, "It is as I told you before, Fiona. A woman who would survive war must overcome her worries. Those worries cannot aid our menfolk, and they make the woman useless at home. If you would help Àdham and his men, do not show them the face you are showing me now. You are brave for yourself, love. You proved that at Lochindorb. Be brave for Àdham and our other menfolk now."

MacNab behaved as if all were normal. He went about helping others prepare their gear and harrying those who were slow, as if he were wholly above the chaos that had ensued. He seemed, to Fiona, to have no feelings.

Although she tried hard to conceal her fears for Àdham, she realized that her ability to do so was not as strong as it had been when she had watched her brothers or her father prepare for battle. They had always seemed invulnerable to her.

Àdham did not, and he had become too precious for her to lose.

He returned late at night two days later. Arriving at the castle with his men, all exhausted from their hasty journey, he spoke briefly with MacNab, a bit longer with Fin, and then sought his bed.

Intending to aid him in his ablutions and talk with him about what she might expect, Fiona followed him upstairs and found him, still in his tunic, washing his face at the washstand.

When he turned and opened his arms to her, she nearly burst into tears.

Having taken Cat's advice to heart, she stifled the urge, walked into his arms, and put her own tightly around him. Looking up at him, she said sternly, "I will be here, sir, awaiting your return. Don't you dare let anyone kill you, or I swear that I will take my own life, follow you to heaven or hell, and snatch you baldheaded!"

He grinned. "Come to bed, *mo chridhe*. I may not be as tired as I thought."

"I do know that phrase," she said as he stripped off her kirtle and shift. "Am I truly your heart, Àdham, my love?"

"Aye, you are, lass. I will oft think of us here together, just as we are now."

CHAPTER 20

Nearly a sennight later, Àdham and his men found the Earl of Mar's army encamped on the east bank of the river Lochy a fast half-day's march south of Loch Lochy's outflow, where he had met his father and young Rory two years before. From their hilltop approach, Àdham saw men-at arms camped southward on the river's banks as far as he could see. Although he knew that some of the area beyond the Lochy to the west was Cameron country, he had never come so far south before.

He also had a clear view of the spectacular snow-capped mountains south of him and easily picked out Ben Nevis, oft called "the mountain with its head in the clouds." Instantly, he recalled Fiona's awe at seeing those mountains at a distance. The view of them from where he stood now stopped the breath in *his* throat.

On nearby forested slopes, the colorful banners of Highland chiefs and chieftains flew, indicating where they and their lieutenants camped. Myriad tents and banners dotted the area, including Ewan MacGillony's oak leaf on the opposite shore, clearly supporting the King, but Àdham had expected to see many more.

That scatter of tents and men continued as they walked on south toward the massive curtain wall and four projecting towers of a Norman-built stronghold surrounded by a moat. The Lochy's confluence with a much wider expanse of water half a mile beyond, doubtless the narrow end of the great sea loch, Loch

Linnhe, assured him that that stronghold was the royal castle of
Inverlochy.

A short time later, he recognized the banner flying atop the
primary tower as the Earl of Mar's. That of the Earl of Caithness
flew below it.

Telling MacNab to report to Malcolm and then get himself and
the other men settled on one of the forested slopes, well above
the flats, Àdham headed for the castle. Crossing the drawbridge
to the entrance, he gave his name to a guard who allowed him to
approach the tower keep, where he gave his name again.

"They be expecting ye, Sir Àdham."

He found Mar and Caithness sitting opposite each other at the
high table, casting dice for pebbles. No one announced him, but
Caithness, facing the lower hall, saw him as he approached.

"So, ye're here at last," Caithness said, speaking Scots, his words
echoing through the cavernous, nearly empty hall. "How many
men did ye bring us?"

"Something over fifty, but Sir Ivor should have more than a
hundred and the Mackintosh many more," Àdham replied in the
same language. "They left before my men and I could join them.
I saw no sign of them as I came down from the hills, so I thought
that one or both of them might be here with you."

"They came two days ago," Mar said, pushing a graying strand
of auburn hair from his face. First cousin to the King and Alexander of the Isles, and bearing the same given name as the latter, Mar
had similar Stewart looks but was taller and thinner than James
or Alexander. "Finding food for so many is hard," he added. "So
Malcolm organized men tae find more and led them southward,
seeking cattle tae drive back and slaughter. Ivor took archers into
the hills for deer and small game."

"Has Donal Balloch begun moving this way yet?"

Mar raised his eyebrows. "He dares not, although, with all the
rumors, I ken fine why ye'd ask. None o' his allies in Glen Mòr,
including Lochiel, ha' shown themselves. Ye dinna think your da
will change his mind again and leave, do ye?"

"I doubt that Ewan would risk his friendship with Malcolm
or their truce," Àdham replied calmly. "Mayhap, if Ewan were

suddenly to learn that his grace might treat Tor Castle as a pawn in some royal game . . ."

"He is a gey wily man, is our Jamie, but he does keep his word," Mar replied with a slight smile when Àdham paused. "Moreover, Jamie isna here, and I have spoken tae Ewan. He promised me all the support he can give us."

"His word is good, too," Àdham said, suspecting that Mar trusted Ewan no more than James did. "What news *have* you had of Balloch and his army?"

Mar made his next cast, shook his head at the result, and passed the dice cup to Caithness. When Mar turned back to Àdham, Caithness—behind Mar—grimaced and rolled his eyes, stirring a tickle of unease in Àdham.

But Mar said lightly, "Jamie's orders tae me were tae extinguish such sparks o' disaffection wi' the Crown as might still flicker hereabouts, after Alexander's defeat at Lochaber and ultimate submission. I doubt that his grace expects any great battle here, though. Not wi' such a force as we be gathering tae prevent one."

Shooting another look at Caithness to see that gentleman's lips tightening, Àdham resisted the urge to tighten his own. Diplomatically, he said, "Mayhap you are unaware, sir, that his grace's people have intercepted messages between Balloch and Alexander, in which Balloch threatens to attack before mid-September, which is now less than a sennight away. That is why his grace ordered reinforcements."

"Och, aye, but 'tis still gey peaceful here. We have a jug of claret and mayhap a clean goblet, so help yourself and join in our dicing. We needna fret over Donal Balloch today, for we heard this morning that he has convened a meeting of some sort on the Islet of Carna in Loch Sunart. So, he is dunamany miles away yet."

"He may be nearer than you think, though," Àdham said dryly as he stepped onto the dais and moved to pour himself some claret.

"'Tis true that Balloch has only just reached Loch Sunart, your lordship," Caithness said. "So, although I lack your experience in these matters, I believe we should be making more exact plans to defend ourselves. We should, at the least, set watchers along both coasts of Loch Linnhe."

"We'll discuss tactics and such later," Mar replied. "Make your cast, lad."

"With respect, your lordship," Àdham said carefully as Caithness shook the dice in the cup and spilled them out, "I must agree with Alan."

"Then ye both forget that I led the royal army against the *second* Lord of the Isles at Harlaw and defeated him soundly. *He* was a seasoned warrior. Donal Balloch be nae more than a scruff wi' eighteen years o' life tae his credit."

"But Harlaw was two decades ago," Àdham protested. Seeing Caithness wince, he added hastily, "Again, I do speak with respect, your lordship."

Caithness grinned but clapped a hand to his mouth when Mar glanced at him.

"Aye, I feel your respect, Àdham," Mar said sardonically. "But I should no ha' tae remind ye that I defeated Alexander *and* his army o' ten thousand nobbut *two* years ago at Lochaber. And, whatever ye think, we ha' nae army o' Islesmen tae fret us today. Loch Sunart lies miles beyond yon mountains tae the west."

Controlling his consternation, Àdham looked again at Caithness.

"Likely, he's right," Caithness said. "I dinna ken where this Islet o' Carna lies in Loch Sunart. But unless it be right at the mouth, by the time they row out o' the loch, south to the Sound o' Mull, all the way through it, around that long point at this end, and up the length of Loch Linnhe, the distance must be more than fifty miles. We've had nae wind since I arrived, and even the best oarsmen need rest."

"I expect that Balloch had reason to convene his forces at Loch Sunart," Àdham said, gazing at a point between the two. "See you, both Malcolm and my uncle, Fin of the Battles, have spoken of a five-mile river glen that connects Loch Sunart with Loch Linnhe. You might ask Malcolm about that."

"Sit," Mar said, indicating the stool beside his own. "If ye mean tae suggest that Donal Balloch might order his men tae carry their galleys such a distance uphill and down . . . Sakes, man, 'tis a daft notion!"

The dice cup was still. Caithness made a half-hearted attempt to pass it to Àdham, who ignored it and looked again from one man to the other.

"Does either of you know of an area a dozen miles south of here, where Loch Linnhe widens into a vast sea loch some three times the width of what it is here?"

Mar nodded, frowning. "Aye, sure, but if ye're telling me that that is where your river glen meets Loch Linnhe, ye must still be thinking that Donal's men could carry galleys up over a mountain and down for a distance o' five miles or more."

"That river glen is called Glen Tarbet, your lordship," Àdham said. "I have never seen it. But you know as well as I do that a tarbet is where men did once carry or drag boats from one body of water to another. I'd wager that with small galleys and thirty or more oarsmen to carry each one, Donal's men could portage them to Loch Linnhe. That would reduce your fifty miles to less than fifteen."

"Blethers," Mar snapped. "I ken fine that men ha' dragged boats across Kintyre and from Loch Lomond tae Loch Long, because men talk o' such. But ye must think yon glen be flat as a board, Àdham. The hills o' Morvern be too high and treacherous tae carry any boat that could hold thirty oarsmen over one o' them."

"Nevertheless, what if—" Àdham began only to have Mar cut him short.

"I'll grant ye that I ken more about the central Highlands than I do about the Isles or yon lochs betwixt here and them. But I'd wager that Glen Tarbet be nobbut a watershed o' burns flowing intae both lochs from hills above them. The name may mean only that men use it now and now as a pass through those mountains."

"But if that pass is low enough and the river flows down into Loch Linnhe, they could drag the boats up. And, even if they don't *bring* boats—"

"Sakes, lad, d'ye never give up?" Mar demanded testily. "I tell ye it be a watershed, which it is. So now ye suggest that Donal Balloch would come *without* his boats! Sakes, how could he get safe away back tae his Isles without them? The man may be daft enough tae challenge me and my ever-growing army, but he's no so daft as tae leave his boats behind in Loch Sunart whilst he fights us!"

He glowered at Àdham, tacitly daring him to argue more.

When he did not, Mar said in a more temperate tone, "Now, sit yourself down and take the dice that Caithness be offering ye. Lest ye're worried about losing yer gelt, I'll tell ye that we play only for that pile o' pebbles betwixt us. Atholl keeps our poor Caithness too short o' gelt tae play for aught o' worth."

Àdham took the cup, rattled it, and cast the dice. Then, having cast highest, he collected a third of the stones and left the rest. Casting again, he passed the cup to Mar but continued to worry about Donal Balloch . . . and about Mar.

Despite having many years' more experience than either Àdham or Caithness, the older man seemed dangerously overconfident about what lay ahead.

As far as Àdham could tell, Mar had considered no strategy beyond a vague certainty that he would beat Balloch because he had beaten his kinsmen at Harlaw and Lochaber. But, lacking a true strategy, whatever tactics Mar employed would more likely lead to unintended consequences than to victory.

The Earl of Mar, Àdham decided, should show Balloch more respect.

Fiona had discovered that setting one's worries aside was harder than Catriona had made it sound. She had stoically watched Àdham leave, somewhat reassured by the number of men he led. He had left Sirius behind, though, saying that battle was no place for a dog, even one as smart and well trained as Sirius was.

However, Sirius missed Àdham and had little interest beyond trying to sneak outside the wall to follow him. Even Rory failed to distract the dog.

Fiona was nearly as fretful. What if the Comyns had ambushed and killed Àdham and all of his men before the battle began? How would she learn of such a disaster? How long would news of it take to reach Finlagh?

"They are likely not even fighting yet," Katy said when Fiona asked her a few days later as the three young women were returning to Finlagh after taking herbs from Clydia's garden to Granny Rosel and visiting tenant women whose husbands were away with Àdham. "I heard MacNab say it takes days to reach Inverlochy."

"As to Comyns attacking him," Clydia said, "Father says *they* risk more danger of attack hereabouts than our people do, because on this side of our hills, all the land is Clan Chattan land. More of our member clans also hold lands north and east of Raitt Castle. The Comyns keep safe only because of the royal order to let them keep Raitt. If they attacked any of us in number, even his grace would support the Mackintoshes' retaking Raitt. In any event, by now, most of the Comyns and their men-at-arms will have slithered off west to join the forces friendly to Alexander."

"Slithered?" The word made Fiona smile.

"Aye, like the snakes they are," Katy said. "What do you think of Àdham's MacNab? I think he is oppressive and likes to make himself important."

"He seems kind enough to me," Clydia said.

"Everyone is kind to you," her sister retorted. "What do you think, Fee?"

"He is reticent," Fiona said. "But he does serve Àdham well, I think."

"If you mean to think only about Àdham," Katy said, "we must distract your thoughts. It is warm enough today to swim. Shall we go to the pond this afternoon?"

Fiona agreed and soon found that the twins, when mutually agreed on a course of action, left little to chance. Scarcely a free moment passed after that without a suggested activity from one twin or the other.

Although grateful for their efforts, after two sunny afternoons came three days of pelting rain that Fiona feared must hinder the royal army. The downpour also filled Finlagh's hall with noisome odors of wet rushes, smoky fires, and too many people and dogs shut indoors. Fiona longed for open spaces, solitude, and sunshine.

The heavy rain had dampened the warriors' spirits but merely reinforced Mar's belief that Donal Balloch was nowhere near Inverlochy.

Àdham, in helmet and mail, spent the first semidry day helping his men check any chain mail they had for rust and ordered
every man to make sure that all of his weapons were in order. He
had just finished cleaning his sword and replaced it in its baldric
when he heard shouts in the hilly southern distance.

Dashing toward them, he saw MacNab to his left, pelting
downhill to intercept him.

The squire said urgently as he handed Àdham his bow and
quiver, "Some lads met me in them hills yonder, sir, saying they'd
run since midnight when they saw galleys miles south o' here on
Loch Linnhe, too many boats tae count in the dark. They must ha'
passed intae the loch's narrower part by now, so I kent fine ye'd
want such arms as ye were no carrying. Them lads was spent, sir.
Will ye tell Lord Mar or must I?"

"I'll go," Àdham said. "Likely, someone has already warned
him. But I'll make sure of it. I sent you earlier to report to Sir Ivor.
Did you find him?"

"I did, aye. He were a mile or so up yon hillside, nearly straight
above our encampment. Last I saw of him, he and his men had
shot two deer and dunamany rabbits. He expected tae get a third
deer."

"Did you tell him about the galleys?"

"Nae, for I saw him afore I knew o' them and came straight
here tae ye."

"Then hie yourself back to Sir Ivor. And tell those of our lads
that you see on your way to rig themselves for battle. I'll see Mar
about those galleys."

He tried to sound firm, but he knew that Mar, Caithness, and
a few other men were playing cards at the castle, as they so often
did—*too often*, he thought.

Nevertheless, slinging his quiver over his left shoulder and carrying his bow, he hurried downhill and across the plain, wondering just how many men they had, how many Mar had sent off in
search of provisions, and how far he had sent them. He knew that
Mar had asked Malcolm to take his Mackintoshes as far as Ard-
namurchan. But the wily old Captain of Clan Chattan had persuaded one of his eager chieftains to attend to that task, saying that

although he was not too old to fight, he was surely too old to travel so far first and then fight.

Gaining entrance to the castle, Àdham hurried into the great hall.

"Àdham, lad, come and take a hand with us," Mar shouted from the dais.

"I bring urgent news, your lordship," Àdham said as he stepped onto the dais. "My squire, MacNab, a man to be trusted, just told me that many galleys passed into the narrows of Loch Linnhe last night and are heading this way."

"In all the rain, they must ha' put up somewhere betwixt here and there, for the night," Mar said. "We should post more lads tae watch for them, though."

"Aye," one of the other card players said. "Had they rowed all night, they would be here by now and too tired tae fight."

Àdham saw Caithness and two of the other men exchange looks of concern, if not exasperation.

Mar said to one, "Draw your card, man. We'll have plenty o' time when our lads can see their boats from the tower. *And* we'll win the day, for we have superior armor. Also, our men keep better discipline than the barbaric Islesmen do."

A brief image of Fiona's belief that Highlanders were all barbaric flashed in Àdham's mind before he recalled that Malcolm was still in the hills somewhere to the south with his foragers. He said, "If I may offer a suggestion, your lordship?"

"Aye, sure," Mar said. Then, looking directly at him, he added, "I'm thinking ye'd offer it even an I said nae."

"I'd hold my tongue if you ordered me to, sir, but I'd dislike it," Àdham said, hoping to win support from some of the others. "I do suggest, though, that we send runners to warn all the men who are out foraging for food and firewood. Deer and rabbits cannot aid us. We'll need Malcolm and all of our other men-at-arms here."

"He's right, my lord," one of the older men said. "It has occurred tae me that Balloch's men need only beach their boats a mile or two south o' here tae ambush us. Anyone who might see them do so and try tae warn us would be just minutes ahead o' them. Moreover, one canna see that upper part o' the loch shore from here, even from your tower, due to yon great hill southwest of us."

"Sakes, we have time tae finish this game," Mar protested. "Àdham, send some of our lads tae warn the foragers that Donal and his boats be nearer than we thought. Tell them tae get their people moving, and then see tae your own men. Ye may shout for my armorer, too, whilst ye're about it, and send him tae me."

Instead, Àdham stopped the first man-at-arms he saw wearing the Stewart badge and ordered him to find Mar's armorer and help him prepare their master for battle. "Donal's army may have landed and be heading for us now," he added.

Turning, he heard someone shout his name and turned back to see Caithness trotting toward him. "I'll send runners to the chiefs and chieftains betwixt here and Loch Lochy," he said, as he halted before Àdham. "Ye look after your own lads. And, cousin," he added, "if we dinna see each other again, I want ye to ken that, although my da doesna make it easy for anyone, ye've been a good friend to me."

"Don't talk blethers," Àdham said sternly. "I'll be happy to knock you on your backside again any time you like, *cousin*."

Chuckling, Caithness clapped him on the shoulder, and each went his own way.

Shifting his quiver strap higher to overlap the wider strap of his baldric, Àdham strode across the flats to the woods where his men had set up their encampment. There, he shouted for the few men he saw to find as many of their comrades as they could, spread word of imminent battle as they went, and then assemble back in their encampment until he gave further orders.

"If battle erupts *before* I return," he added, shifting his gaze from one to the next, "take your orders from MacNab or any another commander until I do."

Remembering Mar's description of their army, he gave a sigh. It was true that most of their men were well trained and disciplined. It was also true that others were just thieves and thugs. Such was true of any hastily gathered army.

And, although many of their leaders boasted fine armor, many others, like Àdham, wore only chain mail between their plaids and their tunics and would cast their plaids aside to fight. Come to that, though, Mar himself rarely wore full armor.

When Àdham had fought with him at Lochaber, Mar had not bothered even with a helmet, saying that his men would more easily know him without it. The man was a fearsome and fearless fighter and a fine leader in any battle. Likely, he would soon take command and would win the day, just as he had said he would.

Deciding to make his way uphill through the forest in hopes of gaining a view of the enemy's boats and also to hurry Sir Ivor and any others he met as they came down, he had gone less than a half mile when he heard someone or something crashing down through the shrubbery above him, cursing as he did.

"*Loch Moigh!*" Àdham shouted. "Who comes?"

"Sir Ivor's Tadhg! Be that ye, Sir Àdham?"

"Aye, what's amiss?" Àdham called back.

"Stay where ye be, sir, and speak low," Tadhg said, his voice quieter now. "There be dunamany others in these woods as dinna be our friends."

Àdham saw him then, shoving shrubbery out of his way as he leaped over deadfalls and other obstacles. The man had his sword still in its baldric but his dirk in hand. As he ran, he kept looking over his left shoulder. Breathing hard, he stopped short of Àdham and gasped out, "They . . . be heading . . . this way, sir."

"From the lochside?"

"Nae, from above us tae the south, in the hills. They carry a banner, and Sir Ivor said it belongs tae Alasdair Carrach o' Lochaber, who be—"

"Alexander of the Isles' youngest uncle," Àdham interjected.

"Aye, that be what Sir Ivor said. He also said I should no go back up there, sir. But I'm thinking—"

"You can stop thinking of aught save what Sir Ivor will say or do to you later if you disobey him," Àdham interjected sternly.

"Aye, sir. Then should I stay here with you?"

Àdham started to tell him to run on down the hill and warn Caithness and Àdham's other men when a great war cry came from somewhere southward to his right and another answered from above them, much too nearby.

Grabbing Tadhg's arm, he pointed to a large bush with a boulder in front of it and gestured for him to dive into the bush and keep quiet. Finding thick shrubbery in a nearby copse of trees, Àdham took cover, and none too soon.

The hillside was suddenly alive with archers, running full tilt down the hill.

Pandemonium reigned below, too.

Realizing that Carrach's archers had stopped at the edge of the woods and had begun raining arrows on the plain below, Àdham stayed put long enough to be sure that no more of them were trailing the onslaught. Then, easing his way from the shrubbery, keeping his eyes and ears open for any nearby noise that might herald an enemy creeping about, he sent a prayer aloft for MacNab and the rest of their men and moved toward the bush where Tadhg lay hidden.

"Art there, lad?" Àdham murmured.

"Aye, sir. Be it safe tae come out?"

"As safe as anywhere hereabouts might be. They're raining arrows down on everyone below us on the plain. D'ye ken this area well?"

"No to say well, sir," Tadhg replied hesitantly. "I ken the road we took from Rothiemurchus tae the river Spean. And I ken some o' what lay ahead as we came. But I dinna ken the loch south of us, nor where all them men came from. Forbye, the clouds be lower on the mountaintops, and a mist be growing below."

"I don't know the area, either," Àdham admitted. "You must go back uphill, then, and find Sir Ivor. He and his archers are sorely needed if they can hie themselves back down here without meeting more of Carrach's men. Malcolm is south of here somewhere. He had too few men with him to attack galleys full of Islesmen, so he may be trying to approach through those towering hills behind us."

"Sakes, sir, did ye see how high some of them mountains be?"

"Just find Sir Ivor, Tadhg. Tell him I'll set up above the archers who ran past us and see how many I can pick off by myself before they find me. I know of no way to get past them to our other men, so I'll doubtless do more good from here."

"Ye should keep me quiver then, sir," Tadhg said, slipping that article off and offering it. "I ha' me dirk and me sword, so I'll be safe enough," he added. "God kens, ye'll take down more o' the bastards wi' them arrows than I could."

Accepting the quiver and Tadhg's bow, as well, Àdham bade him farewell. Then, moving cautiously downhill, he kept to the thickest part of the forest and tried to ignore the din of shouts and terrified screams below. Impulse urged him to run down to aid his men or anyone else of the royal army that he could help. But the part of him that Mar, Malcolm, and Fin together had trained knew better than to fling himself into a fray where he would likely die before he could aid anyone.

He would aid them by taking down Carrach's archers.

CHAPTER 21

Fiona had awakened early that morning from a terrifying, if vague, nightmare and had experienced much stronger concern for Àdham since then. She feared for his safety, even for his life, and hoped desperately that God had *not* granted her Granny Rosel's gift of the Second Sight.

Whether it was the magical Sight or not, Fiona did not want to talk about her dream or her feelings. Not only was she certain to make the other women fret more than they already did, despite their insistence that women must not, but if she could hug her worry to herself, surely she would soon come to her senses.

Fortunately, the rain had stopped, leaving only a mist. So, they were able to open the shutters again, giving the women fresh air and light enough to attend to the mending they had neglected during the darker, rainy days. Fiona was grateful for the task and found it calming.

Later, she would help Catriona and the twins prepare baskets of food from Finlagh's supplies to take to families whose men had gone with Àdham. When they delivered the baskets that afternoon, they could take all three of the dogs with them.

She would have to leash Sirius, though, until she was certain that, thanks to all the rain, he would no longer be able to track Àdham's scent.

❖   ❖   ❖

At midday, the hillside below Àdham was red with blood and lit-
tered with the dead and dying. But he no longer heard clashings of
steel nearby, and he had run out of arrows. How many of the enemy
remained alive above him or hidden between him and the plain
below he did not know. But the distant, gut-wrenching cacophony
of cries and shrieks of pain down there seemed interminable.

He heard no sound of human, beast, or bird near him in the
forest.

Returning to the ancient oak where he'd left Tadhg's bow and
empty quiver, he climbed it. Hidden from below amid its branches,
and despite the mist, he could see a wide slice of the plain, bor-
dered by a hill to the south on his left, the mouth of the river Lochy
ahead, the castle just north of it, and a length of the plain beyond.
Thicker mist hid more distant hills in the north and west. The
plain lay in carnage.

Evidently, Alasdair Carrach's archers had attacked from the
hillside at the same time that Donal Balloch's men had swarmed
in from the south, likely just north of what he had learned was the
river Nevis, which tumbled into the upper end of Loch Linnhe
from its formidable mountain range above and to the south.

A sea of men still moved on the flatlands below him. Not one
looked like an ally. Each man seemed to be seeking out and killing
any of the fallen who moved.

Not many did. Most men on the ground lay dead still.

The battle had ended in disaster for the Earl of Mar and the
royal army.

The only encouraging sign Àdham could see was that the castle
drawbridge was up and Mar's banner and that of Caithness still
flew from the tower keep.

Deducing from such signs that Donal Balloch had beached his
boats on the shore between the river Lochy's mouth and that of the
Nevis, Àdham considered finding and destroying them to prevent
Balloch's escape. But why, he asked himself with a grimace, would
Balloch need an escape route now that he had won?

Moreover, he would have left men to guard those boats, and
one man with a sword could do little against what would likely be
many more.

The plain truth was that the Islesman was as clever a tactician as others had said he was. If his men had *not* carried their boats through Glen Tarbet, they had either stolen some from Loch Linnhe's west shore or allied clans neighboring the loch had provided boats for them. But it no longer mattered how they had got there so quickly. They had, and they had won. He hoped that Malcolm and the men with him somewhere on the west shore of Loch Linnhe had kept themselves safe.

Aside from the two banners atop the castle's tower keep, Àdham recognized none belonging to allies or member clans of Clan Chattan. Moreover, the two earls' banners still flying might mean only that although Donal had seized the castle, he had not yet ordered the banners lowered. In any event, neither Mar nor Caithness would have stayed inside, so both men were likely dead.

Even if one or both had survived, Àdham knew he could not count on them or himself staying that way. Nor could he return by the route he had taken to reach Inverlochy or go anywhere until he could gain some idea of what had happened to his clansmen. Those still alive must fear that he had abandoned them or was dead. The Camerons and others on the far side of the rain-swollen river might yet live.

To divert his mind from such thoughts, he reminded himself that he had killed thirty to fifty of Carrach's archers before running out of targets and usable arrows. As it was, he had had to move frequently, because enemy archers had soon noticed that their own men were falling with arrows in their backs.

Survivors likely still searched for the archer or archers who had shot them.

The woods remained eerily silent. No animal or man made a sound. Even so, Àdham descended from the oak tree as silently as he could and moved cautiously upward through the forest, determined to find a vantage point from which he could see more of the field below. Moving in any other direction, he was certain, would cast him right into enemy arms.

As he made his way amid the trees, aware that others were likely doing so, too, he kept careful watch ahead, behind, and below, glancing occasionally upward.

So it was that, as he passed between two tall trees, the blow from above struck without warning. Blackness descended.

"Bless me soul! Àdham, speak t' me! Ye canna be dead. I willna *let* ye die."

The urgent, yet strangely hushed voice echoed irritatingly through a vast black distance, its Scots words barely understood to mean that he had somehow erred and must collect his wits to make things right.

Was it Uncle Fin who called him? Was he in trouble again? Might Fin punish him this time or simply warn him again? He hated to disappoint Uncle Fin.

"God bethankit, ye're breathing," the voice muttered. "I see that. Now open your eyes, damn ye. 'Tis nae time for sleeping, for I need ye! Wake *up!*"

Not Uncle Fin's voice but a raspier one, and the man was shaking him. Uncle Fin did not shake people. He might take a stiff tawse to one's backside, but no shaking. It was someone else who issued orders and demanded obedience.

So many men had given him orders that sometimes their voices . . .

The thought ended in a groan that sounded too loud for safety. Safety was important, although why . . . he could *not* think. . . .

"Àdham! Open yer eyes, or I swear I'll clout ye again, although I be weak as a newborn kit m'self."

Mar! Àdham's eyes opened instantly. The rest of him threatened to lie right where it was, though, every inch of it and for a good long while.

The man who loomed over him looked less like an earl than anyone Àdham had seen before. The face was right, but the man was muddy and bedraggled from head to toe. Moreover, he was still shaking him.

"Stop," Àdham muttered. "Don't shake me, sir. My head aches as if someone had split it right down the middle."

"That was me. And if ye dinna come tae your senses quick, I'll do worse tae ye. Nae, lad, dinna shut yer eyes again!"

Memory returned in a flood, forcing Àdham to collect himself.

"Mar, stop bellowing at me!" he growled. "You'll bring Balloch's men down on us, or up to us if we're still where I was when—"

"Aye, sure, we still be here. Where else would we be? I canna carry me own self, let alone a great gowk like ye be. But we canna stay here, lad. They still be busy the noo, searching amongst the bodies below, seeking more good men tae kill. They'll swarm this hillside anon tae do the same to us. Here now, I'll help ye."

"How did you get here, sir? Where are the rest of our men?"

"I got here 'cause one o' me own lads fell on me when he was shot, and then another fell atop him," Mar said. "I couldna move, because I'd got an arrow in me thigh. So I stayed put, perforce, trying no tae screech, till I sensed that there be few o' them villains remaining nearby and managed tae wriggle out from under me protectors whilst doing me best tae avoid more damage tae me leg."

That explained his bedraggled appearance. "Where were you?"

"North o' yon hill as shoots up southwest o' the castle, the one as keeps us from seeing all o' the loch's northeast bank. So I crept round tae the hill's backside, which I'm thinking now may be how those villains came down upon us."

"I think so, too," Àdham said. "Have you any water?"

"Nary a drop. But the river Nevis lies none so far south o' here. I'm thinking that may be the best way for us tae go, too. If we can ford it—"

"It will be as rain-swollen as the Lochy, and Donal will have left a good-sized force there to guard his boats," Àdham said. "If it were possible to skirt the battle site and get to Tor Castle—"

"Skirt the field or no, we'd ha' more rivers tae cross, and Tor Castle be a day's march or more north o' here in conditions like this," Mar said flatly. "We'd never get so far alive. I dinna think ye comprehend the damage below yet, lad.

"Anyone on our side who *were* still alive," he added, "unless he be royalty or gey wealthy, be dead the noo. Balloch's men strolled about earlier, 'putting men down,' as they said. I heard one say that Donal Balloch and Alasdair Carrach together lost only seven-and-twenty o' their men."

"They lied," Àdham said grimly, forcing himself to ignore the painfully pounding dizziness in his head as he sat up. "I had two full quivers of arrows and then collected all I could find. And every arrow I shot hit its mark. I doubt I killed everyone I hit, but I know that *I* killed more than seven-and-twenty."

"Good, because they ha' besieged Jamie's castle. My men can hold it for a sennight or longer, but the sooner we get word tae Jamie tae hie hisself here . . ."

As Mar muttered on, Àdham conducted a silent survey of his own body, concluding that, other than a nearly broken head and scrapes and scratches from shrubbery through which he had passed, he was in one piece and relatively fit.

Mar said gruffly, "I was a fool, Àdham. This disaster be nobbut mine own doing. I was their commander, and I behaved like a feckless bairn. Sakes, young Caithness showed more sense than I did, and so did ye."

"Then Caithness will make an even greater commander than you have been because of this experience," Àdham said firmly.

Mar was silent for so long that Àdham turned his head despite the pain and looked at him. Seeing tears well in the older man's eyes sent a chill through him.

"What happened?" he asked quietly.

"That damnable rain of arrows happened," Mar said. "Caithness was struck in the first volley, right through the neck. He collapsed and died where he stood. Atholl, God rot him, need nae longer worry that the son who so strongly disagreed with him might one day inherit his titles and estates."

Àdham's throat closed. He felt tears in his eyes and had all he could do not to howl.

"I will blame myself for his death till I meet my own," Mar said.

Àdham had no words of comfort to offer him.

"Wi' them lasses a-walking out by theirselves as they do, as often as they do, 'tis a rare pity we canna get closer," Hew Comyn muttered on a mist-shadowed hillside northeast of Finlagh as they watched the ghostlike figures of Fiona and the twins heading down into the woods west of the castle. "I'd no let my sister behave so."

"I've seen how ye treat your sister," Dae replied. "But Raitt be surrounded by Mackintoshes. Them woods yonder be full o' crofts wi' who kens how many men and lads left on them tae help look after yon tower. *I'm* no going near 'em, and ye be the one as said last time, Hew, that we canna get too close tae the castle."

"Dinna be such a Lowland feardie, Dae. Ormiston's daughter will still make a grand hostage. I havena heard nowt about leaving her be, neither."

"Sakes, I dinna ken what good we'd be a-doing by abducting the wench the noo," Dae grumbled. "If ye'd wanted tae help Alexander o' the Isles, we should ha' gone west wi' all them others tae fight wi' Donal Balloch and them."

"Balloch doesna need us," Hew said curtly. "Moreover, me da said tae stay here, lest them Mackintoshes and Fin o' the Battles take advantage o' the fighting in the west tae steal Raitt from us."

"Like your lot stole it from them during Harlaw, d'ye mean?"

"Hush yer gob," Hew hissed. "That's blethers, that is."

Fiona's mood darkened more as the day went on, and the strong feeling that something was amiss with Àdham refused to leave her. As she made her way with Katy and Clydia through the rain-and-mist-damp woods, she hitched the wool shawl she'd borrowed from Catriona higher to cover her hair as well as her torso.

She enjoyed aiding Finlagh's people as much as she had enjoyed similar duties on her father's estates. Her spirits lifted when the first woman they visited—a middle-aged wife with two youngsters still at home while her older sons and husband were away with the warriors—welcomed them with pleasure and dignity.

Fiona's proficiency with the Gaelic had improved, although she still needed someone to translate most of what others said to her and what she said to them. She, Catriona, and the twins had filled six baskets, so they soon moved on to deliver the others.

Just as they were leaving the fifth cottage, a renewal of fear for Àdham struck Fiona forcibly. Swallowing hard, fighting her own tension, she said with forced calm, "Katy, I'd like to stop and visit Granny Rosel on our way back, if we may."

"Aye, sure," Katy said. "We'll take this last basket to her, although she will likely refuse it, as she usually does, and tell us to take it to someone who needs it more."

"And if she doesn't," Clydia added, "we'll be coming out again tomorrow with more baskets, and Granny Rosel will be gey pleased to see us today."

The old lady welcomed them with her toothless smile, but when her gaze met Fiona's, she spoke briefly to her in the Gaelic, clearly asking a question.

"What's troubling ye is what she wants to know," Clydia said quietly.

"Ask her if the Second Sight has visited her since our men left," Fiona said. "I have felt frightened for Àdham all day. I felt better when we visited and talked with the other women, but I fear that that was just my own sense of duty and not wanting to burden them with my feelings. Does she know if there's been a battle?"

Nodding, Clydia spoke to Granny Rosel, who put a gentle hand on Fiona's shoulder and looked directly at her as she replied.

Katy said, "She says she experienced the Sight only the day her man died in battle, never again. However, Fiona," Katy added hastily when Fiona's eyes filled with tears, "she also says that if a man and woman have a strong enough union, they may, by some unknown way, share feelings or emotions even at great distance."

When Granny Rosel nodded and spoke again, Clydia said, "If you and Àdham have such a union and that *is* what is happening, Granny says she believes that Àdham still lives and that we must believe that, too. And, she says, we must pray for him, hard."

Wiping away her tears, feeling reassured despite her hitherto general feeling that what she had heard of Second Sight and such notions was illogical and therefore suspect, Fiona reminded herself that she did believe that God would hear her prayers. Whether he would act on them was another matter, though.

The next day, hoping for the best, Fiona prayed for Àdham's safety while she helped deliver more baskets and assisted the twins with chores to which the youngest menservants—now away with the army—usually attended, such as sweeping the small bailey and removing and replacing moldy rushes from the great hall floor.

She prayed so often that she began to fear that God might decide she was sending up more than her share.

Four days had passed since the rain and the disastrous battle. The chill of autumn had set in, and a thick Scottish mist still shrouded the landscape. Not only had Àdham and Mar failed to find Sir Ivor, Malcolm, or any other ally, but they had also run out of food and gone astray in the mist.

Àdham's fine sense of direction had fled, and he was sure they were lost.

They had followed the river Nevis for a short way into the steeper mountains, but Mar had struggled with the terrain because of his injury, so they turned northeastward while they could still vaguely see Loch Linnhe below them.

Àdham, well trained by Ivor and Fin to tend archer-inflicted injuries, had been able to break off the barbed end of the arrow in Mar's thigh, extract the shaft, and bind the wound as soon as they were well away from the battlefield. He had also found a stout branch that, shorn of its appendages, served the earl as a crutch.

Even so, their progress was painfully slow.

The hills east and northeast of Glen Mòr were likely still alive with enemy Islesmen and their allies, seeking anyone who tried to evade them. But avoiding searchers had meant moving, often through underbrush and dense forest, with little awareness of direction other than that they went up or down or right or left.

For the first day or so, turning right meant heading south and left meant north. But the high glens they followed had twisted and turned so, now, since neither he nor Mar was familiar with the range of mountains in which they found themselves, Àdham was certain they would likely run into trouble.

Mar's injury continued to impede their progress.

Àdham knew they were well east of the rivers Lochy and Nevis in that vast mountain range, and they were still—he hoped—making their way more eastward than north. However, they had yet to see the sun, moon, or any stars, and he strongly suspected that their route had occasionally taken them in circles.

They found water easily in those hills. But, other than berries and a rabbit and trout that Àdham caught and skinned or cleaned, they had found no food. They dared not build a fire, even if they could have in the heavy mist, and although Mar tried to eat the raw rabbit flesh and fish, as Àdham did, his stomach recoiled, and he lost more than he had eaten.

At night, they wrapped themselves well in their damp plaids to sleep, and the dampness was welcome. Wet woven wool swelled, allowing the tightened fibers to confine their body heat.

Having hoped to find Sir Ivor or Malcolm, Àdham feared that each had either perished with his men or managed to escape the area. Neither man had had enough men-at-arms with him to stand alone against such a force as Balloch's, and both experienced leaders would have known their cause was lost.

The fate of the few Cameron factions whose banners he had seen, or of Ewan MacGillony, was unknown. They were on the west side of the rain-swollen river Lochy, though, unable to cross safely even if they had hiked back to the crossing Àdham had used during the Battle of Lochaber. He suspected that unless Balloch had sent men up the west coast of Loch Linnhe, Ewan, able to witness the attack, would have soon counted the cause as lost and returned to Tor Castle with his men.

Also, Mar would have spoken of such a division of enemy forces. In any event, to defeat Balloch now would take another royal army matching the one that had captured Alexander at Lochaber. And even James might have trouble gathering such a force to go against Balloch. The Earl of Mar, Àdham realized, was not the only one who had underestimated young Donal.

The question now was what Balloch would do next. From the extent of the carnage, Àdham suspected the Islesmen had lost at least half or more of their army, and Balloch was clearly astute enough to believe that more Highland forces—even James with a new army—might be on their way. Strong contingents of Stewart and Mackintosh men still occupied the royal castles of Urquhart and Inverness, as well as Nairn Castle. So, the likelihood was that Balloch would need reinforcements before he could wreak much more damage. Even so, given the man's history, he would surely act shrewdly and persist in his promise to seize the North.

The light had changed little since dawn, but Àdham still had his keen sense of time and knew the hour was near midday when Mar collapsed by a rivulet.

"We must rest," Mar said hoarsely.

He was weak enough now for Àdham to fear that the earl might die before he could get him to safety.

Hearing feminine voices a short time later, he left Mar by the stream and crept silently toward them. Seeing two middle-aged women and a dog herding sheep to the rivulet, he moved into the open and stood quietly until they saw him.

He said calmly in the Gaelic, "I'll not harm you. My friend is injured, and we have run out of food. Can you help us?"

"Aye, sure," the older one said, patting a fat pouch tied to the sash around her waist. "We ha' barley, and there be water in the rill if ye ha' summat tae mix it in. We ha' a shieling over yon hill, where we bide nights. But we dinna carry a kettle, for we keep the barley by us only tae keep it from the critters."

Evidently hearing them, Mar pushed through the bushes, leaning on his staff.

"Faith, but the poor man can scarcely walk," the younger woman said, hurrying toward him. "Ha' ye no a pot tae mix barley in?" she said to Àdham.

He shook his head.

"Aye, but we do, madam," the earl said, taking off his filthy shoe, while Àdham stared. "Rinse this out, lad, and whilst ye're mixing yon barley, discover if these kind ladies can point us toward the town o' Nairn."

The women did not know Nairn, but the older one did know that they were some miles northeast of Loch Linnhe. She suggested that if they wished to continue northeastward, they should follow a nearby glen that would take them that way.

"Thank you, mistress," Àdham said. "It is good to learn that we have not been going in the wrong direction."

Mar said, "We'll set out at once, when I finish my gruel."

They traveled steadily then, if slowly and cautiously, and the next evening they came to a grassy clearing with a thatch-covered cottage in its center.

Leaving Mar to rest at the edge of the woods, Àdham strode to the door of the cottage, which opened as he neared it. A grizzled head of shoulder-length hair and a shaggy beard poked through the narrow opening, and two bright blue eyes stared at him. A long, weathered nose twitched, and the mouth beneath it grimaced.

Then a gravelly, rather weak, but nonetheless gruff, voice said, "Sakes, ye look like a wraith. Who d'ye be?"

"I am Àdham MacFinlagh of Strathnairn," Àdham said. "My friend and I have traveled a long way, after a defeat in battle at —"

"Sakes, lad, I'm old but I havena lost me senses. I ken fine about the loss at Inverlochy. But if ye be heading back tae Strathnairn, what brought ye doon along the glen here instead o' making for the river Nairn?"

"My friend was hurt, and we've lost our way in the mist," Àdham explained. "If you could spare—"

"Where be this friend o' yours?"

"Yonder in the woods."

"Well, dinna stand gabbling. I canna carry him, but I ha' food inside and embers I can stir tae a fire. Ye're welcome tae what I can offer ye. So fetch him in, and we'll see that we soon set ye on yer road again."

Àdham obeyed, and when he and Mar entered the hut, they found a basin of water on the floor before the sole chair and the old man awaiting them.

"Sit ye doon, mon, or lie upon the floor, an ye prefer," he said to Mar. "The water be warm, so we'll wash yer wound and then ye can wash the rest o' ye."

With Àdham's help, they soon had Mar on a thin pallet on the floor, his wound looking better than Àdham had expected, although he had carefully tended it whenever they stopped near a stream. Certain that the food and drink the old man offered them was all he had, both Àdham and Mar were reluctant to accept it.

But the old man scolded them. "I ha' been looking after m'self these sixty years past, lads. I'll look after m'self a good many more, too. But ye've sought hospitality, so I'll thank ye tae take it when it be given right willingly."

Chastened, the two ate what he gave them, and Mar slept on the old man's pallet that night. By morning and mutual consent, both Àdham and Mar declared themselves fit again and prepared to set off.

"Ye'll take that path yonder till it begins tae head hard uphill," the old man said, handing them a sack with the remains of the previous night's meat. "There be a stream there as heads round to the east and downhill. That be the Arnieburn, so follow it till it merges wi' the river Nairn. I'm thinking ye'll then ken your road.

"I've heard nowt o' Islesmen hereabouts," he added. "So ye should be safe. But keep a keen eye, especially an ye mean tae go intae the town o' Nairn."

Mar shook his hand and said, "I have experienced less hospitality from men who think themselves well-tae-do, sir. If ever ye find yourself in difficulty, ye must make your way east tae Kildrummy Castle, the seat of the Earl of Mar. When ye get there, demand tae see Alexander Stewart, who will see to it that the earl rewards ye for the kindness ye've shown us these past two days."

"Aye, then, and I thank ye for your counsel, sir. I dinna reckon I'll need it, but if ever I do—"

"Aye, if ye do," Mar interjected firmly, "ye're tae do just as I've bade ye, and dinna take any sauce from them ye see wha' tell ye the man doesna exist. He does."

As they walked away, Àdham said, "Alexander Stewart?"

Mar shrugged. "Aye, and why not? *Nae* one would recognize me as I be now, all ragtaggle and filthy. Few hereabouts or anywhere else think of me so, in any event. Sakes, few ken aught o' me save my title, which is what I've used since I acquired it when I married my late countess.

"Moreover," Mar went on, "thanks tae the willingness and rapidity with which my Stewart kinsmen have for generations spread their seed, Scotland must contain any number o' Alexander Stewarts. At present, though, I am the only one who may be found at Kildrummy Castle."

"So you will not return to Inverlochy?"

"Look at me, lad," Mar muttered. "D'ye no think Jamie needs someone stronger and more fit tae be constable there now? I'm for Kildrummy, I am."

"We must first find the Nairn and safety," Àdham reminded him.

CHAPTER 22

Adham tried to persuade Mar to go first to Castle Finlagh, where he knew they would both be safe. But the earl insisted on going straight to Nairn's harbor, where he kept a galley that would take him east along the southern coast of the Moray Firth, then a few miles due south to Kildrummy.

"I ken fine that ye'd like tae see your ain folk straightaway, Àdham," Mar said, "But I'd liefer ye stay wi' me till I'm shipboard. I willna command ye, but—"

"I am still yours to command, sir," Àdham said sincerely. "I'll see you safely aboard your ship, but I will admit that I am concerned about my lady. See you, her father had expected to be married by now and—"

"Tae the lovely Lady Rosalie Percy, aye," Mar said. "Caithness told me they had not yet wed."

"They were to have visited Finlagh before summer's end. When unrest in the Highlands put them off, my lady was gey disappointed. I ken fine that she must be worried about me now, too. But I will go to her as soon as I see you safe."

"Aye, then, ye may tell her that I'll send word tae Ormiston that he and Lady Rosalie can marry at Kildrummy in the spring if they would like that. Winter be fast approaching. And, after this dreadful loss, the western Highlands will likely become more dangerous than ever. Even so, traveling east from here should be safe enough by spring for ye and your family, so ye'll be able tae attend the wedding, too."

"I'll tell her, sir, and I thank you," Àdham said.

It took them another day to reach Nairn. Although they recalled their elderly benefactor's advice, they saw nothing to suggest an infestation there of Islesmen.

Àdham did see two men he knew as tenants from the nearby Thane of Cawdor's estates. He paused long enough to exchange greetings with them, identifying his shabby companion only as a fellow survivor of the battle.

From the two, he learned that the town was as peaceful as usual, because Mackintosh forces at Inverness Castle and Nairn still controlled access to the Moray Firth. The two had heard of the disaster at Inverlochy. "But we ha' heard nowt o' Balloch's men moving northward, let alone as far as Loch Ness," one of them said.

As Mar had expected, his galley awaited him in the harbor. After making himself known to his captain, he turned to Àdham and said, "I'll get word tae Ormiston, and I'll expect tae hear from ye when ye're ready tae travel eastward."

"Thank you, sir. But you need not—"

"Say nae more, lad. Recall the words of our kind benefactor and accept the hospitality I offer tae ye and yours. I owe ye more than I'll ever repay."

Parting quickly after that, Àdham turned southward. As he passed through an oncoming group of travelers just outside the town, with only a few miles to go before he would hold Fiona in his arms again, he felt a sense of deep contentment.

Bruce MacNab reached Finlagh late the following afternoon.

Fiona, helping Clydia and Katy finish picking the last fresh herbs from the kitchen garden for drying on racks above the bake oven, saw him striding toward the tower entrance from the gateway and looked eagerly for Àdham.

MacNab, however, was alone.

Moving to intercept him, with the twins at her heels, she said, "Where is Sir Àdham? And the others," she added as an afterthought.

Stopping, MacNab gazed bleakly at her and said, "I had hoped that Sir Àdham were here wi' ye, your ladyship. As tae the others, we lost dunamany men."

Before Fiona could speak, Katy said, "But Àdham was with you, was he not?"

"Aye, but . . ."

When he paused, Clydia said gently, "We should all go inside, I think. Mam and Da will also want to hear what MacNab has to say."

"Aye," Fiona agreed, swallowing hard. "Let us find them at once." Moments later, looking right into his eyes as she entered the keep, she said, "You have not kept anything horrid from me, have you, sir? About Sir Àdham, I mean."

"By my troth, m'lady, I dinna ken where he is," he said. "The last time I saw him, a sennight or so ago, he sent me tae tell Sir Ivor that our lads had seen Donal Balloch's boats in the northern part o' Loch Linnhe. I havena seen him since then."

Doing all she could to control her emotions, Fiona turned away and hurried into the great hall with the others following. Gillies had arranged the trestles for supper and Fin was on the dais, so she let MacNab lead the way to him.

"Welcome back," Fin said, shaking his hand. "How many are in your party?"

"Just me, I'm afraid," MacNab said wearily. "I traveled wi' the Mackintosh and Sir Ivor tae Loch an Eilein and came here on my own. Five o' Castle Finlagh's wounded lads came with us as far as Rothiemurchus, but Sir Ivor will keep them there till they be fit tae come home. We lost dunamany men, sir."

"Where is Àdham?" Catriona asked, approaching from the privy stairs.

"I dinna ken, madam." He explained how they had met and parted. "I ha' no seen him since. But Sir Ivor's Tadhg did see him afore the battle started. Tadhg said a host o' Alasdair Carrach's archers spilled down the hillside, sending him and Sir Àdham tae cover," he added. "When they had passed, Sir Àdham sent Tadhg tae hie Sir Ivor and *his* archers along down tae help him attack the enemy from the rear." His gaze drifted then to Fiona and the twins.

"I'll want to hear the rest of the details later, and mayhap my lady will, too," Fin said lightly with a smile for Catriona. "We will all eat our supper first, though."

Having no appetite, Fiona did little more than rearrange food on her trencher.

After a time, Catriona gently asked if she were feeling sick.

"Nae," Fiona replied, forcing a smile. "I am tired but not hungry. I think I will seek my bed now, if I may."

Catriona gave her a long look, and Fin leaned forward to say, "Àdham *will* come home, lassie. So, you would be wise to sleep well until he does. You have been looking a bit wan these past weeks, and he will be eager to reunite with you. You won't want to disappoint him by being sick then."

"No, sir," Fiona said. "If you will excuse me . . ." Anticipating his nod, she stood as she spoke, bade them and the twins good night, and made her way to the room she had shared with Àdham.

Bridgett, having watched her leave the dais, soon joined her there. She aided Fiona with her ablutions, swiftly tidied the chamber, and left her to sleep.

Although Fiona had expected to lie awake, imagining horrid things having happened to Àdham, she fell asleep before the first such thought entered her head and slept deeply until the dawn's light wakened her.

After breaking her fast, she helped with the chores as usual. But directly after the midday meal, unable to find Sirius, she took Argus and Eos with her and went out through the main gates and down into the west woods to find Granny Rosel.

Warmly welcomed into the dark, earthy cottage, she managed to smile and to give the dogs the sign to lie down, but when Granny raised her eyebrows in silent query, Fiona shook her head.

"Art sick, m'lady?" Granny asked her gently in the Gaelic.

"*Nae, iomagaineach,*" Fiona said. "*Worried* for Sir Àdham."

Pointing to a nearby wooden settle, Granny silently urged her to sit. Then, with gentle fingertips, Granny shut Fiona's eyelids, put one hand lightly on Fiona's forehead, the other against the back of her head near her nape, and began to hum a soft tune that sounded to Fiona's ears like a bairn's lullaby.

She soon found herself relaxing, and might well have gone to sleep where she sat had Granny not stopped humming and said gently, "Ye be strong, m'lady. Be strong enough tae trust God, and be he willing, all will be good."

"You speak Scots!"

"Nae more than ye speak our Gaelic," Granny said. "We learn taegether."

Although Fiona knew no more about Àdham's fate than she had before, her spirits had lifted considerably by the time she took her leave with Eos and Argus.

Instead of taking her usual path, she continued up the hill behind the castle and made her way through the trees, keeping southward until she looked down on the several paths that led to Castle Finlagh, including a portion of the narrow fork she had taken the day that Àdham had found her with Gilli Roy. If Àdham were to come home, she wanted to meet him before anyone else did.

Instead, less than an hour later, she saw Rory running full tilt through the woods below her from the north. Catching up her skirts, she scrambled down on a diagonal line to meet him and reached a small clearing northeast of the castle just as he entered it from the northernmost end.

Àdham opened his eyes, wondering where he was. The room was as black as pitch and whatever he lay upon felt as unyielding as stone. Worse, although his head had ached after Mar clouted him, it pounded now.

Memory followed slowly after thoughts of Mar. They had traveled long to reach Nairn, and he'd seen the earl off on his galley toward Aberdeenshire.

Then, what? He remembered thinking of Fiona and how near she was. After that, he recalled nothing, but thinking of her brought her image achingly to mind.

He tried to find a more comfortable position and realized that he lay supine with his arms stretched over his head and tied in place. His legs were also stretched and tied, so he was helpless, and he could hear water lapping nearby, close enough that he wondered if he was somewhere near the Moray Firth shoreline.

If the tide was coming in . . .

Rory had apparently run for some distance, because when he met Fiona, he bent over, hands on his knees, and gasped, "Sir Àdham's MacNab be . . . in the woods yonder a-talkin' tae . . . a pair o' wicked Comyns . . . their Hew and some other 'un."

Only then did Fiona see that Sirius was at the boy's heels.

"Where have you been, Rory? Did MacNab send you to me?" She realized as she spoke that she could not imagine Àdham's customarily reticent squire sending the boy to her as a messenger. Perhaps, though, she had misjudged them both.

"Nae, m'lady," Rory said, shaking his head, "MacNab didna say nowt tae me, nor did he see me. Sirius and me saw them, though, all three o' them, together."

"But how do you know any Comyn well enough to identify him by name?"

The boy shrugged.

Raising her eyebrows and capturing his gaze, Fiona said, "Rory . . ." As she did, she heard Davy's sternest tone in her voice.

Apparently, and despite its having affected only that single word, Rory understood that her tone was one to obey. Swallowing visibly, he said, "Sir Àdham and Sir Fin say that a chap should ken the lands round anywhere he finds hisself. And ye ken fine that I roam about when I'm no wanted for summat else, tae see what I can see." Giving her an oblique look, he added, "Just as ye do, m'lady."

Ignoring both the look and the gibe, she said, "Surely, MacNab is not talking to two well-armed Comyns all by himself."

"Nae, he has three o' our lads with him. All o' them be armed, too."

"Where were you then?"

"Yonder on the hillside," he said, jerking a thumb over his shoulder. "Like I said afore, from the top, ye can see Raitt Castle. But the last time I went, I near ran into a pair o' them damna— them *wicked* Comyns. So that be some whiles ag—"

Falling abruptly silent at the sound of male voices approaching through the trees north of them, Rory darted into denser woodland. Sirius ran after him.

Although strongly tempted to follow them, Fiona resisted the impulse and waited. When MacNab and his three men appeared, Eos and Argus stepped in front of her but stood quietly when the four men entered the clearing.

Visibly surprised to see her, MacNab exclaimed, "In faith, m'lady! Ye should no ha' come this far from Finlagh, no by this path. Ye must ken fine that ye stand nearer Raitt Castle here than Sir Àdham would like."

"I have met no Comyns, though," Fiona said, pleased that her voice was steady. She waited to hear if he would admit to talking to the Comyns himself.

"Had ye wandered further," he retorted grimly, "ye'd ha' come upon two o' them glittous hellicats less than a quarter mile from here."

His men nodded, also looking grim.

"Mercy, what were *they* doing so near?" Fiona asked them.

"They *said* they were hunting rabbits," MacNab said. "But Sir Àdham said they do count all the land for miles around Raitt Castle as their own. They had talked o' possessing much of it, even Lochindorb, for many years, ye ken."

"You cannot mean these current Comyns," Fiona said. "Sir Àdham told me that Clan Comyn sacrificed most of their estates more than a hundred years ago."

"Aye, sure, but men dinna always agree about property rights. And some old ties keep strong forever."

It was the longest talk she had had with McNab since Àdham had introduced him, but that thought stirred a more urgent one. "Did you ask if they had seen Sir Àdham?"

"Aye, sure, I did, for have I no been asking folks that verra question all day?" he replied. The trio behind him nodded again.

"But from *them two*," he added, "I had only insolence. In troth, they seemed tae find humor in our having mislaid him, as they would have it we ha' done."

"But did they answer your question?"

"They did not, m'lady. They offered only mockery."

Fiona wondered if that was true or if he was keeping what he had learned to himself. However, although Rory had run full pelt to her, MacNab and his men *had* been close behind. She recalled, too, that Rory said only that he had seen MacNab talking with the Comyns. But the other three men were Àdham's men—or Fin's. Surely they would not be supporting MacNab's version of events if it was untrue.

She said to him, "You ought to have pressed them harder, even so. Have you learned aught of importance from anyone today?"

"I did hear talk o' two ragged men striding through Nairn as if they owned the town, seeking the Earl of Mar's ship. A boat did set sail soon afterward, but whether them two men were aboard, nae one could say.

"One other chap did say he thought he'd seen Sir Àdham in town," he added. "It were at a distance, he said, when one bearded man looks like another, so he couldna be sure. 'Twas the muddy green plaid made him think o' Sir Àdham, but o' course, nigh onto every man hereabouts owns a green hunting plaid."

"And Àdham would not have gone anywhere without first coming to Finlagh to tell us he was safe," Fiona said. "If he was in Nairn then, he would be here now."

"I agree, madam," MacNab said. "But Sir Àdham be well known hereabouts, and I ken some o' his acquaintances in Nairn. Nary a one o' them had heard from him. In troth, though, we should no stand here talking. Those Comyns I met seemed of an ilk as might instigate a mischief."

"Aye, we must go back," she said, fighting an urge to cry. "I did hope . . ." Her voice failed her, and she fell silent, catching her lower lip between her teeth.

"Sir Àdham be a survivor, m'lady," MacNab said, his tone gentler than she had ever heard it. "Also, the man never goes unarmed. You must cling tae that and tae the fact that we ha' had nae word o' his having fallen at Inverlochy."

"But who would know? Any men still there are either prisoners or dead."

"Ye can believe me when I tell ye that had Donal Dalloch's men found a knight o' Sir Àdham's repute slain on the field or amongst their prisoners, Donal Balloch would ha' sent word hisself *and* demanded ransom." Pausing, he added firmly, "Sakes, he would ha' demanded ransom even had Sir Àdham been dead."

Fiona wanted to believe him. But the faith she had in so many of the Highlanders she had come to know did not extend to the shameless villains who still stood hale, hearty, and victorious at the horrid place they called Inverlochy.

As they turned toward the castle, MacNab said quietly, "I'll tell Sir Fin what little I did hear today, m'lady, but I doubt he'll think any more of it than I did."

She had to agree and remained silent all the way back to the castle.

No one asked what path she had taken while MacNab was with her, so he had no reason to mention it. She knew that he might tell Fin when he reported meeting the two, but she was sure now that the squire had not lied to her about that meeting. More likely, Rory had overreacted to the brief exchange of words.

Having no more appetite for her supper than she had had the previous night, she forced herself to eat, knowing that she would do herself no good by starving. However, as soon as she was finished, she begged to be excused.

Catriona eyed her narrowly. "Art sure you are well, dearling?"

"I am not sick, just unusually tired," Fiona said honestly. "I did sleep well last night, though, so doubtless another night's sleep will do me much good."

Signing to Bridgett to finish her supper, Fiona felt Catriona's gaze still upon her and hoped that her weariness had not caused her kind hostess undue concern.

Performing her ablutions hastily, she put herself to bed and fell asleep, only to awaken with a start when a small hand clapped over her mouth. Her eyes flew open to dusky light and the dark shadow of a head and shoulders close to her face.

"Dinna shriek," a hoarse voice muttered. "I think I ken fine where he may be, m'lady. But we dinna want tae raise a fuss till we think more on it, quiet like."

"Rory?"

"Aye, 'tis m'self," the boy murmured. "Be your Bridgett close by, or nae?"

Fiona sat up, drawing the coverlet up to cover herself. "I don't know where she is, but she lives with her granny. Do you mean you know where Sir Àdham is?"

"Aye," he said. "Least, I think so."

"Then why do you come to me instead of telling Sir Fin?"

"He got a message from some'un on Cawdor's estate that straightaway took him there. 'Sides, I wouldna ha' told him anyhow, 'cause if he takes a host o' men there, he'd be like tae get Sir Àdham killed afore he could stop them villains."

"Where is Àdham?"

"On an island in a loch a ways or so from Raitt," the boy whispered. "Mind, I canna be sure he's there, but that be where Hew and them kept captives afore."

"How do you know that, Rory?" Fiona demanded, albeit quietly.

He hesitated.

"I shan't repeat what you tell me, laddie. But I must know the truth."

He remained silent, frowning. But, when she did not prod further, he said at last, "I were used tae live at Raitt, m'self. Hew's big brother, Rab Comyn, made me go wi' them tae that place they called Lochaber tae fetch and carry for them. When the battle started, I tried tae run away, but Rab caught me. He called me a feardie, and he were a-taking his tawse tae me fierce when Sir Àdham stopped him. Then he tried tae kill Sir Àdham. But Sir Àdham killed Rab instead and Hew ran away."

"So you lied to me before, when I asked you about that day."

Rory shrugged. "I twisted the tale, is all, lest ye might repeat it tae the wrong sorts. I warrant Sir Àdham willna like it that I told ye, though, 'cause I never did tell him that I knew they was Comyns. I were too scared he'd give me back tae Hew, so I told 'im they just found me in them woods and made me fetch and carry."

"I will not betray your confidence, Rory. I do think that you must tell him yourself, though, before one of those Comyns sees you and tells Àdham or Sir Fin."

The boy shrugged again but did not say anything more.

Deciding that was enough, she said, "What do you expect me to do?"

"Tae help me think is all," he said. "I darena go alone, 'cause if that Hew catches me, he'll kill me. I didna ken the other one as was with him today, but a Comyn be a Comyn, and wicked withal. Certes, *ye* canna go wi' me. But we ha' talked many times, and I thought ye might ha' a notion or two in your cockloft."

"Sir Fin would have notions, too," she said gently.

"Aye, but we canna wait for him. I dinna think he'd believe me about stirring bad trouble if he takes a host o' men wi' him tae Raitt, neither, even did he still ha' such a host the noo. Old Comyn o' Raitt be there hisself, ye ken, and he'd raise a din and likely tell the King, 'cause the King did say they mustna fight over Raitt."

"I do know about that," Fiona said thoughtfully. "Still, I believe Sir Fin *would* confront Comyn of Raitt if they have captured Àdham. And he would likely need only a few men to do that, Rory, because everyone's manpower is reduced now. But what makes you so sure that Àdham may be on that island?"

"Sithee, I heard MacNab a-tellin' ye he'd heard Sir Àdham might ha' been in Nairn. So, I took Sirius tae the edge o' town and told him tae find Sir Àdham, like I taught him in Perth. He turned right round and led me straightaway toward Raitt, but he cut off eastward afore going on tae the castle itself. So, I bethought me o' that island. I couldna go all the way tae the loch, o' course, without them likely a-seeing me, but I kent fine by then that them dam—them *wicked* . . ."

"Call them damnable if you like," Fiona said grimly. "If they abducted Àdham after he'd escaped the carnage at Inverlochy, those men belong in hell."

When Rory nodded, she said, "Could you show me where that loch is?"

"Aye, sure. But we'd ha' tae be daft tae go there on our ownsome."

"There is still some light out, though, aye?" She glanced at the open window.

"It'd be dark afore we could get there." He hesitated, then added, "There do be a bit o' wind, though, as might clear away some o' the mist and the clouds."

Making up her mind, Fiona said, "I want you to show me where that loch is. You need go no farther, Rory, but do you know how to get out of the keep without running into any of the family?"

"Aye, sure," he said, frowning. "But ye *mustna* go, m'lady. There'll be consequences for us both, bad ones, an we get caught."

"Then we will not get caught," Fiona said. "I just want to look. Everyone thinks I'm asleep, so no one will look for me. You say that the loch is near Raitt?"

He thought about that. "It be east o' the castle and a wee bit southlike."

"Can we reach it without being seen from there?"

"Och, aye, over yon pass Sir Àdham uses tae avoid Raitt. That be how Sirius and I came back t'night. But Hew will likely leave guards near the loch."

"I must get dressed. We can still get outside the wall, though, aye?"

"Aye, sure, although if ye mean tae take the dogs—"

"We cannot take them. They would bark or growl if anyone came near us."

"Sakes, m'lady, Sirius doesna bark *or* growl, and I ken all o' his signals, even his whistles. Moreover, if ye go alone, Sir Àdham or Sir Fin will—"

"We cannot think about that," Fiona interjected hastily. "We'll take Sirius, because if Àdham is a prisoner, we *must* find him. Do you have any weapons?"

"I ha' me knife," he said, patting the small pouch hanging from his belt.

Fiona eyed it dubiously. "It cannot be very long."

"Nae, I just use it for cutting twine or making arrows for me bow. But I could stick someone with it an I had to," he added.

Deciding that that would have to do, since she had no weapon of her own, Fiona asked Rory to wait on the landing. Then, hastily donning her shift and kirtle, she snatched her dark hooded cloak from its hook by the door and stepped cautiously out of her chamber, shutting the door silently behind her.

Rory led the way down to the scullery, clear of servants now, and they slipped out through the postern door to the garden.

Keeping close to the wall, they waited until the man on the gate moved a short distance away in the course of his duties; whereupon, Rory revealed a small postern gate in one of the two tall iron ones that swung open to let a person out without having to open the heavier gate.

Sirius slipped out ahead of Fiona to follow the boy, who headed around to the east side of the knoll.

"Keep close tae the wall," he whispered. "They dinna look straight down much, and this be the dark side anyhow, even when there dinna be mist and such."

"There are a few stars, at least," she murmured. "The mist must be clearing."

"Aye, that be the breeze. We dinna want it tae clear too quick, though."

She followed him, mimicking his movements and striving to move as silently as he did. She heard men talking quietly on the ramparts, but none raised an alarm.

They were soon over the hill, doubtless on the route that Àdham had taken to reach Finlagh from Lochindorb. But Fiona soon lost track of their direction and could only trust Rory to know where he was going.

They moved through dark and chilly woodland that seemed to lack any path and walked for much longer than she had expected. Suddenly, she saw the loch, no more than a sheet of blackness, rippling slightly in the breeze.

Rory crouched in shrubbery, motioning for her to do likewise.

"That be it," he murmured. "Ye canna see the island from where we be. But we'll go round that way"—he gestured to his right— "and ye'll see it, then."

"How far offshore?" she asked.

"Hoots, I dinna ken. Farther than I'd want tae swim on a cold night."

"If Àdham is there, I must see him. How many guards might there be?"

"I dinna ken that neither. But I ha' a notion *where* they'd be. I could creep round and see do I find 'em. I dinna ken how ye think ye could see him, though."

"Let me worry about that. But you *must not* let anyone see you."

He didn't respond to that, and she didn't blame him. The laddie had a strong sense of self-preservation and would do his best to avoid discovery.

She held Sirius back, fearing that the dog might give the boy away if it followed him, but Sirius leaned into her, as if to reassure her that he would protect her.

She knew what she wanted to do, but she didn't know if she could do it and get away with a whole skin.

After all, if the Comyns didn't kill her, Àdham might.

CHAPTER 23

The lapping water sounded no closer, but the air in Àdham's prison was icy cold, making him wonder if his jailers meant to freeze him to death in his tunic.

They had not talked to him or to each other, nor had he seen their faces, but he did vaguely recall flopping facedown over what must have been a garron, and later into a tipsy boat. With his hands bound behind him and an opaque sack of sorts covering his aching head, he had been sure they meant to drown him.

Then, the boat had bumped onto land, and when they hauled him out, he'd lost consciousness again.

Fiona huddled in the shrubbery with Sirius, listening intently for any sound to warn her that someone else might be nearby. But the first awareness she had of Rory's return was when the dog stiffened alertly and then began wagging its tail just before the boy murmured, "It's me; dinna shriek."

"Did you see guards?" she murmured.

"Aye, sure, so he must be there, 'cause naebody else be missing that I ha' ken of," Rory whispered. "But they be at t'other end o' the loch, round a wee fire tae keep theirselves warm and out o' the wind. Hew Comyn canna be here, and if he does come, they'll be gey sorry about that fire. But I were glad tae see it."

"Are they between us and the place where we can see the island?"

"We'll go t'other way. Ye'll see their fire then, so ye'll ken where they be."

"Might they have left other guards to keep watch over the island or on it?"

"'Haps they might, but I didna see nae one the way I went, nor did I see a boat at that end o' the island. I'll go ahead o' ye tae show ye the way. Ye need only keep low and kilt up your skirts so ye willna make a din a-dragging 'em."

"I can go quietly," she said. "Just show me where that island is."

Rory did not respond but moved ahead, so Fiona followed him, trying to keep silent. She soon saw the tiny fire on the upper shore across the loch and realized that, like most lochs she had seen, this one was at least twice as long as it was wide. She saw the island, too, a third of the way up from their end but closer to the opposite shore. The water glistened, revealing the shape of the heavily wooded island. More stars reflected on the water, so the mist was dissipating.

Glancing up, Fiona noticed light showing through clouds in the east. The moon, usually her friend, threatened now to betray her.

She tried to imagine how far a count of two hundred would take her.

He walked along a narrow, silvery path, surrounded by blackness. An odd herbal scent stirred his senses but revealed nothing about his location. Nor did he seem to have a destination in mind . . . if he had a mind. Perhaps he was dead.

He thought about that as he followed the path. His feet moved without any sense of hard ground beneath them. Perhaps he walked on clouds.

His body seemed abruptly to upend then and drift until he was lying down. Sirius sat beside him, lapping his cheek. Lips touched his, stirring confusion.

Dogs did not have such lips. Then Sirius vanished as if he had never been, and he was in bed with Fiona. His body stirred pleasurably. He pulled her closer and began to fondle her, eager to awaken her passions as he could so easily do.

Water dripped on him . . .

. . . icy water that soaked through his tunic as a freezing hand cupped his cheek and a soft, familiar voice said, "Oh, Àdham, love, prithee speak, but quietly! Say it is you, for I cannot see you. Oh, my love, please do *not* be dead!"

Much nicer than Mar's shaking and bellowing at him.

He blinked, and there was light enough now to see her shape. But surely he was still dreaming, for she could not possibly . . .

"Àdham, say something."

"You're dripping on me." His voice, to his own ears, was harsh and not his but someone else's, more proof that he still dreamed. "What did you call me?"

"What do you mean? I said your name."

Water dripped on him again, and his senses reeled. He was certainly not in bed with his wife, but his wife was with him and had no business to be anywhere near wherever he was now. He tried to sit up, but his stretched-out limbs painfully recalled him to his current circumstances.

"Where the devil are we?" he asked. "How did *you* get here?"

"Some Comyns captured you," she said. "You are in a dreadful shack on an island in a loch southeast of Raitt. At least, so Rory told me."

"Rory? Is he here, too, then?"

"Aye, on the shore, watching for wandering guards."

"Shore? Island? Do you mean to say that you swam here?"

"Aye, but underwater, just as I did in the Tay. I was in no danger, for no one saw me. The guards are keeping warm by a fire some distance from here."

"By the Fates, I am going to take a tawse to both of you," he said more sharply than he had intended.

"Aye, sure, and so you may when you are safe," she replied gently. "But first, we must get you home. And before we can do that, let me see if I can untie you."

"Why be we a-sneaking past your ain guards, Hew?" Dae asked his cousin as they crept down to the loch shore, where he could see a narrow boat drawn up on the land. "I thought we came here tae make sure they was seeing tae their duties."

"'Tis true, we did," Hew agreed. "But they be lazing by yon fire, so I been a-thinking, Dae, and what I think is that Àdham Mac-Finlagh has crossed a line. At first, I were a-thinking we could use the man tae force Sir Fin o' the Battles tae give us the lass, but from the time I saw that wee laddie I pointed out tae ye whilst we watched their party making for Rothiemurchus, I ha' had some other thoughts. That laddie were at hand when our Rab were killed at Lochaber, so I'm thinking now that Àdham MacFinlagh were likely the lout I did see kill Rab."

"Did ye no ken the man at the time?"

"Nae, then, I did not. I hadna seen him in years, and everyone there had such shaggy beards that nae man could ken much more than that the one he were fighting were likely an enemy. But I ken him now, aye? So I'm thinking that Sir Àdham MacFinlagh may just breathe his last breath tonight. And, thanks tae those louts yonder, nae one save us two will ken how that came about."

Fiona shivered. Although the water in the loch had felt warmer than the air at first, by the time she had crept ashore on the island, more terrified with each move that someone would shout an alarm, she was freezing. To her relief, the door had only a bar fitted into iron brackets at each end. With effort, she had lifted it away, gently set it down, and pulled the door open.

Even now that Àdham was awake, and with that door ajar, she could barely see him right in front of her. But the faster they could get moving, the better.

As she battled the knots, using Rory's wee knife, Àdham's threat echoed briefly in her mind. Giving herself a mental shake then, she decided that she didn't care what he did, as long as he was alive and back at Finlagh to do it.

With his hands freed, he sat up and leaned forward to deal with the knots at his ankles, but an involuntary cry of pain escaped when he tried to reach forward.

"Ay-de-mi, lass, I can scarce move my arms, let alone my fingers."

"Let me do it," she said. "Keep trying to move your arms and hands, though, because you will have to swim, and quietly. I do not suppose they were so helpful as to leave your weapons here with you."

"In troth, I do not know," he admitted. "Someone must have attacked me when I left Nairn and then, I think, knocked me on the head for the second time in a sennight. I came somewhat to my senses twice, once on a garron and then when they dumped me into a boat. I expected them to drown me."

"You can tell me the rest later, but your legs are free now," she said. "Try to move them, and rub life into them whilst I feel around in here to see if they did leave a weapon. At present, I have only this wee knife of Rory's."

"By the Rood, lass," Àdham murmured wearily as he massaged his legs and feet, "I ought to bellow at you and order you to go home where you would be safe, but all I want is to take you in my arms, hold you tight, and tell you what a mad, brave thing you have done by coming here to rescue me."

"You'll likely come to your senses before we reach home," she said dryly, "but I hope you do not, because I want you to do those other things, just not right now. So rub harder," she added, "so we can leave this dreadful place."

Obeying her orders, Àdham struggled to bring feeling back into his extremities. He was certain that the Comyns would not have left weapons in the shack, so he was startled to hear a soft exclamation of triumph from her a few moments later.

"What?" he asked, keeping his voice down as much as he could.

"Someone left a sort of club here," she replied in a whisper. "It is not a mace or as good as a sword or a dirk, but it may be useful if we meet any Comyns."

"Likely, it's the one they bashed me with," he muttered grimly. "I do not suppose you had the good sense to tell Fin or MacNab that you were coming here."

"We have no time for scolding," she murmured. "Fin went to Cawdor, but Rory heard MacNab tell me he'd met someone who thought he'd seen you in Nairn. So, Rory took Sirius near Nairn and told him to find you. When Sirius led him on east of Raitt, Rory came back through your pass and told me about this island."

"How the devil did Rory know about it?"

"I am sure he will tell you about that when you are safe," she said softly.

He realized that she was talking to him as if he were an ailing bairn. But just as he was about to point out to her that he was naught of the sort, a wave of dizziness struck him, and he realized that his head still ached like fury.

Likely, her judgment was not as impaired as his own was.

"Can you stand yet?" she asked.

"I will." But he quickly realized he would need her help even to do that. "Sakes, lass, I'm as weak as a babe."

Doing her best to help him to his feet, she said, "When did you eat last, and why did you go to Nairn instead of coming straight home?"

"I was with Mar," he explained, wishing his head would stop pounding. "He keeps a galley in Nairn harbor, and he'd been wounded, so I stayed with him."

"Do you think you can swim?"

"Aye, sure, more easily than I can walk," he said. He *was* standing but hesitated to take a step, lest he find his legs less interested in doing so than he was. His head pounded more than ever, but the dizziness had begun to ease.

"I'll just fetch that club," she said. "See if you can walk to the door."

Even as she was talking, she heard a songbird's chirp-chirp from the shore. "Someone's coming," she whispered. "That was Rory. I told him to make a stir to draw the guards off if they raised an alarm but to give an owl's hoot or a night bird's call if he saw someone coming toward this island."

"Fetch the club, lass. I'll step out into the trees and look about."

Moving quickly to the club, Fiona picked it up and was turning toward the door when she heard a new voice outside the shack speaking Gaelic. Although she could not speak it well, her understanding had improved enough for her to get the gist of his words:

"So ye've managed to free yourself, have ye? I vow, I'll string those louts up and take the hide off them for their idleness. But ye'll get nae farther, Àdham MacFinlagh. I ha' me sword, as ye see, and this time ye have none."

Peeking out through the doorway, thinking the voice sounded distantly familiar, she saw a bearded man nearly as tall as Àdham but less broad, wearing a plaid and tunic. Àdham had turned to face him but was backing slowly away toward the shore. A cloud that had occluded the moon was easing past it, and as its light brightened, she saw the other man's profile. Something about it seemed familiar, too, although his thick beard made identifying him impossible.

Nevertheless, he had threatened Àdham and seemed not to know that Àdham was no longer alone. He said tauntingly, "Ye'll no get far if ye try tae swim away. If ye ha' nae ken o' me, I'll tell ye I be Hew Comyn o' Raitt, and I need only tae shout for me lads tae bring 'em down on ye wherever ye might swim ashore."

"But you cannot best me alone, can you?" Àdham said in Scots. "If I mistake not, the last time I faced one of your lot, *you* turned tail and ran."

Recalling what Rory had told her about the day he'd met Àdham, Fiona gripped the club in both hands and began to move into the doorway. Hearing a gasp and slight cough on the other side of the door, she stopped abruptly and kept still.

Afraid to breathe, she watched as a second man passed the opening. He, too, wore a tunic and plaid and carried a sword. He did not speak, but she was as certain as she could be that he was another Comyn.

Àdham had seen the second man, too. He had easily recognized Hew Comyn as one of the two men who had punished Rory at Lochaber. Not that it would aid him now that Hew had the upper hand. He just hoped that Fiona would stay inside the shack and that he could draw the two men farther away from her and regain some of his strength in the doing. If he could not, Hew would kill him.

If his lass remained quiet, she would have a chance to get away . . . unless the Comyns entered the shack again after they killed him.

The second man had not spoken. But he had coughed, so surely Hew Comyn knew he was there. They were both dry, so they must have come to the island in a boat. As the thought crossed his mind, he saw Fiona step out of the shack and had to bite his lip to keep from bellowing at her to get back inside.

Hastily, but still in Scots, he said to Hew Comyn, "What the devil do you two dastards hope to gain by killing me? If you had wanted me dead, you could have killed me straightaway instead of taking the trouble to bring me here."

"Aye, well, me cousin Dae and I had a first thought o' trading ye for your lady, who might be o' use tae some o' us in persuading her da tae speak tae the King on Alexander's behalf," Comyn said, shifting to Scots himself. "However, after our victory at Inverlochy, me da says Jamie will *ha'* tae let Alexander go, or he'll see the whole o' the western Highlands laid waste by Donal Balloch. But I'd also seen our lad Rory wi' ye and suspected ye were the murderous snaffler wha' killed our Rab. Now that ye've spoken o' Lochaber, I be gey certain o' that."

"'Twas your Rab who attacked me, if you can recall the truth of it."

"Ye were interfering in what were our business and nane o' yours."

Keeping his gaze on Comyn's eyes and, he hoped, Comyn's eyes on him, Àdham was nonetheless aware that the second man stood watching them and that Fiona was stealthily moving toward him. His fear for her nearly distracted him from the fact that Hew Comyn had set himself to attack.

Praying that Àdham could keep his attacker's attention fixed on himself long enough for her to deal with the second man without letting the first kill Àdham, Fiona fixed her gaze on the back of her quarry's head.

Ignoring her near certainty that even if she clubbed the man before he sensed her behind him, the other villain would kill Àdham and then turn on her, she knew she could not hesitate. If she did, the likeliest outcome would be Àdham's death and her immediate capture by Rory's "damnable Comyns."

Gripping the club in both hands, she moved swiftly but furtively toward her target. Her bare feet made no sound on the grass and dirt beneath them as she moved toward him, raising the club, and then swung it as hard as she could, catching him a resounding crack behind his right ear.

The man dropped with a thud and lay still.

His sword slid silently to the grass beside him.

Sensing motion behind him and hearing the thud, Hew glanced back to see Dae drop his sword and fall. In the growing moonlight, he recognized Ormiston's daughter, Lady MacFinlagh, standing over Dae in her wet shift, holding their club.

That wet shift held his gaze a split-second too long, for when he turned back toward Àdham with his sword at the ready and murder in his heart, he placed his chin perfectly to meet Àdham's fist as it flashed past the upheld sword and knocked Hew Comyn flat.

"Lass, get back into the shack and collect those ropes. Quick, now, for I doubt that Hew here will oblige us by staying unconscious much longer, and I've little energy left to deal with him if he comes to."

"What about the other one?"

"Has he moved?"

She shook her head. "Do you think I killed him?"

Her voice shook, and he hated to hear that. Keeping one eye on Hew, he moved to the other man's side and felt for a pulse in his neck. It was there, weak but steady. "He's not dead yet, so we'll tie and gag them, and then we'll leave them. Go now."

She went and came back with the four lengths of rope and his plaid.

"I found this in the corner, but there were no other weapons," she murmured.

"The plaid will be useful," he said as he deftly tied Hew's hands behind him with one rope and his feet together with another. "You must be cold."

"I've had no time to think about it," she said. "How will you get your plaid back to shore, though? It cannot be easy to swim with it or wise to get it wet."

"Bless you, sweetheart, it's been wet many times. But these two dastards have doubtless had the kindness to fetch us a boat." He moved to the one she had clubbed, Dae Comyn, and tied him as he had tied Hew.

"Won't the guards yonder hear us or see us if we row back across? It would be safer to swim underwater, would it not?"

"Nae, lass, we'll take their boat. We'll keep the island between us and that fire, and if those louts have heard naught yet, they'll not hear us rowing. Wrap my plaid round you whilst I finish tying up this chap. Do you still have Rory's knife?"

"Aye, I carried it in my teeth when I swam over here," she said with a smile as she handed it to him.

"We'll discuss your swim later," he said. "Wrap yourself up well now."

He was sure that it had been the sight of Fiona in that clinging wet shift that had held Hew Comyn's gaze long enough for him to catch him with that punch. He was glad to have had that time. But the idea that Hew had seen her in such disarray made it hard to resist strangling the man or splitting him with his own sword.

Instead, Àdham used the wee knife to cut strips from Dae Comyn's plaid. Stuffing one into Dae's mouth, he used the second to tie it there. Then he moved to Hew and did the same. As he was tying that gag in place, Hew's eyes opened.

"Don't glower at me like that," Àdham said. "You were a fool to spend time taunting me and staring overlong at my lady. I'd liefer kill you for that, but I won't. It will shame you enough, I think, for your lads to find you like this. Also, if you freeze to death overnight, it will be God's doing, not mine. After what I saw at Inverlochy, you should be glad I don't take my revenge for that out on you."

Straightening, glad that his legs felt like his legs again and that his fingers had managed the ropes, he knew that he still had to get Fiona, Rory, and himself away from Comyn land before the louts near the fire decided to tend to their duty.

They found the boat and saw that the Comyns had thought-fully wrapped the oars to keep them from banging against the oar-locks. After that, it was easy to keep the island between them and the guardsmen as Àdham rowed gently to shore.

Keeping low, so that their moving figures would draw no attention from the opposite shore, they made their way back to where Rory and Sirius waited.

"I saw ye a-coming, or I'd ha' hooted," he told them in hushed tones as he handed Fiona her kirtle and she quickly donned it and laced its bodice. "Sirius alerted a wee while ago, so I think some'un else be a-coming yonder."

Fiona murmured, "We'll be trapped between them."

"Nae, then, m'lady," Rory said. "His tail be a-wagging."

"Come, lass," Àdham said. "We'll go to meet them."

"S-Sir Àdham?" Rory's voice faltered.

"What is it, laddie?"

"Be ye vexed wi' me, sir?"

"We'll talk some later," Àdham said quietly, resting a gentle hand on the boy's shaggy curls. "But you did me a great boon tonight, guarding my lady."

"Ye shouldna be vexed wi' her, either, I think," Rory said with more of his usual confidence. "I dinna ken how anyone else could ha' swum there without making the water move about. The stars were out, ye ken, so even them fool louts yonder might had seen big ripples and got up tae see what caused 'em. But she stayed underwater the whole time."

"I am sure she did," Àdham said, urging the boy forward. "You lead the way now, and go quietly, lest your judgment about Sirius's welcome was faulty."

He soon learned that the boy and Sirius were right, for he heard a quiet "Loch Moigh" ahead and recognized Fin's voice.

So did Fiona, for her footsteps behind Àdham came to a stop.

Recognizing that quiet voice as Fin's, Fiona froze where she was, certain that he would react more vehemently than Àdham had—thus far, anyway—to finding that she had deceived everyone and sneaked out of the castle with Rory.

She stood still for only seconds, though, before Àdham turned and reached for her. Drawing her near, he bent to speak into her ear. "There will be a reckoning, *mo chridhe*. But it will come from me, not from anyone else."

At that moment, his words were less than reassuring, because she knew that he was as answerable to Fin as she was. But she had to continue walking, even so.

They met Fin moments later, and to her further chagrin, MacNab was with him. Even by moonlight, she could see disapproval in the lanky squire's expression when his cool gaze came to rest on her.

There was no more conversation until they were away from the loch and nearing the top of the pass with the moon behind them and Castle Finlagh below on its knoll, making a shadowy picture against the starry northwestern sky.

Then, at last, Àdham broke the silence. "How did you know, sir?"

Such was their kinship and ease of discourse that Fin answered matter-of-factly, "We learned that two of the Thane of Cawdor's tenants had mentioned meeting you near Nairn. So MacNab and I went to Cawdor to talk to them. MacNab had also spoken to Hew Comyn and a cousin of his, whose insolence to MacNab stirred his suspicions that they knew more than they admitted knowing. I had heard about that island prison of Comyn's, so we came along to see if they had put you there. Evidently," he added gently, "someone else had heard about the island, too."

Fiona shivered at his tone.

Rory, walking beside her, looked up at her and opened his mouth, but she shook her head. She knew if he spoke, he might admit to having insisted that Fin would take too many men along if he hastened to Raitt's loch.

That, she decided, was no admission to make just then.

Àdham remained quiet for a time before he said, "It was fortunate for me that the two of them did come along, sir."

"Which of you is going to tell me just how you escaped?"

Àdham looked at Fiona.

CHAPTER 24

⦿⦿⦿

With a sigh, Fiona said to Fin, "Rory figured it out, sir. But he knew that you and MacNab had gone to Cawdor, so he came to me. He also knew that the Comyns sometimes kept prisoners on that island, and—"

"Do I ask how he came to know that particular fact?"

Fiona was trying to think of an innocuous way to explain when Rory straightened his shoulders, looked directly at Fin, and said calmly, "I lived wi' them, Sir Fin, so I ken much that I wish I didna ken about them, that's how. I didna say nowt about any Comyns when I came tae Castle Finlagh, 'cause I knew ye were enemies wi' them, and I feared ye wouldna want tae keep me if I told ye."

"Is that why you didn't tell Sir Àdham who they were at Lochaber?"

"Nae, but I didna ken him then, and I feared he'd send me back tae them. Hoots, though, he saved me from Rab Comyn and scared Hew off. Then he brung me here. So when I heard MacNab tell her ladyship that some'un may ha' seen him in Nairn, I took Sirius and we followed his trail well past Raitt. I kent then that them Comyns—likely Hew hisself—had got him. But ye'd gone, so I told her ladyship, thinking she might ha' a notion o' what we could do.

"I didna think she'd want tae go and find Sir Àdham herself," he added, glancing at Fiona. "But it be as well she did, though. I dinna ken how anyone else could ha' got tae him without them guards a-seeing or a-hearing 'em."

They walked on in silence for a time, each with his or her thoughts. But as they topped the pass, Àdham said, "Hew had come to suspect that I killed Rab Comyn at Lochaber, so he and his cousin sneaked onto the island without alerting their men that they were there. Before Hew tried to kill me, he talked some blethers about having expected to trade me for Fiona so Ormiston would persuade Jamie to release Alexander. But that—"

"Faith," Fiona exclaimed, "*that's* who that man is!"

"Which man, lass?" Fin asked. "We know that they are Comyns. I suspect, as well, that they are responsible for the attack on you near Lochindorb."

"Aye, sir, but I just realized why Hew Comyn's voice sounded familiar, although the bearded man I saw tonight did not seem to resemble anyone I had met before. But, Àdham, he is the fop who accosted me in the assembly hall that night. He *said* I'd be sorry that I'd rebuffed him. Do you think he wanted to kill me, too?"

Àdham shook his head. "Not if he thought he could hold you for ransom, *mo chridhe*, especially if he believed Ormiston could get James to release Alexander."

"James does listen to him," she admitted. "He even seeks him out when he wants his advice. Even so . . ."

"Hew Comyn failed to capture you, lass, so his reasons need not concern us now," Fin said. "Moreover, in the wake of the royal army's defeat at Inverlochy, James will have much to do to restore order. I doubt that Ormiston would seek his aid at such a time, even to save his beloved daughter. His reply to such a demand would more likely be made in person, at the head of his own army."

Fiona smiled then for the first time since she had set Àdham free, knowing that Fin was right about her father.

Seeing Fiona smile, Àdham glanced at Fin and saw that his uncle was looking directly at him, his expression somber.

"We could use such an army now, ourselves," Àdham said. "Our forces are sadly depleted."

Fin grimaced. "Would you truly welcome a host of mad Borderers to the Highlands, lad? I have fought them, and I can tell
you, they take no prisoners and know not the meaning of mercy."

"With respect, sir, you could say the same of our fellow Highlanders. But from what I have hitherto heard of Borderers, much
of their ability lies in their horsemanship. That would avail them
naught in our treacherous mountains."

Shifting his gaze to Fiona, he saw that she was frowning.

"What is it, sweetheart? Does our discourse offend you?"

"No, sir, for I have learned that Scots are much the same wherever they live. I was thinking about tonight's events on that island.
Do you think that man will die? Not Hew, but the other one."

"He was still breathing when we tied him up," Àdham said. "He
is apparently Hew Comyn's cousin, Dae."

"I met only the one called Hew in the assembly hall. . . . Why
do you frown, sir?"

Àdham shook his head. "I do not frown at you. You awoke a
memory. Someone else mentioned a chap called Hew . . . Sakes,
it was Gilli Roy! I saw him talking to that fop *after* he'd accosted
you, and Gilli said his name was Hew but that he knew naught else
about the man. Now, I wonder about that."

"Many men are called Hew," Fin said. "'Tis as common a name
in the Lowlands—or in England and Wales—as it is here."

Fiona's expressive face told Àdham that their words had stirred
an unwelcome thought in her mind.

Ignoring Fin, he said, "What troubles you now, lass?"

She hesitated, eyeing him warily.

Gilli Roy had not told anyone how far north she had gone the day
they'd met Àdham on his return to Finlagh, and Fiona still felt deeply
grateful for that kindness. She was therefore reluctant to betray him
or herself now. But if Gilli did know Hew Comyn better than he had
suggested, surely she ought at least to tell Àdham so.

Would it be the truth, though? Gilli had seemed like a lost
soul in Perth and behaved much more confidently in the Highlands. That transformation was one that she could understand,
because she had experienced an initial loss of confidence in the

Highlands that she had rarely felt in the more familiar Borders and Lowlands.

"Fiona?"

Starting at Àdham's single word and realizing that she had forgotten what, exactly, he had asked her, she struggled to remember. As they passed through the gateway into the bailey, she said, "I cannot believe that Gilli Roy purposely made a friend of Hew Comyn, sir. I was trying to imagine such a thing, but it will not serve.

"Gilli knows that the Comyns are enemies of Clan Chattan, so I doubt that he would purposely encourage one in a town where others in the Confederation might see them. Faith, did *you* recognize Hew Comyn in town?"

"Nae, but if I'd ever seen him before I met him at Lochaber, I do not recall it. Also, in town, I saw only a foppish churl to whom my complaining cousin talked more amiably than he did with his own people."

"Mayhap, his own people were not as sympathetic to his unhappiness about being in a town he did not know or like, with people whose language he did not properly understand or speak. Mayhap Hew Comyn took unfair advantage of that."

Àdham gave her a more searching look then, and something in that look disturbed her senses in more ways than one.

Rory, whom she had completely forgotten was still with them, took advantage of the pause to say, "Be ye vexed wi' all of us, Sir Fin?"

Fin turned his attention to the boy. "Should I be, laddie?"

"As tae m'self, I couldna think o' aught else tae do but talk tae her ladyship. I didna think ye'd like it if I told Lady Cat, instead. But 'haps I should ha'—"

A gasp from Àdham and a look of comical dismay on Fin's face interrupted the boy, permitting Fin's dry admission that he would have disliked that very much. He added, "I do think, though, that I shall pay a visit anon to Comyn of Raitt."

"MacNab and I would go with you," Àdham said, thus, unbeknownst to himself, forcing Fiona to stifle her protest at the thought of his walking into danger again so soon.

"Nae," Fin said. "I'll take my men. But I will send word to Raitt that I seek a peaceful meeting. I doubt that Hew will have told his father the whole of this tale, and I do think that Comyn should hear it. He will understand as well as I do that endangering a knight of Jamie's own making *and* that knight's noble lady might well persuade James to change his mind about who should lawfully possess Raitt."

The porter, evidently hearing their approach, opened the door then, and Fin thanked him, adding, "As for you others, I will bid you good night. I'd wager you are all longing for your beds."

"I am," Àdham admitted. "Good night, sir."

Fiona echoed him, but when she looked at Àdham again, he had turned to Rory and was telling the boy to take himself off, that they would talk more on the morrow. Having expected Fin to have stern words for her, she decided that he expected Àdham to attend to her and wondered if Àdham would feel obliged to be more severe than he might otherwise have been.

Interruping her thoughts, Àdham acknowledged MacNab, saying, "I shan't need you tonight, so go to bed." Then, he turned back to Fiona. "We'll go right up, too, sweetheart. I'll admit I'm worn right through."

"Truly, sir?" she asked, raising her eyebrows and smiling at him.

Giving her a probing look, he said quietly, "I may recover more swiftly when I'm safely in mine own bed." Taking her hand and tucking it into the crook of his arm, he escorted her to the stairway and then urged her on up the stairs ahead of him.

She could not read him and, for once, had no idea what he was thinking. He seemed to be interested in bedding her, but, since he had said nothing yet about her venturing into Comyn territory with only Rory and Sirius to accompany her, she knew not what to expect when they were alone.

He reached past her to open the bedchamber door and then, with a gentle hand to her back, ushered her in and shut it behind them.

She stood still, waiting.

"Look at me, Fiona-lass."

Swallowing, she turned.

"I shan't eat you, I promise," he said, his eyes twinkling.

With a sigh of relief she walked into his arms, and he held her tight.

Leaning her head against his chest, Fiona heard his heart beating and thought of how she might never have heard that sound again had the Islesmen or the damnable Comyns killed him.

Realizing that her hair was still damp, Àdham said, "We need to get these wet clothes off of you. I suspect that your shift is still dripping."

"It doesn't feel wet," she said. "I feel only the welcome warmth of your body." After a pause, she added softly, "I feared you were angry with me."

"Sweetheart, I'd have to be as much of a rogue as Hew Comyn is to be angry with the woman who rescued me, especially since I'm in love with her. I do have some things that I want to discuss with you, but they can wait for another time."

"What sorts of things?"

"Not now," he said firmly. "You must know that I am not a violent man—"

"Faith, sir, the first thing you said when you learned that only Rory had come with me was that you were going to take a tawse to both of us!"

"I did, aye, and you were so terrified by that threat that you said I could do so as soon as we were safe. And we are safe now, are we not?" he said, reaching for her bodice laces and letting his hands brush the tips of her breasts as he did.

"Aye," she said breathlessly. "Art sure you are not vexed?"

"If I have a complaint, it's about the *way* you said that I could beat you. You spoke to me then as if I were a simpleminded bairn."

She smiled then, tremulously. "You seemed so dreadfully weak and helpless that it frightened me. Did you mean it when you said you were in love with me?"

"I did, I was, and I am, *mo chridhe.* I can no longer imagine life without you. I think I realized I'd fallen in love when I had to leave you here. I had never given much thought to those I left behind when I went off to serve as a warrior. But it was nearly all that I thought of for days on our journey to Inverlochy. I also meant it when I said that I'm not angry, but I will insist that you take more care when you walk out alone. Would you like me to ask where you were, exactly, when you met Rory and MacNab earlier today?"

"I would rather not have to tell you," she admitted.

"Then I think you know how I would react if you were to venture there alone again." He slid her kirtle off her shoulders, and she let it slip to the floor. "I was right about your shift," he said then, whisking it off over her head.

"I trust you are not in your courses," he added.

"Umm . . . no."

"Why do you hesitate? Do you fear they may begin tonight?"

"No," she said, this time visibly trying not to smile.

"Fiona, is aught amiss with you?"

"No, sir, but I am not certain how you will react to what I must tell you."

"Tell me, anyway."

"Very well," she said. "I am nearly certain that we are going to have a bairn, because I have had most of the symptoms that Joanna had."

He gasped with shock, delight, and then anger. Catching hold of her by her upper arms, he peered into her face and said, "'Tis as well that you say you are not sure, because if you *were* sure, then what the *devil* were you thinking?"

Having watched the play of emotions on his face, Fiona knew exactly what thoughts had flown through his mind. She said, "I was thinking that I had no intention of raising a son without his father, sir. *That's* what I was thinking!"

"But—"

"Nae, now, you listen to me," she said firmly. "When Rory told me that the Comyns likely held you on an island, I knew that unless they also housed their guards on that island, I might have a chance to set you free. I did not tell even Rory what I meant to do, though, so you must not blame him."

"I won't," he said grimly. "Go on."

Suppressing a smile and hoping that he did not discern as much, she said, "I told Rory only that I wanted to see the island. We left at dusk, so it was dark and cloudy when we arrived. But we could see stars reflected in the water, as well as the island, and I knew I could swim that far without the guards seeing me."

"What if there had been guards on the island?"

"I expect that I'd have heard them before they saw me. In any event, I did search briefly before I lifted the bar from the door and set it aside. I could hear them talking across the water. The tone of their voices did not change."

"You did not see Hew and Dae in their boat," he pointed out.

"They did not see me, either."

He nodded, then picked her up in his arms and carried her to their bed. "I have one more question for you before we sleep," he said.

"I want you to make love to me, if that is what you would ask."

"I am glad to know that, because I do mean to make love to you until you squeal for mercy," he said. "But the question I would ask has more to do with the answer you gave me earlier about why you thought Gilli Roy had made friends with Hew Comyn. Do *you* still feel the way you think he felt? Are you unhappy in the Highlands, trying to speak the Gaelic?"

"No, I'm not, nor do I worry that people here dislike or mis-understand me. I thought that I had made that plain when I said that I believe all Scots are much the same wherever they live. Fin called Borderers 'mad' tonight, just as I once called all Highland-ers 'barbarians.' Do you not think that makes us similar if not the same?"

He chuckled. "I am not even going to try to answer that ques-tion. I do have one more for you, though."

"What is it?"

"Might we hurt the bairn, if there is a bairn, if we make love?"

"No, because James and Joanna . . . That is, I asked Cat, and she said no. And, before you ask, I have not told her or anyone else about the babe yet, but I am sure about him, Àdham, just as sure as I am that I love you more than you love me."

"Nae, you do not, and I know how to make you agree that I love you more."

He failed to make her agree to that, but he did make her squeal for mercy.

EPILOGUE

—⌒⌒⌒—

Aberdeenshire, May 1432

A feather-soft rain was falling, creating a misty, gray view beyond the long, north-facing line of arched windows in the great hall of the Earl of Mar's Kildrummy Castle.

Despite the number of people still present after the wedding feast, the hall was quiet enough for Fiona, standing by one of those tall windows, to hear the crackling of the fire on the nearest hearth.

The great hall's length ran east to west with a fireplace at each end. Its north wall formed a portion of the castle's north curtain wall, and as she gazed out upon that vast northern view, she felt the same awe that she had felt the first day of their visit, when she realized that that line of windows penetrated the curtain wall.

The castle, as she had seen on their approach three days before, sat atop a motte, its entrance protected by a drawbridge that, when raised, provided a giant, impenetrable door between twin gatehouses.

Àdham, Ormiston, and a number of the other men had disparaged the great hall's wonder-inspiring windows but not nearly as roundly as they disparaged Mar's chapel. The east end of that marvel projected right through the curtain wall, providing a fine view of the eastern countryside through three tall single-light casements with pointed arches that defined them as lancet windows.

"I have always wondered what fool decided to weaken the curtain wall in such a fashion," Fin had said to Àdham when the chapel projection piercing the wall came into view, clearly having no further foundation of its own.

Intrigued, Fiona asked if they had ever asked Mar who had built the chapel.

"He doesn't know," Fin said. "But Jamie would hang any noble of his who weakened his wall in such a way. That fellow was at least sensible enough to leave the original thickness of the wall below it, and the chapel itself is splendid."

Having now seen it, Fiona agreed. During the wedding, the skies had been clear except for drifting clouds that began to gather before the ceremony ended. She had been able to watch them gather, because the tall windows were behind the altar.

The ceremony and feast were over, and her new stepmother now sat beside Mar, chatting with Catriona, Katy, and Clydia. Àdham talked with Ormiston and her older brother Davy near the fireplace at the other end of the hall.

Catching Lady Rosalie's eye, Fiona smiled and received a smile in return.

Rosalie spoke briefly to Mar and began to gather her skirts, clearly, Fiona thought, meaning to join her by the window. Just as Rosalie stood and turned toward her, Mar's steward entered and strode quickly to the earl.

"What is it?" Mar asked him.

"Beg pardon, m'lord," the steward replied with a slight nod. "There be some trouble at the gate."

"I thought the bridge was up."

"Aye, it is, but the auld fool outside be raising such a ruckus, a-shouting and throwing big rocks at the gate, and he's such a fierce auld bangster that the porter said I should let ye know."

Mar frowned. "Did this man tell the porter what he wants?"

"Not what, sir, but who," the porter said. "He be enquiring for one Alexander Stewart. The porter told him we ha' nae such man here, but the fool be that stubborn and willna believe him. He just keeps a-heaving his rocks at the gate and insisting that his man must be inside our wall."

Fiona, watching them, saw Mar look toward the west fireplace. Following his gaze, she saw Àdham grinning widely.

Chuckling, Mar said to his steward. "By the Rood, it must be our rescuer! Fetch him in at once. And, mind, ye treat the man as if he were his grace, the King."

"Aye, m'lord, straightaway," the steward said. He turned on his heel and strode away more swiftly than he had entered.

Mar stood and watched him go with a look of delighted anticipation.

Realizing that her breasts were overfull, Fiona turned toward Lady Rosalie, now approaching her, and said, "If you would talk with me, madam, we must adjourn to my chamber. It is time to feed my bairn."

"But we cannot go yet," Rosalie said with her mischievous grin. "Much as I love you, dearling, I must see this man who dares to order Mar's people about, and I expect that your curiosity is also bursting. Do not you want to see him, too?"

"I do, aye," Fiona admitted. "Mayhap another few minutes, then."

The steward soon returned with a scrawny graybeard who looked about as if he could not believe his bright blue eyes at the splendor of that vast chamber.

"My lord," the steward said with formal stiffness, "this gentleman would speak with you."

Fiona saw that Àdham had moved to stand nearby.

Mar, still standing, smiled and said, "Do you remember me, my friend?"

The old man peered at Mar and then shifted his gaze to Àdham. "By the Rood," he said gruffly, looking back at Mar. "Ye do clean up well, the pair o' ye, and ye've fattened up well, too. But where be this Earl o' Mar ye promised me?"

"You are looking at him," Mar said. Then, to the crowd at large, he added, "This gentleman saved Sir Àdham and me, when I was nigh to starving. But what trouble brings you to me, sir?" he asked his visitor.

"Them thievin' Islesmen ha' wrecked my shack and turned me out," the old man said. "They went wild for a time, layin' waste tae all they saw. They've gone back tae their isles, but they threatened tae come back anon, so I thought . . ." He eyed Mar doubtfully.

"Ye've come to the right place, my friend," Mar assured him.

Meeting Àdham's gaze then, Fiona exclaimed, "Good sakes, Rosalie, I must meet that man and thank him!"

Àdham intercepted them as they drew nearer. "'Tis feeding time for my heir, is it not?" he asked with a smile.

"Aye, and past time," Fiona said, leaning into him when he put an arm around her. "But if this man is your rescuer, I want to meet him."

"He is, and you will," he said, hugging her. "Mar is a generous man, and his word is good. So, having practically ordered the man to come to Kildrummy if ever he was in need, he will do all that he can to aid him. If he does not introduce him individually to everyone here, I shall be amazed. But now, take me in to see my son, for when you have settled him, we will return to add our thanks to Mar's."

When he opened the door to the chamber allotted to their little family, he walked past her and straight to the cradle. Gently removing its tiny occupant, he looked down into the bairn's long-lashed, silver-gray eyes and smiled.

Watching Àdham croon to their wee son while she unfastened her kirtle to feed him, Fiona realized that—Highlands, Lowlands, or Borders—she would feel at home wherever her two precious menfolk might be.

Dear Reader,

I hope you enjoyed *The Reluctant Highlander*.

Since several sources specified that James II was born in October, following the Battle of Inverlochy, I have used that as James's reason not to lead the royal army again into the Highlands. However, James II's birthday is officially October 30, 1430, and most experts now agree that Inverlochy was fought in September 1431.

Dating events can be tricky, because clan histories often contain errors. For example, *Clan Donald*, by Donald J. MacDonald of Castleton, (1978, 2006), one of my favorite sources for the Lords of the Isles, dates the submission of Alexander to James as Easter Sunday, 1429.

However, Alexander's defeat at the Battle of Lochaber did not occur until June 23 of that year, so he could not have submitted to the King at Easter (March 27). The more likely date, since Alexander is said to have gone to Ireland and submitted a year or so later, is St. Augustine's Day, 1430, as other sources suggest.

Information for the city of Perth comes from many sources: *Perth: the Fair City* by David Graham-Campbell and John Donald (Perth, 1994), *The Ancient Capital of Scotland*—for the King's tennis court at Blackfriars—by Samuel Cowan, J.P. (London, 1904), and *The Ordnance Gazetteer of Scotland* (Glasgow, 1884).

Ambergris is a waxlike substance that originates in sperm whales and is a very expensive additive to perfumes such as Shalimar and Chanel N°5. Its use had begun by 1000 BC. The word itself comes from the Arabic *anwar*.

Many of you will have recognized the *croquembouche* at the feast as the forerunner of profiteroles, my favorite dessert. Sweet cakes were rare in medieval Scotland (and England, come to that), but a French chef visiting medieval London supposedly saw a pyramid of fried rolls there and took the notion back to France.

Playing cards first entered southern Europe in the fourteenth century, probably from Egypt, using suits of "cups, coins, swords, and polo sticks," that still appear in traditional Latin decks, according to *The Big Book of Tarot*, by Hajo Banzhaf (Rome, 1994, pp. 16, 92). Wide use of playing cards in Europe dates with some certainty from 1377 onward, and most sources do say that Mar and some of the chiefs were playing cards before Inverlochy and were reluctant to stop.

The hill Tom na Faire, southwest of Inverlochy Castle, blocked the royal army's view of the approaching flotilla of galleys.

Glen Tarbet, between Loch Sunart and Loch Linnhe, does exist and could well be the route that Donal Balloch took to ambush Mar's army at Inverlochy.

Some of you will have recognized characters from my Scottish Knights series: *Highland Master*, *Highland Hero*, and *Highland Lover*, as well as Fiona, from *Devil's Moon*. If not, those books are all still available in stores and online.

My sources for clans Chattan and Cameron, and the Earl of Mar, include *The Confederation of Clan Chattan, Its Kith and Kin* by Charles Fraser-Mackintosh of Drummond (Glasgow, 1898); *The House and Clan of Mackintosh and of the Clan Chattan* by Alexander Mackintosh Shaw (Moy Hall, n.d); and many others.

The incidents involving Àdham, Mar, and the strangers (as well as details about both battles) appeared in *The Clan Donald* by Reverend A. MacDonald (Inverness, 1881); *The House and Clan of Mackintosh*; and "The History of the MacDonalds and the Lords of the Isles," by Alexander Mackenzie, *The Celtic Magazine* (v. 5, April 1880).

Information about the battles of Lochaber and Inverlochy comes from those sources, as well. The Earl of Mar wrote the Gaelic couplet at the beginning of this book in honor of the ladies who gave him the barley gruel made in his shoe.

Malcolm, tenth Chief of Clan Mackintosh and Captain of Clan Chattan, also known as "the Mackintosh," fought at the Battle of Harlaw in 1411 and at both Lochaber and Inverlochy. He died in 1457, when he must have been at least in his late eighties or nineties. A number of the Mackintosh chiefs were notably long-lived.

I did take certain liberties with the Earl of Caithness. His birth date is unknown. However, his father, Walter Stewart, Earl of Atholl, the youngest son of Robert II, King of Scots, was born in 1360, so Caithness likely was born between 1380 and 1400. I chose to make him young enough to be a friend of Sir Àdham and Fiona. He did die at Inverlochy, and he was a strong supporter of Mar and James I.

I must extend special thanks to Bruce E. MacNab for the generous donations he made in 2015 and 2016 to the St. Andrews Society of Sacramento, which allowed him to become a squire in *Reluctant Highlander*, and for his extreme patience with the delays due to my husband's illness.

I also extend a special thanks to Bridgett and Bruce Locken for their 2016 donation to the St. Andrews Society of Sacramento. You'll see them again as continuing characters in my next book, *The Kissing Stone*.

I also extend my abject apologies to Corinne and Jim Schrader for misspelling their last name in my author letter in *Devil's Moon*.

As always, I'd like to thank my long-suffering agents, Lucy Childs and Aaron Priest, as well as my amazing and wonderful editor, Maggie Crawford; master copyeditor, Sean Devlin; senior production editor, Lauren Chomiuk; editorial assistant, Annie Locke; and everyone else at Open Road Integrated Media who contributed to this book.

I also extend a special thanks to all of you, my readers, who have so strongly supported my books over the years. I think of you every day, and I love hearing from you. I could not have accomplished what I have without you.

If you enjoyed *The Reluctant Highlander*, please look for the story of Katy MacFinlagh and the fate of Raitt Castle in *The Kissing Stone*, coming soon to your favorite bookstore and online retailer.

Meantime, *Suas Alba!*
Amanda Scott
www.amandascottauthor.com
www.facebook.com/amandascottauthor
www.openroadmedia.com/amanda-scott

ABOUT THE AUTHOR

A fourth-generation Californian of Scottish descent, Amanda Scott is the author of more than sixty romantic novels, many of which appeared on the *USA Today* bestseller list. Her Scottish heritage and love of history (she received undergraduate and graduate degrees in history at Mills College and California State University, San Jose, respectively) inspired her to write historical fiction. Credited by *Library Journal* with starting the Scottish romance subgenre, Scott has also won acclaim for her sparkling Regency romances. She is the recipient of the Romance Writers of America's RITA Award (for *Lord Abberley's Nemesis*, 1986) and the RT Book Reviews Career Achievement Award. She lives in central California with her husband and a cat named Willy Magee.

AMANDA SCOTT

FROM OPEN ROAD MEDIA

OPEN ROAD

INTEGRATED MEDIA

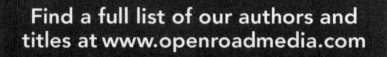

Find a full list of our authors and
titles at www.openroadmedia.com

FOLLOW US
@OpenRoadMedia